The Tales of Iryvalya: Bloodlines

ଔଔ

LeAnn Kelley

This book is a work of fiction. Names, places, and events are all fictitious with no tie to any past or present person, place, or event.

The Tales of Iryvalya: Bloodlines Copyright @ 2016 LeAnn Kelley

Published by:
LeAnn Kelley Enterprises, LLC
www.LeAnnKelley.com/LAKLLC

ISBN-13 (paperback): 978-0997535211
ISBN-10 (paperback): 0997535210

Editing and interior design by:
Lisa Gilliam

Cover design by:
Lem Montero

For Joe, Joey & Ivy, the three loves of my life…

❧ Western Realms ❧

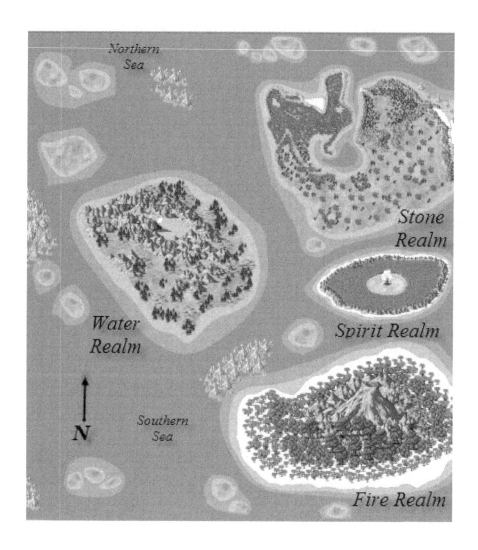

❧ Eastern Realms ☙

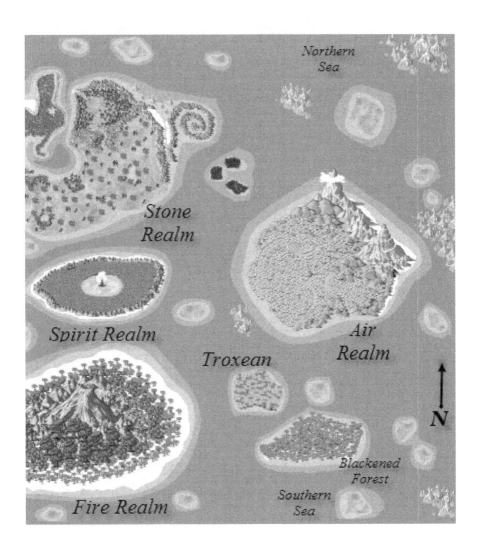

❧ Stone Realm ❧

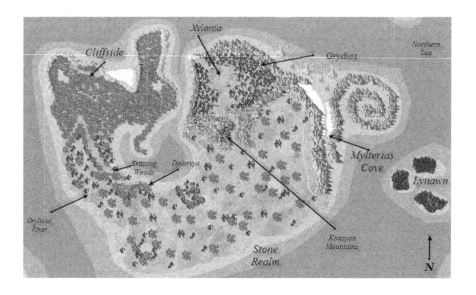

☙ 1 ❧

THE NORTHERN SUN PEEKED through my small window, allowing the warmth of the light to dance across my skin, gently rousing me awake. I finally convinced my eyes to open and look out at the bright blue sky, and I realized the promise of a beautiful day would be short-lived with the threat of the ominous clouds approaching. Storm clouds were rolling in from the North Sea rapidly, so I knew I better get going. I was expected to help prepare for the harvest. Rowzey wanted me to help her preserve a variety of different foods for the season's change coming soon because, as I am reminded often by her, she needs to be able to make her sauce.

I walked over to my dresser to pick between my few old and worn clothes. As I looked through my dresses for the pale green one—the one Rowzey always seems to like seeing me in—something in my looking glass caught my eye. I noticed a small faded mark on my left shoulder. I had never seen it before, and I couldn't seem to figure out what it was in the shape of. I poured some water from the pitcher into the wash basin on my dresser and tried to scrub the mark away with a piece of cloth, and it didn't fade. The skin only changed to brighter pink. I needed to dress quickly and go see Miaarya, the head Fairy here at the Cliffside's home for unfortunates.

Miaarya was a very sweet Fairy, with golden tanned skin from working outside in the gardens, and long beautiful hair comprised of many different shades of pink. From the softest pink like in the start of the morning light, to some of the most vibrant shades of darker pink, all in long flowing curls that reach to the lowest part of her back. Her eyes were also very beautiful, with alternating swirls of the light and dark pinks which accent her pale pink eyebrows.

Miaarya had been the head of the manor for Fairies, and a few other creatures that did not have any family, were abandoned, or did not have a place to live, since I can remember. She had to be close to seventy-eight Leaf years old, but she didn't look a day older than twenty-three. Miaarya had always been very kind in trying to answer any questions regarding my past; even if she did not have much information to give me, she has always seemed eager to try to help me the best she could. She told me before to talk to Iclyn about some of my past, but the few times I had, she was always vague about any information, so I quit asking her.

I knocked gently on Miaarya's flower-carved wooden door and heard her moving around.

She said sweetly, "Come in, Nyrieve."

"How did you know it was me?" I asked, surprised, as I opened the door and saw her tying the end of her long braid together.

"Because you are the only person in the manor who could walk up to my door, and I never hear you before you knock. Everyone else, I can usually hear them moving throughout the manor, but you, my sweet Ny, you are as quiet and swift as the gentlest of breezes when you move," she said, beaming at me.

"Thank you, I think," I said, remembering that I tend to surprise people often when I walk up to them if they were not looking at me.

"What can I help you with?" she asked. "Does Rowzey need more helpers on getting her supplies ready for the cold season?"

"No, it's not for Rowzey... I actually have the problem... I have a spot on my shoulder that wasn't there before, and I cannot seem to get it off of me. I am wondering if there could be something wrong," I said with worry creeping into my voice.

Miaarya gave me a weighted look and told me to come in and shut the door behind me. After closing the door, I walked over to her and pulled the neck of my faded green dress over to show Miaarya the marking on my shoulder. She looked at it without surprise, but with curiosity, and lightly touched the area of the mark. After a few moments, she stopped touching the mark, looked up and spoke.

"Nyrieve, the marking is nothing to worry about, you are fine. This is something that is common to happen to..." Miaarya started stumbling on her words. She paused, took a deep breath, and looked me in the eyes. "This is common to happen to Elves nearing their seventeenth Leaf Day."

I stared at her as if what she said was in a language I could not understand. After a few moments of trying to process what Miaarya said, I stated, "But... I am not an Elf, I am a Fairy."

"No, Ny, you are not Fairy like us, you are truly an Elf. I had hoped that you would be a late bloomer and the markings wouldn't show for a while. I am sorry that this is how you had to find out, but it is okay, everything is going to be fine," she said, as I began to pace back and forth.

I felt like there was a big sticky ball in the middle of my throat that wouldn't seem to move. I couldn't comprehend how it could be that I wasn't a Fairy. After taking five deep breaths, I was finally able to swallow, and I found my voice again.

"How is everything going to be fine? I mean, how is it, in all these years, no one thought it was important to tell me I am not a Fairy like most everyone else here and that I am of all things an... Elf?" I spat the word out like it was sour. I stood still looking at Miaarya, wondering how one of the people I trusted most could keep such a secret from me.

"Nyrieve, there is a lot to explain, but I think before anyone can answer your questions you first need to see Rowzey. She has something important for you that might help you to understand what is going on. I will go with you and let her know it is time for her to give it to you," Miaarya said, taking my rugged hand into her tiny soft hand and leading me out of her room.

I walked without effort or focus, allowing Miaarya to lead me down the back staircase that goes right into the kitchen where you could almost always find Rowzey.

When Miaarya saw Rowzey, she walked over and said something to Rowzey in a language I have only heard Rowzey muttering in when she burned her sauce. Rowzey finished talking to Miaarya and looked at me with her kind mauve-and-silver swirled eyes, pushing back the fallen pieces of her matching long streaked hair away from her weathered face, showing her silver eyebrows. Rowzey looked older than anyone else who lived in Cliffside, and that is saying something when even some of the oldest Fairies around three hundred Leaf years still looked close to their fiftieth–Leaf Day selves. Rowzey was also very short—the top of her head reached the bottom of my chin—but she could never be mistaken for someone who couldn't take care of herself. To be honest, I would be afraid for anyone who crossed her.

Rowzey walked over to the cabinet in the far corner of the kitchen, took out a key hidden in her skirts, and opened a small door in the cabinet. I could see about a dozen or more papers inside. She shuffled them around until she pulled out a very old and worn-looking one that was sealed.

Rowzey came to me and looked in my eyes, handing me the worn letter, and said in her strange accent, "This I's be saving for yous since before yous was born."

The seal on the outside of the letter was not stamped with any symbol, which is highly unusual, as normally all letters are sealed to show from where or whom they were sent. I looked up at Miaarya and Rowzey with so many questions, and yet no words would come. I slowly broke the seal on the letter, hearing the old paper crackle a little as I opened it. The top of the letter was addressed to me.

To our dearest daughter Nyrieve,

I know you have many questions, and while I wish I could answer them all for you, it is not safe for me to give you more information that what you need. The most important thing I have to tell you is that we love you so very much, so much that it crushes us to know that the safest place for you is as far away from us as possible. Your father and my love is forbidden, and the fact that we created you, if ever found out, could lead to not only our deaths, but yours as well. That is the one thing we cannot allow to happen.

We had to hide you with the Fairies far to the north… the Fairies have always hoped for peace to be brought back into the world and were willing to risk their lives to hide you, raise you and keep you safe.

Hopefully you will understand why we had to give you up, and how you are the only hope for Iryvalya to once again know peace.

We love you so much, Nyrieve, and we hope the Fairies will be able to give you this when the time has come.

Love Always,
Your Parents

Warm tears spilled down my face, and I could sense that Miaarya and Rowzey were just standing there watching me. I looked up at the familiar faces of these women I had known my whole life. These were the ones who I usually went to first with my injuries, those who I also shared my sadness and joys with. They stared at me with tears in their eyes, and that is when it really hit me that they had known this all along and they kept it from me. Miaarya I could almost understand, but Rowzey had always told me I could trust her. Anger began to overtake me a little.

"Why, Rowzey? Why would you keep this from me? Didn't you think I had a right to know… to know what I am?" I yelled at her.

"Ny, I's couldn't tell yous such truths, as the truth would have surely led to yous death," Rowzey said in her thick strange accent. I remembered hearing her try many times to say my actual name, and would stumble and eventually give up and just call me Ny instead. Now her talking to me in such a close familiar way was hurtful. How could she talk to me like we were family, when she knew all along who I was, and what I was?

"No, Rowzey, you promised me you would never lie to me, and you did. You kept this a secret from me."

"Ny, that is not true. Yous never ask me all about who yous is. When yous asked about yous, I's would say as simple as I's could. It like the sauce, yous ask if meat in the sauce, and I's says yes, but that not mean I's says if it's good pieces of boar or slimy pieces of slugs. Meat is meat, and if yous want to know more, yous always got to know how to ask."

"You know you kept this a secret, and you knew I wanted to know about who I was and where I came from."

"I's did, Ny, I's knew, but I's knew it best for yous to not know until the time was right… like my sauce, it's not ready to be feasted on, until I's cook it long enough."

Her words of wisdom always seemed to come back to her sauce. I always thought it was mainly because she was the cook for the Fairies here in Cliffside. Now I am wondering if she is just plain crazy.

I stared at Rowzey, wondering if she could keep this from me, what else has she, or everyone else I have ever trusted here, kept from me. I couldn't talk to her anymore or anyone else right now. I turned, grabbing my worn tattered cloak off the hook near the door, and ran out the back door from the warm sweet-smelling kitchen into the cooling air. The clouds had darkened out the Northern Sun and it had started misting outside with the fog rising through the trees and the distant village of Cliffside.

As I ran down the familiar worn path into the woods, I realized that I was running away like a child, but I didn't know what else to do, so I kept going. I followed the path all the way down to the cliffs, just above the North Sea. I climbed down the cool wet path to the cave I found back when I was just a small child, the one I always go to when I need to get away from the world. This cave had always given me peace and solace, and now it seemed to hold no comfort for me at all.

Now that I was alone like I wanted to be, all I had were walls of rock to sit in silence as I yelled my questions at them, asking why this happened and why I was only now being told. I sat down on the old woven blanket Rowzey had made and given to me as a child to keep here for the times it was cold. I continued to cry and yell at the empty walls around me until I couldn't anymore. I leaned back against the cave wall and took five deep breaths, one for each of Iryvalya's exquisite moons: Rydison, Nydian, Lowyll, Joauxy, Ivynilo. I curled up on the blanket and closed my eyes, willing this to not be true. After crying so much, I slowly drifted off into sleep.

⊂ℨ℘

I heard the crackling of a fire near me, and that's when I realized that it was no longer freezing in the cave. There was at least one other person in the cave with me, but I was not ready to sit up and talk to anyone.

I lay there for a long time just listening to the crackling of the fire and the waves crashing against the vast cliffs. I knew I needed to sit up and face who was there with me and, more importantly, face the fact that I am not who I thought I was and nothing of my life would ever be the same.

I slowly sat up and kept my eyes directed down towards the fire, watching the beautiful orange flames dancing across the glowing logs and embers. A pair of boots lay next to the fire. They were worn dark brown leather with a small patch on the front of the right one. I knew instantly who the boots belonged to, and who it was in the cave with me.

"How long have you been sitting here, Kaleyna?" I said softly, still not wanting to look up at her, my best friend since as long as I could remember.

"Since Rowzey told me you had run away from the village... when we got here you were asleep, so we figured it would be best to make a fire to keep you warm while waiting out the rainstorm," Kaleyna said with her soft silky voice.

I let my eyes adjust from the fire light and realized it was just Kaleyna and me in the small cave. "Where is Rowzey now?"

"She went to fetch us something to eat. She should be back presently." Kaleyna smiled at me. She had her long snow-white hair in a messy twist upon the top of her head with a few locks falling around her face. Kaleyna had always been shorter than me by a bit, her hair was super straight, and she was much fairer skinned than I. She also had very beautiful eyes like me, only hers were the deep blue color of the North Sea.

Even with her smile, I could tell she was concerned about me. "So what happened with you? Rowzey wouldn't tell me. She just said in one of her cryptic ways that 'Ny wills give yous the information when it yous time to be told.'"

"Oh, Kal, I don't even know how to start."

"Sure you do, Ny... from the beginning," she said with a slight giggle. It was a phrase we had said to each other many times when we did not know where to start about an issue we were having.

"I was given a letter tonight from... from my parents."

"Your parents? How is that even possible? I thought Iclyn told you that your parents had died during one of the raids in Everglyn Woods in the Air Realm?" she asked with a puzzled look on her face.

"I am guessing that she was lying to me. The letter was written before I was born, according to Rowzey. And not only did I find out that my parents gave me up, I also found out I am not even a Fairy."

"Not a Fairy... How... then what... I mean, did the letter say what you are?"

"Elf. I am an Elf." The words felt amiss and rancid on my tongue. We had learned that the Elves had done nothing recently but bring destruction and death to our world. Without the Elves, Iryvalya would still be living in harmony and not with everyone needing to hide in their different parts of the world.

"An Elf? How could you be an Elf? I thought they had pointy ears and markings all over their bodies? You have neither of those things," Kaleyna said, looking me over, making sure she was not missing something on the face of her best friend whom she had seen daily for her whole life.

"Oh, there be no mistaken Ny being an Elf," Rowzey said as she entered the cave with a small cast iron pot of what smelled to be her sauce and a loaf of fresh hot bread. It wasn't until that moment I realized how hungry I actually was.

"But she looks nothing like the Elves that we have seen here in Cliffside," Kaleyna said.

"Oh, that's Miss Lydorea's works. She knows just how to do the magyc to make someone's features appear not as they really is," Rowzey said with a smirk on her face, like she knew more secrets. "Who would like the sauce and noodles with some bread?" she questioned, while already ladling a bowl out for Kaleyna and me.

I wanted to tell Rowzey that I wasn't hungry and she shouldn't act like everything was okay with the secret she kept from me. Even with all I wanted to say, I couldn't deny that I was hungry. As always, her sauce smelled so good, and I knew it would taste even better so I didn't say everything I was feeling.

I took the bowl from Rowzey without looking up at her sweet old comforting smile, as I knew that right now it would not give me the comfort it once did. "Thank you for the food, Rowzey, but that doesn't mean I forgive you for keeping this—"

"Nyrieve!" Kaleyna yelled at me in surprise. "How can you talk to Rowzey like that? She has always been there for us. While it might not be right her keeping this from you, I can't imagine she would ever do anything to you that was not in your best interest."

"Is that what it was, Rowzey?" I demanded, looking straight into her swirled eyes. "Is that what everyone is going to tell me? That it was in my best interest not to know who I am?"

"Ny, I's can't make yous understand why I's kept these things from yous, but it was truly for yous safety, as well as yous parents and all the Fairies here in Cliffside," Rowzey said, looking at me with worry and concern on her face.

"What is it I am supposed to do now? Am I supposed to leave Cliffside and everyone I know to hide away? Am I supposed to go and join those Elves somewhere? I don't know much of anything about the Elves, everything I have ever been told was from those who were abandoned or those who have looked for refuge here away from the Elves," I babbled, with tears starting to fill my eyes again. "And what did that letter from my mother mean about me bringing peace to Iryvalya?"

"Ny, there is much for yous to learn, but right now, I's think it be best for yous to eat, and then we's all go back to the manor and rest. In the morning, we's can meet with Miss Lydorea and Miss Iclyn, and they can help with all the questions yous have," Rowzey said, handing me a piece of cheese herb bread.

As much as I wanted to argue with her, I sat there eating the noodles smothered in Rowzey's delicious red sauce. No one knew what all she mixed into her sauce. It was so fragrant from the tomatoes and the different herbs she cooks in, and the flavor was so bold with so many subtle undertones.

We all finished the noodles and bread, and drank some of the warm honey tea that Kaleyna had brought with her and kept next to the fire to keep warm. I put out the fire with the water bucket I had always kept full in the cave for such things. After the three of us bundled back up in our boots and cloaks, we walked the path back up the cliff, and then followed it back down through the village of Cliffside. There were not many lights lit in the buildings as we passed. With the storm still overhead and having fallen asleep, I had lost track of the time and how late it must be.

We arrived back to the manor, and I found myself looking at the big wooden two-story building with the large covered porch around the whole first story. There were thick green vines of ivy growing up the pillars spaced out around the porch; they had not yet begun to change colors with the approaching harvest season. This home had always felt like a place I was welcome, but not necessarily the place I belonged to. I had always thought it was due to being without my blood family, but now I wonder if it was that, or that I was in fact an Elf.

I climbed the few steps up to the porch and walked silently behind Rowzey and Kaleyna, thinking how much has changed in less than one day. Rowzey was right, there was no point in talking about the fact I am an Elf anymore tonight, so I just walked in and decided to go up to my room. Rowzey stopped me at the bottom of the stairs and gave me a hug and told me she still loved me. I couldn't respond. I still loved Rowzey, but I just couldn't find the strength to say it back. Kaleyna walked upstairs with me and also hugged me outside my door. She said I could talk to her at any time tonight or any other time. I thanked her and hugged her back. After going into my room and shutting the door, I took off my boots, walked over to my bed next to the small window and lay down.

Maybe this was all a dream and tomorrow it will just be another normal day here in Cliffside. I figured it couldn't hurt to hope.

⋄2⋄

THERE WERE PEOPLE ALL around me, but I could not see their faces. It was like my eyes could not focus. They were speaking in the language Rowzey sometimes used when talking to herself or some of the older Fairies in Cliffside. While I could not understand their words, I could understand the concern and worry in their voices.

I tried to ask someone what was going on, but they continued on their way as if they could not see me. I walked into the middle of the large round room, where a group of people sat at a long table. A person at the head of the table was writing down something in an ancient language I had seen once in Rowzey's recipe book. I walked closer to the person writing and could tell she was a Fairy. She had long flowing bright yellow hair, like the color of sunflower petals in the height of the warm season, and throughout it there were thick groupings of dark blue hair. It was so beautiful, I wanted to touch it, but thought better of it. I leaned over what she was writing and looked over the document. I could not understand it; Rowzey had never explained to me many of the symbols. There was, however, one I recognized near the top of the paper. It was a symbol of an ivy leaf in front of a big tree, and in the middle of the ivy leaf was a single spiral line. I knew this symbol, because I asked Rowzey what it meant. She had told me it was a very important symbol. It represented our path in life. The middle starting point represents where we start out in life and the spiral outward represents the path that we choose.

A tall man, also a Fairy, with broad shoulders and long variegating aqua-colored hair, walked into the middle of the room, silencing everyone with his presence. He looked around at everyone and spoke in words I could understand. "We all know what will come and what the prophecy states. A mixed Elf who bears the mark will someday bring the

Klayns together, we just do not know when. Until that day comes, we must vow to protect any and all mixed Elf children."

Everyone stood and responded in unison, "Volnyri."

ᏣᏍᎻ

I woke startled, the wolves howling in the nearby woods. It was still dark with the Rydison moon in front of the Northern Sun. I did not want to move yet. The dream was still so clear and vivid in my mind. I remembered the symbol I saw of the spiral on top of the ivy leaf, and that they were talking about someone who would bring peace to Iryval-ya. They had said a mixed Elf, like me, but they couldn't have been talking about me. I guess it doesn't really matter, it was just a dream, nothing real. I have enough other things going on that I need to concern myself with that are real instead of silly dreams.

I got up off of my bed and used my flint rocks on the mantle to light a small fire inside the hearth in my room. It was not cold, but I wanted to have a bit of light, as I knew I would not be able to fall asleep again anytime soon.

After getting the small fire going and standing back up, I looked over at the looking glass at my reflection, feeling like I have never really seen myself at all. I looked at my long thick white hair falling out of the bun I had put it in earlier. Taking out the pins holding it in place, my wavy hair fell down around my shoulders, over my chest, and down to the top of my waist. I do not often wear it down, as it always seems to get in the way. I have the same boring hair color as all of us who haven't reached their seventeenth Leaf Day, so it is not like it'd stand out if I wore it down. Soon my hair will start changing colors. I had always hoped it would turn a beautiful color like most of the other Fairies, but feared I would be stuck with white or gray like some are. Now I don't even know what colors my hair might turn, seeing as I am an Elf. I know they start with white hair too. We had learned in school that the only race who is born with their permanent hair color is the Dwarves.

I looked to my eyes, which were currently a solid shade of violet, the only feature I had ever regarded myself in having that was pretty. It was also the feature that others had said was nice too. Soon I will get a second color swirled in with the violet, yet another change that starts sometime after our seventeenth Leaf Day. I wonder what color eyes

Elves have. The few I have met have had eyes similar to the Fairies, but that does not mean much.

I am a bit under the average height of Fairies. I am also a bit more curvy in the hips than most Fairies, which I had noticed most of my life, but never thought it was anything but me just being different from everyone again. I could have nice golden tans like some of the Fairies here in Cliffside, but I always seem to prefer to be outside more when the Northern Sun is hidden behind one of the two moons.

Now I guess I knew why I tend to be different from most everyone else here, because I was not like most everyone here. Other than Rowzey, Kaleyna was the only other person who was similar to me in a many ways, but also different from me in complimentary ways, such as, where I was shy, she was bolder. It was almost like we were opposite sides of the same gem.

I remember the moment Kaleyna and I had become best friends. As children everyone got along for the most part. Sure there was some teasing here and there, but nothing much, as the older Fairies would not allow too much disrespect to one another. There was one day, though, that a Fairy boy named Montryos had been picking on me, making fun of the fact that my eyes were violet. He said that no normal Fairy had violet eyes, and Kaleyna walked over to him and pushed him down into the mud and told him that no normal Fairy boy would ever talk to someone like that. I had been on the verge of crying, but when Kal had done that for me, the tears retreated and I started to smile. I had never had a friend stand up for me like that, and I knew at that moment I would always do the same for her without question. Montryos never talked to me again after that, but the few times I saw him, he always looked at me with hatred and disgust.

Not looking at our physical differences, Kaleyna and I had always had the same interests, helping Rowzey out, sneaking off to explore the Eritsong Woods, and practicing some of the basic magyc skills we had been taught. While neither of us had yet mastered the ability to make fire without flints, we both were really good at making small, light objects float in the air for a short time and some other basic magyc skills.

After all this thinking of Kaleyna, I realized how much I needed to go talk to her and thank her for being there for me tonight like she always has been. I tiptoed out of my room, turned to the left and went down one door to her room. I lightly knocked on the door and waited to hear if she was awake. It was only moments before I heard her stepping to the door. The knob turned and she looked at me, worried.

"Are you okay, Ny?" Kaleyna whispered.

"I don't know what I am, Kal," I said truthfully.

"Come on in, we can talk or just sit together," she said with a forced smile.

I walked inside her room, which looked just like mine, except her window was a little bigger than mine, which I had always envied.

"Do you want to talk about it, Ny?"

"I don't know what to say about it. I just feel scared and alone. I feel like I was abandoned all over again and I have no one." Tears threatened to spill down my cheeks.

Kaleyna hugged me to her and said, "You are not alone, Ny. You have me and you always will. We might not be sisters of blood, but we are sisters of spirit, and that is stronger than blood." Another familiar phrase we had said to each other often.

The tears won the battle and began to fall gently down my cheeks. Kaleyna went and sat on her bed, propping the pillows so I could sit next to her. She put her arm around me and let me lean into her, and I cried as she ran her fingers through my hair. After a while I ended up with my head on a pillow in her lap, lightly sobbing. I felt safe with my best friend, my spirit sister, the person I could always count on. Here I had finally been able to let go of all my fears and anger, and feel something of familiarity. It wasn't long before the sobbing took the small amount of energy I had left and sleep took me over.

I woke before Kaleyna, and I did not want to wake her. The light through her window from the Northern Sun was bright and warm, telling me that the storm had passed. I quietly got up, padded back to my room and closed the door. The fire in my hearth was long since out, so there was a slight chill when I walked in. I went over to my dresser to get some fresh clothing to wear. I picked out a pair of worn brown light leather pants that matched the color of my knee-high laced-up boots I put on over the pants. I decided on wearing the soft lavender-colored shirt that I had made for myself a few years ago for my fifteenth Leaf

Day. It was comfortable and allowed me to move well in it even when it was tucked into my pants.

That is when I realized that today was in fact my seventeenth Leaf Day. This was a day I had been waiting for, for so many years, and now that it was here, I was not sure I was ready for what this special day would hold for me.

∞3∞

I DECIDED TO BRUSH MY HAIR out and retie it back up to get my mind off of it being my seventeenth Leaf Day. As I started to brush my long snow-white hair, I noticed something in my brush. There was one long green hair sitting amongst the few other white hairs that had fallen out. I pulled the hair out of the bristles and held it up to the sunlight. It was a very beautiful shade of green, neither dark nor light, and it looked almost like the green shells of the North Sea turtles. It was solid in color, yet in the light, it looked almost of a green iridescence, where the depth of the color could almost change. After examining this hair, it hit me that it came from my brush, which was just brushing my hair.

I walked over to my looking glass to see if it could really be my hair, and sure enough there was a small streak of this beautiful green hair going from the right side of my temple all the way down to the end. The streak was about as thick as the width of my pinkie, so not very big, but against the rest of my snow-white hair, it stood out. I stared at myself for a long time trying to think of how I could hide this beautiful color that was in my hair.

This is a common change for someone on their seventeenth Leaf Day, so it is not something I should feel the need to hide, yet I had never seen anyone among the Fairies with any shades of green in their hair. If I didn't hide this, everyone would know that I am not Fairy, and while I knew it would come out eventually, I didn't think I was ready to deal with that along with everything else today.

I pulled my hair back tightly in a large bun and searched through my top drawer for something I could wear over my hair. The only thing I could find was the black scarf Rowzey had given me years ago when some tomato juice had lightly stained part of my hair. I wrapped the scarf around my head, making sure that all of my new green hair was well hidden.

After I had my hair hidden, my stomach grumbled. I needed to get something to eat, so I walked quietly out of my room, gently closing my door behind me. I went down the back stairs to the kitchen, and noticed it was quiet. I did not see or hear Rowzey anywhere, so I quietly grabbed a couple pieces of bread and a bright large orange before walking out the back door to eat out near the lake.

I walked down the short dirt path to the water. A light mist still hung over the lake. There was a long wooden dock that crossed the water over to the small island in the middle of the lake. The dock was slightly zigzagged to the island, and I walked across slowly. There were moments I could not see far in front of me, and I did not want to miss a turn and walk off into the water. Once I reached the small island, I went over to a large old weathered tree stump and sat down facing back towards the manor.

I cut the peel off of the orange using the old straight razor Rowzey had given me to help cut vegetables, fruit, or herbs for her. I always kept it in my right boot. I had even sewn in a small little pocket for it, so it was easy to grab, yet not noticeable. After peeling the orange, I ripped up the peels into smaller pieces and tossed them towards the ducks, who came up and started feasting. I ate all of the orange and a piece of bread. I ripped up the other piece of bread, tossing it as well to the ducks and some of the fish in the lake. It is frowned upon to throw any of our extra food away, but I never saw any harm in sharing with the other creatures.

I had been coming to this lake since I was little, after I learned to swim. I had been so scared to even walk out on the docks in fear that if something would happen to them, I would have no way back to the other side. This island used to have a small house on it, but all that was left to show for it were the chimney bricks still stacked up. I remember many of us kids would come here to practice making a fire with magyc in the old fireplace. Only once was I able to actually get a fire started by rubbing my middle finger and thumb together. I remember how shocked I was and wished that someone else had been there with me to see that I actually did it. The only person who seemed to believe me when I told everyone was Kaleyna.

After sitting out by the calm lake for at least an hour, the rest of the mist had burned off of the lake and I could see the manor clearly, as well as parts of the village not too far away. A few people were out and about doing their daily tasks without a care in the world of anything different. As much as I am not sure if I am ready to hear what Iclyn and Lydorea have to tell me about myself, I also know that I cannot wait around any longer and I needed to get going.

೧೩೮೦

I walked up to Iclyn's room, took a deep breath and knocked three times on her door with beautiful butterflies carved into it. Iclyn's cool smooth voice told me to enter, so I slowly opened the door and looked inside her room. She had a large window in her room and a bunch of chairs in a circle in the middle area, and near the window she had a small desk covered in papers. Off to one side was her bed, neatly tucked away, and a few books on the side table.

Iclyn was a very beautiful Fairy. She had shoulder-length hair with darker gray near the roots, and it faded to snow-white towards the tips. She had a fair complexion, as if she never spent any time out in the sunlight. Iclyn also had unique eyes—her two swirled colors were both gray, but one was a lighter gray and one was a very dark shade of gray—and her eyebrows were the same light shade of snow-white as her hair. She smiled at me as I walked in, with her beautiful white smile. I do not think I have known anyone else with such bright white teeth. Iclyn looked only a few Leaf years older than me, but she had recently celebrated her sixty-ninth Leaf Day.

"Hello, Nyrieve. Please come in and have a seat," Iclyn stated in a soft but sure voice.

"Thank you, Iclyn," I replied as I walked in and took a seat closest to the window where the warm glow of the sunlight fell on me. "Who else is coming?" I asked, pointing to the empty chairs.

"Lydorea, Rowzey, Miaarya, Baysil, and Relonya," Iclyn said easily as she walked over to the chair across from me and sat down. She wore a long white gauzy dress that was tight around the chest with layers that flowed downwards to her feet. The sleeves were snug on her upper arms and belled out towards her wrists, which were adorned with a few silver bands on each.

"Relonya is an Elf, isn't she?" I asked.

"Yes, we thought it would be best to have an Elf here to help give you some more information about what you might expect or answer any Elf questions," she said with her normal smile as if this was just any other day for her.

There was a light knock on the open door, and the rest of the group stood in the doorway. I now started to feel more nervous about what I was going to learn, but also a little excited as well, to know I would finally start getting some answers.

"Please, please come in," Iclyn said pleasantly. "Just take a seat, and please, Baysil, close the door behind you."

Baysil was a tall and tan Fairy with incredibly handsome features and a full head of deep turquoise hair. His hair was unusually short for a male Fairy, as it was cut above his ears but slightly longer on top, but I had overheard him once telling someone that it tended to get in his way too much to keep it longer. His eyebrows were the same color as his hair, and he had intriguing eyes, a gold and turquoise swirl. Baysil was around seventy-two Leaf years old, but looked like he was only a few years older than I.

Baysil closed the door, walked over to the open chair next to Iclyn and sat down. He had on fitted long black pants with a white loose shirt, and was wearing a pair of expensive black leather boots. I had not spent a lot of time with Baysil and was curious why he was at this gathering. Next to me on my right was Miaarya, and going around were Rowzey, Baysil, Iclyn, Relonya, and Lydorea on my left.

I looked around the room nervously waiting for someone to start talking. After a few hushed moments, Rowzey decided to get the conversation started in an awkward way. "Ny, why is yous wearing that silly head wrap?"

I could feel myself blushing and knew everyone else in the room could see it. After a few short moments I had decided to tell the truth instead of lying, because I figured it was not really fair of me to be angry at people who lied to me and then for me to lie as well.

"When I awoke this morning and brushed my hair, I noticed a streak of color in it, and I was honestly not comfortable yet walking around with it exposed to everyone," I stated with feigned confidence.

"That is silly, Nyrieve. You should not be ashamed of your hair changing. It is what happens to most everyone around their seventeenth Leaf Day," Lydorea stated in her airy voice.

Lydorea was another fair-complexioned Fairy. She had a long braid down her back in the colors of a soft pink and a dusky purple. Her eyes were swirls of pink and purple framed by dusky purple eyebrows. She was around the same height as I was, but she tended to wear boots with a lifted heel in them, which gave the appearance that she was an inch taller than me. Lydorea had a young face, I would swear that she was my age or even younger, but she was sixty-seven Leaf years old. I had asked her once how she looked so young, and all she did was giggle and say "Magyc." Now I was wondering what kind of magyc, since, according to Rowzey, she is the reason I have not appeared to have Elf traits. Lydorea was wearing a long flowing purple and pink gown that was cut in an empress shape, tied below her chest with a soft yellow ribbon. The sleeves on her dress also belled out very large before her wrists, where her hands could be easily hidden away if she wanted.

"Now why don't you take that dark scarf off of your head, Ny, and let us see the new coloring of your hair," Miaarya said smiling.

I hesitated at first, and then found my fingers untying the scarf and slowly taking it off of my head. I didn't look at anyone, I kept my eyes to the floor out of embarrassment knowing everyone was looking at me.

"Oh, Ny, that is a beautiful shade of green, I's do not remember a time seeing such lovely shade before," Rowzey said, making me smile a little, knowing at least someone liked it.

"I agree, Nyrieve, that is a very unusual and yet beautiful color," Iclyn said.

I looked up and saw everyone in the room staring at my hair with amazement and wonder, and for the first time today, I thought perhaps this new color wasn't so bad, seeing as everyone here seemed to think it was a good thing. I started to smile, and decided to make it easier for them to see the color. I unpinned my long hair and let it fall.

"Well, Nyrieve, as you can see, there are some perks to being an Elf. You get to have one of the most unique hair colors even *I* have ever seen, and I have seen all the different colors of the Elves of the Pyrothian

Klayn," Relonya said, allowing me to hear her deep yet very feminine voice for the first time.

Relonya appeared to be a little taller than me and had a beautiful deep golden tan. She had curly hair that was shades of a bright cherry red and a pale pink, which almost seemed to be white if you did not look closely enough. She had the same pale red eyebrows, and her eyes were a swirl of the same cherry red and a very pale shade of blue. I had never looked closely at Relonya before, and did not think it was possible for Pyrothian Elves, the wielders of fire magyc, to have blue in the eyes. She wore a pair of light black leather pants and a tight black leather vest, as well as matching laced-up boots that went above her knees. The most unique and striking thing I kept going back to was her ears, her pointed Elf ears. I had seen Elves and their pointed ears before, but this was the first time I studied them, knowing this is something I should have. I found myself touching the normal rounded tips of my own ears wondering how that could be.

Lydorea noticed this and smiled at me sheepishly. "I am very good at the magyc I wield, Nyrieve. Your ears are just as pointed as Relonya's are, but you cannot see that or even feel it."

"Your magyc surely is very impressive, Lydorea, but can you change them back for her?" Relonya asked.

"Is the sauce at its best when hot and fresh?" Rowzey asked in her usual sauce references. "Of course she can."

"Rowzey is correct. I can undo the spell that keeps her ears looking like a Fairy's. I wanted to wait to see if she was ready to do so," Lydorea said. "Are you ready, Nyrieve, to have your normal ears shown?"

"Uhm... yes, I think I am ready to have me appear as... well, me," I stammered.

Lydorea reached over to her right wrist and pulled back her belled sleeve to reveal a few silver bracelets that looked just like Iclyn's. I looked closer at these silver bracelets, realizing whenever I had seen Lydorea's wrists, she had always worn bracelets. There was a small pattern in the metal I couldn't quite make out, but it was very beautiful. As she grabbed one bracelet with her left hand, she said something I couldn't quite make out. Suddenly the bracelet broke apart into five pieces and fell into Lydorea's hand. She just looked up at me and smiled.

I reached up to feel my ears. They were no longer rounded at the top, but sloped upwards and ended in a definite point. I couldn't believe what I was feeling. I turned to the window and saw a light reflection of my pointed Elf ears peeking out through my snow-white hair with the one green streak hiding behind my right pointed ear. At first I thought it looked so strange and weird, but after a few moments a smile spread across my face, and I realized I was finally seeing the real me.

A moment later, I was pulled back into the reality that I wasn't alone, and I wasn't here just to see my Elf ears for the first time. I was here to learn the information about who I am, what the next steps I need to take are, and to understand what my mother meant in the letter that I was Iryvalya's only hope for peace.

I turned away from my reflection, looked at everyone in the room, then turned to Lydorea. "Thank you so much, Lydorea, for breaking the spell. I wasn't sure I would like them, but I do."

"You are most welcome, Nyrieve. And now, I do believe we should start getting to some of the more pressing topics," Lydorea gently stated.

"Okay, so… what is going on with who I am and what I need to know?" I asked outright. It was not normal for me to be so forward, but I figured this was not the time to be timid or demure.

"Well, Nyrieve, as you are aware, you are an Elf," Relonya said. "After the wars of the Elves against everyone else, the Elves split into two different Klayns, the Luminary Elves and the Pyrothian Elves. I am sure you learned the basics in your studies about each Klayn, that the Luminary powers are mostly focused around water and stone, and the Pyrothian powers are focused for the most part around fire and air."

"Yes, I remember learning about that before…" I said, wondering what more she was going to tell me.

"The thing is, Nyrieve, you are not either Luminary or Pyrothian Elf," she said nervously. "You are actually both."

I looked at Relonya, confused. "Both?"

"Your mother, whose name is Osidya, was born a Pyrothian Elf, and your father, Arnayx, was born a Luminary Elf," Relonya said.

"But, I was taught that the two Klayns do not speak or mate together," I stammered, not understanding how this could be.

"Your parents had met during a meeting of the leaders of each Klayn. They were there as the representatives' assistants. They were forced together for a period of time, and during that time, they had fallen for each other, against everything they had ever been taught to do," Relonya said. "Your parents were very much in love, but they did not think they could be together because of the Klayns, and shortly after, they found out your mother was pregnant with you."

"Okay, I understand that they were not to be together, but I do not understand why they had to hide me away from the Elves," I said, still confused.

Iclyn interjected, "Ny, what you do not understand, and what we do not talk about, is that right after the Elves had split into the two Klayns, there was a prophecy about a mixed Elf bringing peace to Iryvalya."

"But what does that have to do with me? I mean, I am sure that I cannot be the only mixed Elf there has been in the last few hundred years."

"No, you are not the only mixed Elf, Nyrieve," Iclyn continued. "However, when your parents knew that your mother was pregnant, they went to a Fairy enchantress who lives in the Spirit Realm, near the Leaf Day tree. Her name is Zyjoyvi. She is very old and very powerful, and she can see things that have not yet come to pass. When they went to see her, they wanted to make sure you would be safe with either your mother or father. Zyjoyvi could see that you are the Elf that was prophesized to be the Bringer of Peace to Iryvalya."

"Me?" I asked, looking at everyone in the room. How could anyone think I was the Bringer of Peace to anyone, let alone our whole world?

"Yes, yous, my dear Ny," Rowzey chimed in. "Yous were not safe with either Elf Klayn, so yous parents asked Zyjoyvi who they could entrust yous with, and she told them about me."

"My parents gave me to you, Rowzey?"

"Yes, Ny, they did, but I's knew I's couldn't keep yous safe all by I's-self, so I's brought yous to Cliffside, to be with the Fairies. I's knew the Fairies had powerful magyc that could help I's keep yous safe," Rowzey answered with a look of pride on her face.

"When Rowzey told us who you are and who you would be, we knew we had to help keep you here and safe until you were of age to find out," Lydorea added.

"I just don't know how I can be the Bringer of Peace, I am just me, Nyrieve. I am not special. I have always just blended in with the background..."

Iclyn said, "That is what we wanted for you, to blend in, not stand out, because that way, when Elf scouts would pass through town, you would not be noticed by them. You needed to be kept safe and educated on the world, so when the time came, you would be able to fulfill the prophecy."

I just sat there for a few minutes, not looking at anyone or speaking at all. I was trying to wrap my mind around the idea that I am supposed to bring peace, that I am some sort of savior for Iryvalya. How could I be this person? I was no one. I looked up at everyone in the room. "How do you know I am the one in the prophecy? How do we know there isn't someone else who is supposed to be this Bringer of Peace?"

Lydorea smiled at me kindly, and took another small bracelet off from the same wrist. This time she only slid it off of her hand and said to me, "You bear the mark of the Bringer of Peace. You have had it since the day you were born, but like with your ears, we wanted to help you blend in and stay safe."

"What mark?" I asked.

"Look at the inside of your right wrist," Iclyn told me.

I looked down at my wrist and turned it so I could see the inside, and what before was my normal pale skin, there was now a marking of a symbol. It was a single spiral line, very dark green at the center, that gradually faded to a softer light green towards the end. The spiral was not perfectly shaped, but wrapped around itself in imperfect beauty.

I lightly touched the newly visible mark and traced my finger from the center of the spiral to the end and back. It was strange to see such a mark on the skin, let alone on my own. "How do you know this mark states I am the one?"

"The prophecy said the one who bears the mark of the path of growth and changes would be the Bringer of Peace," Lydorea said simply. "Before you were born your parents found out you would be a girl and that you could be the Bringer of Peace. The day you were born, that marking was on you. It was without any question that you, Nyrieve, are the Bringer of Peace."

I sat there staring at my wrist and touching the tips of my pointy ears, thinking of how so much has changed physically and also in my thoughts of my future. Suddenly my dream came flooding back to me, people talking about a prophecy, and the one who would bear the mark.

As I looked at the marking on my wrist, I softy said, "I do not know what to say or think right now. I am feeling very overwhelmed by so much. I don't even know what questions I should be asking or what I should be doing right now."

"I personally think it would be best right now to take a break for Nyrieve, let her absorb all this new information, and when she is ready, later today or tomorrow, we can meet back together and answer any other questions she might have," Baysil said, standing up. He walked over to me, held out his hand. I took it and he helped me to my feet. "Nyrieve, you are a smart girl, and you have so much being placed before you. I am sorry it has to be like this, but it is the truth and the way of life." And for the first time ever he gave me a hug, tight and close to him, and he whispered into my ear, "Be careful who you trust. I will do anything I can to help you, even lay down my life if needs be."

I couldn't believe he said that. Who would lay down their life for me, and who did he think I shouldn't trust? As he pulled away, he gave me a big smile. He then turned and walked towards the door.

"I agree with Baysil. I think we need to give Nyrieve some time to think and come up with the questions she has," Miaarya stated, standing as well and giving me a smile. "And you always know you can come to see me for anything I can help you with."

"Nyrieve," Lydorea said, "why don't you take some time to think, but please do not go far from the manor. We have people out keeping watch that no one new comes into Cliffside without us being prepared, but just try to stick close."

"One more thing, Ny, before you go. I think you should also be aware of your full name. Only a few Elves are given first and last names," Relonya said with a big smile. "Your full Elf name is Nyrieve

Vynlync. And in the old Elf scrolls, Vynlync was used often to describe heroes and those who brought people together."

"Why do not all Elves have last names?" I asked.

"Usually only royalty have them; however, sometimes parents give them to honor a departed family member or hope it gives the child extra protection."

∝4∝

"NYRIEVE VYNLYNC," I SAID out loud to myself, still trying to make it sound right to me.

After Relonya told me about my name, she had left the room with Baysil, and as I walked over to leave the room, I noticed Lydorea had the pieces of the broken bracelet in her hand.

"Have you been wearing those bands since I came here, Lydorea?" I asked her curiously.

"Actually, since before you came here. Once we received word from Rowzey that you'd be coming, I made them and started wearing them. On the night you were brought here, I invoked them, and they have been concealing your true nature ever since."

"Could I... could I have the bracelets... even the broken pieces?" I asked. "I would like to keep them as a reminder of what you did for me."

"Of course you can," she said, carefully handing them to me. I thought about her and Iclyn's other bracelets, and I figured I should ask while I had the nerve. "Are the other bracelets you and Iclyn wear for other people you are concealing?"

Iclyn made a small sound of surprise as she touched one of the bracelets on her left wrist.

Lydorea smiled at me saying, "Yes, Nyrieve, you are not the only Elf we are hiding here. I think you would be surprised to realize that you know at least one of the other Elves here. Though I am not sure if you or this other Elf is ready to know yet."

I thought for a moment of all the people I know in Cliffside who I thought could also be an Elf, and only one person came to mind.

"It's Kaleyna, isn't it? That is why we get along so well, because we are both different," I blurted out, hoping I'd be right.

Iclyn tilted her head, smiling. "Well, Nyrieve, like Baysil said, you are a very smart Elf. While your friend Kaleyna is also an Elf, I do not believe it is the best time to tell her. She has her seventeenth Leaf Day in fortnight. She will begin to find herself changing as well, so it might be best to not shock her ahead of time."

"I didn't plan on telling her, I just thought... well hoped it would be her. She and I have so many differences from other people our age here, but we are usually the same. We had always just thought we were outcasts of sorts," I said sadly, knowing we were never outcasts, but just different from them. "At least I will be able to be here for her when she does find out, so she will know she's not alone."

"You might not be able to be here for her, Nyrieve," Iclyn said matter-of-factly. "You will likely be leaving within a fortnight or less to meet up with The Drayks, Elf rebels. Sometimes they go by Drayk or Drayks as well, they were named for the dragons of Iryvalya that used to roam all over the world. They will be filling you in on what has been going on with the Elf Klayns and what is needed to be done. Don't fret though, someone will be here for Kaleyna."

"Oh, so soon... I had not even thought about that... that I will have to leave Cliffside," I stammered.

"Sadly, you will likely be leaving soon. Something else, Nyrieve," Lydorea said, "while it's nothing to be ashamed of, do not show the mark of the Bringer of Peace to everyone just yet. It is safer for you to keep that a bit quiet if you can. I have something to help you with that." She took a bracelet out of a pocket hidden in her skirts. It was a long bracelet of beads that were woven in between two black leather strips. The beads were a variety of different gem stones. I had only seen a few of them before, and they were all beautiful.

"Thank you so much, Lydorea," I said as I wrapped it three times around my right wrist and fumbled with the clasp until I hooked it. "It is very beautiful and covers it perfectly."

"You are very welcome, Ny. I made this for you a while ago, and I am happy to see you wear it. Now you best be heading out. Take some time to let everything process, and feel free to come see us if you have any questions or concerns."

I nodded to Lydorea, turned and walked out of Iclyn's room and back up the stairs to my room. Not even a moment after I shut my door, there was a knock on it. I turned back towards the thick wooden door and opened it.

"Hello, Jehryps," I said, surprised to see him standing outside my door. Jehryps was another of the abandoned kids I had grown up with, who still lived in the manor as well. We hadn't been friends, though we have talked here and there, but never before has he come to my room. "What can I do for you?"

"Hello, Ny. I was wondering if I could come in and talk to you for a few moments," he said with his honey-like voice, smooth and calm like he always seemed. Jehryps always had an appearance of confidence and control in everything he did, and today was no different.

"Uhm... sure you can," I said. I stepped aside to let him in. He sat in the only chair in my room, which was next to the door, and I sat down on my bed. After I sat down, he leaned over and closed the door. He settled back in the old faded pink overstuffed chair, resting his right ankle on his left knee.

Jehryps was near my age, a bit older I think, as I can vaguely remember that during the planting season he had a Leaf Day cake that he shared with everyone in the manor. He was taller than me by a little, and he had a beautiful tan that looked like he was almost glowing. He kept his golden yellow and orange hair usually cut halfway down his ears and left tousled. When his hair was still white, he kept it long and tied into an intricate braid all the time. Once it started to have streaks of color in it, he had it cut to where it just covered his ears. His eyes were a light and dark swirl of golden yellows, framed by his golden yellow eyebrows.

"So how are you doing, Ny?" he asked, as if he already knew the answer.

"I am doing okay," I lied. I did not want to talk to Jehryps about my being an Elf or anything else that I have found out.

"Well I doubt that you are just okay, as I know there have been some changes going on for you," he teased.

"And how would you know anything is going on with me?" I asked, doubtful.

"Well that beautiful streak of green is one telltale sign, and if that wasn't enough... those cute pointed ears peeking through your hair is another," he pointed out with a big grin on his face.

I could feel my cheeks redden at the mention of my pointed ears. While I liked seeing them myself, I had forgotten that others would notice them and know I was an Elf.

"Your blushing is pretty cute too I think," Jehryps said coyly.

"I am not sure what to say, but I guess thank you would be appropriate," I said sheepishly, "but I am still wondering why you wanted to see me."

"I wanted to see how you were doing with finding out that like me, you are an Elf," he said, pushing his thick hair behind his right pointed ear.

"I... I didn't know you were an Elf," I said, surprised, continuing to look at his pointed ear.

"I haven't made it a point to tell anyone. I was not ready to be the only abandoned Elf here in Cliffside, and when I found out you were an Elf, I figured it would be good to have someone else like me to, you know... talk to," Jehryps said with a sly little smile, telling me he did not seem to be only interested in someone to talk to. However, that cannot possibly be the case.

Jehryps is the guy who every guy here tried to be friends with, some more than friends, and almost all the girls wanted to pairyn with him, which is simply enjoying a romantic relationship together. How could he be interested in me? He always had a reputation for pairyn with girls for as long as it would take to get them to twyn with him. He was never mean to them afterwards or anything, he'd just moved on, and they always seemed to be okay with that.

"Uhm... how did you found out I was an Elf? And more so, when did you find out?" I asked, getting a little concerned and wondering that if Jehryps knew, how many other people would know already.

"I have known since yesterday. I was actually outside the kitchen last night when Rowzey gave you a letter telling you that you're an Elf, and also from the sounds of others talking, a special Elf," he said coyly.

"And who else knows besides you, Jehryps?" I asked, getting annoyed that he would listen in to such a personal conversation. It also had me worried that other people were talking about me.

"Do you really think I would tell anyone else? I haven't told anyone else that I am an Elf yet," he said with surprise in his voice, though I couldn't tell if it was forced or not.

"You cannot be surprised that I'd wonder if you told anyone, seeing as you are friends with basically everyone in Cliffside, and yet have never gone out of your way to talk to me before," I said. "And besides, I have only just been made aware of who and what I am, so it is kind of surprising to know that someone outside those I have talked to knows about it."

"Look, Ny," he said, standing up and sitting down next to me on the bed, "I just wanted to come and say I am here for you, if you need anyone to talk to. I know it is a lot to absorb finding out you're an Elf. I was quite surprised when I found out I was."

We sat in silence for a few moments. I should apologize for assuming that he came here without honest intent to be there for me, and as I turned my head to face him, he smiled at me and I froze.

Suddenly he stood up and took my right hand in his and placed his lips gently on my hand. He stayed that way for what seemed like minutes, but was only seconds, and then he stood back up and smiled at me.

"If you ever would like to talk to me, come find me. I will always be willing to stop what I am doing to talk to you." With that line, he turned, and without looking back, he walked out the door, shutting it softly behind him.

I don't know how long I sat there for, but my heart was fluttering and I was so confused by what happened. I had seen Jehryps many times with other girls he liked, and only a few times I saw him kiss their hands like that. He never did that to just anyone, so why did he do that to me?

I had only been sitting a few minutes when there was another knock on my door. "Come in," I said automatically.

The door opened and Kaleyna was standing there smiling. "So, was that Jehryps I saw leaving your room a few moments ago or am I seeing things?"

"Yes, that was Jehryps... however, I am still a little unsure of why he wanted to see me..." I said, still wondering about him kissing my hand. As I looked up at Kaleyna's face, it dawned on me that my best friend is also an Elf and has no idea, and I frowned.

"Okay..." Kaleyna said, closing the door behind her and crossing the room to sit down next to me. "What is going on? You seemed kind of happy when I opened the door and now you look super sad or confused."

"What do you mean?" I asked, forcing a smile.

"Oh no, Ny, you cannot put on that fake smile with me and actually believe that I will fall for it. I know you met with Iclyn and Lydorea today. Is it something about that?" she asked, concerned.

"That is part of it," I confessed, hoping she would leave it at that.

"Okay," she said, sitting down across from me on the bed, "so first, I love your new hair and, oh my, look at your cute pointy ears!" She leaned across the bed and lightly touched the tips. "I love them, they are so you, and the green hair. I know it is rare, so that makes it perfect for you!"

Kaleyna is the sweetest person to me. She has always tried to convince me I am something better than I think I am, and whenever I have tried to brush it off, she reminds me how I always do the same for her. I guess this is just what best friends do for each other. But keeping secrets, like me knowing she is an Elf, isn't.

"Thank you, Kal," I said, taking a very deep breath. "There are a lot of new things that my head is just spinning from today. The hair, the ears, learning more about being an Elf... Oh, and I have a last name."

"Oh yeah, I remember hearing that Elves have last names. What is it?"

"Vynlync," I said, and even while saying it, it felt strange, yet so very right.

"Vynlync," Kaleyna repeated. "I like it, it fits you! So what else did you learn?"

We talked about everything that was discussed during the meeting in Iclyn's office, including Baysil's offer to die for me, the bracelet that crumbled off of Lydorea's wrist, and the one that she had that covered my marking. I showed Kal the pieces Lydorea gave me. I took off the bracelet so Kaleyna could see my marking. She looked closely at it on my wrist, tracing it with her dainty finger, smiling the whole time. After I put my bracelet back on, Kaleyna looked at the broken bracelet pieces from Lydorea and tried to put it back together. After a while she gave up and laid them on the bed.

"So they told you that you will be the savior of Iryvalya?" she asked seriously.

"The Bringer of Peace they kept calling it. Me? Can you believe that?"

"Honestly… yes."

"How could you think I could do something like that?" I asked with a surprised laugh.

"Ny, you are special, I have always known that. You are just now only figuring that out. This oddly doesn't surprise me."

"I haven't told you one of the worst parts… I have to leave Cliffside to meet up with the other Elf rebels, called The Drayks, to learn what is going on and what exactly they think I can do," I said sadly.

"Leave Cliffside… I guess that doesn't surprise me. You can't do much from here I'd imagine."

We sat in silence for a little bit, then Kaleyna took my hand and smiled at me. "It's okay, Ny, I will come with you to wherever you have to go. Though I don't know if anyone else will like a tag-a-long Fairy."

"Well that shouldn't be an issue," I said before realizing it.

"What do you mean?"

"Uhm… nothing… just… if I am some peace bringer, you'd think they'd let me bring who I want," I said, trying to sound convincing.

"What are you keeping from me, Ny?" Kaleyna said, looking me in the eyes. "I know there is something you are not telling me."

"It's nothing, Kaleyna, honest," I lied.

"We promised that we'd never keep secrets from each other. Please don't start breaking that promise with me."

"I don't want to keep anything from you, but I was told I am not supposed to tell you, Kal… if I tell you, you must promise me, that you will never tell anyone I told you this. Never," I said with a low whisper.

"I'd never break a promise to you, Ny, as you would never break one to me," she whispered back to me.

"Do you remember how I told you about the other bracelets that Lydorea and Iclyn had on?"

"Yes," Kaleyna whispered, raising her eyebrows curiously.

"One of those bracelets..." I said, taking a deep breath, "one of those bracelets is yours."

Kaleyna looked at me for a few moments blankly. All of a sudden a smile started to spread on her face. "You mean I am an Elf like you?" she asked so quietly that I almost couldn't hear her.

I nodded my head, and she grabbed me and hugged me. When she let go and sat back, I could see tears running down her cheeks. "Why are you crying?" I whispered.

"Because I had hoped that I would be an Elf too, like you. I did not want to be so different from you that people might try to keep us apart," she said, smiling brightly.

"Nothing will ever keep us apart, Kaleyna. We are spirit sisters. No matter what, we will always be together," I said, sure of my words to her.

"Okay, since we can't talk about... something... now you have to tell me why Jehryps was in here and why you looked all flushed when I walked in!" Kaleyna said, back in her usual happy voice.

I laughed. "I have no idea. He told me how he's an Elf too, and that now that he knows I am as well, he wanted to 'be there' for me. He had overheard me in the kitchen yelling last night after I read the letter from my parents. It just seems odd, seeing as he's never really talked to me before, let alone come to my room to talk to me."

"Maybe he has always liked you, and this was a way for him to be able to talk to you without needing another reason?" she said, sounding like even she didn't believe that.

"You and I both know that if Jehryps wanted to talk to a girl, nothing ever would stop him from doing it. I don't know, I just think maybe it is because I'm an Elf and he is interested only because he thinks Elves are different?"

"Well, I personally think you are quite the catch, so I could see why he would be interested in you!"

"I sincerely doubt he is interested in me like that, Kaleyna!"

"You never know, Ny, maybe this made him finally notice you..."

"I don't think that would be a good thing. I mean, if he wasn't interested in me before, when he thought I was a Fairy, why in the world would I want him to be interested in me now, just because he knows I am an Elf?"

"That is a good point, so my advice would be to talk to him and see what he actually wants, but keep your guard up. I will keep my ears open in case I hear anything about it from anyone."

"Thanks, Kal. I think that is what I'll do… if he comes to talk to me again."

"Well, I think I have kept you busy for just enough time now… so let's get up and go downstairs for the celebration," Kaleyna said with a sly grin on her face.

"What celebration?" I asked.

"Your seventeenth Leaf Day celebration, silly! Did you honestly think that today would go by without a celebration?"

"I honestly didn't think about celebrating it with everything else going on…" I mumbled.

"That is what friends are for, to celebrate you even if you do not think it's important. You are important to me, so it's time to celebrate your Leaf Day!"

ಐ5ಜ

THE CELEBRATION WAS AMAZING, so much more than I had ever expected or could have hoped for. Everyone from the manor was there, and even a few others from around Cliffside. They all seemed quite surprised to find out I was an Elf, but everyone was very supportive and complimented me on my hair and ears. I made sure that my bracelet was always covering the mark on my wrist, out of fear that someone might find out what I am.

There was a lot of food, provided by Rowzey of course. She had made her sauce with my favorite noodles and with breaded baked chicken covered in cheese. Everyone was laughing and enjoying the atmosphere, reminding me of all those in the manor who I have grown up with, and how different and yet still the same we are.

After the meal was finished, there were even a few presents given to me. A new pair of soft black leather pants, a pair of matching black boots that laced up above my knees, and a deep moss-green shirt that had silver leaf buttons. Those were from Relonya. I had been surprised to get a gift from someone I had just met, but was thankful for such a beautiful and useful gift.

I also received a silver bracelet from Lydorea, one that looked exactly like the one she had worn to cover up my ears and marking. When I received it and looked up at her, she smiled and told me, "This is a reminder to be proud of who you are." When she leaned in to give me a hug, she whispered, "And it also has the ability to cloak who you are and make you appear as someone else. To invoke it, all you need to do is put three drops of blood on it and say 'Obscure.' It will only last for half a day, and there are only five charges in it."

There were other simple but wonderful gifts, like some new hair ribbons, some of my favorite chocolate-peanut-butter fudge, and a perfume that smelled of apples infused with water from the North Sea. Jehryps also gave me a present, a rose blossom carved out of wood. It was the size of the palm of my hand, and it had very intricate details on it. I was flattered he made this for me.

I couldn't believe all the items I received and that everyone took time out of their day to celebrate my Leaf Day. After all the presents were done, Rowzey came out of the kitchen with a cake for me, and I could tell she had made my favorite one. It was a red velvet cake with a sweet yet subtle white frosting covering it. On the top, she had written out "Happy Leaf Day, Nyrieve." After she set it on the table and showed me it, she proceeded to cut the cake for everyone, and Miaarya was sweet enough to pass some out to everyone who wanted a piece, which was everyone.

After everyone had a slice, Rowzey looked at me and said basically the same speech she gives to everyone on their Leaf Day. "Nyrieve, today we's celebrate yous Leaf Day. The day yous Leaf opened on the great Leaf Tree. Yous Leaf is special and delicate, and will remain growing on the great tree next to everyone else's in Iryvalya until yous last day here. Once yous go on, yous beautiful Leaf will fall to the ground and remain among all of those who has left our world before, but never forgotten. Today we's be grateful for another Leaf Day for yous, and many more to come."

Everyone cheered and said, "Happy Leaf Day, Nyrieve!" We all spent time talking and enjoying the cake. After a while, people started to leave the celebration, and soon enough it was just Kaleyna, Rowzey and me sitting at the table in the kitchen talking and enjoying some hot tea.

"Nyrieve, I did not want to give you your gift in front of everyone else," Kaleyna said, handing me a wrapped package. "I don't mind Rowzey seeing it. She helped get it for me after all."

I looked at Rowzey, and while part of me was still unhappy with her for keeping such a big secret from me, I also knew what she did had to be out of love for me. I smiled at Rowzey, knowing that even though I will be frustrated with her for a while, it will pass and I still love and need her in my life.

I took the package from Kaleyna, smiling at her. "Thank you."

"You have to open it before being able to thank me!"

I unwrapped the white paper that was carefully put together, and when I could see what was inside, I was intrigued. There were three leather-bound books, one green, one blue and one pink, each with a metal latch on it. I took the top book, the green one, which wasn't latched shut, and inside the cover there was a short message: *To Nyrieve, this is to ensure no matter how far apart we may be in distance, we will always be close to one another. Love, Kaleyna.* All the pages after the cover were blank, I looked up at Kaleyna smiling at me with a huge grin.

"Have you figured out yet what the books are?" Kaleyna asked me.

"I think they are journals of some sort?" I said, guessing.

"Kind of… You see, the green journal is yours of course, the blue is mine, and the pink is Rowzey's."

"So these are for each of us to be able to write our thoughts in, and then we can share them with one another?" I asked, still slightly confused.

"Not exactly. These are not typical journals, Ny. I have been working with Rowzey on this for months to get them enchanted. They are Mirror Journals!" Kaleyna said excitedly.

"Mirror journals?" I asked, very surprised. "I thought it was impossible to find someone to make these anymore?"

"Impossible for many," Rowzey said, "but was not impossible for I's to make them for yous both. This is our secret that we's have these though."

"Oh I won't tell anyone!" I said excitedly. "How do they work?"

Kaleyna took her blue mirror journal and tapped the top of the latch with her finger. There was a small drop of blood on the tip now, and she placed it on the center of the latch, which then opened. She then took a small portable quill and ink box out. After dipping the quill in the ink, she wrote on the first page of her journal the word *Greetings*. After a few moments, I saw the word *Greetings* appear in Kaleyna's handwriting in my journal in the exact same location on the page.

"I can't believe this! I love it so much!" I said, giving Kaleyna a big hug, and then walked over to Rowzey and gave her a big hug too. "Thank you so much, both of you. It is the best gift ever."

"I's was thinking that with yous leaving soon, this a way we's can keep in contact. Then if either of yous ever need me, yous can always reach me," Rowzey said with a warm smile.

"And also no one but the three of us can write in them, and all the journals will mirror into each other," Kaleyna added.

"Why is that?" I asked.

"If someone else try to write in it, they can't pretend to be yous," Rowzey said with a sly smile on her kind weathered face.

"Oh... that makes sense then," I said, wondering why anyone would try to.

"Just remember, to open the latch, you do have to put a drop of blood on it. The top of each latch has a small point sharp enough to make a prick on your finger," Kal said with a smile.

After a long time of sitting and talking to each other, I noticed that both Rowzey and Kaleyna were getting sleepy, so I suggested that they both head to bed. I said that I was likely going to sit by the fire in the front room for a bit, as I wasn't tired in the least. Rowzey took her pink book and locked it in her cabinets, and Kaleyna said she would put mine inside my room under my pillow for me, as she took her blue one up with her to her room.

After they left the kitchen, I got up and walked into the front room, but the fire was almost out. I didn't feel like adding to it, so I decided to take a quick walk outside and get a little fresh air. I went back through the kitchen and grabbed a cloak off the hook near the back door. I walked out, not knowing exactly where I was heading, but just enjoying the crisp air and the sounds of the ground under my feet. I walked down the path near the lake, and realized I wanted to see the North Sea, so I changed directions and walked towards the dirt path that lead to the top of the cliffs outside of the village.

As I walked through the village, I found myself staring at these buildings I had seen throughout my whole life. The shops were either connected or very close together, and formed a crescent shape. There were apartments above some of the shops and houses scattered around them. Most of the people in Cliffside lived in the village area. Only a few had homes near the lake or in the woods. As far as the shops, there was a bakery, where we would sometimes get bread when Rowzey didn't have time to make some. Next to that was the butcher, whose daughter also made little sweet candies for the children when they came in with their parents. There was also a fabric and leather shop to get materials for clothing, plus a shoemaker and the blacksmith.

When I reached the cliffs, I sat down on some of the rocks overlooking the huge drop down into the beautiful North Sea's strong waves as they crashed against the rocks below. I must have been sitting for quite a while, as I started to feel the hardness of the rocks beginning to become uncomfortable. Right before I stood, I heard movement off to the right behind me. I turned to look, and Baysil walked towards me in the bright Nydian moonlight.

"Baysil, what are you doing out here so late?"

"I was waiting for you back at the manor, but when you did not come back, I figured it would be best to look for you and make sure you were okay," he said with concern in his voice.

"I am fine. I have just been enjoying the beautiful night and listening to the waves crashing below."

Baysil reached me and sat down on the rock next to me. He was carrying a semi-large package.

I looked up at Baysil, noticing the worry on his face. "Why do you look so worried, Baysil?"

"Nyrieve, I don't think you fully understand how much danger you are in, and I want to make sure you are safe at all costs," Baysil said quietly, as if someone could overhear him.

"I appreciate you worrying about me, but I didn't think I'd be in danger just walking out to the cliffs for a little bit," I said, unaccustomed to the idea that I needed to worry about my safety.

"I understand this is very new to you, but I need you to start thinking about your actions and those you are around. While there are others you can trust, you really need to have your guard up a little and realize that even people you might think are trustworthy, might not be," he said, turning the package in his hands over and over.

He noticed me watching him with the package, and smiled at me. "This is for you, Nyrieve. It's a Leaf Day gift from me. I had this made for you a few years ago, and have been holding onto it until today."

"What is it?"

He handed me the package. It was a carved wooden box with a small latch on the front. The box was approximately the length of my arm and only half as wide. I looked up to Baysil. He smiled and nodded at me. "Open it."

I unhooked the latch and slowly opened the intricately carved box. Inside was something I had never seen before. It was reflective in the moonlight, and after a moment, I could see it was not simply a shiny trinket, but a well-polished deadly weapon. I looked back up to Baysil and asked again, "What is it?"

He slowly leaned over me, taking the weapon out of the crimson-velvet–lined box. I gently set the box down on the rock next to me and turned to give my full attention to Baysil. After a moment of seeing the weapon in his hand, I knew it was a knife of sorts, but I had never seen one with the blade in the shape of a crescent before. Baysil gently took my right hand and guided it to the handle of the knife, which was a strong solid-feeling metal with three holes to slide in my first three fingers, and it was wrapped in strips of soft black leather.

Over the top of each hole for my fingers, there was a metal point that came up, for if I used it to hit someone, it would hurt pretty badly. At the end of the handle was a beautifully set stone. In the moonlight, though, I could not fully tell what it was. On the other end of the handle was a slightly curved blade, that when held in my hand, first curved away and then back to a point near the middle of my forearm. The blade was sharp on both sides. I lightly traced my finger down the one side and felt it bite into my skin. The metal of the blade was a high-polished silver color, reminding me of some of the best swords I had ever read about or seen.

"What exactly is this, Baysil?" I asked, still curiously looking at the knife.

"It is a specialty weapon I had not only made for you, but the rain-bow moonstone in the top of the knife has been enchanted with a spell to make it feel light and easy to maneuver. The silvery metal is something unique, something I have never seen before. When I requisitioned this item, I was told this metal was mined from the heart of Iryvalya herself, and there was only a small amount of it left in the world. The maker also said this metal will give the bearer the backing of Iryvalya herself," Baysil said with a small smile on his face.

"Thank you so much, Baysil, but honestly, I'm a little nervous. I've never held a weapon like this before," I said truthfully.

"You should not be afraid of a weapon, it is but a tool. It is how you carry and use a weapon that will determine if you should be nervous. And this particular blade has a name."

"A name?" I asked.

"Yes, the person who made this said that all his weapons get named, and this one's name is Klaw."

"Klaw..." I said, thinking how the blade really did resemble the nails of an animal. "So I am just supposed to carry Klaw out with the blade exposed at all times?"

"No, not at all," he said, grabbing something from inside his cloak. It was a black sheath that had to have been made especially for this weapon. It had straps around the top and bottom. "This will hold Klaw and have it strapped to the top of your pants and around your thigh. This will allow you to have very easy access to it in an emergency."

I took the sheath and he showed me how to tie it to my upper and lower thigh. Afterward, Baysil showed me how to slide Klaw into the holder properly, to keep from cutting myself. Once it was in place, I tried to move my leg around to see if Klaw would fall out, but it would not budge. So I put my right hand into the holes of the handle and brought my hand up towards my chest with ease and Klaw smoothly slid out with it.

"Thank you, Baysil. I truly appreciate this, but I honestly am not sure how I am supposed to use it."

"When you meet up with the other Elves, you will go through training to learn different fighting techniques and how to protect yourself. You already know how to use a bow to hunt, or a knife, but you will learn how to use a sword, new magyc spells, and also Klaw, so you can better protect yourself."

"I didn't realize I would need to learn things like this... but I guess it makes sense after you said that there are people around me I cannot trust."

"You will learn how to read people after time, and know who you can and cannot trust. I will be going with you, along with a small group of people from Cliffside, to meet up with The Drayks in a fortnight or so. When we meet with the Rebel Elves, you will be taught the ways of the Elves, and one of those will be teaching you the magyc of the Elves as well as different fighting methods."

"I am glad that you will be coming with me, Baysil. I trust you and I know you will always be honest with me."

"Yes I will, even if my truth hurts you," he said. "I think it is time, though, that we head back to the manor. It is late and you need some rest. There are still some details that need to be worked out before we leave and I am sure you want to spend time with those here you care about that you might be leaving behind."

I stood up with him and we walked the path towards the manor in silence. It felt strange having Klaw rubbing against my thigh at first, but by the time we were halfway to the manor, I almost did not notice it there anymore.

When we got back to the manor, Baysil said good night, and went to the stairs that led down into the basement. I watched him go down the stairs and disappear into the darkness. As I walked up the stairs to my room, I could hear the silence of the manor. I realized I had enjoyed the sounds of everyone this evening laughing and talking during my Leaf Day celebration.

After I was in my room and had changed into my sleeping gown, I crawled into bed and felt the mirror journal beneath my pillow. I left it there, thinking how nice it will be to always have a way to contact both Kaleyna and Rowzey if we are ever far apart. Sadly, that would likely be happening a lot sooner than I wanted.

ℭ𝔰6𝔰℣

I WOKE WITH THE LIGHT shining through my small window, feeling that I finally had been able to get some rest after the last couple days. I stretched out on my small bed, and when I placed my hands under my head, I felt my journal from Kaleyna. I slowly sat up, taking the journal out, and looked at the green leather binding. It was truly a beautiful shade of green. I wondered if Rowzey somehow knew my hair was going to be green and that is why she gave me this one, or just because she knew I liked the color. Though with Rowzey, nothing ever seemed to be by chance, as she seems to always know more that she lets on.

I pricked my finger and dabbed the blood on the latch. I opened and flipped through the pages of the journal. There had to be at least three hundred pages all together. Near the back of the journal, there was something stuck between the pages. I opened to that part and found a few folded pieces of paper that were sealed with Rowzey's symbol, a caldron.

I carefully broke the seal and opened up the papers. It was a letter addressed to me from Rowzey. It was written with the correct spelling for everything, but I couldn't help but mentally add her accent to the words as I read it.

Dearest Ny,

Today is yous 17th Leaf Day, and I's extremely proud of yous. Many things be changing in only a short time and many more things will begin changing for yous too.

I's wanted to tell yous about when I's met yous mother and father. They came to me after talking to Zyjoyvi. I's was living with the Pixies on the island of Troxeon, south of the Air Realm and east of the Fire Realm in Iryvalya. It was very strange for me cooking such small amounts of my sauce, as the Pixies is no bigger than the palm of yous hand, so they have quite small appetites. I's was also the main caretaker of two little twin Pixie sisters, Ayllac and Callya. They was the sweetest little things, whose parents passed away when they were so young. Their parents had been remarkably powerful Pixies, and sadly, were killed when they tried to help some of the Elves who's wanted to escape the Klayns.

When I's first met yous mother, Osidya, and father, Arnayx, I's realized they were very much concerned for yous safety. Yous was still in yous mother's belly, though close to being born. Osidya was very tan, tall, and lanky, but was a beautiful Pyrothian Elf, with long curly hair that started near the top of her head as dark red wine color that faded down to a deep orange and finishing as a light orange color. Her eyes was a swirl twist of light and dark orange, and framed with the wine red eyebrows. Osidya had the kindest smiles I's had ever seen. She was a very sweet Elf who was very worried about yous well-being and wanted to be sure I's would keep yous safe.

Yous father was also a very handsome Lumaryia Elf. Arnayx was almost the complete physical opposite of yous mother. The only thing that was the same for them was they were the same height. Otherwise yous father was much lighter-skinned, and he's had big muscles on his shoulders and even his thighs. I's remember him having his bright blue hair tied back every time I's saw him, his eyebrows was the same blue, but his eyes were the biggest attention grabber. His eyes was a swirl twist of the clearest blue and also of the truest violet I's had ever seen, until I's saw yous violet color. He's had a very strong, almost squared jaw line, and very full lips. He's did not seem to smile as much as yous mother did, but I's think he was just very scared for yous.

Shortly after they had come to Troxeon, yous mother went into labor. The Pixies were great at assisting me to help yous mother to bring yous into the world. I's remember when you first opened yous eyes, yous father started to cry seeing part of his eyes in yous. Yous mother was so happy that yous were healthy and full of life. Yous did not cry like most babies, yous just looked at everything smiling. We's could also see immediately yous bore the mark of the Bringer of Peace on yous inner right wrist.

Yous had a few days with them before I's had to take yous all the way to Cliffside. While yous parents had yous, they tried so hard to figure out what to name yous. Yous last name was the easy part, Vynlync. They felt it fitting for *the bringer of peace. Eventually they told me yous name was to be Nyrieve, though they never told me how they got that name.*

They loved yous very much, Ny, and like them, I's love yous very much too, like yous is my own daughter. I's know yous were also raised by the Fairies here as well as me, but I's still always made sure to keep me eye on yous at all times.

I's sorry for keeping this from yous for so very long, but it really was for yous own safety, and because I's wanted yous to be happy and not worry so much about the future. I's know I's cannot protect yous from it anymore, but know that is why I's did what I's did.

I's love yous very much, Ny, and I's wish yous the best Leaf Day. I's do have another gift for yous. Look in the top drawer of yous dresser, and yous will find something that was not there before. Say nothing of it, just take it and know it's yous.
Rowzey

Tears slowly trickled down my cheeks. It was such a phenomenal feeling to finally know something about who my parents were, to know that they did care about me and that they did spend some time with me when I was born. Somehow I just thought I was born here in Cliffside, as if they never saw me at all, even though I logically knew that could not be true. Not only did I now know something about them, I could almost envision them in my mind. It made me smile and cry at the same time. I couldn't be upset with Rowzey at all anymore, especially now that she shared these wonderful memories with me.

As I wiped the slowly drying tears away, I remembered that her note said there was something else for me in the top drawer of my dresser. I got up and walked over the cool floor to my dresser and quickly opened it. Sitting right in the middle were two things that were not there before. The first one I opened was a small portable quill and ink box. It had to be from Kaleyna, she had one just like it. The other item was what looked like a very old box with intricately carved vines knotted together. Inside was the most exquisite pair of small silver circles that appeared to open. On the opposite side of where they opened there was a small polished gem. It looked like the same rainbow moonstone on top of Klaw.

After staring at these silver gems, I finally figured out what they were. They were ear adornments—earrings, I believe they were called. I remembered hearing about those from the Fairies and the Elves who had come to Cliffside. The Elves wore them through the middle of the outer ear rim. Which means to wear these, I would have to have a needle put through my ears. I couldn't believe Rowzey would expect me to do that just to wear these.

I placed the bejeweled earrings into the box, set it back inside the drawer and closed it. I guess I will discuss that one with Rowzey later, even if she said to 'say nothing of it.' I needed to get up and to get dressed. As I picked out my clothes for the day, I wondered what new things I would learn about today. There would have to be something, seeing as there hadn't been many days lately I haven't.

I put on my worn gray cloth pants, tucking them into my brown knee-high leather boots. I also put on a light pink shirt that I had shortened the sleeves on to just above my elbow. While I was brushing out my hair, I checked to see if there was any more color in it, but it was still only the one streak so far. I decided to leave my hair down for now, but I put some hair pins in my pocket in case I wanted to put it up later.

As I opened the door to my room, a piece of folded paper lay on the floor in front of my room. I picked it up and opened it. It was a short note from Baysil. All it said was *Wear Klaw always. Baysil.* So I hurried back into my room, set the note on the top of my dresser and strapped Klaw onto my right thigh. It was going to be strange to explain to people when they saw me wearing it, but that shouldn't be the reason why I don't wear it.

After leaving my room, I hurried down the stairs to get something to eat. When I reached the kitchen, Kaleyna and Jehryps were both sitting at the table talking, and Rowzey was behind them cooking something as usual.

"Morning?" I said with a small question in my voice.

"Morning, Ny," Kaleyna said with her usual bright smile.

"Hello, Nyrieve," Jehryps said, slightly drawing out my name.

"Can I's get yous something to eat, Ny?" Rowzey asked.

"Sure, Rowzey, I'd appreciate it. I am starving," I said, giving her a quick hug, and then sat down at the table next to Kaleyna.

"What is that, Ny?" Kaleyna asked, pointing to Klaw.

"It was another gift for my Leaf Day. I figured I should wear it and get it broken in. Perhaps practice a bit with it to get more comfortable with using it," I explained, pulling Klaw out of the sheath so she could see how beautiful it was.

"I have trained with different weapons before, and I have never seen anything like that," Jehryps said with a look of envy on his face. "Who did you get that from?"

I slid it back into the sheath and said, "It was a gift from Baysil. He said that he had it made for me. It even has a name—Klaw."

"That was very nice of him to get yous, Ny," Rowzey commented as she set a plate of hot pancakes and bacon in front of me, along with a glass of water.

"I agree. And speaking of gifts, Rowzey, I have a question for you about—"

"Now now," Rowzey said abruptly, "I's did not have time to get yous any gift, so I's very sorry, Ny."

I sat for a moment, looking at Rowzey confused, and concluded she must not have wanted Jehryps to know about the letter or the earrings, which seemed odd. "That's okay, Rowzey... I was just going to tell you not to worry about it, because I think the meal and cake last night was more than enough of a wonderful gift to me."

"I's will still get you something, Ny," Rowzey insisted.

I sat quietly eating while listening to Kaleyna and Jehryps discuss daily matters, such as the weather, the upcoming harvest and other unimportant events. I enjoyed the little bit of normalcy it conveyed while eating, though it was far from normal for Jehryps to be here sitting in Rowzey's kitchen talking to Kaleyna or me.

"So what do you have planned today, Ny?" Kaleyna asked, turning the conversation towards me.

After I finished chewing the last bite of my bacon I responded, "Personally I do not have anything planned; however, I know I need to meet up with Iclyn and Lydorea at some point today, and I know that Baysil wanted to talk to me, as did Relonya."

"Actually, Ny, they all is in a meeting, and asked me to tell yous that when they is done, they will come get yous," Rowzey said, taking my plate away to wash it.

"Oh, okay. Thanks for letting me know."

"So... could I possibly interest you in a walk out to the island in the middle of the lake?" Jehryps asked me.

"I think that would be a great idea," Kaleyna replied for me before I could protest the idea. "I think it would be good for you to get some fresh air before being in meetings with everyone later today."

"Uhm... I guess I could... for a little while, but I don't want to go far, in case I am needed for anything," I said, standing up.

I walked over to the door behind Jehryps and turned, giving Kaleyna an annoyed look, and stuck my tongue out at her. She just silently giggled at me. She knew I was not very comfortable going anywhere alone with a guy, especially Jehryps.

Jehryps held the door open for me as I walked out. We walked down the path towards the bridge to the island. I did not wait for him to catch up, but he managed to without much effort, as he had longer legs than me. We walked in silence down the path and across the bridge.

When we reached the island, he asked if I remembered trying to make fires with magyc in the fireplace here on the island when we all were younger. I told him I remembered, though I didn't want to admit that I was never very good at it. Jehryps suggested we try making one now, so I figured it couldn't hurt to try. Worst case, my failing streak of trying to make a fire with magyc would not change anything today.

We put some wood into the small fireplace. He rubbed his middle finger and thumb together, and smoke started to show up but the flame never caught. After him trying a few more times, he suggested it was my turn. I walked up to the small pile of wood, remembering to concentrate and, as Lydorea had told me many times, "believe you can do it." I started to rub my middle finger and thumb together and fire sparked to life. It was only moments and all the wood in the crumbling fire place was ablaze. I couldn't believe it, I did it. Jehryps smiled at me weakly, as if this wasn't the most amazing thing.

Likely for him it wasn't anything new, so why would he get excited? I didn't care if he wasn't impressed, I was so happy and proud of myself for starting the fire so easily. I knew that our powers started to become stronger around our seventeenth Leaf Day, but I had no idea how much easier something like this could be. I sat down on one of the large old benches that were left on the overgrown island, feeling really good about myself, and only after about ten minutes did Jehryps speak again.

"Nyrieve, why does it feel to me like you were avoiding me and didn't want to come down here with me?"

"Avoiding you? When did I avoid you?" I asked, my eyebrows furrowing together. I couldn't remember a time I purposely avoided him.

"Last night, at your Leaf Day celebration, I kept trying to have a seat open by me so you could sit next to me, but you avoided looking at me and seemed to always sit away from me. The only time you looked at me was when you opened the present from me and thanked me."

"I was not trying to avoid you, Jehryps. I have never sat near you before, so it was not an intentional thought to me to go sit next to you," I said, truly surprised that he was trying to get me to sit near him. I do not even remember seeing the seat near him open.

Jehryps straddled the bench right next to me, so close I could feel the slight warmth of him along my side. He was facing me and he reached out, putting a hand on each of my shoulders, turning me to face him uncomfortably. I looked up at his handsome face, wondering what we were really doing here together. Jehryps answered my silent question when he leaned in to me and placed his cool lips on mine. I jerked back, surprised.

"What are you doing?" I exclaimed, scooting further away from him.

"I was just giving you a kiss. I thought you'd want me to—"

"What would make you think I would want you to kiss me?"

"Most of the girls want me to kiss them when we are out here…" he replied, his voice starting to falter.

"I am not like most of the girls here, obviously. I am offended that you could even assume it would okay to just kiss me without even knowing anything about me, or me knowing anything about you," I said, standing up and walking away from him, heading back towards the house.

"Wait, Ny. Didn't you ever think about kissing me before? Haven't you ever wondered what it would be like?" he asked arrogantly.

I paused halfway across the bridge and turned back, facing him. "You know, I honestly had before, because you were always handsome and seemed to be nice to everyone, but now... now I am kind of ashamed I ever did. I never thought that you would be the kind of person to steal someone's first kiss..." I hissed at him. I turned my back on Jehryps and stormed off back to the manor. I heard him plead with me a few times to stop and come back, but I didn't care. I had dreamed my first kiss would be something special, with someone special, and now I just feel like it was not only stolen from me, but it wasn't even a decent kiss.

✂ 7 ✄

I WAS FUMING AS I WALKED back towards the manor. I could not believe Jehryps just kissed me without any warning or me expressing desire to kiss him. Here it was, a moment where I was so happy and proud of being able to use magyc to actually start a fire, and then Jehryps had to ruin it by kissing me like that. I know most of the girls here would be so happy and excited to have his attention like this, but I have seen him give his attention to almost every girl in Cliffside. How could he ever think I'd feel special by him kissing me like I was just any other girl in Cliffside?

I stomped into the kitchen through the back door and slammed it shut as hard as I could. Kaleyna and Rowzey were sitting at the table playing cards, and at the sounds of me coming in I startled them, stopping their game.

"What is wrong, Ny?" Kaleyna asked, concerned.

"He stole my first kiss! He stole it! Why would he think that he can just kiss anyone he wants when he feels like it?"

"Jehryps kissed you?" Kaleyna questioned with her right eyebrow raised at me.

"Yes... I was so excited because I was actually able to set a decent-sized fire with magyc, and then out of nowhere he leaned in and kissed me! He didn't ask... he didn't even ask if I was interested in him. He just... kissed me..."

"I's think that Jehryps is the kind of boy who most girls want to have him kiss them. I's think that he believed that yous would enjoy a kiss from him," Rowzey said thoughtfully. "I's also think that people think Jehryps is a good boy, and I's think yous should remember that just because the sauce smells like it a good batch, don't mean that it is."

I sat down at the table feeling disheartened. "I don't know Jehryps, and I don't know why since finding out who I am he is now interested in me at all. I mean… I get him saying that he wanted to talk to me because we are both Elves, but… we have known each other for years, and this is the first time he has ever showed any form of interest in me… it seems like a lot more interest than our time together deserves."

"Maybe he is wising up and seeing the real you and how great you truly are?" Kaleyna said, but the look on her face couldn't hide the fact that even she didn't believe that was the reason.

"I's think it would not be wise to ignore him completely, but I's do think that yous should let him know what yous expect and what yous don't."

"Right now I do not want to speak to him at all…"

Just then, the back door opened and Jehryps walked in.

Jehryps walked towards me and stopped quickly when I flashed him an angry glance. "Look, Ny… I am sorry… I just… read the moment wrong… I did not mean to upset you at all… I am sorry…" Jehryps stammered, sounding sincere. "I just don't know how I read everything so wrong."

"I think I can give you some insight to that, Jehryps," Kaleyna stated matter-of-factly.

"Please tell me," he begged, sounding desperate.

"Jehryps, you are used to spending time with girls that fawn all over you, want to spend time alone with you, and other such things. Now don't get me wrong, you have always come across as a nice-acting and good-looking guy, but you have never given the time of day to Nyrieve. I don't know why that is, as I personally think Ny is amazing, but girls like her," she said, pointing at me, "do not pine away for boys who have no interest in them. Now, all of the sudden you are wanting to spend time with Ny, and kissing her after only spending a small amount of time together. That alone would make most people question your motives."

"But… I don't have any motives… I just figured we are the only Elves in our age group here. It just makes sense that her and I should be together."

"That, my boy, is a motive. Yous think that yous should be together based on the idea that yous be Elves, not because yous like one another."

Jehryps looked so confused and embarrassed, and I started to almost feel pity for him. He seemed to believe that, because he was handsome and well-liked, I would just automatically want to spend time with him and pairyn with him. I could almost pity him, if I wasn't still so upset with him.

After a long silence, Jehryps looked at me and said, "Nyrieve, I am so sorry... I guess I just didn't realize that you would not naturally want to pairyn with me. I feel stupid right now, and I will back off and not bother you. I just hope that we can at least become friends, as I would like to have another Elf to talk to."

I couldn't think of what I should say, so I said the only thing that came into my head. "I am upset right now, so I need some space... however... I will not likely stay mad for long, as I tend to get over things pretty quickly..." I shot a glance at Rowzey, realizing I wasn't mad at her anymore, and her hiding that I was an Elf is a much bigger reason to be upset.

"I will give you space... again I am very sorry..." Jehryps whispered, looking down at the floor and not meeting my eyes.

"Jehryps, whys don't yous come with me to the basement and help me find a few jars to put the sauce in?"

"Sure," he said flatly and followed her to the back stairs. He stopped for a moment to look over at me before turning back around and following Rowzey into the basement.

After they had been gone for about five minutes, I looked at Kaleyna. "Can you believe the nerve of him?"

"Honestly... yes," she responded, half smiling at me.

"So you condone what he did?"

"Oh no, not at all, but I get it. I mean, think about it, Ny. Besides you and me, and a handful of other girls here, what other girl here would be offended by Jehryps coming up to them out of the blue and kissing them?"

I sat down next to her, running my fingers along the worn wooden table, and thought about it for a few moments. "I can't think of anyone else who would have complained. Most of them would have loved it..."

"Exactly. Jehryps grew up here with a different set of rules than most people. The average person here would never think to do that, but Jehryps was always told how 'handsome' he is and was always flirted with. You are likely the first rejection he has ever had, and he's very confused by it. You could tell by the look on his face. He reminds me of a little kid seeing magyc for the first time. It is something that seems unbelievable and yet they see it happening, so it has to be real, but it doesn't mean they understand it."

I kept looking at the table. I was tracing my finger down a long cut mark that had been there ever since I could remember. Kaleyna had a point, but part of me was still frustrated, but I know my emotions shouldn't override logic. "Maybe I did overreact," I said sullenly.

"I personally think you yelling and walking away was a better reaction than what could have happened. Shoot, you could have given him a closer introduction to Klaw!" She giggled.

"I never even thought about Klaw." I chuckled at her idea, happy she didn't think I overreacted. "I forgot I was even wearing it. I guess that's a good thing. I wouldn't want to ever hurt someone out of an emotional reaction."

"You have better control than most, Ny. I don't know what I would have done if I had been in your place," Kaleyna said. After a short pause she smiled. "So, was it a good kiss at least?"

"Ugh," I said, pushing at her playfully. "Even if it was a good kiss, how would I know when I have nothing to compare it to?"

"Good point."

"I don't know…" I sighed. "I just had always hoped that my first kiss would be special or romantic… or even with someone who liked me for me and not just what I am. And I definitely had hoped it would have been a mutual kiss, not just me getting kissed."

"Think of it this way, your kissing experiences can only improve from here!"

"Way to cheer me up, Kal!" I said, smirking back at her.

"Nyrieve?" Baysil asked.

I jumped at the sound of my name. I hadn't even heard Baysil come into the room. "Oh, hello, Baysil," I said. "Is everything okay?"

"You are needed for some… training of sorts," he said with a slightly mischievous grin.

"What kind of training?"

"Nothing with weapons, but more… educating," Baysil said.

"Could Kaleyna come with us?"

But before Baysil could respond Kaleyna stood up. "Oh I can't, Ny. I have other things I have to attend to, but thank you for asking."

"Oh, okay. So… I guess we should go," I said, standing up and walking towards Baysil and the doorway that went to the living area of the manor. "I will catch up with you later then, Kal."

"Okay, see you later," she said, smiling.

CR80

Baysil took me to a room I had never been to inside the manor, a room off of the basement. I had never noticed the hidden door before, making me wonder if there were other hidden places in the manor as well. When Baysil and I walked through the entrance, I looked around noticing there was a long table off to one side. It looked like there would be enough spots for at least ten people to sit with a comfortable amount of room between each other. The walls were covered in tapestries of serene meadows and valleys, places I had never seen before. There was also a sitting area, with a couple of couches and a few single chairs.

On the table there were maps spread out with labels on them. There was also a large open box of flat crystals. I had seen crystals like them before, back when we were being trained in magyc. They were viewing crystals. One could see, and sometimes hear, messages hidden inside of them. The one we watched in magyc training was for learning how to make an object float. When you held the crystal, an image would appear on it, and as long as you were holding the crystal you could hear what the person in the crystal image was saying. I dropped it once, and the sound stopped. I thought I had broken it, but when I picked it back up, I could hear the instructions again.

We were told the viewing crystals were an extremely rare magyc, that there were only certain people in Iryvalya who could actually conjure this type of magyc. There were some viewing crystals that could be viewed by anyone, like the one I used when I was younger. Then there were some that could only be viewed by intended individuals, but to view them, you would have to put a drop of your blood onto the crystal itself. I remembered thinking how strange it was to see someone talking and doing something in the crystal like they were right in front of me.

Inside the room, Iclyn, Lydorea, Relonya, Baysil and Prydos were standing around talking to one another. Prydos was also a Rebel Elf, a former Lumaryia Elf. I had seen him in Cliffside once before a couple Leaf years ago, but this was the first time I had ever met him.

Prydos was slightly taller than me, his skin was deeply tanned and looked almost rugged. His hair was pulled back into a long braid that reached to the middle of his back. It looked like the blue-green color of the North Sea right before the Nydian moon crosses the Northern Sun. Prydos was dressed in black leathers, quite worn, but still in good condition. The last thing I noticed about him was his eyes. They were the same blue-green as his hair, but the alternating swirled color was a very dark gray, almost black.

Prydos was only a few Leaf years older than me, but definitely had lived a much different life than me. Prydos was here to teach me about the Lumaryia Elves, as he was raised with them and lived with them up until he was around sixteen Leaf years old. When I asked why he left, he looked at me expressionless and simply answered, "You." I didn't know what to say, so I said nothing at all and only gave a weak smile to acknowledge him.

After the polite introduction between Prydos and me was completed, Iclyn suggested we all take a seat at the long table to go over what was going to be happening today.

After taking the chair at the head of the table, as Baysil suggested, I sat down and felt awkward with everyone looking at me. It felt so strange to go unnoticed for my whole life, and now everyone was looking at me. I felt like I was naked. After a few moments sitting in silence, I felt they were waiting for me to say something, so I did.

"I just want to thank you all," I said, trying to keep my voice from shaking. I have never been very good at speaking to groups of people, and this was no exception.

"Thank us?" Lydorea asked sincerely. "For what, Ny?"

"I know you all have either gone to great lengths to protect me, or traveled here to teach me, or even just have been someone to support me. While I still do not fully understand everything that is going on or what I am expected to do, I just want you all to know that I appreciate you taking time to be here for me."

Baysil lightly placed his hand on mine. "Nyrieve, you are a very smart young Elf, and while there is a lot being asked of you for the peace of Iryvalya, if any of us had a doubt in our minds if you could do this, we wouldn't be here." Baysil gestured to everyone at the table. "We all realize you are being put upon a path you did not request or have been prepared to walk, but that is why we are here. We have come here to help prepare you the best we can."

Prydos quietly spoke next. "We do know, Ny, that this is a huge request, to ask you to be the Bringer of Peace," Prydos said quietly. "I honestly cannot imagine being requested to do this, especially since I am more of a fighter than peacemaker. Even after just meeting you though… I do not know if you are aware, but you have a very powerful presence about you, very refined and sure of yourself."

I was again at a loss for words from Prydos's insight. I do believe I know right from wrong, and I cannot imagine allowing harm to others for any reason, but how could someone know that much about me just after meeting me, I wondered. I also do not think I really know myself. I feel like I do not know myself at all now. I always thought I was a Fairy, but now I am an Elf.

"Not to ruin the conversation," Iclyn said, her way of keeping things on track, "but we have a lot to cover, and not a lot of time to do it."

"Agreed," Relonya said. "Now, Nyrieve, there are quite a few different things we want to go over with you. One will be different maps of Iryvalya. I know you are aware of basics from the education you've received, but there is a lot that was left out on purpose."

"Oh," I said, surprised, wondering how much of Iryvalya is different than the world I thought I knew.

"The maps you have seen are generic. Iryvalya is basically the same in shape, but still a bit different than you learned," Lydorea said sweetly.

Relonya continued, "Another thing you will be doing is viewing some crystals. We have a few different ones. Some just show different parts of the world, and others help explain some of the other people of the world."

Baysil sat back in his chair and said, "The one thing I want you to remember, Ny, is that some of the information you receive here from us will differ from what you have been taught throughout your life here in Cliffside. This was not done to trick you, but much of it was based on the information we had at the time, and also some information that we wanted to keep from everyone for their safety."

I sat there quietly for a moment, absorbing everything they were telling me. Everyone was watching me. I realized they were again waiting for me to say something, so I said with a forced enthusiasm, "Let us get started."

०४8४०

TRAINING WAS THE MORE accurate word, instead of just being educated. I felt I was retraining my brain on everything about Iryvalya. Lydorea had gone over a basic map showing the outline of Iryvalya as I knew it with the different Realms. The lands to the east were the Air Realm, to the south was the Fire Realm, to the west was the Water Realm, in the middle where the Leaf Tree resides was the Spirit Realm, and where we were in the north was the Stone Realm. Then there were a few different maps showing Iryvalya as it actually was. While the shape was the same, there were a lot more different villages I had not known about, and I had never fully understood where everyone other than Fairies lived.

The maps took a very long time to go over, as there was a big overall map and then a bunch of smaller maps that showed detailed areas of each little section, so I would know where each river or village would be located. She said that she had a copy of all of these maps already set aside for me with a bunch of notes added.

The one thing that I think surprised me the most in the maps was the idea that the majority of our world was one big mass of land, yet there was so much anger and fighting inside of it. I kept thinking that perhaps Cliffside is the best place in all of Iryvalya. We all seem to get along just fine here, but perhaps that's how people in the other villages feel as well.

Around the time we were finishing up with the map training, Rowzey came downstairs with Kaleyna. They brought down an assortment of fruits, cheeses, bread and some noodles with Rowzey's sauce for everyone to eat. I asked Kaleyna if this was what she meant when she said she had plans, and she smiled and let me know Rowzey had asked her while I was out on my walk with Jehryps.

Jehryps. I had actually forgotten about him and the kiss while being occupied down here trying to learn so much. Perhaps that was for the best, not to think about it now. I was sure I would get plenty of time at some point.

After taking a break and eating some food with everyone, training began again.

Relonya began explaining to me about the Pyrothian Elves. They lived in the Realm of Fire in the south of Iryvalya in a village called Prax, up in large petrified trees. She said that the trees were as big around as the large houses here in Cliffside, and their homes were actually carved out of the inside of the trees. They generally had a main living area, and there were bedrooms scattered going up the tree, which were accessible by stairways. She also noted that while she had a nice bedroom in the tree home she lived in, most of the time she would use a sleeping sling to sleep outside under the sky. Relonya said that the Elves use stairs or ropes and pulleys to get up to the living areas inside the trees, and many of the trees were connected to each other by bridges.

The Pyrothian Elves' main magyc force was fire and second was air, so they wanted to be up in the trees surrounded by air and as close to the Southern Sun as they could be.

Relonya explained that when she was young, the home she grew up in was almost as high up in the air as the cliffs by the North Sea. She said she missed sleeping high up in the sky, and felt odd sleeping down on the ground, especially inside of a building.

She gave me details regarding different areas of Prax, such as approximately where the leaders met, the areas where they kept different records, as well as tactical and magycal training areas for younger Pyrothian Elves. Relonya took one of the viewing crystals out of the box and handed it to me. I looked at it, wondering what this crystal would show me.

"This is a crystal that I... borrowed from the records room in Prax," Relonya said with a knowing smile. "It is a record of just images throughout parts of Prax itself, there is no sound. It will show you a few locations for a few moments and then move on. There should be three different locations it will show you."

"Three?" I asked, curious to see the place where my mother would have likely grown up.

"Yes, the first is the actual record room in Prax. The second will be inside one of the homes there, and the third is of a classroom where young Pyrothian Elves are educated."

I stared at the large flat crystal. It was a bit bigger than the size of the palm of my hand, the flat center very smooth and almost translucent, and the edges slightly rough yet worn.

"How do I get it to start showing me?"

"This is not one that requires blood, but it does require a word. Just hold it and say 'Pyrothian.'"

I held the viewing crystal closer to my face and whispered, "Pyrothian."

The image was remarkably clear. It was a circular room, and the walls all looked like wood, which makes sense as this had to be carved out of one of the petrified trees Relonya mentioned. There were windows carved out as well, with plates of glass placed in them. The light shone brightly into the room. I could see many shelves filled with leatherbound books. There also was a large case that had hundreds of little cubbies all over it, and in each cubby was a scroll or two, many covered in dust.

After looking around at this beautiful room, full of so much information, I looked down at the floor in the image and my jaw dropped. The floor looked like a normal tree stump in its shape; however, in the spaces between the rings, places where it looked like there were cracks, there was a beautiful gemlike appearance.

"What is that on the floor?" I asked.

Iclyn chimed in, "When the trees became petrified thousands of years ago, the areas where the sap would have flowed turned into something that looks like an opal."

"It is so beautiful," I said.

After another moment of looking at this amazing room and trying to memorize everything I could, the viewing crystal went a little hazy and then started focusing in on the next image. This was inside someone's home. It looked to be a very large place. The image was from the point of view of their living room area, and the walls, windows and flooring were similar to that of the records room. There was furniture spread out, with what looked to be a big and very soft couch that was in the shape of a half circle. A staircase spiraled up around the room and stopped in different sections. The first stop on the stairs was a kitchen. I couldn't see much in it, but it looked like a much fancier version of Rowzey's kitchen. The stairs went up to a small landing with a door, and then up again to another landing and door. I guessed these were doors leading into separate bedrooms.

As if hearing my thoughts, Relonya said, "The doors lead to the bedrooms for the Elves of that house. There are sometimes stairs inside those rooms going up or down, or sometimes the stairs are on the outside of the room that can be accessed through a large window."

To me, this home looked lavish and beautiful, but it did not look lived in like our home here did. Nothing seemed to be out of place, no cloak lying on the couch or cup left out on a table.

The image began to get hazy, so I knew it was about to change to the last image, the school for the Pyrothian Elves. I was quite excited to see this, to see if the Elves there were educated in a similar way to how I was.

The image came into focus. It was in another tree room; however, instead of windows being at a level to see out of, there were windows in a full circle around the top of the room. They were at least double my height, and while it appeared to allow in a lot of light, it felt like the room was a cage, as I couldn't see anything outside the room.

On the walls of the room were writing boards. Some had basic letters written, others had images of different magyc spells with illustrations on how to perform the spell. The last wall had multiple signs all over it. I could not read many of them, but the few I could made my stomach turn. "Pyrothian Elves are the only true Leaders for Iryvalya," "If you are not Pyrothian, you are not a true Elf," and "All those who consort with Lumaryia or Rebel Elves will be exiled from Prax." The image grew hazy until there was no image at all.

I could not believe this was what the Pyrothian Elves would teach all their young Elves. Why would they teach hate and that only their race was the right one? Anger built inside of me. How could I be half of these Elves, when I did not hate or exclude others because of who they are?

After a few moments of staring into my own hazy reflection in the crystal, I looked up at everyone else at the table. I handed the crystal back to Relonya and decided I needed to ask her the question in my head. "Do all the Pyrothian Elves believe what they had posted on the walls?"

"I was taught those same exact things when I was young, Nyrieve, and for a long time, I really believed them. I believed that the Lumaryia and Rebel Elves were the enemies of Iryvalya, that those Elves would be the destruction of our world," Relonya said with a sad look on her pretty face. "After I finished my basic schooling, we were sent to work in different areas of Prax to see which would be the best fit for us. One work area I was sent to was the Records room. That is what changed everything for me. While I was there, the older Pyrothian Elf who was in charge of the records, Sweyton, told me to take a few days and read through some of the old scrolls, 'just to get familiar with their sorting.' What I read changed everything. I read about how the Elves all used to be one. There was not Pyrothian or Lumaryia Elves, there were just Elves. Sweyton kept me as long as he could in the Records room, allowing me to read everything I could, but once the leaders realized I was reading more than working, they moved me to another area. The thing is, Ny, it is not just black and white with who is good and bad among the Klayns, because a lot of people are good at their core, but they only know what they have been taught."

"And if you are only taught that water would make your skin melt, you will always avoid water of any kind," I said, repeating a phrase Lydorea had once said to me when I was afraid to try something new I heard was bad. I looked to Lydorea and she smiled gently at me.

"That's right," Relonya said. "Most of the Pyrothian Elves only know what they have been told, and I believe that if they learn the truth, they will open their eyes and embrace the dissolving of the Klayns. I hope they do, because if they don't... I will never again see some of my family or friends."

"Nyrieve," Lydorea said, "would you care to take a break now or continue on?"

I looked at the faces of everyone at the table. All of these people had taken time to help train me on so much. Even if I did not feel like doing or learning more right now, I didn't feel like letting any of them down.

"We should continue, I think, unless anyone else wants a break."

"I could personally use a good drink right now," Prydos said with a laugh, "but seeing as I will be showing you the Lumaryia Elves next, I think it's best I wait until we are done. However, would it be possible to have some honey tea brought down here?"

"Sure we can," Lydorea said, getting up and walking towards the stairs. "I'll be right back." After a few moments she walked back down the stairs. "Rowzey said she will have the tea made and brought down in just a few moments."

"How about we sit at the couches," Baysil said. "I think we could all use a little more comfort for a while."

Everyone agreed, getting up and walking to the small area with the different couches and chairs. I didn't know where I should sit, as I didn't know who would want to sit by whom. Luckily for me, Baysil suggested I sit in the single chair closest to the end of the couch where Prydos was sitting. The chair was old, but so overstuffed that it was like sitting on clouds.

After everyone was settled, someone came down the stairs, the sound of tea cups moving about. Kaleyna entered with a tray of full tea cups. She walked into the center of the area where we were all sitting and started to hand everyone a cup. When she handed Prydos his, their eyes locked on each other, and I noticed a brushing of his hand across hers. I could almost swear I saw her blush, but she calmly walked to me and handed me a teacup as well, giving me a big smile.

"Thanks, Kaleyna. I appreciate it," I said.

"No problem, Ny. I even made yours with mint instead of honey. I know you prefer that," Kaleyna said. She had such a good heart, and it made me want to have her sit here with me and not go, but I knew I had more training ahead and that she wouldn't stay anyway. After making sure everyone had what they needed, Kaleyna went back upstairs.

I slowly sipped my mint tea, enjoying the aromatic smell as Prydos began explaining to me about the Lumaryia Elves.

"Noygandia is the village that the Lumaryia Elves live in. It is in the Water Realm to the southwest of here, but buried deep in the Crystoval Mountains. They live underground in a large cave. It looks like a village similar to Cliffside, but basically placed inside a hollowed-out mountain. The roof of the cave is the bottom of the lake. It is made out of an almost transparent crystal. The water that is trapped inside the lake flows down through a small waterfall into a winding river that flows throughout the whole village. During the day, there is some light from the Northern Sun that shines through, and at night, the same lake water illuminates in an iridescent light purple. It is from all the crystal flecks that run through it, and along the top of the lake and down through the river, some of the crystal flecks get planted into the ground and new crystals grow and glow at night as well in different shades of iridescent purple."

"That sounds beautiful," I said in awe.

"It is," Prydos said, "but there are a lot of the same problems the Pyrothian Elves have that the Lumaryia Elves have. The teachings are similar, but just against the Pyrothian and Rebel Elves. However, I will say, from when my parents were being educated to when I was, I found I was taught a little more acceptance of the Pyrothian and Rebel Elves. I think it is because our teachers were not convinced of the Lumaryia Elves being the only right choice."

Prydos took the viewing crystal he was holding and handed it over to me. "In this you will see another three images like with Relonya's crystal. You will first see part of the lake from inside Noygandia, to the waterfall and into part of the river. The second image will be also inside one of the homes of the Lumaryia Elves, and the last image will be of the entrance to Noygandia."

"Do I have to say anything to get this viewing crystal to work?"

"No, you just have to hold it, and after a few moments it will start to appear."

I took the viewing crystal into my hands. This felt much the same as the first one. I was looking at the flat surface of the crystal when an image started to appear. I was looking at what appeared to be a huge bowl of water, and after a moment I realized this had to be the lake above Noygandia. It was not a perfect circle, there were a lot of different land shapes above, and so I imagined there had to be little peninsulas all around the lake. There was a waterfall off to the right side of the lake, but how it flowed in I could not tell. It was long, relatively thin and so very beautiful. The pool where the waterfall ended and then flowed into a small river couldn't have been more than four feet wide, but there was at least a foot or two on each side of the river where beautiful crystals grew out of the ground in different directions. The water flowed away from the fall towards houses where the river passed between them. There were small little foot bridges that went over the water between the houses. The houses looked very much like the ones in Cliffside, except that they were built of smooth stacked rocks instead of wood.

The image began to get hazy, and the second image came in. It was inside one of the stone houses. It was quite large inside, and there were some of the crystals that grew near the river placed in between some of the stone walls. This house appeared to only have one floor level. There was a large living area with a bunch of big fluffy cushions all over the floor for sitting on. I could see the kitchen off to the back, and it looked very much like Rowzey's, very cozy and definitely used, as there was a stack of dishes that had been used and were in need of washing. There were a few doors off to the left and right. I am guessing one was for entering the home and another for a possible bedroom. Then the image began getting hazy again.

The last image came in clear and I was looking at what appeared to be part of the base of a mountain with tons of trees and bushes growing all over the place. Off to the right there was a strong stream running downhill, making about a twenty-foot waterfall into an actual river that flowed away from the mountainside. Prydos said this was the entrance into Noygandia, but I couldn't see one at all. After a moment of looking, I realized that had to be the point, to not see the entrance. I looked harder at the spots where there were subtle differences from what I thought should be there. It wasn't until I looked closer at the stream running down the mountain that there looked to be a small cove behind the little waterfall areas. That had to be where the entrance was into the large underground village. I was looking to see if there was a path of any kind leading to this entrance, and I couldn't find one. Then the image faded away.

"I couldn't find the pathway to the entrance of the cave," I said to Prydos.

"Did you find the entrance though?" he asked curiously.

"Yes, it was behind the waterfall, it has to be, but there was not a path leading up to it," I said, confused.

"That is because no one walks on the ground to the entrance. It'll leave a path, and others who are not welcome could find it then."

"So it's the water then? You walk up the river, so there are no tracks left in the open?" I asked, feeling a little proud I figured it out.

"That's correct. You are quick to pick up on it," Prydos said. "What did you think of the rest of Noygandia?"

"It is very beautiful. I can only imagine how beautiful those crystals must be when they are glowing at night. That does make me wonder, why are there crystals inside the walls of the houses?"

"Yes, at night, those crystals will glow inside the homes so it lights up the rooms without having to use fire or candles unless wanted," Prydos said with a smile of pride.

"I must say, it is quite amazing to see the different places that both of my parents came from," I said, thinking of what it would have been like for me to have grown up in either of those places, and realizing that in the end, I am very glad I was raised here in Cliffside. While both villages are beautiful, I did not get a full sense of the freedom I had always felt here.

"I think it is getting late, everyone," Iclyn said. "I am sure Rowzey will have dinner ready for everyone very soon. So why don't we all stop here for the night and get freshened up before dinner."

Everyone agreed. I got up and walked up the two flights of stairs to my room. I walked inside, flopped onto my bed, and stretched out. All my muscles were sore from sitting for so long. I decided I would close my eyes for only a moment just to rest them, but my body had another idea in mind.

A loud steady banging woke me with a jolt, scared something was wrong.

☙ 9 ❧

AFTER A MOMENT OF HEARING the banging again and getting my head together, I knew it was just someone knocking on the other side of my door. I sluggishly got up, walked over to the door and opened it. I tried to get my eyes to fully focus from being in the dark room and now into the lighted hallway. After finally being able to focus, I realized I didn't recognize who was standing in front of me.

The person was the same height as me, and she had long straight black hair with streaks of bright yellow throughout it. Her eyes were alternating swirls of the two colors of her hair, and had black eyebrows framing them. She was pale and sullen-looking, but at the same time, she had a look of youthful innocence about her. Her ears were peeking through her hair and had points on them just like mine, so she had to be an Elf too.

"Hello," I said. "How can I help you?"

"Nyrieve?"

"Yes, I'm Nyrieve."

"In the future, do not tell anyone who you are until you know who they are. Wait until you know if they are a friend or foe," she said with a hint of annoyance.

"Who are you?" I asked, becoming annoyed as well. This was my room, my home, and anyone who was in Cliffside would know exactly where to find me, so it didn't seem like a big deal to me.

"I am Koyvean, and you are late for dinner." She sighed, and after giving me a final look-over, turned on her heel and left to go downstairs.

I stood there for a moment in my doorway not knowing what to think about this Elf I had just met. With how dark it was outside, I was really late for dinner. I took off down the stairs without even checking myself in my looking glass. While Rowzey was pretty easy going about most things, she did not like it when people were late for meals, especially dinner.

When I walked into the dining room, it was empty, the table was clean, the chairs all in place. Wondering where everyone was, I walked into the kitchen and saw Rowzey bustling around.

"Where is everyone, Rowzey?"

"'They decided it was a nice night to dine outside," Rowzey said, annoyed.

"Where outside?" I asked. The long table we normally used for outside meals had been packed away over a week ago.

"They is just out back near the lake. No one minded just grabbing a plate and sitting on the ground," Rowzey sputtered. Rowzey was not one for eating away from the table. She felt sitting at the table gave everyone a more together feeling as they dined.

"So we just take a plate and go find a place to sit?"

"Yes, Ny. Yous plate be on the counter. Everyone else already be outside."

"Before I go out, can you tell me who that was who came to get me?"

"Koyvean. She be an… Elf. She be part of The Drayks and told Baysil she wanted to get yous, so she could size yous up," Rowzey said rushing around working on what looked like dessert.

"Another Elf? It's like they are all coming to Cliffside now."

"They is, they is coming to meet with yous, to help yous with yous journey to meet up with the other Drayks. They is worried about any possible… resistance yous might be facing along the way," Rowzey said cryptically. "Now yous go and eat yous dinner before dessert be ready."

I took my plate and a glass of water with me as I walked out the back door and looked around to see where I should sit. Iclyn, Lydorea, Miaarya, and Baysil sat closely together having a heated conversation, and that didn't make me feel comfortable to sit with them. Jehryps sat with a few of his friends. He looked out of place, as his friends were all talking and laughing and he was quiet and looking out of sorts. Kaleyna was sitting with Prydos, and they looked like they were enjoying their conversation, so I did not want to interrupt them.

Everyone else was sitting in small groups, and none of them I felt like joining in with. So I walked quietly, not wanting to attract anyone's attention, and I sat down on the dock bridge to the island. It was very calming and relaxing in the increasing darkness, provided by the eclipse of the sun by the Rydison moon. Every night, one of the two moons fully covers one of the suns for ten hours, giving us fifteen hours of daylight while the moons rotate towards the other sun. Rydison was still moving in front of the sun, allowing a little bit of light still. I knew it was the Rydison moon over the Nydian moon because the Rydison moon gives off a bluish glow while covering the Northern Sun. The Nydian moon gives off a greenish turquoise glow.

I finally looked at my plate. Rowzey had made me a plate of her pulled and seasoned chicken. She usually cooks it in her big caldron for the better part of the day. She has the chicken cook down in there with a decent helping of her spicy sweet sauce. This sauce was very good and sweet, while I never would think to complain to Rowzey, sometimes I think she was a little heavy handed with the amount of sugar she'd put into this particular sauce.

The chicken was accompanied by a sweet piece of corn on the cob, sprinkled with one of her mystery seasoning combinations. It always was very good. The only thing I did not like about having corn on the cob was how messy it could be, with the butter, seasoning and corn juices running down my chin. I was just glad that I grabbed an extra cloth napkin to wipe it all off.

I was enjoying sitting out of the sight of everyone and being able to watch all their interactions. I had always enjoyed just watching people. I love seeing the passion on someone's face, even if they are arguing. I know most people always try to put on a front, or a good face, so to speak; however, once in a while, when no one realizes they are being watched, they relax and you catch a glimpse of the real them.

The dock bridge creaked behind me, and I realized someone must have been on the island in the lake and was walking back. I turned to look at who was behind me, and there was no one there that I could see. I quietly got up and walked down the dock bridge to the island. The moon was fully covering the Northern Sun now, so everything was cast in the bluish glow of the Rydison moon. I looked around and could not find anyone, but I knew that I had heard someone. As I walked around, I noticed there was a small piece of folded paper that was partially burned in the fireplace. I took it out and looked at it. It did not look old, and only one of the corners had been singed off. I opened it up easily, as the seal was already broken, but in the moonlight, I couldn't read it. I folded the paper back up, placing it inside my pocket. I would read it when I get back to the manor.

As I turned around I bumped into someone and shouted in surprise.

"Ny, it's me, it's me!" Jehryps said quickly and loudly, trying to grab my arms to keep me from getting Klaw.

"What in Iryvalya are you doing sneaking up on me like that?"

The voices from back on shore starting to come towards the island. I shouted to them, "Everything's okay! I am okay! I was just startled by Jehryps."

The voices quieted and the movement stopped. Then I heard Baysil's concerned voice. "Let me know if you need anything, Ny." After a moment, I could hear them all start moving away from the shore again.

"What are you doing out here, Jehryps? Are you trying to scare me to death?" I asked, annoyed with him for the second time today.

"Look, I saw you when you started walking towards the island, so I wanted to come and check on you and make sure you were okay," Jehryps said, sounding frustrated. "Why does it seem like I can never do anything right with you?"

"I don't know, maybe it's because you do not know anything about me, so you have no idea how to interact with me?"

"Fair enough... so let me get to know you. I mean, I want to know you, if you will let me."

I thought about it for a few moments. I could just blow him off again, but what if he is being sincere and he wants to know me. Could it hurt to have another friend on my side?

"Fine," I said, throwing up my arms in an act of defeat. "But let's go sit back out on the dock. I like the sound of the water moving." I walked over to the middle of the dock bridge and sat down with my legs crossed together in an x shape.

Jehryps moved quickly to where I was and sat down closely. For a few moments he just sat there looking at the water.

"So what do you want to know, Jehryps?"

"Honestly, I cannot think of what to ask. There are many things I want to know, but I don't want to insult you with any questions I might have."

"Well… I remember a game we all use to play as kids to get to know each other. We can just make it a little more grown up. We will have three rounds of questions. Each round, we each get three questions to ask one another. The first round, simple things you might ask a person you have just met. The second round, these can be more in-depth questions for someone you might have known for a while. The third and last round you can ask anything at all." While I was not very comfortable with the third round idea, it would only be fair if he was answering questions too.

"That sounds like a good idea."

"However, there is one rule… if either of us start to become uncomfortable, the questions stop, and no one can get upset if it's done."

"I can agree to that."

"Good, then you can start the questions," I said nervously, as I did not want to go first.

Jehryps thought for a few minutes, and finally looked up at me with a smile and asked, "What is your favorite flower?"

I smiled back, not expecting something so simple. "It would have to be the Moon Lily. I love that flower because it's the only one I know of that blooms at night, glows in the moonlight, and the smell is just very intoxicating to me."

"I have never seen a Moon Lily bloom before."

"You should see one bloom sometime. So my question, what is your favorite time of the year?"

"I would have to say the warm season. I love being able to swim in the North Sea or the lake here, and to be honest, I enjoy seeing all the girls swimming as well."

I raised my left eyebrow up looking at him, trying to think if I could remember anytime swimming around him in the past.

"You said to be honest."

"I did say that, didn't I?" I asked rhetorically.

"My question is, why do you prefer the night over the day?"

"Because I feel like in the night there is another whole world that not everyone can see and appreciate. Sometimes I enjoy being able to be one of the few people who realize it."

"I never thought about it like that," he said, sounding thoughtful.

"Why is the day your favorite time?"

"Because I like being able to see everyone and everything as it is, not have to wonder or guess. And to be real honest, I am sometimes nervous in the dark."

It was very brave to share something as personal as a fear. I smiled and said, "I can respect that."

"Okay… what is your favorite color?" Jehryps asked with a slight smile.

"Uhm… honestly I don't know. I used to think it was blue, or purple. I guess I like many different colors, but to be truthful I love the green color of my hair," I said with a chuckle. "What is your favorite color?"

"I always loved the color red, and go figure that my hair would start turning it, but that green hair of yours is making me reconsider."

I was happy it was darker out, so Jehryps could not see the blood rushing to my face. I could feel my cheeks getting warmer. I was definitely not used to getting complimented like that.

"So, I guess it is time for the second round of questions," I said. "You can start if you like."

After a couple seconds, Jehryps started the second round of our questions. "Okay, Nyrieve, why do you seem to enjoy wearing pants over dresses?"

"Huh?" I said, confused by the question.

"Over the years I have noticed you, and most of the time you are wearing pants, and I have even seen you with pants on under your dresses. I have always thought girls looked more soft and sensual in dresses, so why do you not like wearing them?"

I thought about his question for a moment, and finally responded, "I guess I always looked at the fact that when wearing a dress, I am more limited on my moving abilities. And also I do not enjoy having the skirts blow up and flashing myself to people."

"Oh, okay. I just was wondering, because I always thought you looked very pretty in the dresses when you wore them."

"Thank you... so my question, what made you notice me over the years?"

"Truthfully I always thought you were kind of pretty, but just that you seemed happier in hiding behind everything else than to try to enhance your beauty and make guys notice you."

I didn't know what to say. While it was truthful, it was also a little hurtful. I never thought I should have to enhance the way I already look.

"What is the craziest thing you have ever done, Ny?" Jehryps asked with a smirk on his face.

"Nothing," I said. "I have never done anything crazy or out of control before."

"Really?" he asked, almost surprised.

"There have been times I had thought of doing crazy things, but I guess I was too scared or shy to do anything. What about you? What is the craziest thing you have ever done?" I asked, realizing most of my questions seem to be me asking him what he's already asked me.

"I guess I would have to say the craziest thing I have done lately would be kissing a girl that had no desire to have me kiss her. Normally my plans are better thought out than that."

"Ha ha," I said sarcastically.

"So my last question of round two, has the mark you got being an Elf started to form something you could recognize yet?"

"Actually it hasn't changed at all. It still looks like a small little smudge," I said. I forgot that it will eventually change into something recognizable. The marking on my wrist was already visible, marking me as the Bringer of Peace. I pulled my bracelet around my wrist a little more, making sure it was over the mark, and realized it was my turn. "Oh, my question, do you have a marking already?"

"Yes I do. It is still kind of hazy though."

We both just sat there. I loved the sound of the water lapping against the dock. I knew this last round of questions would be awkward, and I kind of just wanted to get it over with. "So do you want to start the last round, Jehryps?"

"I started the last two rounds. How about you start this last one?"

"Oh, okay. Uhm… I guess there is no easy way into this round, so here goes. How many girls have you actually twyned with?" I asked, shocking myself that I could have the courage to ask him this. I remembered having conversations with Kaleyna, wondering this very thing. We both had guessed a different number, even though we were pretty close in our guess. She guessed eighteen and I guessed sixteen.

"Wow, uhm… let me think," he said, pausing for a moment. "I would have to say… if I was completely honest… I would guess that the correct number would be around thirty-four."

My jaw dropped open. I could not believe there were so many. After a minute I shook my head and forced a smile. "Sorry, I just was not expecting that… number," I said as politely as I could.

"That's okay. I am not ashamed of it. So my turn… in any way, did you actually enjoy the kiss I gave you?"

"I don't know," I said truthfully. "It was such a shock and so quick, that the only thing I remember was that your lips felt cool."

"Oh…" he said, disappointed.

"My question… why have you been with so many girls? I mean, don't you think that actually twyning with someone should be more… special?"

"I do think it is special to be with someone, but whenever I was with any of those girls, they knew upfront, before we did anything, that it was not anything more than the physical act. I told them the truth. I have never been in love with someone, and I did not want to hurt their feelings by letting them believe there was more to it than there was."

"I couldn't do that, because I am not sure I could ever separate the two, but I give you a lot of credit for always being honest."

"Thank you. So, Ny, while you said I stole your first kiss, I have wondered, and I know others have too… do you mean your first kiss with a guy? Because a lot of us had thought that you and Kaleyna were possibly more than just friends."

I busted out laughing. It was the funniest thing I had heard in a very long time. I knew I had to answer his question, but the laughter would not stop. My side began to hurt and I had tears falling down my cheeks. "No, no, no, no, no. Kaleyna and I are just best friends. Well, more than friends, but not like that. We are basically sisters as far as we are concerned."

"Oh," Jehryps said, surprised. "I wouldn't have minded if you and her were more… intimate. To be honest, I kind of like the idea of you kissing another girl."

I stopped moving and just stared at him. I was not against any form of love, but why did a guy who claimed he was interested in me like the idea of me kissing another girl? I knew there were some who had more than two people in their intimate lives, but this still surprised me.

"So my last question for the night," I said, ready to get this over with and go back to the shore and find Kaleyna and tell her about people thinking we are pairyn. "What are your true intentions towards me?"

"Honestly, I want to be intimate with you, twyning even, but I also think you and I could be more than just that. I think we could be a very powerful pairyn that could maybe do a lot in this world. I already know who you are, bringer of pe—"

"Shh… how do you know that? Who told you?" I asked, nervous that someone could have overheard him.

"I am sorry, Nyrieve. You have already asked your last question for the night," Jehryps said with a sly smile. "So it is time now for my last question."

"What is it?" I asked, quite annoyed by him not telling me how he found out who I am.

"Now that you seem to know me a bit more now, and even though I can tell you are frustrated that I will not tell you how I know who you are, if I were to ever try again to kiss you, would you allow it?" Jehryps asked with a seductive grin.

I thought for a moment. Would I actually want to feel his lips on mine? Feel that cool touch again? The truth is, I don't know. While I've longed to have someone who wants to spend time with me and perhaps be with me intimately at some point, I don't honestly know if I want it to be him. But I guess the question isn't if I want to do all those things with him, but simply if I would like to try another kiss with him. Seeing as my first kiss was already taken and gone, I couldn't see any reason not to answer him as honestly as I could. "Yes, I would allow it."

❧10❧

I DON'T KNOW WHO WAS more surprised by what I said, me or Jehryps, but I knew when I said it I had meant it. For years I had wanted to be desired by someone, and here was the guy almost everyone was attracted to, and he was interested in me. While I do not believe that you should easily be intimate with someone, I don't believe it's wrong to want and desire that warm touch of another.

We sat there for a few moments in silence. Suddenly Jehryps looked into my eyes with confidence and leaned in to kiss me. Our lips first lightly brushed, and I could feel the coolness of his soft lips. Quickly his kiss turned a bit more urgent, as if he had been without water and my lips were quenching his thirst. It was rather enjoyable to feel his lips against mine and him pulling me closer to him. He ran his hands up my back and over my shoulders until they slowly crested over the shoulder and started to slide down towards the front of my chest. Part of me didn't want him to stop, but I wasn't ready for that yet, so I gently took his hands into mine and held them. After a while, his kiss became deeper and felt almost primal. He started to lightly lick my lips and tried pushing my mouth open, but again I held my ground, keeping my lips together.

He roughly broke his hands away from mine, then took my right hand in his and slowly slid it up his thigh. While I was somewhat lost in the moment of our kiss, this snapped me back into reality and that we had gone way further than I had expected to, or was even ready to go.

I pulled back from him completely, and Jehryps looked at me with complete confusion and frustration. He took me by the shoulders and tried to pull me back into another kiss, and I pulled free and scooted back away from him.

"Why did you pull away?" he asked with a hint of anger to his voice.

"Because this is going too fast for me. All of this," I said, gesturing with my hands to him and to myself, "and you are still kind of new to me too. I want to keep a clear head about everything. I am leaving here before long, and I don't want to get things more confused any more than they already are." I stood up.

"Nothing is as confused as I am," he stated with more anger to his voice.

"I am sorry, it was not my intent. I did want to kiss you, but I did not think you would try to go for more than that... We can talk tomorrow if you want, but maybe it'd be best if we took some distance for a few days."

"Yeah, distance... I can do distance," he said, his voice thick with distain. He stood up and looked me straight in the eyes for a moment, a disgusted look on his face. Then he stormed off down the dock bridge.

I stood up and slowly followed behind him. I watched as he made it back over to his circle of friends. He sat down next to Gwyndal, a pretty white-haired Fairy, and put his arm around her pulling her close to him. She giggled as she snuggled closer to him. He looked back over at me and gave me a smug smile.

I was so hurt that he could do that. While I know I said we should maybe have some distance to think, I didn't think if he truly liked me he would go cozy up to another girl right away. Then again, perhaps they were just friends and this was typical between them. I never paid much attention to his daily interactions with his friends. Though even the thought of that was stupid. It was wrong of him to do that. If they were just friends, he would have never shot me that look.

I walked silently past everyone still sitting outside eating and talking. I went into the manor through the kitchen, which luckily was empty. I walked straight up to my room, closed the door, and lay down on my bed, looking out my small window at the Rydison moon.

I didn't know if I should be upset with Jehryps or myself. I was the one who wanted the kiss, but I didn't think it would lead to more than just the kiss. I should have known better. Rarely do things work out how I imagine they will.

There was soft knocking on my door. "Nyrieve... are you in there?" Kaleyna asked quietly.

"Yes, you can come in," I mumbled, knowing she would hear me.

She quietly opened the door, and shut it again after she stepped inside my room. She had a wonderful smile on her face and almost a glow about her.

"What has you so smiley?" I asked, feeling better seeing her smiling face. I sat up so she would have a place to sit by me.

"Oh, Ny, he is just so... I don't even know the right word. Amazing, handsome, funny, and even a little arrogant," she said with a giggle.

"Prydos I am guessing?" I teased.

"Of course. We spent the whole evening eating, talking, and even went for a walk down by the cliffs." She sighed.

"The cliffs, huh?" I said with a smile. That was the typical spot in Cliffside for a couple to go to enjoy some romance.

"Yes, and he kissed me!" She beamed. "I couldn't believe it! We had been talking, he held my hand as we walked around, and I was hoping he would kiss me, not thinking he would. And then... he did!"

"That is wonderful, Kaleyna," I said, giving her a big hug. "I am so happy for you."

"I feel like I am floating on air right now. He asked if he could take me tomorrow night for a walk again, and I said yes."

"I noticed the two of you tonight talking, and I think you make a pretty cute couple to be honest," I said, feeling truly happy for my friend.

"I noticed you as well tonight," Kaleyna said with a raised eyebrow. "What happened between you and Jehryps?"

"Why do you think something happened between us?"

"Well, after your scream on the island, and you telling everyone it was just him, you both stayed out there for a while. When Jehryps did come back, he stomped over to his friends, sat with Gwyndal, and last I saw when Prydos and I left for our walk, Jehryps and Gwyndal were getting pretty intense out near the lake shore."

"What?" I asked, completely shocked. "They were kissing?"

"Kissing was only the tip of it from what we could tell," Kaleyna said with growing concern in her voice. "Why are you upset? I thought you were not interested in Jehryps?"

"I don't want to talk about it, Kal. I feel incredibly stupid right now," I said, anger rising inside of me.

"Ny, what is going on?"

"I am embarrassed."

"So? We are best friends, spirit sisters, so there is nothing you can't share with me."

"Fine... While we were out on the dock bridge, Jehryps and I kissed..."

"What?"

"We kissed, and he tried to kiss me with his tongue, and tried to put his and my hands in places I wasn't ready for. So I told him it was happening too fast and that we should take a little distance so I could think about this, and you saw the ending result when he sat down with Gwyndal," I said, feeling the color rushing to my face, embarrassed all over again.

"I am going to kill that stupid self-absorbed Elf. His little Elf butt will be beaten, and I will even find some shears to cut that messy mop of hair his thinks looks good..." Kaleyna said, jumping up. I grabbed her arm and pulled her back to sit on the bed.

"No you're not," I said, giving my best friend a hug, feeling so lucky to have her in my life, "but thank you for offering to do that."

She held me for a little bit and then I sat back looking out my small window. "I don't understand why he would do that."

"I do," she said, still sounding upset. "You did not just completely fall for him and do whatever he wanted. So he had to prove it to himself that he is still the 'Elf' he thinks he is."

"That is the last of my dealings with him."

"Don't be so sure... I will bet you that he will beg for forgiveness and try again, because now his pride is hurt and he has to try to win your favor."

"Win my favor?"

"Jehryps is not one to give up so quickly and move on... I am betting he is unaware of me seeing him with Gwyndal, so he will figure that you do not know about it either and try to patch things up with you."

"He'll be wasting his time."

"If you change your mind and want me to go smack him around a bit and give him a haircut, let me know."

I laughed at Kaleyna. "While I know he has to out weight you by seventy pounds, I would still bet on you over him any day!"

We sat for a little while in silence, and then Kaleyna looked at me and asked, "So why were you out on the island in the first place and not sitting with everyone?"

"I had seen everyone was already in groups and honestly I didn't really feel much like talking. So I sat out on the dock bridge to eat, and I heard something behind me near the island side. When I walked over there to see who it was, no one was there."

"That is odd. I wonder if it was just a squirrel or something."

"I did find a paper in the fireplace on the island though," I said, remembering the folded paper in my pocket. "It looks like someone tried to burn it, but it didn't seem to catch." I pulled the paper out of my pocket and looked at the seal on the outside of the papers. It simply had the shape of an X on it.

I handed the folded paper to Kaleyna to see the seal. She handed it back, saying, "I have never seen a seal with just an X on it. What is the letter about?"

"I don't know, I haven't read it yet. It was too dark out on the island."

"Read it now," Kaleyna said excitedly.

I opened the short letter and read it aloud to Kaleyna.

I do not understand the delay. This should have been taken care of as soon as she was found. If you cannot get rid of her by yourself, then you need to find someone who can, and soon. If she leaves Cliffside, our plan will not work and we will have to start over again. You have a fortnight to find a way to get rid of her, which is when our sources said they are planning to move her. The Bringer of Peace cannot leave Cliffside alive. If you need to hurt people she cares about to get her to be vulnerable, then do it. I do not think I need to remind you that all of us are depending on you, and what it will mean for you if you fail us. Kill her, and do it quickly.

X

Kaleyna gasped in horror.

"It cannot be about me, right?" I asked, dumbfounded.

"Seriously, Ny? Is there another 'Bringer of Peace' that you are aware of?" She looked at me like I was crazy.

"What should I do?" My stomach tightened, threatening me to be sick.

"You stay in your room. I will go get Baysil and Rowzey and anyone else," Kaleyna said getting to her feet. "Keep Klaw nearby and do not answer your door unless you hear me on the other side."

Before I could protest her leaving, she was already gone and I was alone with only my thoughts.

Why would someone want to kill me? How could being the Bringer of Peace be a bad thing? Wouldn't everyone want to have peace among the Klayns?

The scariest questions though, the ones I really did not want to think about or ask myself, who was the person charged with killing me and who was the person who was trying to have me killed? I was more scared about the person here in Cliffside, but still wondering who the X person was or represented.

It felt like hours before Kaleyna came back, but it could have only been minutes. She knocked on my door gently. "Ny, it is me, and I am not alone. We are coming in."

Kaleyna opened the door slowly, looking down to see Klaw unsheathed and in my hand just in case. Behind her were Baysil, Iclyn, and Koyvean.

They all squeezed into my small room and Baysil was the first to speak. "Can I see the letter?"

I handed it over to him and he read it aloud to everyone. After a few moments he handed the letter to Koyvean, and she just held it with her eyes closed.

She shook her head and said, "Whoever wrote this has an enchantment upon it. I cannot tell who the writer is or who has touched the letter even. I am sorry." She handed the letter back to Baysil.

"How did they know when we are leaving? Someone is planning or trying to kill Nyrieve sooner than we expected," Baysil said.

That phrase seemed so odd to me, "kill Nyrieve." Not once in my life had I ever thought someone would want to kill me. I had never been important, and the reality of how important people now thought I was began to sink in.

The silence in the room felt deafening. Kaleyna was looking at me with worry. I couldn't take the quiet anymore. I kept thinking about how the letter suggested hurting those I care about, and while I was not sure what was going to happen with me, I could not allow those I cared about to be hurt.

I stood up and said to Baysil, "Seeing as someone wants me dead, and from the sound of it they want me dead yesterday, we need to keep ahead of them in any way we can. The only option I see is to move up our departure from Cliffside to as soon as possible. We cannot tell anyone who does not need to know."

The first one to speak was Koyvean. "I might have misjudged you."

"I don't understand," I said.

"When I woke you, you did not take the time to know who was at your door. But now, when you know you have danger, you are willing to take steps to keep ahead of those who would harm you. That is a trait of a leader, so perhaps I was wrong about you. But only time will tell for sure."

Iclyn slightly grinned and said, "Take it as a compliment, Ny. That is the nicest thing I have ever heard her say."

Baysil kept focus. "You are right, Ny. We need to get you and those you are closest to out of here. That means Kaleyna and Rowzey will need to be moved as well."

"I am going anywhere Ny goes," Kaleyna said right away. "I had planned on going with her anyway, even if I had to follow behind."

Baysil gave her a small smile. "I am not surprised, Kaleyna. Iclyn, go talk to Rowzey in private and explain what is going on. Then talk to Lydorea about what step she feels we might need to take. Remember to keep it quiet, I want no one to know what is going on until we are ready."

"Of course," Iclyn said as she turned and walked out of the room, closing the door behind her.

"Nyrieve, you and Kaleyna need to act like nothing has changed and that everything is... typical." Baysil instructed. "We do not want to tip anyone off that we are about to leave. I am not sure if it will be tomorrow or the next day, but I want it to be within the next two days. You need to get your belongings prepared. Pack anything that you need and anything sentimental you don't want to lose. Whoever is looking for you, when they realize you are gone, they will go through everything left behind for a clue of where we are going."

"And where are we going?" I asked.

"It is best you do not know. That way it is impossible for any trace to be left behind or a slipped word to give indication. Now everyone knows you are leaving in a fortnight. Keep talking as if that is the case if asked. Do not let on to anyone what is going on," he said sternly.

Kaleyna spoke up. "And what do we do to keep her safe all the rest of the time we are here?"

"We will have someone with her at all times. Ny, you have to keep Kaleyna, Koyvean, Iclyn or myself with you at all times. If anyone asks... say it is because you have been having... dizzy spells and we are keeping an eye on you. Sometimes this happens to Elves as they start changing, so people should buy it."

"Okay, never alone. Act like everything is normal. Get ready to leave at a moment's notice. And pretend I don't know someone is trying to kill me," I said sarcastically.

Baysil raised an eyebrow at my tone, then dropped it once he realized I was actually nervous. "Now Koyvean," Baysil said, looking to her, "can you put a protection spell on the manor here and especially one in her room?"

"The room, yes. The manor... I can try, but there is already a lot of protection magyc in this home. I am guessing it is Lydorea's work," Koyvean said, sounding slightly impressed.

"Okay, get the room protected... please. And Ny, keep Klaw on you at all times. Kaleyna, I want you to take my knife to keep on you, seeing as you could be a target as well." Baysil gave Kaleyna his dagger and the sheath for her to tie to her leg as well. He handed me back the letter.

"Keep this safe. It is proof for you to keep for later. You might need it. Kaleyna, I want you to stay in Ny's room tonight. I will bring your bed in here in a little while, and we can push them together to allow room to actually move around."

"So, now we just stay in here tonight and do nothing?" I asked.

"Just stick together, and talk about this to no one. Iclyn will explain everything to Rowzey, and in the morning I will have some more information for you," Baysil said as he and Koyvean walked out the door. Before he closed the door, he leaned just his head into the room. "Do not leave each other's sight. Keep safe and we will help you fulfill the prophecy, Nyrieve. Even if it is with our death, you will be the Bringer of Peace." He then closed the door and was gone.

೫11ೲ

I PACED THE FLOOR, back and forth, but the second bed in the room made it a bit awkward to do. I could not sit still, yet there was nowhere else I could go. Kaleyna was sitting on the bed writing down everything in her room she needed to pack so she wouldn't forget when she was able to go to her room in the morning. I knew I should be going through my few personal items, but I couldn't stop thinking about how there was one or more people here in Cliffside who wanted me dead.

The letter from my parents said they gave me up to keep me safe, and others, like Baysil, have been telling me to keep an eye out and they would protect me, but it never hit me until now that they really were trying to protect me. I did not fully comprehend the importance that seems to be placed on me just being alive, let alone on what they think I can possibly do. The Bringer of Peace, they keep calling me, but how am I going to bring peace to everyone if the only way to get it seems to be with fighting somehow?

I pondered the bigger question. Everyone was saying I was to bring the peace back to Iryvalya, but did I want to have this job? I mean, yes, it would be great to know our world was in peace, everyone could get along and there were not senseless deaths, but was it actually my job to do it? Would it be better for me to disappear maybe, just run away and hide out in one of the islands to the west perhaps? I did not want to leave everyone I cared about, but I did not know if I wanted to do all this. I had always pictured my life just growing older, helping out at the manor with other abandoned children, hoping one day to find love.

I just don't know anymore. I had always hoped life would get more interesting, but this was definitely not what I meant. The more I thought about all the dangers that lay ahead—not for me, but for those I love—I just didn't know if I could do it. I remember hearing travelers who passed through Cliffside saying the islands to the west were secluded and beautiful. I wondered how hard it would be to take some supplies and find a boat to travel across to one of them.

I had been hearing the constant sound of Kaleyna's pen moving while I was pondering what I should do, but all of the sudden, it stopped. I looked to Kaleyna, saw her looking down and not moving her pen, then suddenly she jerked her head up and looked at me with her brow furrowed.

"What, Kaleyna?"

"You are not running away, Nyrieve," she hissed.

"What are you talking about?" I asked, surprised.

"I don't know how or why, but I all of a sudden had a picture of you in my head getting off a small boat onto a little island all by yourself."

I couldn't speak. How could she have envisioned what I was thinking? "How did you see that? I was just thinking about going off to one of the Western Islands."

"You cannot run away from this, Ny. You are the Bringer of Peace if you like it or not, and going to another location will not change it. Until you die, this is who you are."

"I know, but I just... I don't know if I can do this. How can I put others at risk, because I am this... this Bringer of Peace?"

"Ny, I understand your fears and desire to keep everyone safe, but realistically, you cannot do that. If you run away from everything and everyone, they will just do like they said in the letter, hurt or kill those you care about just to hunt you down. Even if we don't know where you are, everyone would be hurt. They will stop at nothing to find you."

My eyes welled up and I broke down. "Kal, it is not fair. I did not ask for this, I did not get a say in this. How is it fair that because of who I am, which I didn't choose, those I care about can be hurt or killed?"

Kaleyna got up and came over to me, pulling me to her. Tears were streaming down my face onto her. "It is not fair, Nyrieve, that so much is being put upon you. Everyone should have a say in their life, and the truth is... you do. While you cannot change who you are, the Bringer of Peace, you do have a say in how things move forward. You can leave and run away and hide out for the rest of your life. Or... you can choose to stay and help Iryvalya, not for everyone in this world that you do not know, but for you and those of us that you do know and care about."

"Is it really a choice when, if I leave, all those I care about can be harmed or killed?"

"Yes, it is a choice. Neither of us chose to be Elves, or you the Bringer of Peace, but we can choose what type of people we want to be. We can be smarter and kinder than those Klayns who choose to believe they are better than others, and hopefully we'll prove it to them."

I sighed, sitting on the bed, and Kaleyna sat down next to me with her arm around my shoulder and said, "And if it makes any difference to you, I honestly think you are the perfect person to be the Bringer of Peace."

"How do you figure that?" I said with a laugh of derision.

"Ny, you've always put everyone ahead of yourself, sometimes more than you should. You never do it to get anything out of it, you do it because you have a pure heart and you are a good person."

"I am not that good," I grumbled.

"Yes you are. No, you are not perfect, none of us are, but you admit your faults and you question yourself. That makes a person good, and that you are. You are the best person I know, and I am so proud to be your best friend, and your spirit sister."

I smiled and hugged Kaleyna. "You are the flip side to me, Kal."

"Yes I am, and you to me."

"Thank you."

"For what?"

"Making me see that running away would not be what I want to do." I sat back, looking at Kaleyna, still with a vague lingering question if this is something I can do, be the Bringer of Peace. "Now we have to address the big question."

"And what is that?"

"How in Iryvalya did you 'see' what I was thinking of?" I asked curiously, pushing out any conflicted thoughts I had on my future for now.

"According to Lydorea, whom I talked to while you were in your meeting earlier today, this is one of my Elf powers starting to come through. She was trying to be so careful when she told me I was an Elf, and here I already knew. I pretended to be surprised, but I doubt she fell for it."

"So can you see everyone's thoughts?" I asked, a little concerned that she would know what I was thinking.

"No, it seems to be directed at you for the most part. Lydorea said that it is likely because we are both Elves and so close. Tomorrow she is going to take off the bracelet that hides my ears, because I wanted to have the dinner tonight without being noticed as different just yet," she said, smiling at me.

"That is amazing, and I am definitely more okay with you being someone who could know my thoughts over other people, though it is a little nerve-wracking, the idea you might know all I am thinking." I chuckled.

"I don't know everything that you are thinking, Ny. But truthfully I don't know how much stronger my ability will get, or if it'll just be limited to thoughts. Lydorea said I could be empathic as well, knowing people's feelings. Also… Lydorea told me I, too, have a last name."

"Really, what is it?" I asked, excited.

"Tarsys. Kaleyna Tarsys," she said with a smile.

"Kaleyna Tarsys… I like it," I said. "It suits you."

"I like it too. It just seems so odd to have a last name, but I do like it."

We sat in silence for a little bit, and I started to yawn repeatedly. I was tired, but I didn't know if I could sleep.

Kaleyna seemed to notice. "I don't want to be a pain, but I think we need to get some rest. We don't know when we will be going and we need to be rested for any journey, seeing as we have no idea how far we will be traveling."

I sighed, knowing she was right. "Okay, let's get some rest, but please wake me if you wake up?"

"I promise, as long as you do the same?"

"I will."

We gave each other a hug and got into our own beds. It wasn't long until I heard Kaleyna's breathing change, telling me she was finally sleeping. It couldn't have been much longer, and I fell asleep as well.

CO80

The sun streamed in through my small window, the sky perfectly blue without a cloud to be seen. I kept still for a few moments, not wanting to wake Kaleyna. It wasn't long and her breathing pattern changed again slightly.

"You awake, Ny?" Kaleyna whispered.

"Yeah, just woke up a few minutes ago," I responded, sounding sleepy. I needed to sit up. After sitting upright and stretching, I took a look around my room. It wasn't much of a room, but it had always been mine, and now I would be leaving here, and I might not see it again. I didn't know if that thought excited me or scared me more. As I continued looking around, I noticed a folded paper on the floor near the door.

I quickly climbed out of bed and padded over to the paper. I picked it up and hopped back into my bed. The floor was slightly cold, which was another indication the harvest season was here.

"Read it," Kaleyna urged.

I opened the short letter and read it aloud.

Nyrieve and Kaleyna,

I noticed you stayed in the same room last night, hope everything is okay. I just wanted to see if you both would want to join me in a quick ride to the salt flats just north of Cliffside. Rowzey said she is almost out of salt and needs some right away for her sauce. She suggested you both to help, as she said you are very good at finding the best salts. If you would like to help me, please meet me in the stables when you wake.
Baysil

"For some reason I doubt that Rowzey needs more salt, and least of all having Baysil go get it," Kaleyna said, unconvinced.

"I know she doesn't need more salt. I was in her pantry a week ago putting some things away, and she had a barrel full still," I said, concerned. "It has to be to get us in private and away from the manor."

We both dressed quickly. Kaleyna had brought some of her clothing last night into my room. We both wore our brown leathers for riding; mine were a slightly darker brown, while Kaleyna's were a lighter shade. We both had similar simple white shirts, so we looked almost like twins with our clothing.

Once we were dressed and downstairs, we saw in the kitchen that Rowzey had left us each a plate of food—some bread, cheese, nuts and fruit. We ate quickly and walked through the back door, each grabbing a cloak to keep us warm in the chilly morning air.

We kept a fast pace down to the stables where Baysil stood with three horses already saddled and ready to go. When he saw us coming, he smiled as if everything in the world was fine.

"Thanks for coming to help me. Rowzey will be happy to have the extra salt she said she needed," Baysil said, continuing the ruse.

"We are happy to help," Kaleyna said, mounting one of the horses.

I got up on the other horse, and we took off in a slow walk down the beaten path by the side of the cliffs to where the salt flats were. As we went along, not a word was spoken. I wanted to know why Baysil wanted us to come out here with him, but I knew I shouldn't say anything until he let us know it was safe.

The salt flats were a big open area of land that was in a long narrow deep valley between the cliffs. It had once been part of the North Sea, but long ago there was a dam built to allow a passage between the two cliffs. The salt flats formed on the ground between the cliffs. I don't know who the first person was to pick up some salt and put it in their food, but I think that had to be a brave and smart person. I love to add a little salt to almost everything, but not usually in front of Rowzey, as I do not want her to think that her food isn't good. I just love a little extra salt.

The salt flats area was exactly that, flat, but it had a faint bluish tint to it, as did the salt we used. I was taught in classes that this was because of certain minerals in the North Sea. Sometimes it could almost look the same shade of blue as the sky, and I would pretend I was walking on air. I was often jealous of the birds and any other creature that could fly. What I wouldn't give to soar above the ground and see everything from above.

We reached the salt flats and went through it to one of the caves at the bottom of the cliffs. I had seen this cave before when I collected salt here for Rowzey, but I had never gone inside. We stopped and tied the horses to a post outside the cave.

It looked like a typical cave, but there was actual furniture inside, old worn wooden chairs and even a bench. Baysil sat on one of the chairs with his back to the rear of the cave so he could easily watch the entrance.

I sat in one of the old worn chairs. I would have thought it would be stiff and uncomfortable, but it was oddly comfortable. I guessed it had been used so much that over the years it was worn and became almost soft. Kaleyna sat next to me on the long bench, her back against the cave wall.

"I am glad you girls didn't ask questions and just came along. Please know I am very appreciative that you trust in me," Baysil started. "We were up almost all night trying to figure out when we should leave and exactly where we should go to meet up with everyone. As of right now, our plan is to leave tomorrow night. Remember, this can change if we feel there is a need to, so make sure today you get all of your things packed up. There will be a trunk and bags in each of your rooms when we get back. Relonya is seeing to that. If there are any supplies you need before we go, let Iclyn or Lydorea know, and they will make sure you get them."

"Have you figured out yet who is trying to kill me?"

"We have a couple of leads that we are looking into. While we are not positive who it is, we are pretty sure the person or people will be trying to make contact with you today, seeing as whoever X is seemed to be urging them to get close to you. So please do not go anywhere alone with anyone. We cannot take any chances, as practically everyone is a suspect until we can rule them out."

Kaleyna took my hand, giving it a gentle squeeze. She looked to Baysil. "So is there anything else we need to know?"

"Yes, Rowzey has already left Cliffside."

"What?" Kaleyna and I said at the same time.

"She left last night. She went to meet with some old friends who had been on their way here to visit her and had planned to travel with us to our next location. She feared for their safety if they arrived after we left, so she went to meet up with them, and then they will all continue on to our meet-up point," Baysil said. "Last night a few of us were having a late snack, and basically we were having a conversation for others to overhear. Rowzey stated that she was leaving to go to the Oryliout River for some herbs that grow along the banks, saying she needed it for a big dinner to celebrate her friends' arrival."

I sighed, feeling a little hurt. "I understand why she left, but I can't believe she left without seeing me first."

"That was part of the ruse. If she didn't wake you and make a big deal of it, anyone listening would think that she is doing exactly what we wanted them to think."

"It make sense," Kaleyna said. "I know Rowzey would never do anything to put you in harm's way, Ny."

"I understand, but I can't imagine if something happens to her and I don't get to say goodbye."

"Nothing will happen to Rowzey," Baysil said. "She is stronger than most people I know."

We sat and talked a bit about some of the things Baysil recommended we pack and things he suggested to leave behind. He said if there was anything at all that we couldn't take, but wanted to keep safe, to put it under our beds, and once we left, someone would put the items in a safe place for us.

We must have been talking for a couple of hours, when Baysil grabbed a bag with some food inside. He passed it out to us and we all ate quietly and quickly. Once we were done, he stood and stretched, saying we should start heading back.

"What about the salt?" I asked. "Won't people know something is going on if we go back without the salt we were supposed to collect?"

"No worries," Baysil said. He walked over to a large hole in the wall of the cave, reached inside and pulled out an old wooden barrel. He opened the lid and it was filled to the top with salt. "I have a few of these hidden inside the wall, in case I ever need a reason to come out here to talk in private or just get away for a little while."

We all mounted back up on the horses and rode back to the stables. We actually had a little fun on the way back. We let the horses run for a little bit through the North Sea, even though we all ended up with a lot of water on ourselves. After we got back, Baysil said loudly with a smile on his face, "Thank you, ladies, for your help. If you wouldn't mind taking the salt inside, I will get the horses put away. And you might want to take some time to clean up. There's a lot of dried saltwater on you both."

We took the salt inside the manor and placed it in Rowzey's pantry. All the salt that had been there last week was gone. I guessed Rowzey or someone got rid of it in case someone looked around to see if her supplies had truly run out.

We walked through the manor to the stairway, and sitting at the top of the stairs was the last person I wanted to see right now—Jehryps. I continued up the stairs as if I did not see him at all, and when I walked past him he jumped up and grabbed my arm tightly and turned me to face him.

"Hey, what do you think you're doing?" I yelled, pulling my arm free and placing my hand on Klaw.

"Look, I am sorry about last night," Jehryps said, trying to lightly touch my arm again and stopped when he noticed my hand on Klaw.

"And what exactly is it you are sorry for, Jehryps?" I asked, annoyed he would even bother me after I found out what he did with Gwyndal.

"For making you feel uncomfortable and sitting next to Gwyndal like I did."

"That's all?" Kaleyna chimed in.

I couldn't help but smirk a little. I loved that she watched out for me.

"What else would there be?" he asked.

I took a step towards him. "Perhaps making me think that you actually cared and were interested in me, or pretending that you were a decent Elf."

"I do care about you. I want to have a real relationship with you, Nyrieve."

"If that was true, you should have reminded yourself about it prior to being seen out by the lake shore, doing a lot more than just talking with Gwyndal," I said boldly.

He looked like someone hit him in the gut and all the air was knocked from his lungs. "How did you know? Who told you? I am going to kill them," he shouted.

"First, how do you know it wasn't me who saw you with my own eyes? Second, it doesn't matter, because you just confirmed what you did with her. Third, go away, and leave me alone. I want nothing to do with you Jehryps. Nothing!"

I pushed past him and walked to my room with my head held high. Once Kaleyna and I walked through my door and shut it, I fell into the chair with a sigh of relief. I had finally stood up for myself, and it really felt good. Perhaps there is something to doing what's right for me.

‹‹12››

KALEYNA AND I WERE PACKING up everything in her room. We had decided it would be best to do her room first, seeing as we would be sleeping again in my room tonight. Her room was similar to my own. She had the same type of dressers and looking glass; the only real difference was the larger window. My window was large enough to possibly peek my head outside of it, while Kaleyna could have crawled outside of hers if she wanted to.

We had the trunk full of her belongings, minus a change of clothes for tomorrow, which we put in her backpack. Her room looked like just another empty room in the manor. There were always at least two or three rooms available for new arrivals or visitors, but there hadn't been many over the years, until recently.

We moved Kaleyna's trunk and backpack just inside my room, trying to do everything quickly and quietly, to not allow anyone to hear what we were doing. Once we were done, we used the key that was left on her dresser to lock her bedroom door. We never used locks in the manor. We were told the idea was that no one should need to hide things or keep secrets. The idea was not completely correct, otherwise I would have known who I actually was and had possibly been in danger earlier in my life. I guess sometimes it is okay to have a secret or something to hide.

Once we were back in my room, we got started packing away all my things. I kept out a change of clothing for tomorrow, and I also put the gift of the new black leather clothing from Relonya in my pack as I could not get it to fit in the trunk with everything else. In my pack I also put the letters I had received inside a hidden ripped seam I found in the front flap, figuring it would keep the letters safe from anyone else who might look for them. I also put on the bracelet from Lydorea so I would know where it was at all times. It slipped easily over my left wrist, but wasn't so loose that it'd fall off. I was about to put my mirror journal in my pack when it dawned on me that I could write Rowzey a message.

I took the journal over to my bed and sat down with my portable quill and ink. I opened it with a drop of blood, only to see that Rowzey had beaten me to the idea. There was a note inside my book, in her handwriting. I turned the book around to show it to Kaleyna, and she smiled at me. "What did she write?"

I read her note out loud, and as always, I had to read it with the accent she always used when talking.

Ny and Kal,

I's sorry I's didn't get to see yous before I's had to leave. I's had to go meet my friends to keep them safe, but we's will meet up again soon. Until I's see yous girls again, keep each other safe and always watch each other's back.

Let me know when yous get this, so I's know yous are safe. I's love yous both more than yous know.
Rowzey

"I was hoping she would tell us who she was going to meet, but I guess not," Kaleyna said, sounding disappointed.

"No, she wouldn't if she was worried someone could take either journal and find out where she was or who she was meeting," I said, realizing it myself. "Something we are going to have to do too when writing in the books, kind of talk in code when what we say needs to be kept secret."

"I agree," Kaleyna said. "Why don't just you respond to Rowzey, so she knows we are okay and she is aware of what is going on."

I wrote a quick and simple note back to Rowzey.

Rowzey,

I am glad we got your message. We are good, and getting ready for the trip, even though we still do not know where we are going. Both of us are excited to see you soon and meet your friends. We love you very much too, Rowzey.
Ny and Kal

I wondered if she would reply, or if we would just have to wait to see her again. I took my mirror journal and packed it in my backpack on top of the leather outfit. There was not a lot of room left, between the leather clothes and boots, but I did not want to leave them behind. I looked at the carved rose bloom from Jehryps, and I couldn't decide if I wanted to bring it or leave it. So I set it out on top of my dresser for now.

Kaleyna and I went down and made something for dinner. It was nothing fancy with Rowzey gone. No one seemed very suspicious of Rowzey not being here, seeing as there were many times she would be gone for days looking for items for her sauce or other things.

Once we were back up in my room, Kaleyna quickly fell asleep while I was still reorganizing my trunk and pack so I could put most of the items I took from Rowzey's kitchen in my pack. I did not know if where we were going would have salt, so I took a salt holder that I put inside my pack, but the extra salt container I grabbed fit into my trunk. I also took a couple of Rowzey's seasoning mixture containers and placed one in my pack and a bunch of others in the trunk. I also took was some of Rowzey's cheese bread. She had just made it yesterday, so I wrapped it in some paper and placed that in my pack too. It would be good to have in case I got hungry on the road. The last thing I took was a liquid container I had seen her use before when she was cooking. It was clean and dried out, so I filled it with some water, just in case.

Once my pack was done and I was alone with my thoughts, I kept finding my eyes looking at the carved rose blossom on my dresser. I decided I did not want it at all. I didn't like seeing it, and it kept giving me a strange feeling like it was trying to pull me, which made no sense. While I knew in my head I shouldn't leave the room without Kaleyna, I just wanted to throw it outside the front door and have it gone.

I made sure I had Klaw securely fastened and I tiptoed outside my room, closing the door behind me without a sound. I moved silently down the stairs and to the front door. I managed to open the door without it making any creaking sounds. I pulled my arm back to throw the carving as far as I could. Right before I released it, I heard someone breathing right behind me.

Arms grabbed me and a hand covered the scream that started to escape my throat. A hoarse voice whispered in my ear with anger, "Your time has come, Feral-blooded Elf. You will never get a chance to destroy our world, and I will be known as the hero of Iryvalya. The hero who killed Nyrieve."

I started to panic trying to figure out who it was and what they were trying to do. A voice in my head told me I needed to relax and think. Once I was able to calm my mind, I remembered Klaw. I dropped the carving from Jehryps and grabbed Klaw. I lifted my right arm up and brought it down as hard as I could, Klaw penetrating the person behind me. I felt a warm, thick liquid cover the side of my hand and start to drip across the top of my hand.

Almost instantly the arms let me go and someone behind me was screaming. I turned, and in the dark with Klaw held up to my chest ready to swing out in defense, I saw the back of a hunched over male. I couldn't see his face, or understand him through his cries of pain. His voice sounded familiar, even through his cries, and before I could think to do anything else, Baysil was running in with Koyvean next to him. They were followed by Iclyn and Lydorea, who came in with a candle that was magycally enhanced to be bright enough to light up the whole room.

Baysil grabbed my hand and looked at it covered in blood. "Are you hurt?" he demanded.

"No... no it's not my blood, it's his," I stammered, pointing to the man lying on the floor holding his right side. The blood had started to flow, covering the flooring near him.

Koyvean kicked him over onto his back, and as I looked at his face, I realized he was someone I recognized, but only barely. Suddenly it came to me. It was Montryos, the boy who had made fun of my eyes when we were young. Shortly after he had been cruel to me, he had moved in with the blacksmith to help him out with work. I saw him once in a while after he left, but never took notice of him.

"Montryos?" I asked.

"Yes, you dirty Feral-blooded little Elf!" he yelled as he spat blood out on the floor.

"Why?" I asked. "What did I ever do to you?"

"You were born! Your parents brought an abomination into our world and you need to be destroyed before you destroy it."

I didn't know what to say, I was at a complete loss. It was only a matter of moments before others started coming to the entrance of the manor. Kaleyna came towards me with a scared look on her face. I knew she would be disappointed in me for leaving without her. Miaarya came with some cloth to wrap the wound, and off in the corner was Jehryps watching everything that was happening.

Baysil was great at getting everyone focused. "Get Montryos down into the basement and let's see if we can clean him up and determine how bad the injury is," Baysil told some Fairies I did not know, who must have just come into the room.

"Shouldn't I get his wound taken care of first?" Miaarya questioned.

"No, he needs to be brought downstairs now, and we can clean him up down there," Baysil said, giving her a questionable glance.

"Nyrieve, why were you out here so late?" Lydorea asked as she looked me over making sure I didn't have an injury.

"I... I was just wanting to throw something outside," I said, realizing how stupid it sounded. I looked down where the carved rose blossom had fallen on the floor. It was lying in the puddle of Montryos's blood, completely covered in the red sticky fluid.

Lydorea looked down at what I was staring at. She gave me a glance when she realized what it was, came closer and put her arms around me giving me a warm embrace. I tried to pull back when I realized my hand had blood all over it, and it would ruin her pale pink dress, but she pulled me back to her. She leaned in close and whispered in my ear, "I know why you wanted to throw that gift away, Ny, I do, but he is not worth risking your life for in any way."

She pulled back and wiped away a tear running down my face—I hadn't even noticed it—and she said loud enough for people to hear, "I'm impressed to see you are more than capable of protecting yourself."

I still was confused and did not know what to say or do. Luckily for me, Baysil chimed in with the utmost confidence, as if everything was fine. "How about you come downstairs to get cleaned up. Kaleyna, help Ny, as I think she might still be a little shaken. Lydorea, could you please help Miaarya clean up this mess? Everyone else, please just go back to what you were doing, likely sleeping, and we will figure out what is going on."

I followed Baysil down the stairs, with Kaleyna right behind me, and we went into the small storage room in the basement. It was only big enough to hold about 9 people at the most. Once the door shut, Baysil turned away from us, and on the bookcase that covered one whole wall, he shifted a dark brown leather-bound book with the symbol of a tree on it, and a door opened behind the bookcase.

We walked into a large room, bigger than what was possible to still be only underneath the manor. There were random support beams throughout the room, but otherwise, it was all open. The room was white, all white—the walls, the floors, the ceiling even. It felt very bright, yet cold at the same time. After we walked through the door, it closed behind us with a push of a lever on the wall behind the bookcase next to Baysil.

Baysil turned around to me with a look of concern and anger. "Are you really okay, Ny? Did he hurt you in any way?"

"I am so sorry, Baysil. I know it was dumb to go anywhere alone. I just did not think I had anything to worry about in the manor," I said quickly. "And Kaleyna, I am so sorry I left you. I should have known better. They could have come and hurt you and not me. I don't know what I was thinking. I am just so stupid. I don't know why I—"

Baysil grabbed my shoulder, shaking me lightly. "Ny, I asked you if you are okay?"

"Yes, I'm fine," I mumbled quietly.

Baysil gave me a huge hug, and it felt almost like he was going to squeeze the life out of me. When he let go, he looked at me. "I am so glad you are okay, and so proud of how you defended yourself. Now let's get you cleaned up."

He led me over to a section of the room that had a wash tub and some water warming up on a stove fire. Baysil poured some of the hot water in to the wash tub and took Klaw, which was still gripped in my hand. As he took it away, the handle slightly stuck to me from the drying blood. Baysil took my hand and dipped it into the warm water and gave me a bar of lavender oatmeal soap to scrub off the blood.

After I had all the blood off of my hand and arm, I had to scrub the blood that was under my finger nails. I would have never guessed that blood was so difficult to wash off. When I was finished, Kaleyna handed me a drying cloth and I dried off my hands, still feeling like the blood was on me.

Baysil was over at another wash tub cleaning Klaw for me, which apparently took a lot longer to clean. The blood must have soaked in through the leather wrappings. I looked more around the room and noticed the one corner had a small white divider set up. It blended in with the walls, so I must have missed it. I started to walk towards it, and when I could see behind it, there was a bed with feet on it. As I got closer, I realized it was Montryos lying on top of it. He wasn't moving or making a sound.

"Baysil, is he alive?" I nervously asked him.

"Yes, Ny, he is alive. We gave him a sleeping spell to knock him out long enough to try and mend his wounds," Baysil said, crossing the room to me with Klaw. When he reached me, he handed me my blade and it easily slid back into my hand. After a moment I put it back into its sheath.

"While he is still knocked out, let's go over everything that happened. I know you said you decided to come downstairs to throw something out the door. What happened?" Baysil questioned.

"When I went to throw the item out, I heard someone behind me and then he grabbed me, saying that I was... I was Feral-blooded... and that I would never get the chance to destroy the world. So I started to panic, but when I remembered Klaw, I grabbed it and I just jabbed it into him hoping it would make him let me go. I wasn't my intent to kill him, but when he said he was going to kill me, I knew I had to try to get away. What does he mean? Why would he think I would ever destroy the world?"

"My guess is he has been brainwashed. I am betting the letter from X was either to him, or he was the messenger someone picked. Now we need to figure out if Montryos knows who X is."

Kaleyna spoke up, "How are we going to find out from Montryos if he is knocked out?"

Just then, Prydos walked into the room from the hidden bookcase, and he lit up when he saw Kaleyna next to me. He walked over, gave her a hug, and whispered in her ear, "I am glad you are okay."

"We are going to wake Montryos up," Baysil said, "and we are going to make him answer our questions."

"And how will you make him answer any question?" I asked.

"Oh... we have our ways," Prydos said with a wicked grin.

Baysil smiled in agreement and nodded to Iclyn, who had walked in with Prydos. Baysil gave us all a confident look and said, "Now let's wake Montryos up."

❧13❧

ONTRYOS WAS MOVED to a chair in the middle of the room while he
was still knocked out, his arms and feet bound to the chair he was
placed in. Even for someone who tried to kill me, I had to admit that he
was still a handsome Fairy. He was only a few Leaf years older than me,
but much taller than I was.

His hair was cut short, almost as if he had recently cut all of it off
and it was starting to grow back in. The hair growing back in was a faint
yellowish color. I remember when he was yelling at me upstairs that his
eyes were yellow and gray, and his eyebrows were the same yellow as
his hair. His ears looked strange, like he had gotten them caught on
something or burned, and they healed in a strange bumpy shape.

After Montryos was all set up, Baysil set some chairs up near him so
we could all sit and face him. Baysil looked at Kaleyna and me. "I need
you both to understand that we do not want to hurt him to get the
information, but if he will not talk to us, we will have to take other
measures to get some answers from him. They might be physical or
magycal, it will just depend on what will make Montryos talk."

"Do you think you both will be able to handle this?" Iclyn asked
calmly.

Kaleyna answered first with anger seething in her voice, "Part of me
wants to say no, because I do not want to be someone who enjoys seeing
others hurt, but after he tried to kill my best friend, I wouldn't mind
causing some of the pain myself."

I was a little shocked with what Kaleyna said, and did not answer
right away. I shook my head, trying to snap myself back to the situation
at hand. "I don't care at this point what happens to Montryos. The fact
that he was going to kill me shows he doesn't care about me, so I guess
I'll just return the favor."

"Good," Prydos said. "Iclyn, I think it is time to wake him up."

Iclyn walked over to Montryos and took a long thin rod off of the table nearest to him. It was an enchanting crystal. Enchanting crystals were used by imbibing them with a spell, and usually you need to invoke it with the person's blood that it's to effect. When you were done with the spell, you'd simply either break the crystal, or if you wanted to use it again, you'd simply put the person's blood on it again. Iclyn took the crystal and wiped it across some of the blood still seeping from Montryos stitched wound, and he instantly jolted awake and shouting out in pain.

"Why is he screaming so much?" Kaleyna asked Baysil.

"Well... we stitched up his wound, but we have not given him anything for the pain... yet..." he responded, loudly enough for Montryos to hear him and turn his angered attention to us and off of his pain.

"You are a Fairy. You should not be interfering with Elf business, Baysil," Montryos snapped.

"And seeing as you are also a Fairy, how is it any of your business?" Baysil queried.

"You don't know enough about who I am to say what is my business, Baysil," he countered.

Prydos sighed loudly enough to get a glare from Montryos. "I can see we at least have your attention," Prydos said. "And seeing as I am an Elf, I guess it is my business, so how about you start talking to us about who you are working for?"

"And what makes you think I am working for anyone and not just trying to rid Iryvalya of the Feral-blooded Elf whore myself?"

"Simply because you are not important enough. If you had been, you wouldn't have been sent, out of fear of you being caught and killed yourself. So I'll ask again, who are you working for?" Prydos sounded as if he was bored.

"I won't tell you anything. You're nothing but Rebel Elf scum. By rejecting your Klayn, you're nothing more than a Feral-blood just like her," he said, looking at me with disgust.

"You say that to me like it is an insult; however, you have never lived among the Klayns, and that means you cannot even begin to fathom how asinine you sound," Prydos said with a light chuckle.

"You don't know where I have been. I will not talk to you, Feral-blood!" he yelled out as he writhed in pain.

"You will talk, Montryos," Baysil said.

"You can't make me say anything!"

"Well, we thought that perhaps the pain might make you talk. That doesn't appear to be working... so what about if we can give you some relief from your pain. Would you talk to us then?" Baysil asked softly.

"There is nothing you can do to me that will make me talk. Cut me more, burn me, hit me, I don't care. I will not share anything with that Feral-blood whore," he said, his voice straining with pain.

"Perhaps we were wrong going the pain route," Prydos said, looking to Iclyn. "Is there anything we can do to help convince him to talk?"

"There is a potion that Lydorea has made that should loosen up his tongue," Iclyn answered, going over to the area where there were different first-aid items, along with pain-removing crystals and other unique healing items. She looked through a bunch of different vials, and finally selected one that had a teal liquid in it. She brought it over to Montryos.

He started screaming, saying he wouldn't drink it and flailing around. Prydos walked behind him and placed his hands on his head, holding it still. Baysil pinched Montryos's nose until he opened his mouth to breathe. When he did, Iclyn poured the potion down his throat and covered his mouth. After a few moments of struggling, he swallowed the liquid and started to calm down and relax his body a bit.

Baysil and Prydos sat back down across from him, and Iclyn sat down next to Montryos and said, "Now give it a minute, and he will start being freer with his answers. He might be guarded with some things, but the potion makes him forget the need to keep secrets. However, he will be as bigoted as he was before. It doesn't change personality."

"Will he give us the answers we want?" Prydos asked.

"It will depend on how well the potion takes. It works differently for everyone. He might be less guarded on some things, but still guarded on others," Iclyn responded.

Baysil sighed. "Why don't you ask him first, Iclyn, and we find out."

"Montryos, you were here in Cliffside since you all were kids, and went to work for the blacksmith. What caused you to begin to hate like this and attack Nyrieve?" Iclyn asked simply.

"Yes, the blacksmith, where you all pushed me away to. You didn't want me around, so you got rid of me," he said, his anger mixing with sorrow.

"No one pushed you away. We gave you that as an option after you kept running away from the manor. You told us you did not want to live here anymore," Iclyn responded. "We gave you an alternative, and you agreed to it."

"It wasn't a choice. I couldn't keep living in a place of lies."

"What lies, Montryos?" Baysil asked.

"That this was a home for abandoned Fairies, when there were Feral-blooded Elves living here," he said, looking at me and Kaleyna.

"How did you know we were Elves?" Kaleyna asked.

"Because I listened. I heard you both being talked about and how she," he said, looking at me, "was to be protected at all costs. I knew that I shouldn't be here. I deserved to be in a place where I would be protected at all costs as well."

"So, you were angry that non-Fairies were living here, and that we were protecting them. Did you honestly think that meant we were not also going to protect you as well?" Iclyn asked.

"You didn't protect me, you pushed me off to the blacksmith, and he didn't protect me either. He allowed me to run away and never came to look for me."

Lydorea silently entered the room, startling only Montryos, when she said, "I have just talked to the blacksmith, and he said you ran away several times. He said when he would find you and bring you home, you were belligerent to him and cruel. That you had left a note the last time telling him if he tried to find you, you would kill him."

"If he had truly cared about me, he would have tried to find me anyway," Montryos said, sounding like a young child.

"When you left last, where did you go?" Baysil said as if he was bored, but I knew he was getting at something.

"I made it all the way to the South Sea, alone, because I am strong and smart, unlike your Feral-bloods," Montryos said, full of pride.

"That is quite an accomplishment, Montryos. Not many Fairies can make it as far as the South Sea all on their own. You must not have had many encounters with anyone to make it so far alone," Baysil said.

"I had plenty of encounters," he said arrogantly. "I saw Centaurs, Gargoyles, Satyrs and even fire Elves."

"Oh, you saw Pyrothian Elves," Iclyn said matter-of-factly.

"Yes I did," he confirmed.

"And how long did you enjoy the company of all these different creatures?" Baysil inquired.

"Mostly just a few days each, but the fire Elves let me stay for months, because they knew how smart and strong I was. They had never even heard of Cliffside, that's how much smarter I was than them. I even drew them maps of how it was laid out and everything. They said they would love to see a place near the North Sea," Montryos said, completely not realizing how much of a fool he really was.

"Oh, that is a big accomplishment. So if you liked being there so much and they realized how smart you were, why would you ever come back to Cliffside?" Baysil asked.

"Because they became too stupid for me. They could not appreciate my skills anymore and I chose to leave," he said with bitterness.

"Are you sure that is it, Montryos?" Prydos asked. "From my experience, being an Elf and all, we always keep around the things we find valuable. My guess... they got the information they needed from you and then they didn't need you around anymore."

"That is not true! I would have been able to stay if I had just been able to pass the fire test!" Montryos yelled at him.

"Fire test?" Baysil asked.

"Oh, so that is why your ears are so scarred. You tried taking the fire test and ended up with your ears burned," Prydos said lightly.

Montryos just sat there with a look of anger and humiliation on his face.

"Prydos, please fill the rest of us in on what you are talking about," Iclyn said.

"Relonya and I had talked about different... competitions, if you will, that the Elf Klayns do to their younger Elves before their seventeenth Leaf Day. For the Pyrothian Elves, if you are powerful enough, you should be able to put out a fire that was started on your head. If you failed, eventually someone would put the fire out for you. I am guessing that Montryos here did not have someone who cared to put the flames out quite as quickly as others."

"Why would they allow a Fairy to do an Elf competition?" Iclyn asked.

"I am guessing that our friend here lied about being a Fairy, and said he was an Elf. We mostly look the same, minus our ears. So how did you hide it from them at first, Montryos, your lack of pointy ears?"

"I kept my hair long and down. When we did the fire test, all my hair lit up, and I was so concerned about them noticing my ears I couldn't remember how to do the spell to put out the flames. They noticed my ears once my hair had all burned away, and then they put the flames out," Montryos said quietly.

"You do not really believe that they had thought you were an Elf, do you? I mean, they did the fire testing knowing you couldn't put the fire out like they could," Prydos said.

"They didn't know. They said they were surprised and felt bad I was burned so badly."

Kaleyna was staring at Montryos and said, "And then they mended you, and told you about a girl of mixed Elf blood in Cliffside who bore the mark, and that she needed to die, because she would ruin Iryvalya. You figured it had to be Nyrieve because you had overheard how she needed to be protected at all costs."

"How did you know that, Feral-blood?" Montryos asked, shocked.

"Because I can see it in your mind," she said simply.

"What else do you see, Kaleyna?" Baysil asked.

"I cannot tell who the person is who asked him to come kill Ny, but it is because he doesn't know. The Elves never trusted him enough to give him any more information. They played on his hatred of Ny and got him to believe that if he could kill her, they would allow him to be one of them, and he actually believes it," Kaleyna said concentrating.

"Get out of my mind, you dirty little Elf," Montryos shouted.

"Can we quiet him?" Prydos asked Lydorea.

"Yes," she said with a sweet smile. She took a different enchanted crystal and let more of Montryos's blood seep on it. Suddenly he stopped making any sounds, even though his mouth was still moving. When he realized we couldn't hear him, he at first looked like he was trying to yell louder, but once it sank in that it wouldn't work, he quieted down and just slumped more into the chair with a look of pure hatred on his face.

"Okay, now that we do not have to listen to his ramblings anymore, Kaleyna, is there anything else you can see with Montryos?" Prydos asked.

"I don't know, let me try," she said, closing her eyes to focus. After a few moments she said, "There are just fragments I am getting, I can see him watching Ny and he is thinking some extremely sick and disturbing things he wanted to do to her when he caught her and had her alone."

"Like what?" I asked, speaking for the first time since Montryos was woken up.

"Ny, I don't want to say it."

"If he had plans to hurt me, I think I have a right to know what exactly he planned on doing," I said, looking into Montryos's eyes.

Kaleyna sighed and began to explain. "I don't know all the details, like I said, it is broken up, but he wanted to torture you with fire, and burn off your Elf ears for one."

"Go on," I said flatly.

"He also wanted to make cut marks all over your body, and he wanted…"

"What did he want?" I asked, still keeping my eyes locked with his.

"He wanted to take something… he wanted to cut out your eyes to keep."

"Oh, my eyes… the ones he made fun of so many years ago."

"Yes. There are other things, but mostly just the same in different variances."

"I see," I said. "And does he know who X is?"

Kaleyna sat there for a minute concentrating. "I don't think he does. All I sense is confusion and him wanting to really harm you. From what I can see, he has been receiving messages only about what to do, and all were marked with X. But… but the images I am seeing, the X is not the same as in the letter. I honestly don't know if the letter we found was sent to him."

"So now what, Baysil?" I asked, still not looking away from Montryos.

"Personally, I think that is up to you, Ny," he said. "You are the one he attacked, and you are the one who he wants to kill."

"Well, is there any place we can put him that is not pleasant for him and will get him out of our way for at least a while?" I asked.

"I know a perfect place," Prydos said with a grin.

"Good. I do not want him to get his voice back anytime soon, so I will be keeping that enchanted crystal," I said, standing and walking over to Montryos. I leaned in close to his face and tried to read any regret in his eyes. I could only see hate and anger, and while I wanted to believe that he was brainwashed, I knew in my gut that he was eager to harm me and that he wanted me dead. I thought about what I would do if he had hurt or killed anyone to get to me, and realized while looking him so close in the eyes, he would have killed without pause.

I took a deep breath and spoke slowly and clearly to him, "You will go away, and if you are smart, Montryos, as you claim to be, you will stay away, far away. It is not in my nature to hurt someone, but I will definitely make an exception for you. If I ever find out you have hurt someone, I will come find you and listen to you beg for a quick death. If you ever cross my path, it will be the last thing you ever do."

The look on his face was pure fear. He must have seen in my eyes I meant every single word of it. I stood there in front of him for a few more minutes, then straightened myself up, reached my hand out towards Iclyn. She placed the enchanted crystal keeping Montryos silent into my hand. I then turned my back on him, walking over to the doorway and into the adjoining room.

I stood there for a few moments collecting my thoughts and shortly the others came over to me. I looked at them and could tell again they were waiting for me to say something. I did not think I would have to take a leadership role quite so soon, but I guess it was time to start.

"When he is taken to this place, Prydos, make sure he is knocked out. I do not want him knowing how he got there or to have any idea how to leave."

"That is not a problem, Ny. I will make sure those who take him will keep him knocked out," Prydos said.

Baysil placed his hand on my shoulder. "What do you think would be our best next move now, Nyrieve?"

"Why are you asking me?"

"Because, this is your life, you are the one everyone is after, and I think you should have some say in it," he answered.

I thought for a moment. "I know we were going to wait until tomorrow night to leave Cliffside, but after all this, I think maybe we should leave sooner instead. When do you think it would be possible to have everything ready?"

"I think we could have everything ready to start out around midday tomorrow. We still need a little time to prepare a few things," Baysil said.

"That sounds good to me, if everyone else agrees?"

Everyone nodded in agreement, and then Baysil said, "If I can suggest, I think you and Kaleyna should go back to your room for the night. I will have someone standing guard outside it. You should try to get some rest. We have a long journey to start tomorrow, and you need to have as much energy as you can. The rest of us will finish up down here and finish our preparations to leave Cliffside."

We agreed and walked back out of the basement and up the stairs to my room. Standing outside my door was Jehryps, who looked like he had been crying. I didn't care to deal with him anymore and went to walk past him as if he wasn't there.

"Ny, are you okay?" Jehryps asked.

"She's fine, Jehryps," Kaleyna answered for me.

"I just want to talk to you, Ny... please..." Jehryps said.

I looked him in his eyes for a moment, wondering if I even cared to hear what he had to say. I realized I didn't, so I said nothing and turned my back on him and walked into my room. Kaleyna came into the room after me, slamming the door in his face.

We both lay on our beds in the dark, and after a little while, Kaleyna said to me, "Do you want to talk about what happened, Ny?"

"What is there to talk about... someone tried to kill me... there are others out there who are plotting to kill me... this is typical, right?" I asked, trying to make light of my worries.

"Yeah, typical... well, you know I will always be by your side supporting you, Ny."

"I know, Kal... thank you... Kaleyna?"

"Yes."

"Sorry for leaving you tonight. I shouldn't have left the room, let alone left the room without you."

"You can make it up to me later," she said, her voice trailing off as she was falling asleep.

"I will, I promise," I whispered, not wanting to wake her. Not long after that, I found myself drifting off to sleep as well.

I awoke to shouting and yelling in the manor. My heart began to race, as I had never heard fighting in the manor before.

∽14∾

THE SHOUTING SOUNDED CLOSE, so I knew it wasn't far from the base of the stairs. I looked over and saw Kaleyna looking back at me, still hearing the commotion. I tried to listen, but everything sounded muffled.

"Do you know what's going on?" I asked in a whisper.

"No, I have been awake for only a couple minutes longer than you, but I can't understand what they are saying," Kaleyna whispered back.

"Can't you feel what is going on?"

"I tried, but it is all emotions and feelings. Anger, worry, nervous, anxious, and desperation. Nothing good."

"Well, if it's not about me or us leaving Cliffside, I will be extremely surprised." I sat up, realizing I never changed into sleeping clothes. I looked out the window, and the Rydison moon was still covering the Northern Sun. We couldn't have been asleep more than a couple of hours.

"How about we go see what is going on together?" Kaleyna suggested.

"We can try. There is supposed to be a guard outside the room according to Baysil," I said, standing and stretching for a few moments. "Let's go see what is going on."

As I walked over to the door, I checked my right thigh and made sure Klaw was still securely attached. It's strange how in only a short amount of time Klaw now feels like it's just a part of me now. As I reached the door, the sounds grew slightly louder. If we could hear whoever it was downstairs arguing, everyone in the manor might be awake too.

I opened the door quietly and saw Koyvean standing right in front of me. "Going somewhere?" she asked flatly with a raised eyebrow.

"Just wanted to see if Kaleyna and I could go see what is going on with the commotion downstairs? I know we are to stick together, so would you want to come down with us?" I asked, hoping she wouldn't give me any problems.

"We can go down. I was given orders to escort you and keep you safe, but not to limit where you can go."

"Thank you, Koyvean," I said sincerely.

All three of us walked gingerly down the stairs. I was quite eager to know what was going on with all the commotion. In the living room was a Fairy from Cliffside that I had seen before, but she was not someone I had many interactions with. Her name was Reayondr. She was short, even for a Fairy, only a little taller than Rowzey. She had a dark golden brown complexion. She was slender, and had beautiful straight bright pink and bright green hair, which was the same color as her eyes, and oddly, had one eyebrow of each color. Every time I saw her she was always bubbly and happy, but now, she looked enraged. I was wondering why she was so upset, until her eyes became fixed upon me, and then I knew the reason. Me.

"She should not be here anymore!" Reayondr yelled, pointing at me. "She is going to bring us more Elves and danger, I have foreseen it. They are coming and will be here in only a matter of days."

"Nyrieve, I am glad you are up," Baysil said in a calm even tone.

"Kind of hard to sleep with all the yelling," I said lightly, trying to sound confident in myself.

"Oh, pardon us for interrupting your beauty rest, Your Highness," Reayondr said sarcastically, "but your sleep is not my biggest concern."

"Highness? That is a new one," I said, my left eyebrow rising in confusion.

Relonya responded to me. "It's a title that actually should have been bequeathed upon you by your parents, but seeing as you have been living here in secret, we figured you'd be fine without the formalities."

"Seriously… why would that be given to me?"

"Your mother is part of the Pyrothian Elves' Royal bloodline. Osidya was the youngest in her family, and while she had not yet had a chance to ascend the throne and join the Pyrothian council, she and her heirs are of the Royal family. For the Pyrothian Elves there is always a council member that is from the Royal family, so they are usually addressed by their formal titles."

"Okay... so this was a little more than I was expecting to hear coming downstairs... I'm not surprised at getting yelled at, but being uhm..." I couldn't even finish the words.

"Royal?" Kaleyna said with a smile.

"Yes, thank you," I said sarcastically. "How about we get back to Royalties later and talk about the issue at hand."

Reayondr looked at me with anger. "Oh, great, she wants to finally talk about the problem she is causing by still being here!"

"Look, Rea," Iclyn said, taking Reayondr's attention off of me, "Nyrieve has done nothing wrong. We chose to keep her here, and that was not just a few of us. The Fairies as a whole agreed it was the best thing, and while you were not old enough at the time to have a say, everyone else of age in Cliffside did. So if you have seen that Elves are now coming here to get Ny, you need not worry, as we will be leaving soon. This is what we have been trying to tell you for over an hour, but you never seem to shut your mouth long enough to hear."

Reayondr's mouth fell open and she looked to Iclyn as if she had slapped her in the face. "How dare you to talk to me, the daughter of Fynnasla. She was the greatest seer the Fairies ever had, and once she died, all her powers poured into me. So when you talk to me with disrespect, it's as if you are talking to Fynnasla with disrespect. And I demand that you give me respect," she said, stomping her bare tiny foot on the ground.

When I looked to Baysil, Iclyn, Koyvean, Relonya and Kaleyna, they all looked like they were on the verge of bursting into laugher at Reayondr's outburst. The only people who didn't look humored by her actions were Lydorea, who looked like she was lost in her own thoughts, and Miaarya, who looked especially nervous. I am guessing she didn't like the confrontation. I should say something quickly before anyone laughed and made the situation worse.

"Reayondr, please understand that we are doing everything we can to leave Cliffside in a quick manner. However, we do need some time to prepare our things and then make haste to our destination."

Reayondr just stared at me as if she couldn't believe I would have the nerve to address her directly. So before she could speak, I started again, "I also wish to humbly ask for your forgiveness for any stress that I have caused you. I have only recently found out about what I am, and as you can see from what Relonya just told me, I still have a lot to learn. I know I am young, but I do want to help Iryvalya, and I appreciate so much what all the Fairies of Cliffside have done for me and any sacrifices they have made on my behalf. I ask that you give us thirty-five hours to prepare and take our leave onto our destination."

I wasn't sure who looked more shocked in the room, as everyone was looking at me like they had never seen me before, and to be honest, I did not feel at all like myself with what I just said to Reayondr. While I meant everything, it was not at all like me to speak so formally. I just hoped that it worked and she would accept my request.

Reayondr stood there staring at me, and after a few moments she finally spoke. "Fine, but if you are not out of Cliffside by then, I will make sure you regret it." She turned on her bare heel and walked out the front door, slamming it as hard as she could behind her, wanting to make sure everyone in the manor heard it.

"Who are you, and what did you do to Nyrieve?" Kaleyna asked, looking at me with false confusion on her face.

"She was upset because she feels she is important and needs to be heard, so I let her know we heard her while making her think we think she is important too," I said simply.

"I'm thinking you are more a leader than any of us realized," Koyvean said, "at least more than I thought."

"Thanks..." I said, confused. "I just wanted to basically get her on her way. I never realized she was the daughter of Fynnasla. I know everyone respected her and mourned the loss of her, and her daughter feels since she has powers like her mother she should be respected too. Right now, we need more friends than enemies, and while I am not sure why, I get the strong feeling that if we do not keep her believing we appreciate her, she might start looking for another group who does."

"That is the same feeling I got from her also," Kaleyna said, giving me an odd look. "You could feel what she was feeling?

"I don't know if I could feel what she was feeling, but more an instinct that she wanted to be appreciated. When she called me Highness, it told me that she felt inferior and I did not want her to think that I thought of myself like that, because I don't."

"You definitely have the beginning traits of a good leader," Iclyn said to me, and coming from her, it felt like a big compliment.

"Thank you," I said, slightly embarrassed.

Relonya asked, "Ny, I was wondering why you told her thirty-five hours, when you know we plan to leave sooner than that?"

"I figured it was better to give us more time, in case something goes wrong," I said, "but also, in case she is already in talks with others who are not looking out for my best interests, they will believe they have more time to get to me or make an attack. To be honest, I think if it is at all possible, we should try to leave before dawn. That would give us about five hours from now to be prepared. Even if we have to break early and get some rest, at least we will be gone and have some distance from Cliffside."

"I agree with you, Ny," Kaleyna said. "I did not get any good feelings from Reayondr towards Ny or many people in this room in fact."

"I also agree," Baysil said. "Does anyone disagree?" Everyone shook their heads no. "Okay, then let's get everything ready. Ny, Kaleyna, do you have all your items prepared?"

"Yes we do," Kaleyna answered for both of us.

"Good, while I know this might seem unnecessary to you both, would you be willing to wait for us to be ready in Nyrieve's room? Koyvean has a very powerful protection spell on it now, and no one wanting to harm you can enter while you're inside it. So you can even leave the door open, but just please wait in there till we get everything ready."

"Sure," I said right away. "While I would be more than willing to help, I do also understand you needing to be able to get things prepared faster if you are not having to keep an eye on me as well."

"Thank you for making this easier, Ny. We all appreciate it," Lydorea said. "We will come get you both as soon as we are ready. Koyvean, can you escort them to Nyrieve's room, and then come back to help us?"

"Of course," Koyvean said flatly, walking up ahead of me to our room, with Kaleyna following closely behind. After we entered my room, Koyvean quietly said to me, "You have improved my thoughts of you, in how you dealt with Reayondr. It shows true leader form." With a slight smile she walked out of the room, closing the door quietly behind her.

Once the door was shut, Kaleyna spun around to me and demanded, "Are you sure that it was an instinct and not something more?"

"I am pretty positive, because I felt nothing different than normal. I just sensed that she was not being fully truthful with us," I said. "I wish I did have that power like you, but I don't think I do, Kal."

I walked over to my bed and noticed a note sitting on my pillow with a small wrapped package underneath it. "Do you know what this is?" I asked Kaleyna.

"No, what is it?" she asked, concerned.

I opened the folded note. "It's from Jehryps." I quickly scanned it and read it aloud to Kaleyna.

Nyrieve,

I saw that my Leaf Day gift was the item that you were trying to throw out earlier. This makes me feel so horrible for how I have hurt you, so much that you almost died trying to get rid of something from me. I could never forgive myself if you had gotten hurt or died because of me. Please give me a chance to prove to you I am not the guy you think I am, and that I want to be a better person, like you. You do not have to keep the carving I made for you, but I did clean it off the best I could.

Jehryps

"Ugh, why is he even trying?" Kaleyna asked.

"I have no idea. I am just annoyed that he managed to come into my room without me in here. It makes me worry if he went through my pack or anything." I started to look through my pack.

"He couldn't have gone through anything. The spell that Koyvean did only allows those with pure intentions to enter the room. So if he had tried to go through anything, it would have likely zapped him or forced him out, wouldn't it?"

"I don't know. They said no one could come in while I was in the room, they never said anything about when I wasn't in it. Though it doesn't look like anything was touched anyway." I looked at the wrapped package of the carving. I didn't know what to do with it honestly. After a few moments, I stuffed it into part of my pack and figured I would toss it away somewhere on our journey.

After a little over a half hour there was a quick and light knock on my door. I crossed over and opened it. Lydorea was standing there dressed in riding leathers. I was surprised. She was normally always in a flowing dress. "Hi Lydorea, would you like to come in?"

"Oh no, I haven't the time right now, but I wanted to see Kaleyna for just a moment," she said in a hushed yet hurried voice.

Kaleyna walked over to the door in front of Lydorea and smiled at her. "What did you need?"

"Nothing, I just wanted to give you something," Lydorea said, showing her left wrist with the silver bracelet, which was like the one she wore to hide my ears for me. She took it in her right hand, whispered something I couldn't understand, and broke it off of her wrist.

I looked at Kaleyna's pointed little ears showing now, and smiled. It was great to see her ears looking almost exactly like mine. Kaleyna ran over to my looking glass and squealed in delight at her new pointy Elf ears. She ran over to Lydorea and gave her a huge hug. "Thank you, thank you, thank you!"

"You are most welcome, my dear," Lydorea said, handing her the broken pieces of the bracelet. "Now I have to get going, lots to prepare for before our journey."

"You are coming with us?" I asked, happily surprised.

"Of course, Ny. Nothing could stop me from coming along with you on the journey, nothing," she said as she took off down the hallway.

As I started to close the door, I saw that Jehryps was sitting on the floor in the corner watching me. It was like he was hoping I'd call him over, but I had too much going on to deal with him, so I closed the door. At least once we leave for our journey, I will not need to worry about him bothering me or trying to get me to talk to him.

A few moments after closing the door there was another knock. I opened it and saw the face of another Fairy I knew, but hadn't seen in a long time. She lived in the manor, but always went on journeys to different places for Iclyn and Lydorea.

"Hello, Marselyus. What can I help you with?"

Marselyus was a very alluring Fairy and quite tall. She was naturally pale, but always seemed to have a dark tan after her travels. Her hair was cut to just above her shoulders, was soft straight hair that was different shades of dark red. Some were more pure red like a ripe apple, others were darker like the plumb wine Rowzey made. She had captivating eyes, a dark ruby red and a bright gold, and framed by dark red eyebrows. She had a friendly smile and a silky voice, though I only heard her speak when she felt there was something important to say.

"I have something for you and Kaleyna," she said quietly, handing me two large wrapped packages. "These are for our journey. There is one for each of you, and they are yours to keep," she said and then turned and left.

I closed the door and turned to Kaleyna with the two large packages. She took the one off the top, which had the letter K written on it. There was a letter N written on the top of the package I was still holding. "I guess we know whose is whose," I jested.

We sat on our own beds and opened the packages. Inside each package was our very own cloak, and it looked like they had never been worn before. I couldn't believe how beautiful they were and how identical they were except in color. Kaleyna's was in a beautiful deep cobalt blue that almost looked black, but when she held it near the candlelight you could see how pretty the blue was. Mine was a deep dark hunter green that also looked almost black away from the candlelight. Along the hem of each, there was an embroidered ivy leaf pattern in a silver thread that felt almost like a metal. The clasps on each cloak also had a silver ivy leaf on each side that connected to each other.

I had seen cloaks in different colors before, but never with such beautiful decorations on them. When I tried it on I noticed how warm it was and as I felt around the cloak, I found a couple different hidden pockets on the inside. I made a mental note of these in case I ever needed them, and told Kaleyna about them as well for her cloak.

After we had tried our cloaks on and were looking at ourselves in my looking glass, there was yet another louder knock on the door. I walked over and opened it, and it was Baysil. He looked worn out but had a smile on his face when he saw us. "Those cloaks look lovely on you both," he said.

"Thank you," we said in unison.

"I guess we will get to see if they will keep you warm on our journey."

"I hope they do," I said, smiling.

"Let's find out shall we," he said. "The time has come. We are leaving Cliffside now."

⟡15⟡

THE RYDISON MOON HAD about an hour before it started to move out of the way of the Northern Sun, so it was still dark outside. Kaleyna and I grabbed our packs, and some of the Fairies helped carry our trunks down to the front entrance of the manor. It looked like all the horses from the stables had been brought to the front, even though I knew it couldn't possibly be all of them. A covered carriage had room in the back for our trunks to be strapped onto it.

Once I stepped onto the ground I heard my name being called from behind me. I turned to see Miaarya standing with a forced smile on her face. She was dressed in her normal attire—a long gown with silk slippers, both in a matching pale yellow. "Miaarya, aren't you coming with us?"

"Sadly, no. Someone needs to stay here and keep watch over Cliffside... and I was the one that was picked..." She sounded distraught.

"I am sorry, but I know that you had to be picked because you know everything here and can keep everyone safe," I said, trying to help her feel better.

"I am sure you are right, Ny. I just want you to know I will miss you and hope you have a safe trip," Miaarya said, giving me a big hug.

I hugged her back. "Thank you, I will miss you also. Please keep everyone here and yourself safe too."

"Oh I will." Miaarya stepped back and smiled at me, and then gave a quick hug to Kaleyna. "Have they told you yet where you are off to?"

"Not yet," Kaleyna answered, "but I am figuring they would rather us not know, in case someone after Ny tries to find out."

"Of course. I am sure you both will find out soon enough. You two best be going now," she said with a forced smile. Miaarya was always offering me and Kaleyna help or just listening to our problems, but I didn't think she would have taken our leaving so hard, as she always offered everyone in Cliffside the same.

As I walked away from Miaarya, I looked to Baysil to ask which horses Kaleyna and I were to ride. He was standing by the twin horses that he had been training for the last year.

One was a male named Storm, and the other was a female named Rain. They both looked like they were covered in gray clouds during a rain storm, which is how their names were picked. I had only ever seen them ridden by Baysil. They had been born about two Leaf years ago, and had a gentle temperament about them. They always enjoyed when I would go to the stables and groom them and give them some carrots.

"Nyrieve, Storm is now your horse. He will treat you good and take care of you. Kaleyna, Rain is now your horse, and she will do the same for you too," Baysil said with a smile.

"Our horses?" Kaleyna asked.

"Yes, if something happens during our travels and you two need to go, these are your horses to take and keep with you. They have been trained to not spook easily, and they are some of the fastest horses Cliffside has ever had," Baysil said.

Kaleyna and I exchanged smiles and walked over to each of our horses. I ran my hand down Storm's neck and looked at the saddle that was placed on him. It was broken in, but did not look overly old. I turned to Baysil. "Thank you, Baysil. I honestly do not feel like I can thank you and everyone here enough for everything you have all done."

"You are welcome, Ny, but it is not without cause. I mean, we do all care about you and want to help you, but we are also investing in you to bring peace to Iryvalya. It is a lot to ask of you, so we are more than willing to help and support you anyway we can."

"Still, it means a lot to me, so thank you again," I said, feeling grateful and nervous that I would not let all these people down.

Baysil walked over to Kaleyna, took her pack and strapped it onto the top of the saddle behind where she'd sit, then did the same with mine. "Now, if for any reason we do get separated, we are heading towards the Eastern Sea," Baysil said quietly. "No matter what happens, you two stick together. We will come to find you. In the side saddle bags, you will find some food and water. If you need more, there are a few streams and rivers we will cross as we go. Just keep heading towards the east, and hopefully we will catch up to you right away."

"Any other advice or anything we should know?" Kaleyna asked.

"Just stick together. You two should never leave each other's sight. If you need me, just ride next to me. I will be riding at the back with Prydos to make sure we are not being followed. Also, keep your knives close at hand, you never know if you might need them."

"We will," I said, wanting to ask more about where we were going, but knowing there really wasn't a point. I know the direction we are heading, and I know it will be farther than I have ever traveled.

"Now, you both get mounted. We will be leaving presently," he said as he walked over to his own horse and did a check to make sure everything was ready.

I put my right foot in the stirrup and climbed up on top of Storm and, after getting my left foot in the other stirrup, I sat down comfortably. I straightened out my new beautiful cloak to fall across the back of my horse. Once everything felt comfortable, I leaned over and petted his neck. I whispered to him, "I promise I will take care of you, Storm, and keep you safe."

I sat back up and looked around. Everyone was mounting up. Kaleyna had a big smile on her face and had her cloak spread out the same way I did. I started to take note of who all would be riding with us.

Baysil sat on top of his black horse, Shadow. Iclyn was settling in on top of Frost, named for her white coat. Prydos was sitting on his pinto horse, but I did not know its name. Lydorea was sitting on top of her brown and white horse named Flutter. Other people on different horses were Relonya, Marselyus, Koyvean and five other Fairies I didn't know very well. There were three male Fairies, Lyosx, Symiar, and Kelvyhan. The two female Fairies were Elyzia and Nulya. Someone else was on a horse behind Iclyn, but I could only catch a glimpse, and could tell it was a male. As Iclyn's horse moved, my jaw dropped. Kaleyna asked, "What is it, Ny?"

"Jehryps," I said, stunned. "Jehryps is on a horse over by Iclyn."

"What?" she said, shocked. "He's coming with us?"

"I don't know, but I'm going to find out," I said, not trusting him coming on this trip with us. I lightly pulled Storm's reins and he started walking towards Iclyn as I guided him. When I was next to her, I pulled back a little and he stopped with ease. "Iclyn, why is Jehryps riding with us?"

"It was not my idea, Nyrieve," she said, sounding unhappy about it. "However, Reayondr came back and spoke with me right after you went up to your room, and she made a fuss that we should make sure that all known Elves leave and come with us on this trip."

"Why would she care?" I asked, annoyed with Reayondr, after I tried to keep the peace with her.

"My personal feeling is someone," she said, looking towards Jehryps, who was sitting on his horse with a knowing grin on his face, "went and informed Reayondr that it might be safer for Cliffside if all Elves would leave on this trip."

"He basically talked her into getting him forced to come," I said with disdain.

"That is what I think; however, I was unable to argue with her why all Elves but him would be leaving, so we had to allow him to come." Iclyn sighed.

"Great... that will just make this trip much easier," I said sarcastically.

"I told him he needs to stay away from you and to keep in eyesight of me at all times," she said. "If he bothers you, let me know."

"Thanks, I will," I muttered.

All of a sudden I heard Baysil's voice above all the mindless chatter. "Everyone, let's head out. Soon Rydison will be moving away from the Northern Sun, and we need to get as much distance as possible between us and Cliffside before that happens. Iclyn will be taking the lead, everyone else, fall in between her and myself. Let's go!"

Everyone started moving towards the trail that goes through the village and then around the outside of Cliffside and heads east. I directed the reins to get Storm to move us back over next to Kaleyna and Rain. We followed everyone, keeping to the back of the group, I wanted to keep as much distance between Jehryps and myself as I could. I told Kaleyna what Iclyn said about him and she shook her head. "It figures. He would do anything to get close to you, Ny. You need to keep your distance from him, yet keep an eye on him at the same time."

"I couldn't agree more," I sighed. "At first I thought perhaps he was serious about being interested in me, but I wonder if his interests run more towards thinking about what he would or could get out of me."

"If I feel anything or see any of his thoughts, I will let you know."

"Thanks, Kal, I know you will."

We rode through all of Cliffside. It was still dark, and everything looked so empty and lifeless. A few windows of houses we passed opened to see what all the noise was, and I even saw a couple of people wave to us, which made me smile and feel sad at the same time. It was good to know not everyone in Cliffside was like Reayondr. I just hoped Miaarya and the others who were staying behind would be able to keep Cliffside and everyone in it safe.

Once we got through all of the houses on the outskirts of Cliffside, I could see nothing ahead but trees. I had been down this path before, when going to collect herbs or mushrooms in the Eritsong Woods. We would be going through those very woods and farther beyond to places I have never been before. I couldn't help but feel excited to see new places and meet new people, but there was still a small knot in my stomach, worried about the many dangers that would surely lie ahead.

After a few hours of riding, the Rydison Moon had left the Northern Sun fully exposed; however, there were many clouds in the sky with a possible threat of rain to come. With the cloud cover and it being almost the middle of the harvest season, I was thankful for my new warm cloak, as it was quite cool outside. As we rode towards the east, I could see the faintness of the Joauxy moon and the Ivynilo moon as they started to cross just south of the Northern Sun. They always moved close to each other, following not too far behind the Rydison moon.

The legend was that they were siblings that had been torn away from their parents, and that is why they stayed together, always taking care of each other. The Joauxy moon was a deep blood red, with the Northern Sun above it. It was a little bigger than the Ivynilo moon, which gave off a beautiful sage green color. I remembered when I asked Rowzey about these moons, and she told me the story of them. I always felt like they were watching over me. Since I also did not have my parents, it seemed like we had a connection.

The ride had been pretty uneventful, and most everyone rode in silence. After about four hours we reached the village of Dalorvya. I had ridden close to the destroyed village before, but never went through it, and today, we were going through it.

If I squinted my eyes, the village could appear a lot like Cliffside, but with my eyes wide open, I knew it had gone through something I hoped would never happen to another place again. While most of the buildings were still intact, there had been a lot of fire damage to them all. The windows were all broken out of the buildings and homes, and the belongings of those who lived there were strewn about the streets.

Tears began to slide down my face when I noticed that there were still bloodstains and bones of those who died in the doorways of the buildings. I remembered in my learnings that the bodies had been left, as they were all so burned they couldn't tell who were Fairies and who were Elves. There were even heartless messages still written in blood on the walls of the buildings saying *There is only one ruler, the Elves, follow or perish.* How could they be so hateful, to kill innocent people like this. I was looking at all the destruction when my eye caught something off in the corner of a broken doorway, and my stomach dropped.

It was a small and innocent-looking child's toy, a small tan bear with big black button eyes, and a half broken stitched smile. What caused my tears to speed up was this tiny little bear, that I am sure a small child loved dearly, covered in old dried blood, and still being grasped by a glove with an unseen hand, attached to the slumped over bones of a little girl. Her blue dress was half burned away, and the rest faded from all the years exposed to the elements.

I know why Baysil had us go through the village, I didn't even need to ask. He needed me to see this, to see the destruction that had happened in Iryvalya because of the Elves. I knew I would likely see things like this again, but I did not think that the image of the little girl with her bear would ever leave my mind.

After we made it through Dalorvya village, we stopped outside the Eritsong Woods near a small river to let the horses rest for a while and have some food. Kaleyna and I were sitting on some rocks near the water sharing bread and fruit when Prydos and Baysil came over and asked if they could sit with us. I knew Kaleyna wanted to have more time with

Prydos, and I never minded his or Baysil's company, so we nodded and told them to join us.

"How has the ride been going for you both?" Baysil asked, sitting down.

"Besides seeing what happened in Dalorvya, I guess I'm doing okay," I said to him.

"I understand, Ny... I know how hard it is to see the destruction like that, but it is also important to see and remember what has happened. It's important to remember the good and bad of the world, so we can enjoy the good again and not repeat the bad."

"I know... I just wasn't really ready for it I guess..."

"No one should be."

"And if they are, there is something wrong with them," I said.

"I agree with you," Baysil sighed.

"This is actually the farthest I have even been away from Cliffside," I said, wanting to change the subject a bit, "so I want to try to keep watch for anything new."

"You will definitely be seeing some unique things as we travel on," Baysil said, turning and listening to the song of a bird hiding up in the trees. "Have you ever heard a bird like that one singing?"

"No, I haven't," I said.

"Me either," Kaleyna added, sitting close and cozy to Prydos. He put his arm around her and her face lit up. I smiled at her happiness.

"It's a Sangrynaw. They are some of the most beautiful birds in song and in color. They have longer necks and a big tail of feathers, very similar to the peacocks we have in Cliffside. These, though, are about half their size. The feathers on their bodies are all black or white, and the tails are a rainbow of different colors," Baysil said.

"They sound beautiful," I said, looking up at the trees and hoping to catch a glimpse of one.

"Yes, they are, but they are also quite deadly," Prydos said, looking up as well.

"Deadly?" Kaleyna asked, staring up too.

"Yes, but they will never attack someone without reason," Baysil said.

"What reasons would they have to attack?" I asked, slightly nervous.

"If they are attacked, if one of their eggs is taken, if you try to trap it, or even if you just try to take some of its feathers," Baysil said.

"Why would anyone try to take its feathers?" Kaleyna asked.

"Because they are rare and so very beautiful. I know in Noygandia, there are people who have some quills made from the feathers," Prydos said. "There are even adornments made out of them for people to wear."

"What makes the Sangrynaws deadly?" I asked curiously, looking back to Baysil and listening to the bird's song.

"Well the Sangrynaw has a small but very sharp beak, and there is potent venom that is secreted into its mouth. When it bites, it always breaks the skin on its prey, and usually within a day or two the person is dead," Baysil said.

"Too bad you couldn't get Jehryps to go get one of those feathers for you, Ny," Kaleyna said jokingly.

"No kidding," I said flatly.

"Jehryps is a piece of work," Prydos said. "For the last two days he has been asking me if he could come with us and where we were going. I told him it was not a trip for him, and he should stay back in Cliffside where it was safe. So of course he had to find another way to be able to come along."

"He wants to follow to where Nyrieve goes," Baysil said, looking at me. "I believe he thinks if he joins with you, he might gain some sort of power."

"I just wish he would leave me alone," I said quietly.

"Isn't there a way we could just tie him up and leave him here outside the woods?" Kaleyna asked seriously. "I mean, when he gets free, he can walk back to Cliffside."

Baysil leaned in to us and spoke quietly. "I have no proof, but I do not think that Cliffside would be safer with Jehryps there. While he always acts nice to everyone, his world revolves around himself and what or who can get him further in life. And for him, the only thing that is important is power and control."

"He told me once that he believed he and I could be a very powerful couple and bring good into the world," I said, looking at Baysil.

"I believe the first part, you and he would be very powerful. I just do not believe the good part with him," he said.

The rest of the time we sat and talked about unimportant matters. After a while the conversations died off, and Baysil left to go talk to Koyvean. Kaleyna and Prydos began talking of different things they liked, and I just sat back and listened to the sounds all around me. I kept hearing the Sangrynaw's song, thinking how strange it was that something that could make such a beautiful song could be so deadly.

As I listened and looked around I noticed the leaves had started to lose their colors above. They would go from their beautiful shades of green to a gleaming silver, and then fall to the ground. They moved so quickly and almost fluidly in the breeze, as if they were doing a dance on the branches, and reminded me how much I had always loved seeing the changing of the leaves. I know many people did not like to see the leaves lose their color, but there was something so beautiful about the trees when the leaves were mixed between the green and silver colors. I had always made a point to save at least one silver leaf a year. Rowzey had started me on the tradition when I was little, and I was glad I made sure to pack those in my trunk, as I did not know if I would ever again get to see the silver-turning leaves. I figured I should take one of the leaves now, because I didn't know if I would ever get the chance again.

I looked around the ground near me and didn't see any, so I told Kaleyna that I was just walking to the tree edge only a few steps away. I walked around and finally saw a perfect silver leaf, as big as the palm of my hand. I went back and sat down, and placed the silver leaf inside my backpack in the middle of my mirror journal for safekeeping.

I heard some movement near the water off to the side of us, and I turned to look. Jehryps was using water to splash his face and take a drink. He looked so innocent, yet I had such doubts about him. I did not think I could ever fully trust him, but did that mean I should also hate him? Iclyn and Baysil even worry about his intentions, but I remember something Rowzey had told me: "When making the sauce, yous want to be making sure yous look at all the ingredients up close before yous decide if they is right for the sauce or not. Do not just trust what others tell yous."

So I told Kaleyna I was going to go talk to Jehryps, since he was only about thirty steps away. She told me I was crazy, and Prydos agreed, but I explained that I needed to ask him something, which is exactly what I did.

I walked the few feet to be close enough to Jehryps to talk to him, but not close enough he could reach me.

"Jehryps?"

"Ny!" he said, sounding overly excited, and began closing the distance between us.

"No, stay there, and I will stay here," I said. He stopped in his tracks, looking confused. "I just wanted to ask you a question, and then I'll let you get back to whatever it is you're doing."

"Sure, anything, you can ask me anything at all. I am just so glad you are talking to me. I told Gwyndal that what happened was a mistake, so she knew and so you don't think that I am interested in her," Jehryps said quickly, like he was worried I would not let him finish.

"Look, Jehryps," I started, "as far as you and I are concerned, I really cannot see a future for us beyond perhaps friends, and that right now I am not even sure of. So it doesn't matter if you spend time with another girl, it's none of my business."

Jehryps looked like I had taken all the hope out of him, and while part of me told me I should feel bad, I didn't.

"What is it you want to ask me then, Ny?" he mumbled.

"I want to know what your real reason was for getting Reayondr to think that you needed to leave with us."

"What makes you think I had Reayondr do that?" He narrowed his eyes at me.

"Jehryps, I know you did. Just answer my question," I said, getting annoyed with him.

He stood there for a moment just looking at me. Finally he said, "I had two reasons. One, I wanted to go where you are going. I just want to be near you and try to convince you I am worth your time. Two, I was scared to stay in Cliffside. After what happened to you with Montryos, I was nervous to be the only Elf left there."

For once, I kind of believed him. "Thank you for answering my question, Jehryps. I am not saying you cannot talk to me at all, but I am asking that you keep your distance and allow me space to decide if a friendship is even possible between us."

"I can do that," he said, looking like he felt some hope again.

I nodded at him, turned around, and walked back over to where Kaleyna and Prydos had been watching like hawks.

"So what was that all about, Ny?" Kaleyna asked.

"I just don't trust him," I whispered, "but I want to keep him close enough to know if something is going on."

"Everyone," Baysil said loudly for everyone to hear, "we need to leave in the next five minutes, so get ready and mount up."

∽16∾

WE MOUNTED UP AND STARTED heading east again. I knew there was something going on for Baysil to have us take off so quickly. I did not want to bother him right away, but after about a half hour of riding, Kaleyna and I fell back enough to be able to talk to Baysil quietly.

"What is going on, Baysil?" I asked.

"We had a couple of visitors while we were stopped, some Satyrs, brothers they said. Leyhroi and Jynkins were their names. They were quite odd and chatty, and they made mention of seeing some other Elves not long before we got to the river."

"I am guessing they were not Rebel Elves?" Kaleyna asked.

"We don't know. They could be, but again they might not be," Baysil said, "so we figured it was best to keep moving."

"What direction did they say these Elves were traveling?" I asked.

"They were not sure, but it is not likely to have been to Cliffside, otherwise we would have already run into them," Baysil said.

"Not necessarily," I said. "If they would have heard us coming, and there was only a few, they could have hidden off the road somewhere."

"We know, Ny," Prydos said. "That is why Baysil decided we should get moving so we were not sitting ducks for an attack."

"Do you think we can trust these Satyrs?" I asked.

"They have no reason to lie," Baysil said. "There used to be a very large Satyr population near the Crystoval Mountains. After the Elf Wars, their population was left at not even a quarter of how many there used to be."

"Why would the Satyrs have been killed by the Elves? I mean, I have never met one, but from what I read and was told, Satyrs are a very peaceful race," I said, confused.

"They are peaceful. However, during one of the wars, the Elves wanted to use the Satyrs as a type of slave to do their bidding for them," Prydos said. "While Satyrs are peaceful, they will fight for their freedom. And that is what they did. They fought against the Elves. However, the Elves vastly outnumbered the Satyrs, so in the end the Satyrs were defeated."

"So now all the Satyrs live up in the north side of Iryvalya?" Kaleyna asked.

"There are some up here, but most of the remaining ones were captured and enslaved by the Lumaryia Elves," Prydos said sadly.

"They are the ones who live in the Crystoval Mountains," I said.

"Exactly," Prydos said. "My family actually has a Satyr, her name is Dazyen. She was always so kind to me, even though she was supposed to be my servant. My only regret leaving the Lumaryia Elves was having to leave Dazyen behind with my cruel family."

"I am sure she is proud of you for leaving and knowing right from wrong," Baysil said.

"I hope so. I hope one day I will get the chance to save her and give her freedom back to her," Prydos said quietly.

There was really nothing more to say. I couldn't think of any words that could comfort Prydos. If I failed at somehow bringing peace to Iryvalya, so many people would be disappointed in me and will have risked so much for nothing. I did not know how I was going to bring everyone together and have peace between the two Klayns. Was I supposed to fight them? Was I supposed to simply get them all to talk to each other and let go of their differences? No one told me how I was supposed to be the Bringer of Peace. While I did want peace for everyone, I was not sure I was the right person for this.

We rode on for the rest of the day through a meadow-like valley called Brydalwind. We continued with a few stops here and there to stretch and give the horses a little time to drink and rest. There were not many trees, just a lot of fields with wild flowers that had died off. Once the Nydian Moon started to cover the Northern Sun, Baysil said we should stop and make camp for the night. I was kind of hoping to keep going through the night. I was not yet tired and I was a little nervous about stopping again without any trees around for cover.

Once I had Storm tied up next to Rain, brushed, watered and fed, I waited for Kaleyna to be done with Rain. When she was finished we both walked over to the campfire to warm ourselves up. It was a lot colder than I was expecting it to be, but then again, I hadn't slept outside in a long time. Lydorea brought both Kaleyna and me a bowl of stew that was warmed up on the fire. We ate quickly in silence. I had not realized how hungry I had become, and ate everything in my bowl and two large pieces of bread.

After a while of just sitting and finally feeling warm and full, Lydorea came back over and got our bowls to wash and repack them. When she was done, she came back over and sat down next to us.

"How are you both doing so far?" Lydorea asked.

"I can't answer for Nyrieve, but I am starting to feel a little sore from riding all day long," Kaleyna said.

"That is common. You will feel tired for the first few days, but then it won't be so bothersome." Lydorea sighed.

"Days?" I asked. "Will it really take days to get to wherever it is we are going?"

"That is what I have been told," Lydorea said. "I think only a couple of people know our true destination. In case someone gets lost or taken, they cannot give up where we are going."

I sighed a bit louder than I had meant to.

"What is it, Ny?" Kaleyna asked.

"The idea that someone could or would be taken and harmed just to find out my location is worrisome to me. I do not want to see anyone hurt because of me."

"Ny, you need to realize that almost everyone is here not because of just you, but the hope of peace being brought to Iryvalya. You are the Bringer of Peace, and with that peace, everyone will truly prosper in many ways. The Fairies will not be forced to live inside Cliffside alone, we could live anywhere we wanted without the fear of being killed. That is not something we have been able to do for hundreds of years. The only places I have traveled to have been in secret with the fear of being killed at any moment. This gives us hope not only for peace, but for freedom," Lydorea said with a bright smile.

"And how am I supposed to bring peace to everyone, Lydorea?"

"That I do not know."

"If you do not know, and I do not know, who does know? Because I get the feeling I should know what I am supposed to be doing here," I said, getting frustrated.

"Yous will know when it time, Ny," Rowzey said from behind me.

"Rowzey!" I spun around, jumped to my feet and hugged Rowzey to me. "I am so glad you are safe!"

"I's glad yous be safe too, as I's heard yous ran into a little trouble with someone," Rowzey said, hugging me back.

"Yes, just a little, but she was able to take care of herself, Rowzey," Kaleyna said. "We are all proud of her."

I let go of Rowzey and turned to Kaleyna. "Why is anyone proud of me hurting another person?"

"Not that you hurt someone, Ny, but that you were put into a position where you had a choice to live or die, and you chose to live," Kaleyna said, getting up and taking a moment to give Rowzey a hug herself.

"So, Rowzey, where are your friends you went to meet?" I asked, wanting to change the subject.

"They were getting pretty cold from our trip, so they were hiding in my bag to keep warm," Rowzey said as she opened her bag. Out flew the smallest people I had ever seen. They had iridescent purple skin and wings, which looked a lot like a dragonflies. Their eyes had a pale green glow. I knew that they had to be Pixies.

"Hello," they both said in unison, flying around Kaleyna and me.

"Hello," I said, "how are you both?"

"We are good," they said again together.

"This is Ayllac and Callya," Rowzey said.

"I remember. You helped raise them on Troxeon," I said.

"The island of the Pixies?" Kaleyna asked.

"Yes," the pixies responded together. "That is where we are from."

"Do you always talk at the same time?" I asked with a giggle.

"No," said the one with light sky-blue hair that looked to be streaked with a dark pink. "I am Ayllac. It is a pleasure to meet you again, Nyrieve."

"It is my pleasure, Ayllac," I said, and I looked to the other Pixie with the bright orange hair with dark purple streaks. "So you must be Callya?"

"Yes," Callya said with a slight shyness to her voice. "I have looked forward to seeing you again since you left Troxeon with Rowzey after you were born."

"I am glad to finally get to meet you both, now that I am old enough to remember you, that is," I said with a smile.

"Please do not be offended, Nyrieve, but it is very cold out here for us. We will talk more tomorrow on our journey," Ayllac said politely as she and Callya waved at me and flew back into Rowzey's bag.

Rowzey set the bag close to the fire to help keep the Pixies warm, then came back over and sat next to us, still in arms reach of her bag. "Those girls have been waiting to see yous again since yous left Troxeon with me all those years ago."

"In your letter you talked about Ayllac and Callya, I just did not realize that they would have known me when I was born," I said, smiling. "So they would have known my parents a little too, right?"

"Yes, they did meet yous parents, but they were young Pixies at the time, so I's don't know what all they might remember," Rowzey said. "They think of yous like their long lost little sister."

That made me smile. I knew they were older than me, but they were just so tiny and cute, and I had this feeling I needed to protect them. I seemed to have that feeling a lot lately. I guess it was part of being the Bringer of Peace, I felt the need to keep everyone safe.

Rowzey explained her journey from leaving Cliffside to meeting us here. She said it was quite uneventful, as either no one cared to follow her, or everyone believed what she said about collecting herbs. We told her about everything that had happened since she left, and after I was done telling her about it all, she came over and gave both Kaleyna and me a hug.

"Yous girls are very special to me, and I's am proud of yous both and happy yous are safe."

After Rowzey sat back down, Baysil walked over to us smiling. "It is so good to see you, Rowzey," he said, leaning down and giving her a hug. "We have missed your cooking."

"Well I's not making anything tonight, but tomorrow, yous will have a good breakfast!" Rowzey said laughing.

"Nyrieve, Kaleyna, I would like it if you both would sleep between me and Prydos. We just feel it will be a better way to keep you safe," Baysil said.

"Only if I can sleep next to Prydos!" Kaleyna said cheerfully.

"I kind of figured that one, Kal," Baysil said. "It is getting late, and we have an early day ahead of us, so let's all try and get some rest. Some of us will take turns keeping watch, but you both do not need to tonight."

We each laid out a blanket to sleep on, and I took my cloak and used it like a blanket to keep extra warm. Kaleyna did the same. Being between Baysil and Prydos did not leave me feeling much like talking, so I just looked at the Nydian Moon covering the Northern Sun with its beautiful turquoise glow and listened to Kaleyna and Prydos whispering and giggling to each other. Their sounds made me feel happy for them, and I fell asleep with a smile on my face.

It continued like this for six more days. We would ride and take small breaks and then keep going. We went through patches of forests and then more open meadows, even past a few abandoned villages, which were sad to see. Though in all the travels, we never came across another person. Over the days traveling, I spent time with the Pixies and learned a lot about their personalities and what they enjoy doing. They explained how rough their journey was over the cold mountains that divide Iryvalya in half. They said if it hadn't been for the middle of the mountains being magycal surrounding the Leaf Tree, they could have frozen to death. They were very vague about the Leaf Tree, no matter how much Kaleyna and I would ask for details. Each night we would make camp and sleep, me always between Kaleyna and Baysil.

CR80

I awoke with a gloved hand placed firmly across my mouth and a cool and sharp blade against my neck. I snapped open my eyes, focusing on who was above me. Whomever it was, I had never seen them before. I couldn't tell if it was a man or woman, as they had the majority of their face concealed by black cloth. I tried to feel to my sides. Kaleyna was still next to me, but Baysil was gone. I looked towards Kaleyna and saw someone else holding her down the same as me.

The person above me shouted, the voice telling me that it was a woman. "Do we know which one it is yet?"

"I think we have her over here," a deep male voice said from across the camp area.

The woman above me looked me in the eyes. "Don't move. If you are not the chosen one, you will live to see the morning."

They were here to kill me, and they thought someone else was me. I should say something, I should make them come after me and not someone else. Kaleyna nudged my hand repeatedly. I knew she was trying to tell me to keep quiet, we had done that to each other before when we knew the other might say something they shouldn't.

My right hand was still under my cloak and couldn't be seen, so I very slowly moved my hand towards Klaw. I let my fingers slide into the handle, and I gripped it as tightly as I could. I knew I should probably just take Klaw and stab the person above me, but I worried the person holding Kaleyna might hurt her. All I could seem to do was just wait for an opportune time to strike if I needed to.

I lay there listening for what felt like hours, but had to have been only minutes. Finally the deep male voice spoke again loudly, "She's not here. She must still be in Cliffside. Let's go and join the others."

The woman above me leaned closer and looked me in the eyes. I could see from the dwindling fire, she had black and gold swirled eyes. She whispered so quietly that I almost didn't hear her, "You are very lucky, little Elf. Do me a favor, the next time someone grabs you in your sleep, don't wait, attack. Because not everyone will pretend that they couldn't find the Bringer of Peace."

My eyes opened in surprise. Was she saying she knew who I was?

"One more thing, not everyone with the Elves are against you, but not everyone with The Drayks are for you. Remember that and speak of this to no one, ever. Volnyri."

The Elves who had us pinned and surrounded sped off into the woods heading back towards Cliffside. I just lay there and breathed, not believing what just happened. I lightly touched my neck and felt a small drop of blood from where the knife nicked me. I turned my head to

Kaleyna, and she nodded at me and whispered, "I heard. I won't say anything."

Suddenly Baysil was next to me helping me and Kaleyna stand up. "Are you okay, you two?"

"We are fine," I said, still not knowing why this woman saved me.

"I heard some movement in the woods and went to see what it was, and they ambushed us. There had to be thirty of them. I am so sorry I left your side, Ny."

"Baysil, it's okay, we are fine. Is everyone else okay?"

"They cut Nulya's throat a little when she tried to fight back, but Lydorea is tending to her and thinks she will be fine. We need to get you out of here now, so let's get our things and leave."

"Why shouldn't everyone leave? I don't want to leave anyone behind to get hurt," I said, looking around at everyone still sleeping.

"They should be fine, and they will start on after us shortly as well, but we cannot wait for them," Baysil said with urgency. "Also, before we were attacked, Iclyn received word that some Elves had reached Cliffside. I'm guessing they were not aware of the second group."

We all walked over to where our horses were, and I asked, "How did you find out that the Elves reached Cliffside?"

"I received a message from Cliffside," Iclyn said softly. "It was brought by one of the ossyr birds that Miaarya keeps in the stables." The stables housed a number of ossyr birds, commonly used to send messages short distances. I remember one being used before to retrieve some Fairies at the Salt Flats when there was a small fire at the bakery and we needed more help to put it out. I had never thought that they were used to send messages over such a long distance.

"What did the message say?" I asked.

Iclyn handed me the note and I opened it and read: *There are Elves coming into Cliffside. We will not tell them where you are, but I do not believe they will be here for long. Volnyri. Miaarya.* There were also a couple strands of Miaarya's beautiful pink hair attached with wax to the message.

"Why did she send some of her hair?" I asked, concerned.

"That is something we do to ensure the person receiving the message knows it is truly from us," Iclyn said.

"And what does Volnyri mean?" I asked, not wanting them to know of the Elf who spared my life and said it to me.

"I's can tell yous that," Rowzey said. "Volnyri is an old word from a language used before I's was even born. It means Peace to Iryvalya."

"Volnyri. Why haven't I heard it said before now?"

"Because, this word is now considered to be a battle cry for The Drayks, and this is not liked by either of the Klayns," Iclyn said.

"How will we know if everyone in Cliffside will be okay?" I queried.

"I had sent back the ossyr bird with a basic message about being met by the Elves here, that all was well and we were unsure who they were looking for, but that we will be continuing our journey to the southwest to gather herbs," Iclyn said. "Miaarya will understand it to know we are okay and received her message."

"Who all is going with us right now?" Kaleyna asked, looking at Prydos with concern.

"It will be you, Nyrieve, Prydos and myself," Baysil said. "The rest will take off as scheduled at dawn, so in a few hours. They'll wake, have breakfast and then head out."

"What about Rowzey and the Pixies?" I asked, looking at Rowzey and wanting to protect Ayllac and Callya.

"They will all leave and catch up to us. We just need to leave to make sure you are safe, Ny," Prydos said.

"Now let's mount up and get going. We want to try to make it to Xylonia before the Rydison moon starts covering the Northern Sun," Baysil said.

I gave Rowzey a big hug, and then mounted Storm as everyone else mounted their horses. We quickly and quietly started making our way back to the path, and once we were far enough away to not wake anyone, we took off in a fast gallop to get us far away as quickly as we could.

After about an hour of alternating speeds on the horses, we were able to drop it down to a normal trot. The horses seemed happy with a break from running. We went along the open meadow in silence. I could not see much with the Nydian moon still overhead, but I could see what looked like patches of rocks starting to sprout up throughout the meadow. It had been a couple hours of riding before Baysil broke the silence. "Are you guys doing okay?"

"Yes," we accidently said in unison, and smiled at each other.

"Good, I am so sorry we couldn't take more time to rest, but we do not want to take a chance, not knowing how long ago Miaarya had sent that message to us," Baysil said.

"With luck she will be able to convince them as well that we are traveling south," I said hopefully.

"I hope she will be able to as well," Baysil responded.

"Did I hear you right, that we are traveling to Xylonia?" Kaleyna asked.

"That is correct."

"Isn't that where the Gargoyles live?" she asked.

"Yes, that is also correct," Baysil said with a smile. I had read about Xylonia and the Gargoyles on the maps I was given, but never heard much about them, only knew of their general location.

"I have never seen a Gargoyle before," I said.

"What do you know of them?" Prydos asked.

"Only that they are creatures by day and person by night."

"You are partially correct, Ny. They are creatures by day, but they are definitely always a person, even when in creature form," Baysil said.

"What kind of forms are they during the day?" Kaleyna asked.

"Each is a little different, but the ones I know look mostly like flying stone beastly men of sorts, even though they cannot fly," Baysil answered.

"Beastly men?" I asked.

"Yes. They believe they are a descendent of Golems and Fairies combined."

"I was not aware that Golems still existed," Kaleyna said.

"I honestly do not know if they do," Baysil said. "They have not been seen in a few hundred years. It is likely they are all gone, but Golems are quite the resourceful creatures, so you never know."

We continued riding in silence again, waiting for the Nydian moon to start allowing the Northern Sun to shine again on us. As we rode, I couldn't stop thinking and worrying about all those still in Cliffside, hoping they would be okay. The only thought that would stop my worry for Cliffside off and on was thinking about meeting the Gargoyles, and wondering if they would be friendly like a Fairy or mean like a Golem.

❦17❧

I T WASN'T LONG AFTER THE Northern Sun had fully emerged from the Nydian moon that I could see more and more rocks and less meadow. Ahead was a high mountain range that we had to cross through to get to Xylonia. Baysil said there would be a trail that we would follow; however, this was not what I would call a trail. It was more like a barely used footpath. The horses were doing great, following in a line. Baysil led, followed by me, with Kaleyna and Prydos at the back. They hardly stumbled or seemed nervous.

Baysil said these were the Kivesyon Mountains. On the other side of them would be a valley and then a forest we'd pass through, and then we'd enter into the Xylonia village. For three days of traveling, we only stopped to eat and rest for short periods of time. Once we were almost off the mountain, we stopped at a small summit area to eat some bread and cheese. The horses rested and drank from a stream that ran near the small patch of grass they were eating. We talked about the journey so far, and Kaleyna asked about what to expect in Xylonia and the Gargoyles.

Baysil said Xylonia was a village similar to Cliffside, but far more modest. They did not have much in the way of adornments, just basic homes and a simple way of living. Like the Satyrs, the Elf Klayns had tried to use them for slaves, and when they fought back, the Elves tried to kill as many as they could.

The more I heard about the Elf Klayns, the more ashamed I became of being an Elf. I did not understand how any group of people could ever decide that they were better than everyone else. I didn't know how I would be able to give all the people of Iryvalya the peace to coexist when the Elves seemed to be so cruel and more than willing to destroy others so easily.

After we ate, we started back down the rocky Kivesyon Mountain. I kept catching glimpses of the Lowyll moon passing above the Northern Sun. It always gave off such a beautiful soft purple color. It reminded me of the lilac bushes that grew around the lake in Cliffside.

Once we reached the bottom of the mountain, I could smell life again, not just dust. While it was the harvesting season, there were still a few wild flowers in bloom here. I had never seen these before. They reminded me of the sun, big and yellowish-orange petals as big as my hands. Their centers were a beautiful light blue color. I asked Baysil if he knew the names of these, and he did not, but he said the Gargoyles would know.

We made it through the dense forest and into a meadow. By the time we could see the outline of Xylonia in the distance, the Rydison moon was already starting to cover the Northern Sun. It would be fully covered by the time we reached the village.

As we approached the small village, I could see that it was similar to Cliffside but also very different. They had houses like we did, but much smaller. The houses were round and looked like they could only have one or two rooms each. The roofs were made of long thick straw that formed a peak at the top of the building, instead of wooden shingles like we used. There was a window in each house, but there was no light coming from any of them.

Their roads were empty as we went through the village, heading to one large round building in the middle. Baysil was taking us towards that building, where I guessed all the Gargoyles would be. When we reached it, Baysil signaled to all of us to get down and keep quiet.

I climbed down from Storm, tied him up to a post outside the building, and reached down to feel Klaw securely fastened to my leg. Baysil walked us to the door and lightly knocked in a strange rhythm. The door slowly creaked open, and Baysil smiled at a man who was hidden in shadows.

"Louv!" Baysil said, shaking the man's hand and pulling him into a one-armed hug.

"Bay!" the man said with a deep, strong, gravelly voice and a thick accent that reminded me of the travelers we had once met from the

North Western Isles. "We are so glad you were able to make it. Please come in and warm up."

Baysil nodded to us to follow him into the dark room. The room was warm, though I did not see a fire burning. There were candles lit, casting the room in a dim light, showing the outlines of tables with benches along one side. On the other side of the room, there was what looked like a large pool of water in the middle with skins of different animals and pillows all around it.

We were led to the pool area. It was the length of three tall Fairies and about two tall Fairies in width. It was in a strange shape, roundish but skewed. As we got closer to the water, I finally figured out why the room was so warm without a fire—it was a hot spring, and it had a glow of light coming from it.

I looked around the room and did not see anyone else in here, just us and the man Baysil called Louv. Louv gestured to all of us to come closer. He looked at us carefully, like he was trying to decide what to do with us. He was standing next to Baysil, and pushed his arm. "Bay, why don't you do the introductions?"

"Oh, I'm sorry, of course," Baysil said, seeming surprised he had forgotten to do that himself. He first pointed to Prydos. "Louvyordal, this is Prydos. He is a former Lumaryia Elf."

"Prydos, it is great to meet you," Louvyordal said, shaking Prydos's hand.

"It is great to meet you also, Louvyordal," Prydos said.

"Please everyone, just call me Louv," he said with a smile and looked at Kaleyna. "And who might you be?"

"I am Kaleyna," she answered, sounding a little nervous.

"I can see you are an Elf," he said, looking at her ears. "What kind of Elf are you?"

"Uhm… I honestly do not know. I was raised with the Fairies and didn't know I was an Elf until recently."

"Do you know what kind of Elf she is, Bay?" Louv asked.

"No, I don't. The only one who does would be Lydorea," Baysil answered.

"Lydorea…" Louv said with a smile on his face. "She coming here too?"

"Yes, she was in the group with us, so she should be here by tomorrow," Baysil said, smiling at him.

"Well, it is a pleasure to meet you, Kaleyna," Louv said, shaking her hand lightly, and she smiled back.

Louv then stepped in front of me. He was a tall muscular man. His hair was a tousled dark gray with what looked like a bluish color highlighting it. He had a weathered yet ruggedly handsome face, with dark gray eyebrows framing his gray and blue swirled eyes. The blue was like the color of the sky on a clear day. Louv was covered in thin linen clothes, which seemed out of place for the weather outside, but after being in here for a little while, I was starting to see why he was more comfortable in less clothing.

Louv extended his hand to me, and I took it and felt his cool and rough skin in my hand. "And you must be Nyrieve."

"Yes, it is a pleasure to meet you," I said, not knowing what else to say.

"No, my dear, the pleasure is all mine," Louv said, sounding truthful. "I have waited a long time to meet you, Bringer of Peace."

I could feel my face redden with embarrassment. It still felt strange to hear that someone has waited to meet me.

"Please do not be embarrassed, Your Highness, I am just very happy to meet you and know you have made it here safely," Louv said, making me blush more with the Highness comment.

"I am sorry for being embarrassed, but I have never thought of myself as someone people would know and want to meet," I spoke honestly to him, "and I am definitely not used to being called 'Your Highness'. So please, just call me Nyrieve or Ny."

"I can do that... Ny," Louv said, gently letting my hand go and giving me a brief hug. "Please know you are safe here in Xylonia. My men are out right now checking the outskirts of the village to ensure your safety. They should start coming back shortly, and will be happy to meet you as well."

"That is great. We look forward to meeting everyone," Baysil said. "Now, I hate to ask, but is it possible to get some food and drink, Louv? We've been on the road for a while, and we're running low on supplies.

If Ny hadn't taken some food from Rowzey's pantry, we wouldn't have had anything today to eat."

"Sure, sure, sure. Why don't you all give me your cloaks. I'll hang them over there," Louv said, pointing to a rack near the door we came in, "and please go sit and get comfortable. I will get some food started for you all. And Baysil, if you could come with me, you can get some drinks for everyone."

Louv took all of our cloaks and hung them up. Kaleyna sat on the floor near the water, so I sat down next to her. Prydos sat down near us, but a little further away from the water, and stretched out on some of the pillows.

"This is so warm and beautiful," I said to Kaleyna and Prydos.

"It is. Don't you want to sit closer, Pry?" she said, using his nickname.

"No thanks," Prydos said, looking around the room like he was taking inventory of everything.

"Why not?" I asked. "It feels really warm to sit near."

"It reminds me a lot of the water that runs through Noygandia, and if I sit too close, I will likely want to get in," he said with a laugh.

Kaleyna and I sat talking about the hot spring and how warm it was. It wasn't long before Baysil came in with some glasses and pitchers. "Louv said he didn't know what we would prefer, so he gave us a few choices." Baysil handed each of us a glass and explained what was in each pitcher. There was hot honey tea, cool Peayalt, and some windoberry wine. Kaleyna had the hot honey tea and Prydos had some of the windoberry wine. I had never had either of the last two, and did not feel like wine or anything hot, so I decided on the Peayalt, which Baysil said was an old Gargoyle word for water infused with cucumbers and lemons.

After the first sip, I realized this was the best thing I had ever drank, and also how thirsty I actually was. I drank down the whole glass in only a couple minutes, and then poured myself another, this time just sipping it.

After about a half hour of relaxing by the water, Louv came back in with some skewers of cooked meat. They smelled so delicious my mouth started to water. Louv handed each of us a skewer and sat down with one of his own. I watched him as he chewed the meat off the skewer, and Baysil did the same. So I tried to eat the same as them, and once the taste of the seasoned meat was in my mouth, it was easy to just eat off the skewer. It was cow meat, tender and seasoned with a strange spice that gave it some heat. The heat was so intense that I ended up drinking all the Peayalt.

Louv was very gracious, and he went and made me more Peayalt. When he came back in, he wasn't alone. There was another man with him. He had a small slender build, light hair that was peeking out of his cloak hood, and was carrying some blankets. I could not see his face, but I heard Louv ask him to join us once he set down the blankets. The man responded, "No. I will help protect them, but I do not need to eat with them." And he stormed out of the large room.

When Louv handed me the fresh pitcher of Peayalt, I asked him, "Who was that?"

"That is Zendiya."

"I am gathering that he isn't happy with us being here?" I asked.

"He, like all of us, has had some bad experience with Elves," Louv said. "He doesn't trust any of you really, even though he knows you are the Bringer of Peace."

"Don't worry about him," Baysil said. "Not all of the Gargoyles think like Zendiya."

"If I may ask, Louv, how many Gargoyles are there here in Xylonia?" I asked.

"Before the Elf Wars, we had over five hundred in a village not too far to the east of here called Grydios. Now we have only seven of us here in Xylonia," Louv said somberly, "and we are all males."

"What happened to your females?" I asked, surprised.

"During the last raid on Grydios, before the Elves burnt everything to the ground, they took all of our females and children and left," Louv said. "After a few weeks, one of the Gargoyle boys had escaped. He came and found us, and said that he had overheard guards saying they killed all the female Gargoyles. The Elves had figured it would be much crueler to force us to watch our race die a slow impending death, and they were right."

"I am so sorry. I don't understand how anyone could do that," I said, feeling guilty, though I had nothing to do with it.

"I appreciate your kind words, Ny, but it is not your fault, and after a couple hundred years, we have just gotten used to the idea that it is just us seven left."

After a little while, the five other Gargoyles came inside to introduce themselves and eat. They all looked like normal Fairy men, but when the sun came up, they would no longer look like this. We met Demetryus, Rhyon, Whyndal, Jytt and Voynder. They were all very polite and kind to us, making us feel very welcome.

After everyone had eaten and the conversations had died down, I asked Baysil if he knew where we'd be sleeping for the night. He told me that it was a good question, and he asked Louv.

"You all will sleep in this building. We have some cots that we will bring in, so you do not have to sleep on the floor," Louv said. "And please feel free to use the spring if you would like to soak your muscles. I am sure you must be pretty worn out from all the riding you have been doing. There is also a privacy screen that I will have brought in, so if you want to change in privacy, you can. As you can imagine, the seven of us Gargoyles have known each other for so long, it doesn't matter to us anymore."

"We appreciate that," Kaleyna said for the both of us.

After a while, Louv and the other Gargoyles brought in the cots, some drying cloths, a changing screen, and some strange clothing I had never seen. When I asked him what it was for, he said that he thought we would want to wear them in the hot spring, to keep covered to an extent. They were basically sleeveless cloth shirts and cloth pants that had been cut above the knee. They were quite large, but had a drawstring to keep them up.

After Louv told us that someone would be on guard outside the building at all times, he excused himself to go to his own home to rest. Once it was just Baysil, Kaleyna, Prydos and myself, I felt like I could relax a bit more. Kaleyna and I decided we would try the hot spring, so we went behind the changing screen and quickly changed. I was not afraid to change in front of her, as we had done that over the years growing up, so I guess I could understand why the Gargoyles were not embarrassed to change in front of each other as well.

Once we had changed, we walked back around to see Baysil and Prydos already in the water. They were sitting on what looked like a stone bench that I had not notice before. There were some small steps leading into the water that we stepped down. Once I felt the hot water, I realized how sore my body was. Kaleyna was talking to Baysil and Prydos, but I just moved into the middle of the pool until the water was up to my chin. After a short time, I took the braid out of my hair and tipped my head back into the soothing waters. I could feel the heat all around me, only my face exposed to the air. For a moment, I felt like all my troubles were gone, and I was finally enjoying some peace.

After I felt fully relaxed, I sat back up and moved over by the others. They were talking about the journey, how great the food was tonight, and other unimportant talk. I smiled, wanting to ask detailed questions about what was to come, but we needed a night to relax and pretend that everything was okay. Tomorrow, reality would come, and I did not know when we would have another moment like this again.

ᛒ18ᚮ

I AWOKE TO HUSHED VOICES. One was Baysil. The other voice sounded familiar and yet it did not. It was deep and gravelly, but there was something about it I knew. I looked around to see who it was, and I almost let out a yelp of surprise to see Baysil talking to a gray stone-looking person. He looked like a Golem, but with the proportions of a Fairy. I studied his mannerisms and realized Baysil was talking to Louv.

Louv was still the same height as he was before, but his whole body looked like it was chiseled out of one large piece of stone. He was a lighter gray, with darker flecks running throughout him. His feet had only three toes, and they looked more like very sharp claws. His legs and arms looked muscular, like he could easily lift one of the houses by himself. He had a wide dark-red velvet sash, which seemed a little fancy to me, wrapped around his waist covering his private areas. I could see all his muscles throughout his torso and chest, again making me realize how strong he was in this stone-like form. His arms were a bit longer now, it seemed, and he had only four fingers, which also looked like strong and sharp claws. On his back he had two wings, similar to bat wings, but they had a points on the top and bottom, four points on each one. Each point looked like a sharpened claw. I could not see his face, as his back was still turned towards me.

It would be rude not to let them know I was awake, so I sat up and said, "Good morning, Baysil. Good morning, Louv."

They stopped talking and turned to look at me, surprise on Louv's beastlike face. His hair was gone, his scalp just a smooth solid stone, minus two long curled horns that came out of each temple area. He had a furrowed brow, which appeared to be stuck that way, and his eyes, surprisingly, were still the same swirled colors of gray and blue. His nose was wider and flatter against his face. His mouth was bigger and protruded more forward, with big thick lips and pointy teeth. He smiled at me, realizing his appearance didn't scare me.

"Good morning, Ny," Louv said in his rough voice. "Did you sleep well last night?"

"Yes, I did, thank you. I wish I could take this pool of water with me everywhere I go," I said, smiling as I stood and walked over to him and Baysil.

"There are in many of these hot springs throughout all of Iryvalya, actually," Louv said.

"There are not any in Cliffside that I know of," I said. It was amazing how well the pool worked, because this morning all my muscles felt well rested and ready to go.

"There is," Baysil said with a smile.

"Where?" I asked, surprised.

"It is hidden inside one of the caves on the northeast cliffs," he answered.

"Why didn't I know about it?" I wondered.

"It is kind of hard to get to, and to be honest, the older Fairies do not want to share it with the younger people," Baysil said, still grinning.

"That is not very nice." I chuckled, wishing I could have used it before, but also understanding why it would be kept secret.

"If we ever get back to Cliffside, Ny, I will show you how to get there," Baysil said.

"Me too?" Kaleyna asked. "Good morning, everyone." As she sat up she noticed Louv, and I could see a look of surprise on her face, so I tried to mentally tell her it was Louv. I kept thinking, *It's Louv, It's Louv,* hoping she'd see the thought. After a moment she smiled at me and said, "Louv, thank you so much for the clothing to go into the hot spring. It was amazing."

An awkward smile rose on Louv's face, knowing that he was recognized and that we were not scared of him.

"You are most welcome, Kaleyna," Louv said with that smile of his.

I wondered if it was hard to smile with those sharp pointy teeth.

"Are you ladies hungry?" Baysil asked.

"I am," I said right away with a smile.

"Me too," Kaleyna added.

"Prydos should be back in just a little while with some breakfast. He went to get it from Louv's house, as he prepared everything for us," Baysil said.

"Thank you, Louv. Your hospitality has been more than I could have ever hoped for," I said, hoping he would know that I really was appreciative to not only have good food and the hot spring, but to have had a good night of sleep without constantly being in fear of someone sneaking up on me to try to kill me.

"You are very welcome, Ny. If you all do not mind," Louv said, "I have to go talk to some of the other men here, and also help do a check of the village to make sure everything is as it should be."

We all nodded to him and Baysil said, "Not at all, let me know if there is anything you need me to do."

"One thing before I go," Louv said seriously. "Most of the men here have not been around other people in a long time, so if they tend to avoid you when in our day form, please do not take offense."

"Not at all, Louv," Baysil said, and we all nodded in agreement. After Louv walked out the door, Baysil said to us, "I am going to go and do a quick survey of the village and see if there are any signs of anyone else yet. They should be here sometime today if there were not problems."

I decided to get changed out of my sleeping clothes, so I took my pack and went behind the screen to put on my leather Leaf Day gift from Relonya. As I opened them up, I also noticed something tucked away in the leather boots— a new black lace supportive undergarment and underwear. I had never seen any like this before. Most are just basic cloth, and I had never seen ones made out of a silky black lace like this before.

I couldn't believe how well everything fit me. The pants were perfect and allowed me to move with ease. The boots laced up and were comfortable and soft to the touch. My moss green shirt from Relonya looked great on me too, form-fitted on the torso, but not stiff, and the sleeves were loose for easy movement. The only thing I was not overly comfortable with was that the shirt was quite low-cut on the top, and every now and again, you could catch a glimpse of the supportive undergarment.

After I was dressed I walked around the screen, and Kaleyna smiled at me. "What?" I asked her.

"You just look very pretty, Ny," she said, still smiling.

"Thanks, I am not sure if I like the shirt like this though." I gestured to the low cut.

"It looks great on you, really grown up, like we are now," Kaleyna said, taking her clothing around the screen to change as well.

I sat down on my cot and decided to try to get my hair brushed out and hopefully let it dry. I was brushing it without paying much attention, when I noticed more strands of the green hair in my brush. I reached into my pack to pull out my small looking glass I brought with us. More than half of my hair was turning the beautiful green color like the original streak I had. Instead of it looking white with a green streak, it now looked green with only a few white streaks. I guess while traveling and keeping my hair back and under my cloak, I hadn't noticed it had been changing more.

My hair was still quite wet from the water last night, so I ran my hands through it to try to squeeze the extra water out. Suddenly I felt a cool breeze across my scalp. I quickly pulled my hands back, and the sensation stopped. I went to squeeze the water out again and the breeze started again. It was coming from where my hands were. I pulled my hands back, looked at them, and thought about pushing away the water, and I could feel myself controlling the air around my hands. I walked over to the hot spring, dipping my left hand briefly into the water, and then I took my right hand and held it in front of the left. I concentrated and watched the water on my left hand get pushed off with a breeze.

"How did you do that?" Kaleyna gasped, standing behind me watching.

"I don't know. I felt the breeze when I was trying to wring out my hair and I wanted to see if it was me doing it or something else," I said, still in shock.

"It is one of the powers some mixed Elves get," Prydos said from behind us. I had not even heard him come inside the building.

"What exactly does the power do?"

"It allows you to control air and water and move them as you want them," Prydos said with a smile. "It is not a very common power to have, or so I have been told."

"How do I control it?" I asked, staring down at my hands.

"I can't answer that," Prydos said, "since I have never had a wind power myself. But if it is like other powers in general, you want to focus on moving the air or water around and with the force that you want it. Normally when you start getting a new power, it is kind of weak and hard to fully control. You want to practice with it, and the more you practice, the better control you will have."

"That is a pretty impressive power, Ny," Kaleyna said.

"It feels strange to have power move from my hands, it almost tickles," I said with a grin.

"Just curious, what were you doing when you first noticed it?" Prydos asked.

"I was trying to wring out the water from my hair, and I thought how nice it would be to either go outside and have the wind blow through it or if I could just wring all the water out."

"Powers tend to show up when you start to need them, though I doubt it is strictly so you can dry your hair," Prydos said. "Though I think I can help you with drying your hair quickly."

Before I could ask how, Prydos raised his hands up in front of him facing towards me, and my hair lifted up towards him, partially covering my face. It was a strange but light tugging sensation. After only a few moments, it stopped and all my hair fell around my head completely dry. I moved the hair from in front of my eyes and I could see Prydos with a small ball of water holding its form between his hands.

"I didn't know you could control water," Kaleyna said, surprised.

"It is not typical to let everyone know what your powers are, and while I do trust you both, I don't always trust the ears of others who might be listening too." Prydos made a gesture of tossing the ball of water at the hot spring, and it flew right to the pool and landed with a splash.

"How many powers do you have, Prydos?" I asked.

"So far I have two, controlling water and also being able to make some crystals glow for a short time."

"So far?" Kaleyna asked.

"There isn't a real way of knowing how many powers an Elf will get. I know some who have only one, and others who have dozens," Prydos said. "Now why don't you both finish getting ready, and come over to the table. I brought in a bunch of food for us that Louv made. It all looks and smells great."

Prydos walked over to the tables on the other side of the room and sat, grabbing some food. I quickly ran a brush through my now dry wavy hair. Once it was untangled, Kaleyna put a braid down the back for me. We went over to the table and sat down. There was a lot of food—pancakes, bacon, fruits, bread and jellies. I couldn't decide which looked best, so I took a little bit of everything. There were two pitchers, one of hot tea and one of the Peayalt I enjoyed yesterday. I took a goblet and filled it with the Peayalt and enjoyed its refreshing taste.

After we had finished eating, the door opened and Baysil walked inside with a big smile on his face. "I have good news," he said as he walked over to us and sat down, grabbing a slice of bacon and taking a bite.

"What is the good news?" I asked.

"The rest of the group is only an hour or so out from Xylonia."

"How do you know?" Kaleyna asked.

"Koyvean was riding out ahead to watch for any issues. I talked to her a few minutes ago. She is riding back to let them know that we are here and okay."

"Are they all doing okay?" I asked, excited that Rowzey and the others were all safely on their way here.

"Koyvean said they had not run into any troubles at all, though she did mention they had a few Satyrs coming along with them," Baysil said, grabbing more bacon.

"I wonder why," Prydos said. "Satyrs do not normally leave their homes. That is what Dazyen had always told me anyway."

"I guess we will find out the reason when they get here," I said. "Is it okay if I walk around the village?"

"Yes," Baysil said. "The Gargoyles are all on watch, so just stay inside the village area."

"No problem. Do you want to come with me, Kaleyna?"

"No, I think I am going to stay with Prydos if you are okay with it?"

I smiled. "It is fine. I just did not want you to think I was trying to leave you behind."

"Good, but if you need me, just let me know."

"I will, and if any of you need me, I will just be outside walking around."

I got up and walked to the door, grabbed my cloak off of the hook, and wrapped it around me and hooked the clasp. I opened the door and the bright Northern Sun shined down on me. I loved the smell of the cool fresh air and it made me feel a little more energized.

I walked around the small village and noticed that all the round houses were built of stacked boulders and rocks. They looked very sturdy. The houses were like Baysil said, very plain and simple. There were no personal touches to any of them, and there were no plants or anything around any of the buildings either. It looked very bare around the homes with only the dirt paths surrounding them all. The doors to each of the houses faced the large building in the middle of the village. There were a few pathways out of the village, one leading to the north, the one to the south we rode in on, and one towards the woods in the east.

As I walked on the dirt path, I turned and almost ran into another Gargoyle. He looked very similar to Louv, but his eyes were swirled with a deep blue and pure white.

"Oh, I am sorry," I said. "I was not paying attention."

"I am not surprised, Elf," he said.

"You must be Zendiya," I said to him. I had met all the other Gargoyles last night, and none of them had his eye color, or his apparent dislike of Elves.

"And what is it to you who I am?"

"It is nothing to me, I was just making note," I said simply, not wanting to goad him and also not wanting to back down.

"That is all we are to you Elves, nothing," Zendiya said.

"Perhaps to the Elves you have known in the past that is true; however, I am not like them."

"How would you know if you are or not?" he asked. "You haven't even really met any of them. Maybe you will realize you have more in common with them than you think."

"Listen, Zendiya, I am not going to argue with you about the Elves in general, because I truly do not know much about them," I said. "However, from what I do know about them, the things they have done to others are not things I could ever do. Harming an innocent person or race for personal gain is not something I believe I could ever do."

I turned on my heel to walk away and he grabbed me gently by the arm and looked into my eyes. "I know you are not a typical Elf, but if you do anything to cause my people more pain, I promise you I will stop you."

"I have no plans to hurt anyone, but if I do purposely hurt those here who have sworn to bring peace to Iryvalya, you have my permission to stop me by any means possible. I do not ever want to be known as someone who hurts those who want peace." I lightly pulled my arm out of his grasp and continued on my walk.

After I had walked around the village a few times and ran into a few more of the Gargoyles, who were very polite, I decided to go back to see what Kaleyna was up to. When I opened the door and went in, I could hear Baysil and Prydos talking. I hung up my cloak and walked over to where Kaleyna sat on her cot. I couldn't help but smile when I noticed as she was brushing out her hair, there were some blue streaks throughout most of the back of her hair.

"That is quite a beautiful color, Kal," I said, sitting down across from her.

"I only noticed them today as I was letting my hair down to retie it up," she said with a smile.

"It is a very beautiful shade of blue. It reminds me of the deep blue colors of the North Sea."

"I was hoping I would have blue hair," Kaleyna said.

"I don't blame you. You have always looked amazing in any shade of blue."

Rowzey or Miaarya would often find clothes for Kaleyna in different shades of blue. And they always seemed to find shades of green for me. I wondered if they somehow knew that those would be the colors of our hair.

"I also found a mark, Ny," Kaleyna said quietly.

"Where?"

Kaleyna pulled up the right sleeve of her shirt, enough to show a faint mark inside the crook of her arm. I couldn't make out what the marking was, but it definitely was something I had never seen on her before. "Has yours started to look more like something, or is it still blurry?" she asked.

"I honestly haven't checked." I pulled my shirt open enough to check where the mark was. It was darker than before, but the shape still was not fully clear to me. It looked like a leaf of some sort, but I couldn't tell if that is what it was. "Can you tell what it is?"

"No, I can't," Kaleyna said.

I covered myself up and lay back on the cot, relaxing a bit as Kaleyna twisted her hair up in an intricate knot. "I still sometimes cannot believe we are on this journey," I said to her.

"Me either. But I am very glad to be on the journey with you."

"As am I."

Baysil's voice was loud as he spoke across the room to Kaleyna and me. "You have about thirty minutes and everyone should be here. Koyvean just got back and everyone else should be here soon."

Kaleyna and I both smiled at each other. We were both excited to get to see everyone again. Even though it had only been a day, a day is a long time to worry about those you care about.

‹‹19››

SOMEHOW EVERYONE WHO left with us from Cliffside made it to Xylonia safely, and they even made it with an extra three Satyrs. I had never met a Satyr before. I had seen a few when they visited Cliffside for different reasons, but had never talked to one. The three who traveled to Xylonia were all male Satyrs. Their names were Leyhroi, Jynkins and Knarfy.

Leyhroi and Jynkins looked the exact same, except in the color of their hair. They were both a lot shorter than me, close to the same height as Rowzey. The upper half of their bodies looked mostly like a male Fairy and the bottom half, starting just below the belly button, looked like a goat. Their bottom halves were dark brown and furry like a goat, and they both had a brown cloth wrapped around their waists. They had brown split hooves, same as a goat. They walked upright, but because their ankle joints went the opposite way of ours, their walk was more bouncy. Their chests were bare and slightly muscular. They didn't look like the toughest of people, but they didn't look weak either.

The faces of both Leyhroi and Jynkins were very broad, their eyes set a little too far apart. They had long crooked noses and teeth, but even if they were strange looking, their smiles were oddly warm and friendly. They had thin lips that barely covered their teeth when they weren't smiling or talking. They also had pointy ears, much smaller than an Elf's, but definitely pointy. The only other thing different from a Fairy's face was they had two little horns in the same spots as the Gargoyles, but much smaller.

"It is a pleasure to meet you, Miss Nyrieve. My name is Leyhroi," the one with long golden wavy hair said.

"It is an even greater pleasure for me to meet you, Your Highness. My name is Jynkins," the one with the short silver hair said.

I giggled at their playful tone. "The pleasure is all mine, good sirs."
I noticed that they both had the same eye swirls of gold and silver. "I
have never seen two people with such closely matching eyes before."

"That," Jynkins said, "is because we are brothers."

"Not just brothers, Miss," Leyhroi said, "we are twins, but I am the
oldest."

"And I am the more handsome one." Jynkins laughed.

The other Satyr was Knarfy, who seemed much quieter than the
other two. He looked the same from the waist down as Leyhroi and
Jynkins, and had the same type of muscular upper body. His face was
more proportioned than the other two, with a slender nose, and deep-set
eyes. Knarfy only smiled and nodded; he never said anything to us. His
hair was cut shorter, and pushed back behind his small pointy ears. His
hair was the color of a ripe strawberry. He's eyes were swirls of the same
red with a much paler version. Normally I would think such colors
might look menacing, but on Knarfy, they didn't.

After we were all introduced to our newcomers, Louv had them
shown to one of the smaller houses so they could freshen up. Everyone
else was split up and shown to the other small homes. No one else was
shown to the large building in the middle.

"Baysil," I asked when everyone else was shown to different buildings, "why is no one in the larger building with us?"

"Louv feels it will be safer for you to keep the amount of people in
the building at night to a minimum."

"Is he worried that the Elves will get to me here without them
knowing?"

"That, and also in case there is a traitor in our group..."

"Do you really think someone in our group is a traitor?"

"If I was worried about someone in the group, I wouldn't have allowed them to come along. However, I think Louv is right to be cau-
tious."

It began to sprinkle rain again. Louv came back out to us and said,
"You should really go back into the building to keep dry and warm. The
rain is going to pick up, I can feel it. After everyone else in your group
freshens up, I will have everyone join you. Jytt and Whyndal will bring
in a large lunch for everyone to enjoy."

The four of us went back into the large building, each of us taking some time to go to our own cots and relax for a bit. Kaleyna and Prydos were talking about when we would be leaving Xylonia and different things they hoped for in the future. Baysil was writing in the book he kept stored in his pack. I couldn't relax, as there was so much happening and so much about to happen. I could not imagine what was going to happen next, or where we were going to go, and who I was going to meet. Suddenly, something that never occurred to me hit me like a ton of bricks. *Why didn't I think to ask this before*, I thought. I sat up and looked at Baysil, who was now looking at me with concern. "Are my parents still alive?"

"What?" Baysil asked, looking confused.

"Are my parents still alive, Baysil?" I asked, not understanding why, until now, I just assumed they were dead.

"As far as I know, they are," Baysil said. "And from what we were told, they are both with their own Klayns."

"They didn't stay together..." I said, more to myself, sad they were apart and yet very excited to know they were still alive.

"They couldn't, Ny. They had to separate, to make sure no one knew about you," Baysil said.

"That would make sense I guess."

"It couldn't have been easy for them to go back, but they wanted to ensure that you would be safe and no one would come looking for you."

"I understand. I don't know why I just assumed they were dead," I said. "I mean, that was originally why I was without parents, but after learning about them and who I am, it never occurred to me that they could still be alive."

Prydos spoke up. "I don't know about your mother, but I do know your father is well."

"You know my father?"

"I can't say I know him, but I knew him. He is high up with the Lumaryia leaders. He doesn't have a powerful position, but he is on the council," Prydos said, sitting up facing me.

"What else do you know about him?" Kaleyna asked.

"Uhm, he is tyed to another Lumaryia Elf. She is well known throughout Noygandia for her kindness."

"Tyed?" I asked.

"Yes, they have been tyed now for almost sixteen years," Prydos said, as if he did not want to elaborate further.

"That means he had to have gotten tyed about a year after I was born... What else should I know, Prydos?"

"What do you mean?"

"I know you are trying to not elaborate on my father, but I would like for you to tell me what else you know about him."

After a few moments, Prydos cleared his throat. "About fifteen years ago, Arnayx and his wife, her name is Clyo... they had a child together," Prydos said quietly.

"A child?" I asked, not sure if I was more shocked or excited.

"Yes, a girl they named Dymma Loycurv."

"So, you are telling me I have a sister?"

"Yes, she is a very smart and pretty young girl. She is always taking in animals and caring for them. She is a lot like her mother."

Just then the door opened and Relonya, Iclyn, Lydorea, Jehryps, Marselyus and Koyvean walked in, shaking the rain off their cloaks and then hanging them up on the hooks by the door.

"Can we talk about this later?" I asked Prydos.

"Sure," he said, sounding relieved.

"I don't want to talk about any of this in front of everyone. I do not trust everyone," I said, shooting a glance towards Jehryps.

"It is no one else's concern," Baysil said to me, ensuring me he wouldn't say anything to anyone else either.

As we walked over to talk to everyone, I couldn't fully decide if I was excited about having a sister, or also upset. Not that I wouldn't want a sister, but I never thought about having another sister other than Kaleyna. I decided it would be best to leave these thoughts for later and to put on a smile and enjoy those around me.

I went and gave everyone a hug, but when I got to Jehryps, I just half smiled and nodded. He seemed upset, as if he figured I would hug him as well.

"I am so glad everyone made it to Xylonia safely," I said to them all.

"We are too, and very glad you guys made it safely," Marselyus said with a smile.

"Why did you all leave us in the night?" Jehryps asked, looking right at me.

"We had our reasons," Prydos answered for me.

"And we do not get to know them, I am betting," Jehryps said sourly.

"Only those who need to know will know," Baysil said to him.

I felt a smile cross my face, knowing that these two men supported me and protected me, even from someone as insignificant as Jehryps. After talking to everyone for a little while and getting some of them to try the wonderful Peayalt water Louv had made for us, we all sat down near the hot spring to talk about the journey here.

While our journey was fast and boring, theirs was longer and a bit more interesting. They told us about the Satyrs and how entertaining they were along the way, the twins mostly. They had a great sense of humor, though according to Jehryps, he did not understand most of the jokes. Lydorea also talked about how Rowzey and the Pixies told stories of Troxeon that were very interesting and helped pass the time.

As if on cue, after Lydorea mentioned Rowzey, she walked in the building with her bag and smiled at us all. Kaleyna and I got up quickly and went to Rowzey for another hug. Rowzey whispered to us, "I's so glad that yous both is safe. Callya, Ayllac and I's were very worried about yous."

"Why?" I asked quietly.

"I's will tell yous more later," she said, looking behind us.

I turned around and saw Jehryps walking towards us to get more to drink at the table next to Rowzey.

"Come, Rowzey, sit by the hot spring. It is so warm," Kaleyna said.

"Where are Ayllac and Callya?" I asked.

Rowzey patted her bag and opened it after we sat down near the hot spring. Callya flew out first, followed by her sister, Ayllac. They both did a flight around the whole building checking everything out and came back to sit next to the hot spring. They took their very tiny shoes off and dipped their feet into the warm water and were giggling to each other about something in a language I didn't know.

"I am very glad to see you both are faring well with the weather," I said to them.

"Us too," they giggled in unison.

"We are also glad to have space to fly around without our wings freezing," Ayllac added.

"Yes, it was getting quite cold outside, so we had to go into the bag often to warm up," Callya said.

It wasn't long after sitting and talking to everyone that Louv came inside and let us know that our lunch should be ready shortly. He came near the hot spring and went to sit on the far side away from everyone. "Louv, why don't you come sit over here near us?" I asked him with a smile.

"Oh, I just did not want to interrupt you all," Louv said, sounding almost embarrassed.

"Nonsense, you and the rest of the Gargoyles have been such wonderful hosts to all of us. I would love it if you would please join us."

Louv smiled his sharp toothy grin at me, and came over and sat down next to me and Kaleyna. "Thank you, Ny. We are very glad to have you all here safe in Xylonia."

After about a half hour, Jytt and Whyndal came in with serving trays full of fruits, cheeses, a hot broth, and a black bread. The trays were set around the group of us sitting near the hot spring so we could enjoy the food where we were. I looked at the black bread for a few moments and Louv smiled at me. "You should try it. It is the favorite bread of us Gargoyles."

"What is it exactly?" I asked curiously.

"It is herb bread made from flour ground out of the black wheat we grow here. I have never seen it anywhere else in Iryvalya," Louv said.

I tried the bread and it was so flavorful. There was a wonderful spice to it and it was also very moist, which surprised me. I ate the whole piece he gave to me, and even took another.

After eating, everyone but Rowzey and the Pixies left to rest for a while. Once we were all alone, Rowzey told me that the Pixies had been spying throughout the forest off and on during stops and overheard Jehryps talking to himself when he thought no one was around.

"He was complaining about being left behind when he should be riding with you, Ny," Callya said to me.

"Why would he think he should be riding with me?"

"He kept saying that he should be tyed to you, and together you both could wield a lot of power, and that if he was tyed to a royal, the Elves would want him to join the Klayns," Ayllac said.

"But we are trying to stop the separation of the Klayns," I said.

"Yes, Ny, but I's think he believes that you and he together would allow for yous two to make one Klayn. Kind of how the Elves wanted it to be originally. One ruling power to see over all of Iryvalya," Rowzey said to us.

"How would he figure that I would go along with it?" I asked Rowzey.

"I's also think he believes his charms are more powerful than they are. I's also think that perhaps the reason he wants to be close to yous is because he think he might convince yous that he is the best option for yous."

"He said it would have happened already if he was near you," Ayllac said.

"Maybe he has a spell he can cast on her or something like a totem charm. But for it to work, she'd have to have it and him near her," Callya said.

"The carved rose," Kaleyna said right away.

"The rose..." I said, looking at Kaleyna. "After Montryos attacked me, it was left on the floor covered in his blood, and Jehryps left it in my room, cleaned, for me to keep."

"Where is it now, Ny?" Baysil asked.

"It's in my pack," I said, getting my bag. I opened it and took the wrapped carved rose out. I handed it to Baysil, who opened it and looked at the carving.

"I cannot tell if there is a spell on it. I am going to take it to Koyvean and see if she can," Baysil said, putting his cloak on. "Ny, you need to stay in here until I get back, just to be safe. Prydos and Kaleyna, do not leave Ny alone please." And he walked out the door.

"While I's would love to stay, I's need to get some rest as well. Louv gave his home for the Pixies and I's to keep extra warm. He said he has the biggest fireplace here." Rowzey got up and opened her pack as Ayllac and Callya flew inside of it.

I walked with Rowzey to the door, helped her put her cloak on, and gave her a big hug. "Thank you, Rowzey, so much, for always being there for me. I don't think I ever told you how much you mean to me."

"Oh, Ny, yous and Kaleyna is like daughters to me, so I's love to be here for yous," Rowzey said hugging me back. "Remember one ting my beautiful Ny, just because the sauce looks good, smells good, does not mean it will taste good. The same goes that it might not look or smell great, but could be delicious. Keep this in mind when dealing with people. They are the same as the sauce."

Rowzey smiled at me and went out the door. I walked back over to Prydos and Kaleyna and sat down next to them. "So now what?" I asked.

"I don't know, but I know that Jehryps is acting very strange," Prydos said.

"We definitely need to keep an eye out for him," Kaleyna said.

"I couldn't agree more," I said to them both, "but I do think it would be best he doesn't know what the Pixies heard. We might learn a lot more about what he is up to that way."

"I agree," Prydos said.

"Me too," Kaleyna said, "but just make sure you do not let your guard down with him."

"I won't. I will just have to let him think that perhaps I want to let the past go. But if we find out from Baysil he is trying to use a spell on me, he will be very sorry," I said, thinking that I would have no problem making Jehryps go back to Cliffside if he tried to use magyc on me to get his way. He was becoming more of a problem than he was worth.

While waiting for Baysil to come back, Lydorea came in and asked if I would go for a walk with her. I was happy to get out for a walk, even if it was raining. I asked her if she thought Baysil would be okay with me leaving without him or someone else, and she told me he had agreed to allow us to walk over to the cliffs, and that one of the Gargoyles wouldn't be far behind us.

I had my cloak clasped and wrapped tightly around my shoulders. The temperature had dropped a little more, but the fresh smell of the dirt covered in rain was well worth it. I have always loved the smell after the rain. It gives me a feeling of peacefulness, like everything in the world can be refreshed and renewed.

After walking for a short time I decided to break the comfortable silence. "What are we going to the cliffs for?"

"I have always wanted to see the cliffs from here, and I thought you would enjoy it, and it'd give us a little time together," Lydorea said with her singsong voice.

"I am glad you asked me."

"I must say, I do have another reason. It is something I wanted to tell you about."

"What is that?"

"Hundreds of years ago, there was an amulet that granted the bearer the protection to be free of mind control or magycal persuasion. It was called Clyr. The amulet was taken and hidden somewhere inside the Blackened Forest, which is an island not far from Troxeon, where the Pixies live."

"That sounds like a useful amulet," I said, not understanding why she was telling me about this.

"The amulet has a curse placed upon it, so it does not work. This amulet was originally made to be given to The Bringer of Peace, but it was cursed and hidden a couple hundred years ago during one of the raids on one of the Fairy villages called Syngladen in the Fire Realm. The only way for the curse to be broken is by the blood of those who cursed it."

"So it was an amulet for me, but it is hidden and cursed... and likely the person who cursed it is no longer alive..."

"You are correct. However, there are... possibilities."

"And what are they?"

"First, I know where the amulet was hidden in the Blackened Forest."

"Where?"

"I cannot say right now; there are ears everywhere," Lydorea said in a hushed voice.

"Even if we can find it on the Blackened Forest Island, if it is cursed, there is really no point in bothering to try to find it."

"The curse can be broken."

"How? Do you have a vile of blood from the person who cursed it?"

"No, but we have my blood."

"Your blood?"

"Yes… the person who cursed it was my great-great-grandmother, Torgany, on my mother's side. Her blood flows through me, so in essence, I have the blood to break the curse. And it is my plan to help you obtain Clyr and break the curse, so you will be able to have the protection it provides."

Lydorea told me that I should keep quiet about this to most everyone, as it could put her at risk if someone knew that she knew the location of Clyr and that she had the blood to break the curse. Though she did tell me I could tell Kaleyna, as she already knew that we did not keep any secrets from each other.

We reached the cliffs and enjoyed sitting for a few moments when the rain stopped for a short time, allowing the Northern Sun to shine down and warm us up a little. Once the rain started to sprinkle again, we figured it would be best to get back to the village to dry off and warm up. I thanked her for trusting me with this and also that she would be willing to try to help me obtain this amulet to help keep me from being controlled by others.

When I got back to the middle building in the village, I shook off my cloak and hung it up to dry. I sat by the hot spring with Kaleyna and told her about what Lydorea had told me. Kaleyna thought it was great what Lydorea was going to do to help.

It wasn't long and dinner was served to everyone. We ate and relaxed for a few hours and then went to sleep. When we awoke there was already a large spread of food out for us for breakfast. The Gargoyles definitely were skilled at keeping their guests well fed.

Shortly after finishing breakfast Louv came through the door, smiling. "Ny, would you come with me? There is something I think we need to discuss."

໑20໒

I FOLLOWED LOUV OUTSIDE and down a path past the other buildings. "Where are we going, Louv?" I asked, starting to feel a little nervous about going too far away from everyone.

"Just past those trees ahead, there is a special building I want to show you... I think it might prove helpful."

As we walked past the trees, I could see a small building. It couldn't be a place where anyone lived, as it was falling apart and old. When we approached it I could feel an energy field around it. I had only felt those before in one of my magyc classes when we were shown how to make a protection spell for something. All the little hairs on the back of my neck rose, making me realize this had to be a very powerful protection spell.

Louv opened the cracked door and allowed me to step inside first. It was very dark with the only light coming in from the small cracks throughout the roof and walls. I stepped further inside to allow room for Louv to enter behind me. The floor boards creaked beneath me as I breathed in a mixture of old wood and dust. Louv shut the door behind him, and suddenly there was a fire in a small pot on a stand beside the door. As my eyes adjusted to the light, I could see there were two mats on the floor with a few pillows and another larger pot between the two mats.

"You can hang your cloak up here, Ny." He pointed to some hooks near the door as he walked past me and sat down. "And please sit opposite of me."

I hung up my cloak and sat down on the mat, still not able to figure out what I was doing here. I kept waiting for Louv to give me more information, but he was placing some things inside the large pot between us. He began talking in a language I did not understand and had never heard before. It sounded more like deep grunts than actual words, but after a short time I could make out a pattern and repetition of some of the words. He mumbled another word, and whatever he had placed into the pot began to burn. It filled the room with the sweet smell of lemongrass. When he had finished, he looked at me and spoke.

"Ny, I know you are a good person, and I know you want to do what is right. However, I also know you are conflicted about the tasks set before you on becoming the Bringer of Peace."

"Have you been talking to Kal?" I asked, worried that she told him.

"No, similar to your friend, some of us Gargoyles can sense emotions, and a couple of us have sensed the struggles you are feeling."

"Oh…"

"Do not feel ashamed, Ny. A lot is being placed before you, and I would honestly be more concerned if you were not dealing with an internal struggle. This is also why I brought you here, this is a place where we come to seek the answers we are struggling to find."

"How do you do that?"

"I am going to give you a tonic made from xylota berries. It will allow your mind to open and you will face different tasks. Some will be things you can only watch happen, others you might have to make choices or actions to complete. These will allow you to figure out what you are afraid of, what is in your heart, and if this is the journey you want to take."

"How many tasks will I face?"

"It is different for everyone and it is focused on your journey, so it will be however many you need."

I took a deep breath as Louv pulled out a small glass vile of glowing orange liquid. He reached across the pot between us and gently placed the vile in my hand.

"How long should it take?"

"I can't say. It could be a few minutes or even a few hours. Though I will stay here with you the whole time and protect you."

"So I just need to drink this and it will start?"

"Yes."

"How will I know it is working?"

"Trust me, you will know. And please, Ny, do not fight what you see or feel. Through this spiritual journey, you will find some inner guidance."

I looked at the glowing vile, removed the stopper and downed the liquid. I looked up to see Louv no longer in front of me. I was standing in a small room where everything had a red haze to it. There were two people sitting in front of me with their backs facing me. As I stepped closer, I could see they were holding a newborn sleeping baby that had the cutest little pointy ears. The people must have been the parents, as they were kissing the baby and holding the child close to them.

The baby gently woke and stared past the parents right at me and smiled. The baby had the same violet eyes I had, and when the baby reached its arms out towards me, I could see on the baby's right wrist it bore the same mark as me. I just stared for a moment, until it dawned on me that I was not just looking at a little baby Elf, I was looking at myself when I was born. I felt a smile crossing my face as I fully realized this is who I was, this is who I am, and Elf.

Suddenly the room was empty and it shifted to an orange haze. In front of me was a table with a puzzle laid out. I knew I had to put the puzzle together, but each piece looked exactly the same. No matter how I put it together, there would be pieces that were left out and would not connect.

I looked around the small room, hoping to find a clue, only to see nothing. I had to be missing something, so I turned one of the puzzle pieces over and noticed it had a different image on it. I flipped all the pieces over and figured out how to put it together. It only took me a few minutes to arrange all the pieces perfectly. When I was finished, the pattern gave way to one simple word written in the puzzle: perspective.

Suddenly the room was gone, and I was standing in the middle of a destroyed village covered in a yellow haze. There were soldiers running around with swords, shoving Fairies to the ground and beating them savagely. I tried yelling for them to stop, but no one could hear or see me. There were people hiding in the buildings nearby, watching what was happening to their people.

I shouted to them to help, but they just hid behind their windows as the Fairies were beaten or stabbed to death. I looked around at the soldiers and wanted to help those who were being hurt, but I needed help. I could not do this alone.

Now I was in the middle of a forest on a worn road, everything now covered in a green haze. Many wounded people lay on the ground and others rushed around to save them. It was mostly Fairies and a few Elves. It looked like a group was ambushed as they were traveling down the road. There were wagon carts filled with household possessions — pots and pans and blankets. Not only were there villagers injured and dead, but there were a few soldiers as well.

One of the soldiers was still alive and screaming in pain. As I walked closer, a Fairy squatted down next to him, and after taking his weapons away, she started to dress his wounds. There was a large cut on his arm, and she took the time to clean and stich it closed so he wouldn't bleed to death. He told her many times to stop and not to help him. When she was done, he asked her why she helped him when he attacked her people. She looked at the man and simply told him, "Sometimes we need to have compassion for even those who do not have compassion for us. Otherwise we are no better than they are."

As a tear fell from the soldier's eye, I was shifted to a place I had only ever heard of. With the blueish haze surrounding me, I stood and looked up at the Leaf Tree. It was so full and beautiful. Each leaf was white at the base, and as they grew outwards, they changed in color. No two leaves were the same. As I walked closer to it, I could see the leaves were nothing like any leaf I had seen before. They looked more like feather plume from a large bird.

While I stood below it looking up, time suddenly started to move at an impossible rate. The leaves would fall here and there at first, and then many of the leaves all fell at once. Rowzey told me that when you die, your leaf falls off the Leaf Tree. There were so many people gone in such a short amount of time. This had to be the Elven Wars.

As I stepped back and stared at the tree, it almost split in half views. On one side, the tree was flourishing again, like it was in the beginning. On the other half, there were no more leaves left and the tree was dying. This was showing me the two possible outcomes to what will become of Iryvalya, either flourishing again in peace, or the death of us all.

Suddenly I was back in my room at Cliffside, with an indigo haze covering everything. The door burst open and two Kaleynas walked into my room shouting at each other. They were accusing each other of not being the real Kaleyna, and demanding I pick who is the real one. They both went on about memories we shared, and the things they knew about me. Neither was wrong, nor could I tell them apart.

I felt overwhelmed and started to cry. I did not want to let my friend down. One Kaleyna started yelling at the other, "See what you have done now? You have hurt my best friend. You are such a horrible liar."

The other Kaleyna ignored her and sat down next to me and put her arms around me. "I am so sorry, Ny, I did not mean to upset you. You do not have to choose."

I knew in that instant this was the real Kaleyna. I sat back and said, "Thank you, Kal. I know you are my spirit sister, all I needed was to listen to my own intuition and I knew the one who was the real Kal would not want me hurt." When I said it, the other Kaleyna disappeared into the air.

Everything became completely covered in a violet haze, and after a few moments, I was standing the in front of a forked road. To one side, the road was worn and smooth. The trees that lined it were full of bright green leaves and the sun was shining down. The other road was bumpy and looked like it was covered in shadows. The trees were dark and foreboding.

I thought for sure I would take the smooth road, but when I looked closer, there were people hiding amongst the trees in fear, constantly looking around for an unseen monster. As the smoother road went further down, the bright light only became dimmer until it was cloaked in darkness. I then looked closer at the bumpy road, which had swords and blood spilled on the ground, but farther down, there was a bright warm light ahead. It was beckoning to me that even though it might be harder to reach the light, it would be much better in the end.

Suddenly I was staring at Louv again in his person form. "What happened?"

"You were on your spiritual journey, Ny."

"How long was I gone for?"

"A few hours. The moon is out, though with the rain you can't see it. So did you figure out what you needed to know?"

I thought about it for a moment, and spoke the truth. "I feel as though I am realigned with myself, and that while I do not know for sure what the future is going to hold, I at least know the path I want to take."

"That is great, Ny. That is what the spiritual journey is for."

We walked back to the large building and I went inside just in time to grab some food to eat and then everyone was sitting around talking, and it was just too many people all at once. I needed to process a bit of what I just went through. I asked Kaleyna if she wanted to go for a walk with me.

We let Baysil and Louv know we would be going for a walk, and they said they would have one of the Gargoyles follow behind to make sure we were safe. While I didn't really want to have someone around listening to everything we said, I knew our safety was more important.

I showed Kaleyna over to the cliffs where Lydorea and I went. "I was thinking you might like seeing something that reminds you of home."

"It is quite beautiful," she said, "but definitely much different than Cliffside."

"I agree." We sat down on a large worn boulder. It was cool and barely dry from all the weather, and the Rydison moon was starting to cover the Northern Sun making it even darker with the cloud cover.

"So, Ny, are you really okay?"

"Yes and no."

"You can tell me more than that."

"It is just the whole thing with Lydorea and now having taken the spiritual journey, I am honestly a bit worn out. There is just so much to process, and it feels like there is never enough time."

"I know, Ny. I would say that things should start slowing down soon, but I doubt that they will. We have no idea what to expect and what is going to happen next."

"Okay, enough talk about all this stuff," I said shaking my hands. "Tell me some good stuff, like how you and Prydos are doing?"

Kaleyna blushed with a big smile. "It is going really good. I can't believe I have met someone like him."

"So it is more than a crush, I am guessing?"

"Much more it would seem... while you were gone with Louv, Prydos and I were alone, so we went in the hot spring... well, we ended up kissing more and..."

"And?"

"I feel almost bad, but we had talked a lot, and he said he feels like he had looked for me his whole life and that he really feels like he loves me... and I know it is fast, only a few weeks, but I feel like he is the one for me."

"There is nothing wrong with that, Kal," I said, giving her a big hug. "I am so happy for you."

"Thanks, I just worry that others will talk about us, like it's a bad thing or moving too fast."

"Who cares what they say? All that matters is that you are happy."

"I really am, Ny."

"So... you never answered my question."

"What?"

"What else did you do after the kissing in the hot spring?"

"Ny!" she said with a giggle and her face turning even more red.

"Oh Kaleyna! In the hot spring?"

"No, no, no, no..." she said quietly, "the pillows on the floor by the hot spring."

I smiled and giggled so hard my face started to hurt. It was great to hear about my best friend's happiness. "So, was it okay?"

"It was... perfect."

"I really am happy for you, Kal."

"Thank you... Prydos asked me beforehand if I wanted to be pairyn with him. He said he wouldn't go further unless I was sure. It was so sweet."

"So my best friend is pairyn with someone. I couldn't be happ—"

Someone shouted out behind us. I spun around to see the Gargoyle who had followed us, Rhyon, lying on the ground slumped over. I grabbed Klaw and stood in front of Kaleyna, looking around to see who had attacked him.

I then saw a cloaked figure moving towards us. Their hood was pulled down so I couldn't see their face clearly. "Who are you and what do you want?" I asked, trying to keep the fear out of my voice.

"I want the abomination," he said in a low rough and yet familiar voice.

"Who are you?"

"Does it matter who I am? No, I don't think it does," he said, slowly approaching us.

"You're right, it doesn't matter who you are, but you will not take or hurt either of us," I shouted, hoping Rhyon would wake up or someone else would hear me.

"No one is going to hear you."

"You will not get her," Kaleyna said, holding the dagger from Baysil in her hand, "without a fight."

"Then a fight it shall be," he said as he lunged forward, quickly closing the distance between us. As he came at me I noticed the flash of a dagger in his gloved hand. I slashed outward with Klaw and cut his cloak near his shoulder. He shouted, so I must have reached his skin.

He then spun and kicked out at me, connecting his foot into my stomach and knocked me on my butt. I saw him reach for Kaleyna to disarm her, and he incorrectly guessed and grabbed at her right arm to keep her still, but the dagger was in her left.

She struck out with the dagger, hitting him in the right shoulder. He dropped his weapon and grabbed at his arm. Kaleyna quickly pulled her dagger back out and went to strike again. Before she could, he spun around and shoved her backward, causing her to lose her balance and almost fall off the side of the cliff.

He advanced on Kal, and I knew he planned to push her the rest of the way off, so he would only have me to fight. I sprang up and crossed the short distance between us. I shouted the word "Down." Kaleyna instinctively dropped to her knees and the man turned to face me, just in time to see me hit him at full force, causing him to lose his balance and fall backward.

He spun to grab onto the side of the cliff and managed to stop sliding down the side. I ran to the edge to see if I could save him, but when I looked I was shocked to see his face. It was Kelvyhan, one of the male

Fairies who left Cliffside with us. He had always been friendly and nice to me. I didn't understand why he would come after me. Then it hit me, he really was after me. He knew who I was, he had to by now. "Why did you want to hurt me?"

"It was my job."

"Your job... and who are you working for?"

"I didn't have a choice. If I didn't come after you, my family would be killed."

"Then tell me who it is, and I can try to save your family."

"You can't," he said, struggling to hold on.

"Hold on, Kelvyhan," Kaleyna said. "We will try to help you up."

She looked at me, and I nodded. We both reached out to help him up. He took my hand and Kaleyna's. He was able to gain some footing and start to help pull himself up. As he started to reach the top, I could feel him slipping from my hand and pulling Kaleyna down towards him. "No!" I shouted.

"If I can't have you, I'll take her with me!" he yelled.

He started to fall backward and Kaleyna was getting pulled forward. I completely let go of his hand and put my arms around Kaleyna's waist and pulled her back. "Let go of him."

After a moment I felt arms around me. I turned and it was Rhyon helping pull us backward. "Kaleyna, you have to let him go." He told her.

After a few moments, she finally let go. We heard him cry out as he fell down the cliff into the water, and then there was nothing but silence. I held Kaleyna in my arms and told Rhyon to go get Baysil and Prydos.

"Are you okay, Kal?"

"I don't think I ever will be okay with this."

"Me either..."

I held her close to me and told her how much I loved her and was glad she was okay. It wasn't long and Baysil was there asking me about what happened, and Prydos took Kaleyna in his arms and walked her back to our building. I walked slowly back with Baysil and Rhyon going over everything that Kelvyhan said and did. I knew that Kaleyna would be upset by this for a long time, but I am glad that she has me and now Prydos to talk to and care for her.

When I reached the building, Kaleyna and Prydos were sleeping on some pillows off to the side where their cots had been. I took a few minutes to soak in the hot spring, to help warm me up and relax my muscles.

I lay on my cot and tried to relax and not think about anything. It must have worked and helped me fall asleep, because the next thing I knew, the door to the building slammed open and Louv, in his Gargoyle form, hurried in through it. "You all have to pack up and get going. There was a group of Elves spotted about a half day's ride from here and they are heading this way."

ଓ21ଥ

BEFORE WE LEFT XYLONIA, I made sure to see Louv and thank him for everything. He seemed especially surprised when I gave him a big hug and a light kiss on his Gargoyle cheek.

"You cannot thank me after what just happen to you. You were attacked."

"Louv, I know that I can and will be attacked often, and likely for the rest of my life. You have done everything possible to keep me and everyone else safe. I cannot thank you enough. You are a wonderful person and I am proud to now call you my friend."

"The pleasure is mine, Your Highness. And anytime you need me or my Gargoyles' services, all you have to do is let me know. Volnyri."

"Volnyri."

We grabbed our things, packed up, and got back on the horses. We rode east towards an overgrown path heading through the ruins of Grydios. It was so sad seeing another village that had been destroyed by the Elves.

Grydios looked like it had been a cozy and large village. There had to have been many more Gargoyles then. Unlike Dalorvya, this village was not burned to the ground; it looked more like it was shaken apart by ground quaking. I could see more writings on the crumbled buildings. They were faded, but I could make out that they were about the Elves ruling Iryvalya, and for people to submit to them. There were no bodies or bones to be seen, but to the north of the village there were many burial mounds, more than I could count riding past so quickly.

Like Dalorvya, I did not think I would ever be able to forget seeing the destruction the Elves caused in Iryvalya, and this was only in the Stone Realm. Who knows what else has been done in the other Realms?

The path was long and winding through a narrow opening in the mountains. It took a few days to get through them, stopping only to allow the horses to rest and drink from the few streams we came across. When we finally emerged through the far west side, all I could see was the mesmerizing waters of the North Sea. Baysil stopped and looked back at us all. We had been riding so long in silence, only hearing the horses' hooves move across the terrain, it was almost hard to hear him.

"We have to move along the shoreline south. There is plenty of beach for the horses to walk along, but we have to keep quiet and move as quickly as possible. I will take the lead, and Koyvean will bring up the rear. Everyone is doing great, but we have to push on until we reach the north side of Mylterias Cove. We have people waiting for us there, so they will be able to monitor if anything is coming towards us," Baysil said to us quickly and quietly. "Ny, I want you and Kaleyna riding up front with me. Prydos, please ride with Koyvean for now. Everyone else, I want you to stick together, two people at most, side by side, and do not leave any large gaps between each other. We need to stick together and be as fast as we can."

Baysil took off at fast gallop. Kaleyna and I had to really push our horses to catch up. Everyone else was about a hundred steps back. Their horses were nowhere near as quick as ours, but I got the feeling that Iclyn, who rode in the front of the group, was trying to keep a distance between us all.

When I was next to Baysil I looked to him, hoping for answers of what happened with the carved rose, if the Gargoyles would be okay, how the Elves seem to keep finding us, and if he knew about Cliffside. I hadn't been able to ask him anything with everyone being so close together through the mountains. I had been quite thankful that when we had slept, I was still between Baysil and Kaleyna; however, it was still not far enough from everyone else to talk. When Baysil looked back to me he gave a forced smile, one that I knew was to try to make me feel better. "Baysil what is it?" I asked, worried.

"Ny, we do not have time to discuss the details of what is going on out here," Baysil said.

"What we do not have time for is you keeping things from me," I snapped at him, immediately regretting it. "I'm sorry, I just know you're keeping something from me, and I want to be aware of everything going on."

"It's okay, Ny. I did not want to worry you, but you are right, you need to know what is going on. The rose did have a curse on it, the one we thought it might, to influence you. Koyvean was able to remove the spell, so you can keep it with you for now to allow Jehryps to think he might have some control over you." Baysil took a deep breath and continued, "The Elves that were on their way to Xylonia, we believe are the same ones who were in Cliffside. We do not know for sure, as we have not heard anything back from Miaarya, which of course has us worried for everyone's safety. The Satyr brothers were going to head back towards Cliffside for us to check on them and see what has happened."

"Why didn't you tell me sooner that you had not heard from Miaarya?"

"Because you do not need to worry about those things. There is nothing you can do. You have to go forward and meet up with The Drayks. That is who is waiting for us at Mylterias Cove. They will be able to hide us for a while and allow us to get everything sorted out."

"What about the Gargoyles?" Kaleyna asked, just as I was thinking it.

"They should be fine. They are strong and smart, and they will not tell them anything. Louv did say once they are gone he will try to contact us somehow to let us know where the Elves are headed next. As long as we reach The Drayks first, it will not matter. They can keep us hidden as long as need be."

Everyone had fallen into silence again, and I couldn't help but wonder what was happening back in Cliffside and Xylonia. We rode on for what had to be many hours, the Nydian moon had covered the sun and we rode on in the turquoise-tinted darkness. We did not make any stops to eat or even to let the poor horses rest this night, as Baysil said we were getting close. By the time the Nydian moon was moving away from the Northern Sun and the light was starting to cover the ground, we could see the end of the mountains on our right and the start of some valleys of grass again. We kept going for at least another hour and gradually Baysil started to slow us down.

He handed me his red silk scarf. "Here, wipe your face, you have water all over it."

When I took the scarf from him, I felt the carved rose inside of it. I made it look like I was wiping my face and managed to tuck the carved rose into my cloak. I handed the scarf back to him, but he waved me off so I would keep it. I folded it the best I could and tucked that inside my cloak as well.

Shortly, the rest of the group began to catch up to us and I could hear the complaints and groans of everyone being tired from riding so long. I did not look back. I could only imagine the exhausted looks on all of their faces, and did not want to feel any worse than I already did. As I looked ahead I could see a faint silhouette of a man all dressed in black on top of a black horse. The sun shone down on him and I could make out that he was wearing a hooded black cloak as well, covering his face from view.

"Baysil, there is a man ahead," I said urgently.

"I see him."

"What should we do?"

"It's okay, I know him. He is a Drayk," Baysil said with a little smile. "I am glad to know we have finally made it to safety. I think everyone is pretty worn out."

Baysil rode ahead to meet to the dark figure. He shook his hand and they spoke in low voices, so we couldn't hear. The man turned his horse around and rode ahead. Baysil looked to us all. "Follow him. We are not far from safety and need to hurry to keep out of sight as much as possible."

We followed the cloaked man for about a half hour. The mountains on the right had faded away to valleys and green hills, but where the water had been on the left, new mountains and cliffs emerged, protecting the shoreline. As we followed the cloaked man, he rode his horse through a small waterfall along the mountains to our left. Baysil went behind him and I followed cautiously.

As I went through the waterfall, the cool refreshing water pounded down on top of me, but it was not as strong as I would have thought. After passing through the waterfall, I wiped my eyes dry and let them adjust to the darkness. There was a darkened path that Baysil was following downwards. I continued to follow behind him, and checked to make sure Kaleyna was right behind me. When our eyes met in the murky light she gave me a nervous glance. The path led down, then curved and then down again for what seemed like another half hour. When the tunnel finally started to open up, we were deep inside a large underground cave. There was water along the right-hand side that was level with the ground, and to the left there were houses and what looked like a village of sorts, though much smaller than the ones in Cliffside. There were people walking around who would pause and stare at us momentarily and then continue on with what they were doing.

The cloaked man stopped his horse and said something to Baysil, who had stopped as well. "You can all stop here and the horses will be fed, watered and brushed so they can rest for a while," Baysil told us as he dismounted from his horse.

I rode Storm over to where Baysil was with his horse, and I leaned down to Storm to pet his neck as I started to dismount. As my right foot was coming over the back of Storm to get down, the heel of my boot caught on one of my bags and I started to fall. Just before I was about to hit the ground, strong arms reached around me and held me to keep me from hitting the ground. I turned my head quickly to see a pair of bright orange and cobalt blue eyes locked onto mine. After a moment I was able to realize the man in the black cloak was holding me. I quickly stood up, still in his arms, and looked at the man face to face the best I could, as he was a head taller than me. His hood had fallen around his shoulders in his valiancy to keep me from hitting the ground. His hair was quite short around the sides and back, longer and tousled on the top. His hair was mostly dark cobalt blue with bright orange streaks throughout, and he had glowing tanned skin. His beautiful eyes were framed by similar dark blue eyebrows and long dark lashes. He had a prominent nose with a small little bump near the top—it looked to me like it had been broken before—a squared jaw line, and full soft-looking lips.

"Are you okay, my lady?" the man asked me with a deep and masculine voice and the hint of an accent. I had heard an accent similar before, someone passing through Cliffside, but I never knew where it came from. It sounded unique.

"Yes... uhm, yes, thank you," I said. Realizing I was still in his arms, I took a small step back to stand on my own and he let his arms fall back to his sides. "My name is Nyrieve."

"I know who you are, my lady. I am Kylyan," he said, still looking into my eyes.

"Thank you, Kylyan, for helping me. I don't know how I missed clearing the bags on Storm," I said, feeling quite embarrassed.

"It was my pleasure to help the Bringer of Peace," Kylyan said to me, then he turned to Baysil, who was watching us. "If there is anything any of you need, let me know. I am going to go talk to Jyngy and Sudryl and let them know you have arrived."

Kylyan gave me a quick glance before he started walking towards a building right next to the water. He knocked a pattern on the door, it then opened, and he walked inside closing it behind him.

"Ny?"

"Yes?" I asked, turning away from the building and looking at Kaleyna.

"Are you okay? I have been trying to talk to you, but I don't think you heard me," she said, smiling.

"I am sorry. I guess I didn't hear you," I said, feeling confused.

"I think I know why," Kaleyna said, looking towards the building Kylyan went into and giving me a big smile. "I am guessing you saw something... or someone you liked."

"Kaleyna! I don't even know him."

"You do not have to know someone to find them attractive or inter-esting," Kaleyna said.

"Who do you find interesting or attractive, Kal?" Prydos said, walk-ing up to us.

"I personally find you interesting and attractive. However, I am thinking Ny might be thinking about someone else."

I was glad when Baysil interrupted us. "Everyone, we are going to be split up into different buildings again, like in Xylonia." Baysil turned towards the building near the water, where Kylyan was walking back out towards us.

"Baysil, there are four buildings to the left," Kylyan said. "They are all well stocked with everything your people should need. Jyngy said that she would like to talk to you, Nyrieve, Kaleyna, Prydos and Koyvean, as soon as she is done talking to Sudryl. So if you five could follow me, I will take you to wait until she is ready."

"I would like to go with Ny," a sadly familiar voice came from behind.

"You are not invited, Jehryps," Kaleyna said to him, frustrated.

A look quickly passed over Kylyan's face, one that resembled disappointment, and it was quickly replaced by a thoughtful look to Baysil. "Jyngy did not ask to see a *Jehryps*, Baysil, so I do not think it would be wise to bring him into such a meeting."

"I agree," Baysil said, turning towards Jehryps. "You will go get set up in one of the buildings with everyone else. When we want to talk to you, we will send for you. Otherwise, I would appreciate it if you would stay in your building. Iclyn, can you and Lydorea make sure Jehryps does exactly that?"

"Of course," Iclyn said with a sly smile on her face.

"You five, this way please." Kylyan led us towards the building near the water. We all walked in and Kylyan told us we could sit on the wooden chairs in the room near the entrance door. The walls were quite bare, but looked like strange rocks stacked upon each other. I walked over to the wall and lightly touched it, realizing it was not rocks at all, it was made of worn coral.

"I am sorry for Jehryps," Baysil said to Kylyan. "He is not someone we want to know what is going on; however, we do not dare have him roaming free either."

"I understand, Baysil. Besides, if he and Nyrieve are pairyn, I am sure he always wants to be near her," Kylyan said flatly.

"Pairyn?" I asked, appalled. "Who said we were pairyn?"

"No one, my lady. However, the possessive way he looks at you and that he demands to be near you, it is a safe guess." Kylyan looked at the door in the middle of the wall, across from the one we came through.

"Jehryps and I are not pairyn!" I was getting angry.

Baysil lightly grabbed my arm and gave me a look telling me to calm down. "Nyrieve and Jehryps are not pairyn, Kylyan, though I believe he would like that very much," Baysil said calmly.

Before I could say anything, the door Kylyan had been watching opened, and a beautiful Elf stood in the doorway. She was a little taller than me and had pale yet luminescent skin. She had long flowing bright orange and pink hair that reached her lower back. Her face was oval-shaped, and her eyes were swirled with the orange and pink of her hair, and framed with pink eyebrows. She wore a long gauzy dress in a pearl white, tight above her waist and without sleeves. Her arms had bands of silver that wrapped around them. They were unique and quite lovely.

She scanned everyone standing in front of her, and once her eyes locked onto mine, she smiled bigger, walked over to me and embraced me. I was surprised by her strength. Her arms looked thin and lean, but her hug proved she was not all that she seemed. After she finished hugging me, she stepped back and looked at me. "Hello, Nyrieve. I have waited a long time to meet you. I am Jyngy, one of the leaders of The Drayks." Her voice was softer than I had expected. It was light and almost playful, which seemed odd to me for a leader of rebels.

"It is a pleasure to meet you, Jyngy," I said with a smile.

Jyngy looked to everyone else in the room. "I am sorry for my rudeness, I have just been waiting a long time to meet the Bringer of Peace. I am thankful to all of you for coming. Let's go into the other room so we can talk."

Jyngy led us through the door into a large room where half of the floor was beach sand and the other half was water that went all the way to the walls. A couple of couches and chairs sat along the shore of the water, but not too close to get wet. I waited and watched Jyngy, Kylyan and Baysil walk to one of the couches and sit down. I sat on the side nearest Baysil, who smiled at me as I sat down. Then turned to Jyngy and said, "I am very thankful for you bringing us here, Jyngy, and giving us shelter and protection."

"You are most welcome. We have looked forward to your arrival for a while now," Jyngy said. "I have asked you all to come here private-ly because we seem to have a traitor inside the Rebel group here, and I wanted you all to be aware. We are not positive who the traitor is, but you can completely trust in me and Kylyan. If there is anyone you find suspicious, please let one of us know. Now, you will all be set up in one of the larger houses. It is where Kylyan and I stay as well. The rest of your group will be staying in a couple of the other houses."

"Will we have separate rooms?" Koyvean asked.

"Kylyan and I each have our own rooms, but there are four other rooms in the house, so you can all decide how you want to do that."

"We do not normally leave Ny alone anymore," Baysil said with concern.

Kylyan stated, "You can feel assured that if she would like to have her own room, she will be safe. There are wards placed on the house so that no one can enter who plans to cause any harm at all."

"I know I wouldn't mind having a night alone with Kaleyna," Prydos said with a wicked grin, and Kaleyna blushed and lightly punched his arm in return.

"I can handle being in a room alone," I said calmly, even though I was not really convinced that I wanted to be alone at night.

Jyngy smiled at me. "Wonderful. Kylyan, would you please show them to their rooms? I do think it would be best to have Nyrieve in the room next to yours, as you are the strongest and best warrior we have."

Kylyan showed all of us into the large house near the waterfront. It was made of stacked smooth coral, something I had never seen or even imagined before. Kylyan showed everyone to a room. Before Baysil went into his, he asked me if I was sure I would be okay alone, and I assured him I would be. Kylyan took me to my room, which was basically the same as the rest of the rooms in the building, with a large bed in the middle and a table and chair in the corner.

"Thank you for showing me to my room," I said to Kylyan as I walked past him, entering the room.

"It was my pleasure, my lady. Is there anything I can get you before I go?" Kylyan asked me flatly, like he was in a rush to get away from me.

"I don't think so, just... do you know by chance where I can find my bags?" I asked, turning to face him and realizing he was right in front of me. I was so close to him, if I took a deep enough breath we would have touched. My heart started to race a little, not knowing if it was the fear of being alone soon or the strangeness of being so close to someone I did not know.

"I will make sure they are brought to you, my lady," he said. "If there is anything else you need, just let me know."

"Thank you, I will do that," I said with a smile.

Kylyan stepped back from me, opened the door, and before he walked out, said, "Be assured you are completely safe in this house, but if you want to walk around the grounds, let me know and I will escort you anywhere you'd like to go. Even to see that Elf who seems to be pretty infatuated with you."

He walked out and shut the door before I could even try to explain that I was not interested in Jehryps. I turned around frustrated, and lay down on the bed. It was very soft and comfortable. I couldn't believe it had been so long since I had last lain in my own bed. I decided I should take advantage a few minutes alone to rest, so I closed my eyes and let sleep take me away.

I don't know how long I had been sleeping—it felt like only a matter of minutes—but from how sluggish my body felt, it had to have been a few hours. I tried focusing my eyes and looking around my room. My bag and trunk had been brought in and set in the corner near the door. I stood up and stretched out. The roof was so short that I could almost touch it with the tips of my fingers.

I went over to my bag and trunk, and I noticed a large box sitting next to my stuff. I picked up the box and saw a note on the top of it. I set the box down on my bed, took the note off of the box, and opened it to read.

Nyrieve,

Tonight we will be having a feast to celebrate your arrival. Please wear what we have provided in the box for you. Someone will come by shortly to help you prepare for the feast.
Volnyri,
Jyngy

❦22❧

I SET THE NOTE DOWN on the bed and opened the box. There was a beautiful gown inside. The top was form-fitted and made of exquisite green silk adorned with shimmery gems. The bottom of the dress was also silken, but mixed in was a wispy, gauzy material. It looked like they used the full silk down to middle of the thigh and then strips of the cloth for the skirt. When I walk in it, I imagine a lot of leg would show. There were no sleeves or straps on the dress, so I couldn't figure how it would stay up. I couldn't imagine walking around with so much of me exposed.

There was a knock at my door, and before I could say anything, it silently opened and the head of a young girl peeked in.

"Hello, Your Highness. I am here to help you get ready for dinner. My name is Ghilyauna. May I come in?" she asked with a big smile on her face.

"Yes, yes, please come in," I said, surprised. "It is nice to meet you, and please, you can call me Nyrieve, or Ny."

"Thank you, Your Highness, but I am to treat you with the respect that you deserve," Ghilyauna said as she walked in with a case in her hand. The door shut softly behind her. "Do you mind if I get some more light on in here for us?"

"No, please do." I glanced around for some candles to light.

Ghilyauna walked over to the wall where there were some big shells I hadn't notice before, they seemed to blend into the wall. She rubbed her middle finger and thumb together and brought forth fire to light up the oil that must have been inside the shell. She did that for all the shells on the walls, three on each. The room lit up brightly, and I was finally able to see that Ghilyauna was neither an Elf nor Fairy, she was something different altogether.

Ghilyauna was shorter than me by about a head and had shorter hair in large curls that surrounded her round face. Her hair was nothing like I had ever seen before; each curl was a different color, as if her hair was colored by a rainbow. She had pale skin, which looked almost like it was made of pink pearls. Her big eyes were pale pink and a soft teal, with soft pink eyebrows.

She was wearing a bright pink dress that looked similar to the dress in the box for me, though her skirt was much shorter. She also wore shoes I had never seen before, like the sandals we sometimes wore in the summer when relaxing by the water, but made of gold-colored straps with a heel that made her taller. She was even shorter than I imagined.

"Your Highness, like I said, I am here to help you get ready for the dinner, or feast, as the Elves like to call it," Ghilyauna said, very excited.

"Please, Ghilyauna, call me Ny. I am not used to being called Highness or anything so formal."

"I will only call you Ny if you would call me Ghily in return? That is what all my friends call me," she responded with a smile.

"That I can do, Ghily," I said, smiling back.

"You are very nice, like most of the Elves here, The Drayks," Ghily said.

"Do you know Elves other than Drayks?"

"A few. When I was younger I served a Pyrothian Elf. They did not like to call us Nymphs by anything other than 'Nymph.' We were never allowed to be called by our names. It has been a nice change to be with the Rebel Elves who treat us like people too."

"I have never met a Nymph before, but I think who you are is more important than what you are."

"That is why you are the chosen one, the Bringer of Peace, because you see people the way they should be seen," Ghily said. "Since I am the first Nymph you have met, I'll let you know there are different types of Nymphs, and I am a water Nymph. Most of my magyc is associated with water."

"I am very happy to meet you, Ghily. It is always great to meet new people and make new friends," I said sincerely. With a smile I pointed to her dress and the one in the box. "So how is it that these dresses do not fall down?"

"Before you put on the dress, you need to put on a corset. Do you have one of your own?"

I stared at her blankly. "I do not know what a corset is."

"Oh my," Ghily said, "I guess I didn't realize that Cliffside was a bit different than here... or where any of the Elves seem to live."

"I do not know much about the day to day life of Elves, but it seems quite... complex," I said, feeling out of sorts.

"No worries, Ny, I can get you ready for the feast and give you any information I can think of," Ghily said. "First thing we need to do is get you washed up, then we can get you dressed and made up."

Ghily took me to another room near mine. Inside it was hot spring like the one in Xylonia, but this water was a shade of pink and the spring itself was very small, only big enough for one person at a time. She had me undress and get into the water. I did not feel very comfortable being naked in front of someone, but she gave me a thin sheet to wrap around myself for my modesty. She sat behind me and washed my hair with lovely smelling oils, and also gave me something to rub into my skin as well. Ghily told me she had to prepare some items, that I should relax for a little bit, and when ready, get out. After a while of soaking, I looked down at the bracelet covering the marking on my wrist. Everyone here already knew who I was, so I figured for now, I no longer needed to wear it. I got out of the water and wrapped myself in the big robe Ghily left, and took off my bracelet. I opened the door to the small room and saw Ghily standing just outside the door smiling at me.

We went back into my room, the dress I was to wear was hung up, and below it was a pair of those tall strappy shoes, only in silver. The small table was now covered with different size brushes, colorful palettes I had never seen before and small bottles filled with liquids. Next to the table was a tall looking glass, one that you could see your whole self in, from head to toe.

"First, Ny, why don't you sit down and I will get your hair dried and ready."

Before I sat down on the chair, I made sure to place my bracelet inside my pack. Once seated, Ghily walked behind me and held her hands over my hair, and I felt the water pulling away from my scalp, just like it did when Prydos had dried my hair before. After just a few moments, my hair was completely dry and for the first time in days, I saw my hair fully in its beautiful green shade. I leaned closer to the looking glass and looked at all of my hair. I could not see any more white strands it in. I couldn't believe that it had changed so quickly. It felt like only yesterday it was all white and I still had no idea who I really was.

Ghily brushed out my hair and started to twist it up into an intricate knot on the top of my head. There were a few strands left down, and she had the rest pinned securely, meaning she had used well over sixty pins in it. She then took a metal rod that had a leather handle, and she wrapped one of the strands around it. She lightly blew on the wrapped strand of hair. It felt like a hot breeze against my skin, and when she stopped blowing on it, she let the strand down and the piece of my hair came off the metal rod in the shape of a beautiful curl. She did that to all the pieces she left down, I had never seen anyone style someone's hair like this before. Once I saw how she was curling my hair, I decided that I would wait until I was fully dressed to look into the looking glass again.

After Ghily finished my hair, she fit a beautiful metal headpiece on me. It was made of what looked like different strips of silver that was weaved into a beautiful pattern that formed a small point at the middle of my forehead. On the small point was a tiny gem that dangled. It was the same as the gem on Klaw, a rainbow moonstone. The rest of the headpiece tucked behind my pointed ears.

"I do not wish to be rude, but why are your ears not pierced, Ny?"

"Besides that it seems unnecessarily painful, no one had pierced ears in Cliffside," I said, wondering if I could ever find the courage to purposefully shove a needle through my ear.

Ghily continued to put powders of color onto my eyes and face. She even used what looked like a charcoal stick around my eyelids. Ghily also put some pinkish liquid on my lips, telling me that they would be stained a light pink for the whole night. I dabbed some of my beautiful-smelling perfume I received on my Leaf Day on my wrist and neck. I loved how it smelled of fresh green apples and blossoms. I had thought this preparation was slightly taxing and not needed, but what was coming next, was even more of a chore.

There was the undergarment that Ghily said I needed to wear to be able to wear the gown properly, the one she called a corset, and it was a black silk and lace garment that was made stiff in the ribs by something inside of it. I asked her what it was made of, and she said it was bones, which seemed very strange to me, even though I wore leathers. When she put the corset on me, she had to stand behind me and lace the thing up from the bottom to the top. It was too tight when she laced me up. I felt like I was going to pass out from not being able to breathe. I told Ghily I couldn't wear it like that, and she responded saying this is how they are to be worn. After realizing my polite protests were getting me nowhere, I explained to Ghily that if she did not loosen it, I would take everything off and go to the dinner in my leathers. With a sigh of exasperation, Ghily finally unlaced the corset and tried again.

After two attempts, Ghily finally was able to get the corset to where she and I both agreed it was manageable. Next, the dress was placed in front of me open so I could step into it. It fit me perfectly, which surprised me, as I am sure the dress was someone else's that they were allowing me to borrow. After Ghily laced up the back of the dress she made me sit on the chair to strap the fancy shoes onto my feet. Once they were strapped on, Ghily helped me to my feet and I could hardly stand. Not only were they wobbly, they were not very comfortable for walking, but Ghily said that this is what all female Elves wear for such events.

After Ghily did some readjustments of my hair and dress, it was time to look into the looking glass. I took a deep breath and stepped in front of it. I couldn't believe the girl looking back at me was me. She looked all grown up and regal, something I had never been. My hair was soft and delicate, the gown looked so flattering, and while it showed a lot of leg, it was not indecent. Something with my eyes looked different, so I had to take a closer look. I first noticed my eyebrows were the same shade of green as my hair, and in looking even closer I realized my eyes were no longer just violet. They had a swirl of green now. It was the same almost iridescence green shade as my hair. They were fascinating. My eyes had always been just violet and now they weren't. I wondered how long ago they had changed. It had been a while since I looked closely into a looking glass, so it could have been a while ago or just today.

The marking on my shoulder was much clearer than it had been before. It looked almost like lines swirling around. There was still some blurriness to it, and I sighed, hoping it would start to make sense soon. I turned a little to see the back side of my outfit using the handheld looking glass, and I noticed another small marking on the back of my neck right in the middle, it was blurry like the first one had been when I first noticed it.

I turned to Ghily, who was beaming at me with a huge smile. "Thank you, Ghily. I did not know it was possible for me to even look like this."

"No need to thank me, Ny. It was my pleasure to show you another side of yourself."

There was a soft knock on the door and when it opened I almost gasped when I saw Kylyan standing there looking at me. He was dressed in almost all black—pants, shoes and cloak. The shirt was a beautiful shade of orange, the same color as the orange in his hair. When his eyes met mine, he gave me a slight smile. "You look very beautiful, my lady."

"Thank you," I said, feeling my face flush. "You look beautiful—I mean handsome—yourself."

"Oh, this?" he said with a smile and gestured to his clothes. "Thank you. I am to escort you to the feast. Everyone else has arrived and you are to be the last to enter, as the feast is mostly in your honor."

"Great, another chance to stand out," I said sarcastically.

"You would stand out no matter where you are," Kylyan said softly.

"I look that out of place?" I glanced back into the looking glass, worried.

"No, you misunderstand," Kylyan said walking over to me. "You have the most beautiful eyes and smile I have ever seen. Next to anyone I have ever seen, they pale in comparison."

I couldn't help but smile more, and I took his arm, which he had offered to me, and allowed him to lead me out of the room. "Wait, what about Ghily?"

"I will be joining you all in a little bit. Go ahead, Ny, enjoy yourself. Kylyan will be sure to help you get to where you need to go," Ghily said with a big smile.

"I will see you there then, Ghily, and thank you for everything." I gave her a smile, then turned to Kylan. "I guess we should get going then."

❦23❧

KYLYAN WALKED ME OUT of the building, allowing me to keep holding onto his arm, which was helpful with all the stumbling I was doing in these new shoes. He led me down a path through the different buildings until we reached a bridge that crossed over the water on the far side of the cave. On the other side, lights twinkled and people talked and mingled. I slowed my pace, nervous about how I looked. I did not feel comfortable like I normally did in what I wore. I took my free hand and ran it over my skirt to feel the faint outline of Klaw strapped to my thigh. I had to argue with Ghily to allow me to wear it. She only agreed when she saw that it could not be seen when it was on. While I was sure I wouldn't need Klaw, having it strapped to me helped me feel a little more like myself.

Kylyan looked at me thoughtfully. "Are you ready for this?"

I thought for a moment and smiled at him. "I don't think I will ever be ready for things like this... but seeing as everyone has been waiting for me, I guess we should not keep them waiting any longer."

"I will be by your side the whole evening," Kylyan said, and a smile crossed my face. "Jyngy's orders."

"Oh," I said, losing my smile a bit. "I appreciate it."

Kylyan started walking us across the bridge towards the feast. As we approached, everyone got quiet and turned towards me. I had never felt so many eyes on me. There had to be close to fifty people, all of them dressed similar to Kylyan and myself. I spotted Kaleyna in a dress like mine, but it was a cerulean color, and she had a huge smile on her face, standing arm in arm with Prydos. Even Rowzey was dressed fancy, though not in a dress without sleeves or straps, hers was more modest and in a smoky gray color.

The majority of the night was filled with meeting many new people and eating little bits of food when there was time. I was introduced to all the different Drayks of this camp. It surprised me to learn there were other camps throughout Iryvalya. I kept receiving compliments on my hair and clothes, and while I thanked everyone for their kind words, I kept saying that it was all Ghily's work. It felt strange to not only have so many strangers know who I was, but to also have them constantly complimenting me.

Kylyan was great at helping me remember people's names and explaining not only who each person was but how they could be important to me. I had never thought about needing people with different magycal powers, but after having Kylyan explain some of their powers to me, I could see how some could be useful to have around. He also made a point to try to explain the different areas that The Drayks came from and approximate areas of other camps.

When I had a minute alone with Kylyan, I told him how I appreciate his help. He responded that he was under strict orders to keep near me, help with whatever I need and not let Jehryps get close enough to me to possibly cause a scene in front of everyone. I was glad, because I felt awkward enough without having Jehryps making things worse. I did feel a little disappointed that everything Kylyan did tonight was because he was ordered to do it and not necessarily wanting to do it.

At one point, when I had finally been able to sit down for more than five minutes and eat some food with Kylyan, I overheard Jehryps talking with Baysil, saying that he should be the one escorting me and that Kylyan was only trying to take what should be his. He actually was talking about me like I was his property. Baysil informed him that this is Jyngy's call, and she wants Kylyan with me, and that if he didn't like it, he could go back to his room.

"Your boyfriend seems to be worried about you spending time with me," Kylyan whispered to me, giving me a small smirk.

"He is not my boyfriend," I hissed quietly at him.

"I get the feeling that he thinks he is."

"We shared a kiss... well, two kisses actually, but that was it. He was off with another girl that same night."

"Really..." Kylyan said. "That bad of a kisser, huh?"

"I am not!" I said, shocked, and then noticed his teasing smile, which wouldn't allow me to be upset with him.

"I am sure your kiss wasn't the problem. There are a lot of Elves who seem to think they are entitled to whatever or whomever they want. Granted, most of them are a part of the Klayns and usually higher in power, but even average Elves can have such bad habits. I will say, though, that I think it is pretty vile for anyone to jump from twyning with one person to another like that."

"Twyning?" I asked in a hushed voice. "I have never twyned with anyone, and I sure wouldn't have twyned with someone like him!"

"I'm sorry," he said, holding his hands up in defense. "I never meant to insult you. I wouldn't have thought less of you if you had. However, I think it is good that you wouldn't want to waste your time with someone like him."

"Look, I don't know why I am trusting you with this information, but I am hoping I can. One of the other main reasons I do not like or trust Jehryps is because he is trying to use a spell to control me. He somehow thinks we could rule all the Elves together. I am not interested in him, but I also cannot let him know what I know. So I am stuck in this situation where I do not like him, but I cannot fully let him realize it."

Kylyan looked at me thoughtfully for a moment, leaned in close to my ear. I could feel the little hairs on my neck stand at attention feeling him so close to me. Kylyan whispered softly, his warm breath tickling my skin, "Your secret is safe with me, my lady. You can trust me." He pulled back and looked me in the eyes and smiled at me. I don't know why, but I truly did believe him.

There was another part of the evening I had not been prepared for. Dancing. I had never danced anywhere but in either my or Kaleyna's room. We would be silly and dance around, but here they had people playing different music than I had ever heard before. It was beautiful and felt bouncy to me, and others began to dance and I watched on in amazement and dread at the same time. While I partially wanted to join in, I knew I could never dance like everyone else was. They all moved in sync with each other, either as couples dancing or the males doing one thing and the females another. It reminded me of a story being played out.

After the song ended, Jyngy walked up next to me and spoke loudly to get everyone's attention. "Thank you all for coming to celebrate not only the arrival of our allies from Cliffside, but to welcome Nyrieve, the Bringer of Peace, to Mylterias Cove. We have waited many Leaf years for this time to arrive, and we are thankful that our brothers and sisters were able to make it here and keep Nyrieve safe. We still have a long road ahead of us to bring Iryvalya back to its peaceful existence, but now, with Nyrieve here to lead us, it is no longer a dream, it is the future. Please everyone, let's enjoy the rest of this evening celebrating, and tomorrow the work towards our future shall begin. Volnyri!"

"Volnyri!" everyone said in unison.

The music started up again, and Kylyan took my hand. "May I have this dance, my lady?"

"Oh... I uhm... I don't know how..."

"That's all right, I do."

"But I have never—"

"My lady, for this dance, all you need to do is follow my lead, and nothing more. Do you think you can do that?" A charming smile crossed his face. He seemed to enjoy teasing me, and while it kind of felt like it was at my expense, I didn't really mind.

"Yes, I do believe I could do that."

Kylyan led me out to the dance floor, where there were already a dozen couples dancing around in different directions. One of the couples was Iclyn and Lydorea; they looked so happy together. Another was Kaleyna and Prydos. She looked about as nervous as I was, but Prydos kept her close to him and moved with ease.

Kylyan turned me to face him, placed his right hand on my hip, and took my right hand in his left. I placed my left hand on his shoulder to keep balance, and then he pulled me closer and started moving us around the floor. I stumbled and even stepped on his foot, but he just kept going. After a few minutes I began to feel the music helping me move in rhythm with Kylyan. He was a great dancer and I enjoyed being in his arms. While I didn't know him very well, I enjoyed the feeling of being held and the idea of someone wanting me close who wasn't trying to get something out of it. I am sure this was part of what he was supposed to do as my escort tonight, but I decided not to think about that and just enjoy being in his strong arms and smelling the cologne he wore. It was a citrus woodsy scent with a hint of spice. I had never smelled anything like it before, and while I had noticed it throughout the evening, being this close to him made the smell seem intoxicating.

After a couple dances and a couple hours of mingling, a lot of people had left and there was only a handful of people still there. I decided to ask Jyngy if she would be offended if I left for the night.

She smiled and said, "No, Nyrieve, I cannot ask anything more of you tonight. I appreciate you following our customs with the clothing and adornments. You have been very kind and gracious to everyone you have met. Everyone agrees and believes that you are the Bringer of Peace, and we will all follow your commands to bring peace to Iryval-ya."

Jyngy smiled at me, embraced me, and whispered into my ear, "Volnyri." She stood back smiling at me and turned to Kylyan. "Kylyan, please help Nyrieve back to her room if you would, and see to it that she gets anything she might need tonight and the rest of her stay here."

"Of course, Jyngy," Kylyan said, nodding. He took my arm again, like he had all night long, and escorted me back over the bridge towards the buildings. As we walked back, I noticed he was leading me a different way than the way we came.

"Where are we going?" I asked.

"I just wanted to take you to a place so you can have a memory of this evening," Kylyan said as I gave him a confused glance.

We walked to a different house and he opened the door after knocking a short pattern. I was a little nervous to go inside, but I knew at my core I could trust Kylyan. Inside were a couple people from the party, as well as Koyvean, who looked a little surprised to see us. The room was quite dark, lit by only a few candles and oil-filled crystals.

Kylyan walked over to one of the people Koyvean had been talking to and whispered to them. The woman smiled and nodded, getting up and going into the next room. A few moments later the woman returned holding a viewing crystal. She told Kylyan to go stand next to me. He at first seemed hesitant, but she told him it was the only way she would do it.

As Kylyan stood next to me, holding my hand on his arm, he said, "Look at the crystal, hold still, and smile if you'd like."

We both stood looking at the crystal, and my thoughts of the evening came rushing through my head. I found myself smiling, realizing not only did I endure everything I was uncomfortable with, but I actually enjoyed myself and Kylyan's company. After a few moments the woman took the crystal, said an incantation, and handed the crystal to Kylyan. He thanked her and escorted me back out to our building and to my room.

He handed me the crystal. "Here, this is yours to keep as a memory of tonight, and a reminder to you that you are not only the Bringer of Peace, but also a very beautiful Elf."

"Thank you very much, Kylyan, and thank you for staying by my side tonight. I could have never gotten through it all without you."

"It was my pleasure, my lady," he said as he lifted my hand to his lips and gently pressed a warm kiss on the top of my hand. He turned, walked to his room next to mine, and went behind the door. I closed the door to my room, noticing all of Ghily's tools were gone. I sat on the bed, kicked my shoes off and rubbed my sore feet, swearing that I could never get used to them.

I took the crystal and looked into it. An image came of Kylyan and me standing side by side. He was so handsome and had a mesmerizing smile on his face. This was truly a wonderful gift, which I would always treasure.

I stripped off my gown and the corset the way Ghily showed me how to do. I put on a silk sleeping gown that was left for me on the bed, and then I snuggled down into the blankets. Sleep came fast, giving me pleasant dreams of tonight's festivities: the music, the food and even the dancing.

∽24∾

I WOKE TO THE SOUND OF shuffling in my room. I bolted up and focused my eyes to see Rowzey coming in with a tray of food for me. "Good Morning, Rowzey, Kaleyna," I said to them, noticing Kaleyna coming in behind her.

"Good morning, Ny," Rowzey said.

"Morning," Kaleyna added.

"What's going on?" I asked, stretching.

"I's think yous could use a good breakfast after such a long night," Rowzey said, smiling. On the tray was bacon, pancakes, fried potatoes and her herb bread. The smells reminded me of Cliffside, back before there was any hiding or battles that lay ahead, back when everything was simpler. It seemed like that was so long ago, but it was only several weeks.

"Thank you, Rowzey, nothing sounds better right now," I said with a smile.

We all sat on my bed and ate in silence, enjoying the amazing food Rowzey made. It felt so good to be sitting here with Rowzey and Kal. I missed the simple times like this. Even as young children, Kaleyna and I would sit at the table in Rowzey's kitchen, helping her prepare items for the meals, getting to taste different things before everyone else. I didn't appreciate then how wonderful a simple life could be. While I was happy, I felt bored and believed that I would always live just as I always had and nothing would change. I guess I was quite wrong on that one.

"You looked beautiful last night," Kaleyna said as she leaned in close, looking at me. "And Ny, oh my, your eyes have swirls of green in them!"

"I noticed it yesterday before the feast. I have no idea when they changed though."

"Yes, Ny, yous were breathtaking and so was yous, Kal," Rowzey said as she took another bite of bacon.

"She is right, Kal, you were stunning! I had not realized that you did not have much white in your hair until last night." Her hair was in a long braid down her back. There were only a few streaks throughout the whole braid that were still white.

"Thanks, Ny, and I hadn't realized you didn't have any white left!" Kaleyna giggled, tousling my hair. "The green shades are so beautiful."

"As is your blue hair. It reminds me of the North Sea by Cliffside," I said.

"Me too, I love it! It is like I have a constant reminder of home."

"I am betting your eyes will be swirled with another shade of blue." I paused a moment and pulled a small wooden box from my bag next to the bed. "And before I forget, happy Leaf Day, Kaleyna!"

I handed her the small box and she smiled at me as she opened it. "Oh Ny, it is beautiful!" She beamed at the ring I had Baysil get for her.

"It is from both Rowzey and I. The stone is an amethyst, which Rowzey told me is great for helping those who can hear and feel what people are thinking and feeling, and I had asked for it to be made out of silver. I thought it'd match your bracelet."

She slipped it onto her right middle finger and it fit perfectly. "I love it, thank you both so much."

"I's am sorry we's can't have one of my normal Leaf Day meals for yous though."

"It's okay, this is just perfect, spending time with you guys. And you both already know I have never enjoyed my Leaf Day being made into a big affair."

"I do want to also say I am sorry I did not get to spend much time with either of you last night. Jyngy had me meeting so many people, I honestly can't even remember who all I met. I was lucky Kylyan already seemed to know everyone and could help me with their names."

"It's fine, Ny. I's was busy with da Pixies and also keeping an eye on Jehryps," Rowzey said. "Baysil told me what he be trying to do with that spelled carving."

"Prydos and I were watching him too last night," Kaleyna said. "He was very upset when he saw you walk over the bridge with Kylyan and not him. Then when you and Kylyan danced together, he all but lost his mind. I heard him telling Lydorea that he should be the one with you, and that you are destined to be his."

"That is a bit creepy," I said, taking another slice of bacon and wondering if it is in my best interest to allow Jehryps to stay with us here or wherever we are going next.

"Da Pixies have been doing a great job spying on him," Rowzey said with a smirk. "They follow him often, and he is so focused with yous and his own thoughts that he doesn't see them."

"I hope they keep safe, I would not want to see him catch them spying and hurt them," I said, thinking for a moment about whether he could hurt someone just to get closer to me. He was willing to try to enchant me for his own motives, so what else could he do? "If I am really worried that he is going to hurt someone, then why is it we are keeping him around? Doesn't it seem like the smart thing to have him leave here and stay away from us?"

"That is what I said to Prydos, but his argument was that with Jehryps here, we know what he is up to," Kaleyna said. "Prydos also said that Jehryps thinks his Elf bloodlines are Royal. So maybe that is why he believes that you and he could take over everything together."

"I do not want to be in the same room with him, let alone rule Iryvalya with him. I don't want to rule Iryvalya at all, I just want it to be at peace." I dropped my head into my hands.

"What is it, Ny?" Rowzey asked.

"How am I..."

"How are you what?" Kaleyna asked.

"How am I... supposed to bring peace to Iryvalya?" I said with a sigh, looking back up to them.

Neither Rowzey nor Kaleyna had an answer for me. They just looked at me with blank stares.

"No one has told me yet how I am supposed to bring peace to Iryvalya," I said, feeling frustrated. "All I have been told is why I am supposed to bring peace... who my parents were or are... that everyone is depending on me and that I am to bring Iryvalya peace, and yet no one can give me a damn clue how I am supposed to do that!"

"Ny, I know we don't know how you are supposed to do it, but we'll figure it out together," Kaleyna said, taking my hand in hers. "I will be by your side the whole time."

"I know you are, that you both are. I am just scared... scared if I can be the Bringer of Peace that everyone needs... and if I fail, those I love will be hurt in the process."

"Ny, it is not because of you that we'd be hurt. Iryvalya has been in turmoil for a long time, and that was before either of us were even born. You did not cause the problem, and if you are the one to bring peace to it, there is no place we would rather be, than right beside you to help. If I ever want to have kids, I want them to live in a world where they do not have to hide who they are," Kaleyna said. "You are the Bringer of Peace, Nyrieve Vynlync, and you will figure out how to do it. I will always be by your side, we are spirit sisters, and nothing or no one will get in the way of us being there for each other."

"Kal's right, Ny, and I's will always support yous girls. Yous are like my own daughters, and I's will always be here for yous," Rowzey said, taking Kaleyna and my joined hands. "We are family, and we will figure this out."

We sat and finished the rest of breakfast, talking about lighter subjects, such as the party last night, the different foods that were there, how nice I thought Kylyan was to me. I showed Kal and Rowzey the viewing crystal that Kylyan had made for me. They both thought it was sweet. Kaleyna kept hinting that she thinks he has a crush on me, but I assured her that I do not think he does at all, he is just following orders and trying to be polite.

Rowzey and Kaleyna left, taking the plates with them and saying they would see me later. After a little while, there was a knock on my door. It was Ghily, who said she was sent to get me ready for the day and that if I first wanted to soak in the hot spring, I could. I couldn't turn that down, so I walked to the hot spring alone, got into the water and just relaxed, feeling all the aches left in my feet from the shoes last night start to fade away.

It felt like only a few moments in the small hot spring when Ghily knocked on the door and said I needed to get out and back to my room. I sighed and slowly climbed out of the spring and grabbed the long robe

Ghily gave me when I went in. After I was wrapped up, I opened the door and gasped in shock as I was face to face with Jehryps.

"Excuse me," I said, annoyed, as I tried to walk past him.

"No, Ny. We need to talk. Now," he said with anger in his voice.

"Now is not the time," I said, trying to get him to move so I could walk by.

"Yes it is," he said, pushing me back into the hot spring room and closing the door.

"Jehryps, I do not have time to argue with you or anything else. I have to get dressed. I have people waiting for me," I said, trying to figure out how to get around him, wishing I had Klaw on me.

"No, you have been avoiding me for long enough. You spent time with that half-breed Elf last night, time you should have spent with me. Do you know what everyone was saying? They all thought you and he were pairyn!" Jehryps yelled at me. "Everyone needs to know that we are pairyn, Nyrieve, and you need to make it clear that we are! You are not to spend time with him again, and you are to have me at your side at all times. Do you understand me?"

"Have you lost your Elven mind?" I asked. "You do not get to tell me what I can and will do. You and I are nothing to each other."

"Oh, so you want to pretend what happened back on the dock in Cliffside was nothing?" he asked with a nasty grin on his face.

"That? That is what I call a mistake! The biggest mistake I have ever made!" I yelled at him.

"Mistake? I am no one's mistake!" He walked towards me, backing me up into one of the corners in the small room. "Maybe it is just that you can't remember how wonderful it was on the dock, or at least how wonderful it could have been if you hadn't been such a child." He leaned in to kiss me. I shoved him back and he stumbled, almost falling into the hot spring. He quickly regained his balance and turned back to me, enraged. He pulled back his right fist and let it fly, striking me hard in the face, and repeated it one more time.

I felt the room start to spin and kept blinking to try to regain my thoughts. As I tried to get my eyes to focus, a blurry outline of Jehryps came close to me, pressing me against the cool rough wall and pinning my hands above my head with his left hand. He started kissing my neck roughly and fumbling with the tie on my robe with his right hand.

"I tried to make this easier for you, but you had to play hard to get. I will show you how much you want me, Ny. Everyone wants me, and after I have you, you will be angry that you didn't do this back in Cliffside."

I couldn't believe he was doing this. I began to feel physically sick at knowing his plan. I couldn't seem to get my limbs to move together enough to try to stop him. His fingertips slid into the top of my robe and he grabbed at me, squeezing me as hard as he could. He started to slide his hand down further, then suddenly flew backward away from me and landed in the hot spring.

I slid down to the floor, fumbling to pull my robe back together. I rubbed my eyes and tried to focus on the person who was repeatedly hitting Jehryps inside the hot spring. After my eyes refocused, I realized that short cobalt hair that was dripping with water was Kylyan's.

"Kylyan," I barely managed to say. He stopped, with his arm pulled back to hit Jehryps again, and quickly let him go. Jehryps slumped over the side of the hot spring and Kylyan ran to me.

"Are you okay, Ny?" he asked, checking my face.

"I think so," I said, still feeling dizzy and starting to feel the pain in my face throbbing through the panic that was fading.

Kylyan put his arms around me and under my legs, lifted me off the ground, carried me into my room and laid me on my bed. He told Ghily to get Jyngy and to have someone go get Jehryps out of the hot spring room and to take him somewhere he couldn't get away, to tie him up if they needed to. I heard her run out of the room and more shouting.

Kylyan sat down next to me on the bed and moved my hair out of my face. "You are okay, Ny. You are safe here with me, I promise."

With those words, I quit fighting the darkness that was trying to take me over, and I allowed it to swallow me up and take me away from the pain.

෨෬

The room was dark when I started to hear people talking. I could only make out a couple of words: "hit her... nothing broken... grabbing... kill him..." The rest just blended together. It took me many tries to fully open my eyes, and when I did I could see Baysil talking to Jyngy, Koyvean, and Marselyus quietly in one of the corners. Kaleyna was sitting in a chair next to the bed. She was the first one to realize I had opened my eyes.

"Ny!" Kaleyna said, jumping out of the chair and coming to sit next to me. "Are you okay?"

Everyone else quieted and turned around to look at me. It took me a minute to find my voice. "I think I am okay, I just have a bad headache." I tried to sit up. Kaleyna helped me get up into a sitting position on the bed and placed pillows behind me to help support me. I was still wrapped up in the robe, but I was dry, so I had to have been lying here for a while. "How long have I been out?"

"You passed out a few hours ago. You are lucky, though, he did not break any bones. But you have a really nasty bruise across the whole left side of your face. We put something Jyngy had on your eye, to keep it from swelling shut."

"It was something the merpeople gave me," Jyngy said, walking closer to the bed. "It seemed to help a lot with the swelling, but it did not stop any bruising and those will be there for a few days. I am very sorry, Ny, that this happened to you here."

"It is not your fault, Jyngy. We brought Jehryps with us," Koyvean said.

"And I will be making sure he pays for what he did," Marselyus added.

"Before anything happens to anyone, Ny, can you tell us what exactly happened with Jehryps?" Baysil asked.

"Yeah... I was coming out of the hot spring room... Jehryps was blocking the door... He wanted to talk to me and I said no... He got pretty angry with me and pushed me back into the room... He hit me twice in the face... While I was disoriented he pinned my hands above my head and..." I stopped, feeling sick remembering what Jehryps started to do next.

"What did he do, Ny?" Kaleyna said, taking my hand in hers.

"He started to kiss my neck and untied my robe, and he said he would show me how much I would want him," I said quietly.

"Then what happened?" Jyngy said.

"He grabbed at me, squeezing... and then before he could go further, someone... someone grabbed Jehryps and started hitting him. When I realized it was Kylyan and called out to him, he stopped, picked me up and brought me in here. Is Kylyan okay?"

"Kylyan is fine," Jyngy assured me. "He hurt his hand a little, but nothing compared to the damage he inflicted on Jehryps."

"What happens now?" I asked.

"It is honestly up to you, Ny," Baysil said.

I thought about it for a few minutes, and I decided what I needed to do. "I want to go see Jehryps and talk to him, but not alone, I don't trust him."

"You want to talk to him?" Kaleyna asked, surprised.

"Yes, because I want him to answer my questions before I choose what needs to happen to him," I said, trying to be logical.

Everyone but Kaleyna went outside the room to let me dress. Kaleyna helped me find some clothes to put on. There was another dress that was hanging up on a hook on the wall, so we picked that, as it was easy to put on. It was a purple gown, with layers of a thin soft silk, that was tight at the bodice and flowed out from there. There were long sleeves that belled out as well. I made sure Klaw was secured on my thigh. It seems Baysil was right, I do need to keep Klaw with me at all times. There were also shoes for me to wear, but luckily these were like slippers, no heel, easy to walk in. It was then I realized that Kaleyna was wearing something almost identical, but in a pink color.

When I was dressed, Kal grabbed my hand. "Are you actually okay, Ny?"

"I think so... I mean, I do not think it is something I will get over anytime soon though," I said sadly.

"Why do you want to see him?"

"I need to confront him. I need to make sure he knows that even though he hurt me, he didn't break me," I said, fully realizing that is what I felt. "And I need to do it right away, so I, too, know he didn't break me."

"I understand that," Kaleyna said. "I am thankful that Kylyan heard you shouting."

"Me too." I needed to make sure to thank Kylyan after I was done talking to Jehryps.

ಲ25ಬು

I WAS LED TO A BUILDING, which was the furthest building away from the entrance of the cave. It was dark inside; there did not appear to be any windows, and no door to the outside other than the one we were walking through. After I walked through the door, a whimpering sound came from behind the only other door inside the room. I knew right away it was Jehryps. "Why is he making those noises?" I asked.

"He was injured quite a bit by Kylyan," Jyngy said calmly.

"Has anyone tended to him since he was injured?"

"We cleaned him up, reset his nose, which will never look the same, and gave him something for the pain earlier, but that has likely worn off a while ago," Jyngy responded.

"Okay," I said flatly. "Is there anything I should know before I go in?"

"Just that he is in a chair and his arms and legs are tied to it," Baysil said to me. He must have known I was wondering if he'd be able to move around.

"Is it okay if I go in alone?"

"Yes," Jyngy said, "but if you need us, just call and we will come in."

I took a deep breath, opened the door to the room, and stepped in. I let the door shut behind me, and I took a moment to let my eyes adjust to the dim light. The air in the room was different, cooler and moist. The flooring was wooden boards over water. I guess this room was designed so someone could only escape one way, from the door I just walked through.

I could see Jehryps's outline in the chair in the middle of the room. He twitched when he saw me, and grew very quiet. There were a few of the shells on the wall filled with oil, same as in my room. I walked over to a few of them, rubbed my thumb and middle finger together, and made a fire to light them. It came so natural, I didn't even have to think about it or concentrate.

There were a few other chairs in the room, but I really did not feel like sitting down just yet. So I slowly walked around Jehryps, not close to him, but not far enough away that he would think I was scared of him.

"Jehryps?"

He grumbled in return, but didn't say anything intelligible.

"I wish I could say I was surprised by your attack on me today, but in truth I am not," I started as I continued to walk around him. "Ever since I rejected you in Cliffside, you have gotten more angry and frustrated with me, and everyone else for that matter. And for some strange reason you believe that you are entitled to everything you want in life, and if this is not a revelation for you to realize how incorrect you are, I am not sure what will be."

"I am entitled!" Jehryps shouted with pain in his voice. I wondered if it was just physical pain or the pain of him realizing that he would not be getting what he wanted.

"Perhaps you once were. You were always doted upon by the Fairy girls in Cliffside, but you never appreciated it, you just expected it. I was even a bit flattered at first when you started to show interest in me."

"But that all stopped when you were too scared to be with someone who was out of your reach," he said quietly.

"Is that what you think?" I asked. He did not respond, so I continued, "My interest in you wavered a bit after the incident on the dock, you not respecting my wishes to go slower. But it wasn't until I learned of you going off that night with Gwyndal that I realized you could never be a person that I would want to be with. You have no commitment to anyone but yourself."

Again he remained silent. He knew I was right, that is why he could not argue against it. I stopped walking around him, took a chair directly in front of Jehryps, and sat down to look at him face to face. He was beaten and bruised, much worse than me. There was a large cut above his left eye that had been stitched together. His left eye was swollen shut and puffy. I could see where his nose had been reset, and Jyngy was right, his face would never again look symmetrically perfect. While I am sure that Jyngy's people repaired him, I believe they also repaired his injuries at the most basic level possible, and I did not feel bad about it.

"So are you going to answer my questions honestly or do I need to get a charm to get you to tell me the truth?" I asked him flatly.

"You wouldn't do that!" he said, shocked.

"I did on Montryos, so why wouldn't I on you?"

He didn't say a word, just looked at me with his one good eye. After a few moments, he looked away and nodded to me.

"Good, I wouldn't want to have to waste a charm on you," I said flippantly to annoy him. "So, why don't you explain to me why it is exactly, you feel we should be together and then we will get to the events of today."

He took a deep breath and began, "I have always known I was to be pairyn with you. It was told to me before I came to Cliffside. My parents are both Pyrothian Elves. They believed the chosen one was being hidden there, so they gave me up in hopes that I would find you and bring you back with me one day to Prax. I always knew I was an Elf, and I hated that I had to hide it. I had just celebrated my fifth Leaf Day when my parents told me the prophecy, and that I would be the one who'd help lead the Pyrothian Elves to power. I believed them too. For years I tried to make friends with all the girls in Cliffside, but you... I never suspected you would be the Bringer of Peace. You were just too simple and boring... but once I knew it was you, I tried everything I could to get you to be with me and let me lead you in the right direction, but you just wouldn't."

"You are telling me that you had been sent to Cliffside as a child to spy and get close to me?" I asked, astounded.

"Yes. Do you really think either of the Elf Klayns will just let you destroy the world as they know it to be?" he asked seriously.

"I do not want to destroy anything. I just want peace for everyone. One group of people is not more important than another group of people," I said, standing back up.

"You might truly believe that, Ny, but that is not reality, that is not how Iryvalya works. For all the things you'll try to do to bring peace, there are hundreds of others trying to destroy it."

"And you are one of those people?"

"I don't know what I am. I just know that because of my failure, the Pyrothian Elves will have me killed now."

"How do you know that?"

"My parents would send me letters off and on, reminding me of my duty and what I was supposed to do. I am the one who let the Elves know that you were in Cliffside. Why do you think they showed up right after we left? I had overheard you and Kaleyna talking in your room about leaving one evening, but I never heard you guys change it to leave sooner. I figured the note I left behind would help them follow us to wherever we were going next, but apparently they are not as quick as you seem to be."

I had no words for him. He betrayed everyone in Cliffside, and we still didn't know if anyone was hurt or not. "Why did you give me a cursed gift on my Leaf Day?"

"You figured that out, did you? My parents sent it to me, they told me that whoever I gave it to would listen to me and I could encourage them to do as I said. I figured after I gave it to you, if I could just get close enough, maybe I could get you to follow me and do the right thing. But you were too stubborn to let me near you."

"What about today, Jehryps? Why did you attack me like that and try to force yourself on me?" I asked, getting more angry and beginning to walk in circles around him again.

"You wouldn't talk to me, you kept pushing me off. I had a potion I was going to have you drink, and you would have believed that you wanted to be with me and that everything was perfect and you would have listened to me and followed my rules. I knew it would work on you, because it had worked on every other girl I had given it to before. I never needed it to bed one of them, only to get them to be happy with me breaking it off with them afterwards. But you... you just couldn't give me the time to talk to you or at least force you take the potion, so when you tried to push past me again, I lost it."

"Lost it? That is your explanation?" I asked, looking at him shocked.

"Yeah, no one has ever denied me before, no one! I cannot tell you how many women I have had back in Cliffside, but only the one woman I needed to be able to seduce was immune to my charms. I felt like a failure, and that my life was for nothing... I wasted growing up away from the Elves for nothing!" He started getting louder.

"So you honestly thought forcing yourself on me would have worked?"

"No, I didn't think it would work, but I figured that if I told everyone back in Prax what I did, they would have at least spared my life and known I had tried everything I could to bring you to the right side."

I stopped walking and just stood there thinking about what I should do or say. How is it, the man sitting before me who hit me and tried to violate me could make me almost feel pity for him? What he did was wrong, and he needs to be accountable for his actions, but what if he was telling the truth? What if he would have been looked at as a hero for hurting me and had his life spared? It doesn't excuse what he did by any means, and he could be lying to me now, same as he has to everyone else.

"Baysil," I said flatly.

Suddenly the door opened and Baysil came in with a sword drawn and the others all filed into the room as well.

"Yes, Ny?" he asked, concerned and looking at Jehryps to see if he was still secure.

"Could you hear everything out there?"

"Yes, Ny, we all did," he responded.

"Good. We need to first find out what happened in Cliffside. Do you have any suggestions on how to do that?"

"Yes, we received word from Xylonia this morning that the Satyr brothers are on their way here with an update."

"Good, they should be able to fill us in. And what of the Gargoyles?" I asked.

"They are fine. The Elves arrived shortly after we were gone, but left quickly, going back the way they came."

"As soon as we know the status of Cliffside, we will finish dealing with Jehryps," I said coolly. "If anyone was hurt because of his actions, informing the Elves to come looking for me, I want him held accountable."

"Yes, Ny," Baysil said, sounding a little surprised.

"I am sick of people like him and Montryos hurting people because of their stupid ideals. I want to make it very clear to anyone else that if their actions cause pain to the innocent, they will be held accountable for those actions. I may be the Bringer of Peace, but I will not tolerate these kinds of actions. If they want to come against me or those who choose to stand against them and fight for peace, that is fine, but to hurt innocent people or try to violate people in such a way will not be accepted."

"You have the full support of The Drayks, Your Highness," Jyngy said.

"And the Fairies," Baysil said.

"The Death Elves as well," Koyvean said, making me finally realize that is the type of Elf she is. They called them that because they usually have powers that can pull someone's spirit out of their body, causing death.

"Thank you all," I said. "Keep him tied up, provide him with the basics that he needs until I decide what is to be done with him. I need to go take care of something, but would it be possible to have a meeting with all Drayks here in a few hours, Jyngy?"

"Yes, Your Highness, I will make it so," she said as she bowed, turned and walked out the door.

I gave one more look back to Jehryps. I knew he had cringed hearing everyone following my direction, and had to worry about his future, which is exactly what he needed to worry about. I nodded to everyone, thanked them, and started out of the building. Kaleyna followed behind me and waited until we were out of hearing of everyone else. "You are a true leader, Nyrieve, and I will be proud to follow you anywhere."

I smiled at her. "Thank you, Kaleyna. I am entrusting you to keep me in check. I am going to set up a trusted council, and I want you to be on it. I know you will be honest with me and help me question the choices I need to make. I also know you will tell me when I am making the wrong choice, and that is most important."

"It would be my honor to do that," she said with a look of pride on her face.

We entered the building we were staying in. I turned to Kal. "I need to do this alone. I need to thank Kylyan for his help today."

"Of course. I am going to go meet with Prydos and update him on everything." She gave me a quick hug before she turned and walked towards her shared room with Prydos and left me alone in front of Kylyan's door. I hesitated for a moment, took a deep breath, and knocked.

☙26❧

"COME IN," KYLYAN SAID.

I slowly opened the door and peeked my head into the room. It was similar in size and shape to my room, but Kylyan's room definitely looked more lived in and personal than mine. Kylyan lay on his bed in just a pair of leather pants with his arms over his head covering his eyes. I couldn't help but take a moment to look at his muscular chest. Then I quickly noticed his bandaged hands and I gasped.

"Are you okay?" I asked.

Kylyan moved his arms to look up at me and then sat up, swinging his legs over the side of the bed. "Ny, I am sorry, I didn't think it was you. Please come in."

I stepped inside his room and shut the door behind me. "I am sorry to disturb you, but I wanted to come and talk to you."

"I appreciate the visit... what can I do for you?"

"Do for me?" I asked, surprised. "Kylyan, you have done more than enough. I wanted to come and thank you for what you did... for saving me."

"Anyone would have done it."

"The more I seem to learn about people, the less I believe that to be true," I said. "Do you mind if I sit down?"

"Oh, I am sorry. Yes please, please sit down."

I walked over to the chair next to his bed. It was a lot like the one I had in my room at Cliffside, but his was much newer-looking and in a beautiful bright orange color. When I sat down, I was surprised how soft it was.

"Are you okay, Nyrieve?"

I thought about it for a minute and answered with the truth. "Physically I am fine, otherwise, not so much. I have never been so scared, and I doubt that I'll forget about it anytime soon, but I have to keep going."

"Yes, you have to keep going, but you are allowed to feel your emotions. You are allowed to take a moment and feel everything you need to."

"Maybe I will at some point, but right now, I need to keep thinking about what's next. I cannot fully understand why things happened today like they did, and maybe I will never know... but what I can do is focus on what I can control and what I can do..."

We sat in silence for a while. Kylyan just sat there looking at me thoughtfully and then finally broke the silence. "I know you came to thank me, and you have, so why else did you come see to me?"

"I have decided if I am the Bringer of Peace, then I need to start acting like it." I sighed. "I have been very lucky to have some wonderful people around me to help get me to this point, but I need to start being more aware of what is going on and making more of the decisions about what needs to happen."

"I agree with you, Nyrieve."

"Please Kylyan, call me Ny." I said. "Now, I have asked Jyngy to call a meeting with all Drayks here in a few hours, and one of the things I am going to announce is that I am forming a trusted council to aid me in making decisions. I cannot expect to know everything, but I figure if I divide up a group of people I trust to handle different things and report back to me, I will have a much better understanding of what is going on and also be able to make informed decisions."

"That sounds very logical... Ny," he said, and I couldn't but help smile at the sound of my name from his lips. "What made you decide this?"

"I have been thinking about that, and while I am supposed to be in charge, I am not. I do not know everything going on, and it seems I am often being treated as if I cannot handle the truth or that it will break me. I need to know what is going on, good or bad, and I need to be able to know that those I trust also trust enough in me to tell me the truth. While I know that it was unknown what Jehryps would do, I didn't want him coming with us, and if I would have trusted my instincts, perhaps today would not have played out like it did."

"I see your point, though I will say some of the others who traveled with you here, have nothing but your best interests in mind."

"I know, but if I am to be a leader, I need to start making the decisions regarding what I am doing."

Kylyan just nodded in agreement, so I continued, "This brings me to my other reason for coming here. I want you on my council."

"Me?" he asked, furrowing his brow in surprise. "Why me?"

"Because you saved my life today, even if he hadn't killed me, he would have killed something inside of me, and I don't know if I would have been able to emotionally recover from that to be the Bringer of Peace."

"You are a lot stronger than you think, Ny, physically and emotionally. Jehryps hit you pretty hard, and you kept it together long enough to get help. Not many people can do that, they'd pass out right away. And emotionally, you are sitting here with me planning about the next best steps to take, keeping your mind focused on what you feel is important."

"Thank you, I am sure I will have a momentary break down at some point, but today is not it and while I might be stronger than I think, I still know I need to be a lot stronger. Another thing I wanted to ask is if you would be willing to train me for any physical fighting I might have to do?"

"Me?"

"Yes, you seem know what you are doing, and I know I need it. I have never had to really fight before in my life, and I cannot keep hoping that I'll be able to actually bring peace to Iryvalya without fighting for it."

"It would be my honor to help train you, my lady. I just ask that if we are to train, you do not get offended if I do not go easy on you. Easy will not help you fight for your life when you have no other choice."

"I would not have it any other way," I said, confident and nervous at what kind of training lay ahead. "I need to go and prepare for the meeting. Will you be there, and will I be able to announce you as part of my council?"

"Yes to both," he said, taking my hand and placing a gentle kiss upon the top.

After leaving Kylyan, I looked for Baysil and Koyvean to discuss with them my plans, but I could not find them. I went back to my room to prepare myself for the meeting, and I decided I needed to be myself, which meant no fancy dress or shoes this time.

After going through my bags, I pulled out my black leather outfit that Relonya gave me with the green shirt. I put everything on, laced up my boots, and strapped Klaw to my thigh. I checked the looking glass and decided that while I did feel more like me, I was going to try encompassing some of the traditions the Elves had. I went to look for Ghily, and found her just about to walk by the building. I asked her to come and help me with my hair and putting the colors on my face.

Ghily first had to go to her room to get everything, and when she came back she started to do my hair. "Ghily, before you start doing everything, I need to make a few requests."

"Sure, Ny, what can I do?"

"First, I do not want my hair fancy, just nice. I normally put it in a braid, but I would like it to be a bit nicer than a simple braid. Is there anything you can suggest that you could also show me how to do myself?" I asked hopefully.

"There are a few different ways we can do it, and I will show you everything, even how to put on some face colors," she said, seeming to know I had hoped she would.

It took almost an hour with Ghily. She taught me how to do everything myself. When we were done, I had just a small amount of face color on and my hair had a beautiful braid that was not overly fancy, but not simple either. I had my hair pulled tight enough to stay, but it was loose and soft around my face. When I looked at myself, it made me think I looked more grown up, not just a young Elf of seventeen Leaf years.

Ghily promised to help me teach a few others, along with Kaleyna, so we could help each other if need be. Ghily also felt I needed to make a real statement at the meeting, and said I should have someone pierce my ears, as this was a highly recognized cultural status among the Elves that I was no longer a child, but an adult who could be taken seriously. I remembered the earrings that Rowzey had given me, and I decided that I needed to make this statement.

I asked Ghily to go get Kaleyna. I wanted to give her the choice to have hers done as well. If she was going to be on my council, I needed to give her the option to come in at the same level as me if she wanted.

Kaleyna was not thrilled about the idea of piercing her ears, and I didn't have another set of earrings for her; however, Ghily said that she had a pair that she would love to give to Kaleyna as a present. After Ghily returned with the earrings for Kaleyna, she looked at me and asked me if I was ready. I really wasn't, but I had decided this is what I was going to do, and I was not about to back down now.

I got my earrings out and told Ghily to go ahead. She took out a long threading needle and held it in the fire for a while, making it red. She then let it cool and walked to the right side of me and stuck the needle through the middle of the outside rim of my ear. It hurt more than I expected and I cursed a lot while she quickly put the earring in the new hole in my ear. She quickly repeated the process on my left ear, and after I finished cursing about the pain, I gazed into the looking glass.

The silver hoops with the small rainbow moonstone looked odd to me, but it also looked right. Next was Kaleyna's turn. She cursed five times as much as I did, and I even had to practically hold her down to get the second one pierced. Her earrings were also silver hoops, but she had a beautiful pearl gem on them, which Ghily said were from the Eastern Seas.

Kaleyna decided she liked the look after it was completed, and asked Ghily if she would come with her to her room to do her hair as well.

After the two left, I wrote a message in my mirror journal to Kaleyna and Rowzey. I wanted them to understand everything I have been thinking about, and seeing as there never seems time to talk to them both together, this would be best.

With my drop of blood I opened the mirror journal. I checked first to see if there were any new messages written from Rowzey or Kaleyna, but there was nothing new. So I took out the quill Rowzey had given me and wrote a message to them both.

Rowzey & Kaleyna,

I want to first thank you both for caring about me so much and sticking with me through everything. Tonight at the meeting I am planning on telling everyone that if I am going to lead and be Iryvalya's Bringer of Peace, then I need to start making the decisions that involve me.

I hope that I am going to make the right choices, and I ask that if either of you are concerned with what I choose, to let me know. Or if you don't want to say it around other people, write it in here. I know I do not know everything, and I know that I do not know how I am going to bring peace to Iryvalya, but I do know that I will do everything in my power to try.

I love you both very much, you are my spirit family, always and forever.
Love,
Ny

Shortly after I finished the note and hid my journal back in my bags along with the quill, there was a knock on my door. I walked over to the door and opened it. Standing in front of me was Baysil looking disheveled.

"Baysil, what's wrong?" I stepped aside as he walked in and closed the door behind him.

"I just got word back from the Satyr brothers, and it is not good."

I took a deep breath, preparing myself for the worst.

"They said there were a few Fairies still there, but not many. They found Miaarya. She was badly injured, both legs were broken and one of her arms. She told them she was left for dead. They were able to get her and the other Fairies to Xylonia, and Louv is going to help hide them and take care of them."

"What about the missing Fairies?"

"Miaarya believes that they were taken by the Elves to some location to the south. She said that she overheard a couple talking that they figured when you found out about them going to Cliffside, you would return to see what they did and then come save them," Baysil said, his brow furrowed with worry.

I paced back and forth for a few minutes, thinking about how I would love to just charge off and try to find the Fairies and save them, and then punish those who took and hurt them. But I had to use logic over my emotions on this. "Can we send out a group to at least look into where they took the Fairies?"

"Of course."

"Have them research the area, how many Elves there are, buildings, anything else we would need to know."

He nodded in approval. "I can get a group ready to leave right away."

"I would like them to wait until after the meeting. I want everyone who can be there to attend and provide their thoughts... Since you are here, Baysil, I want to let you know what the meeting is about. I am going to set up a trusted council of advisors, and because you have always done everything you can to help me, I would like you to be one of the advisors."

"I think the idea of advisors is a good choice, and it would be an honor to continue to serve you, Nyrieve," Baysil said with pride.

"I appreciate it. You have truly been someone I can count on and I trust that you have Iryvalya's best interests at heart."

There was another knock on the door. I looked at Baysil, questioning whether he knew who it was. He shook his head. I opened the door and Jyngy was standing there. She bowed her head for a moment and said, "In the next ten minutes, everyone will meet in the same location as where the feast was held. Is there anything else I can do for you before the meeting?"

"There is nothing I can think of right now. Thank you, Jyngy," I said sincerely.

"You are most welcome, Your Highness."

"You do not have to call me that. You can just call me Ny."

Baysil stood. "I know you do not feel you need the title, Ny, but I do think it is important to allow some people to at least address you like that in front of others. With your close friends, it is fine, but for those who do not know you, it would be wise to allow those who want to call you Highness the ability to do so. While you do not put much stock in titles, there are many Elf leaders who do."

I thought about it. He had a good point. If I wanted others to start respecting me as a leader, I needed to allow them to call me a leader in any way that would work and be appropriate.

"You are right, Baysil. Jyngy, when we are in private conversations, please feel free to call me Ny if you like," I said with a smile.

"It would be an honor, Ny," Jyngy said. "Now I must get going to make sure everything is ready for the meeting. If there is anything that you will need, just let me know." She bowed again and left the room, closing the door behind her.

"Do you know what you are going to say to everyone?" Baysil asked.

"I think so. I do not have anything written down, but I have a good idea of what I want to say. I am nervous though. I don't like speaking in front of people, but I guess that is something I am going to have to quickly get over." I forced out a chuckle.

"I think you are right," Baysil said with a halfhearted smile. "I think it is time we start heading down for the meeting then, don't you?"

"Yes, I do."

Baysil and I walked down the path through the different buildings and over the bridge to where everyone was already waiting for me on the other side.

"You can do this, Ny," he said, giving my shoulder a light squeeze.

"Thanks, Baysil." I took a deep breath and walked across the bridge to everyone waiting to hear what I had to say.

≈27≈

I STOOD BEFORE ALL THE DRAYKS, some I knew in Cliffside and others I had not even met yet. Standing there looking at all their faces, I found myself humbled that all of these people wanted peace for our world, and they believed that I was the bringer of that peace. Now I needed to show them I was ready to take on that role, and that I planned to do everything I could to fulfill the prophecy.

"Thank you all for allowing me time to speak with you," I started, trying to stop the quivering in my voice and to sound as confident as I should be. "It has been a real transition for me for these last several weeks. Back then, I thought I was an ordinary Fairy who would live out my life in Cliffside. I had dreams of doing great things, but never believed those things would happen. Now the opportunity to do something really amazing and important for Iryvalya is in front of me.

"I was not sure at first if I was the Bringer of Peace, let alone if I had the strength and moxie to handle the situation that stands before us. To those who have been striving for peace even longer than I have been alive, I am inspired by your honor and commitment. Many of you have done things to protect me and keep me safe over the years, intentional or not. Today I am able to stand here before all of you and say I am ready to repay the favor and begin to help us all achieve the peace that Iryvalya deserves.

"Peace and freedom are, sadly, not won by simply wanting them. They are won by fighting for them. Which is what we will need to do — be willing and prepared to fight, even to our death, for freedom and peace. I am willing to sacrifice myself for the peace and happiness of the people of Iryvalya.

"I know the prophecy talked of an Elf of mixed blood who would be the Bringer of Peace. The thing it might not have mentioned is that she did not and cannot do it alone. I need your help, and the help of everyone else in Iryvalya who wants freedom and peace. I do not for a moment pretend I know everything I need to know or have the abilities to win a fight yet, but that is why I am asking for everyone's help and insight.

"I am forming a trusted council of people I know will be honest and inform me of the things I need to know. I also would like you all to tell me at least three people you would feel comfortable with being on the council as well, that will represent you and what you think I need to know and be aware of.

"I will be calling this council the Nomydrac. As many of you may know, the Nomydrac was the name of the breed of dragons that used to protect the Leaf Tree before they died out. Those dragons were sacred and wanted nothing but to protect something we all greatly value, and that is what we will be doing, protecting the people of Iryvalya.

"I welcome any suggestions or ideas from any of you. Those who will be part of the Nomydrac, I want you to feel free to come to me with any ideas or suggestions, or tell me when you think I might be doing something wrong. I am the Bringer of Peace, but I know we are not just one person. We need to be able to depend on each other, and if there is someone who is not for the freedom and peace of Iryvalya, I want you to leave before dawn. This will be your last chance to leave without force or harm coming to you.

"As for those I would like to be part of the Nomydrac, I want at least one person from each race, as I believe every race should have representation. Those races who are not present, and that I do not know anyone from, we will find someone to represent them and their voices. Now, for those I have already chosen for the Nomydrac, those who represent different races and those whose advice I trust. I will simply call their name, and those who are here, I would like you to come join me. Kaleyna, Kylyan, Baysil, Prydos, Koyvean, Rowzey, Jyngy, Louvyordal, Knarfy, Relonya, Ghilyauna, Ayllac and Callya."

Once those I named joined me, I spoke again. "Now, no one who I have asked to be part of the Nomydrac has to join, but if you do, I would be forever appreciative."

"I will stand by your side until the end, Nyrieve," Baysil said.

"As will I," said Kaleyna.

"I will proudly fight beside you," Prydos added.

"Us too," the Pixies said in unison.

"It would be an honor, Your Highness," Jyngy said.

"Of course," Ghily said with a smile.

"I will be honored to represent the Satyrs," Knarfy said.

"You have my word, I will fight for freedom and peace," Relonya added.

Koyvean bowed down and said, "I will gladly represent the Death Elves."

Only one person had not responded yet—Kylyan. I turned to him to see if he was going to say anything. He turned towards me and said, "My lady, I am honored to be chosen for the Nomydrac, and I will do everything in my power to serve it honorably and truly."

I smiled at Kylyan and then looked amongst those I had so far chosen for the Nomydrac, and I knew I had chosen wisely. I looked back to the rest of the crowd watching and addressed them all once more. "Thank you all again for coming. As of now, we need to start training and preparing for whatever may lie ahead. I am going be discussing in depth with the rest of the Nomydrac and we will figure out how to get everything started. When we do, we will inform you all. If you have questions, suggestions or concerns, you may come to anyone in the Nomydrac to talk to us." I took a deep breath, taking the moment to appreciate all these people who were here for me and Iryvalya. I bowed down to everyone, stood back up straight and tall, and said "Volnyri!"

Everyone cheered back in unison, "Volnyri!"

CЯЮ

I spent a couple hours speaking to many of the people individually after announcing the Nomydrac members. Everyone was very positive and excited that we would no longer be forever in hiding, that we would be taking action somehow at least. After I finished speaking to everyone who wanted to talk to me, Baysil came and let me know that Jyngy's people had a meal set up for us back at the building we were staying in, and they would like me to come.

I thanked everyone who was still there chatting, and excused myself to go with Baysil back to our building. As we walked around the paths to the building, Baysil smiled at me. When I asked him why he was smiling, he said, "You have grown so much, Ny, in such a short time. I feel bad that you have to, but I am so very proud of you."

"Thanks, Baysil," I said, smiling back. "I couldn't have gotten to this point without you."

"You would have gotten here, Ny, maybe not the same way, but you are a determined Elf, and you would have gotten here somehow."

"Thank you."

"By the way, many of the Elves were talking about your new appearance."

"New appearance?"

"The earrings. The Elves noticed you did that, and the ones I heard talking all seemed to feel like you doing that was a sign of you officially declaring yourself one of them," he said to me. "I am not sure what made you and Kaleyna do it, but I think it was a very smart move."

"Good, I was hoping the pain of it would be worth it!" I said with a light laugh. "And it is true, for a while it was hard for me to realize I was not a Fairy, and I feel lately that I am an Elf. Not that I love the Fairies any less than I love Elves, of course."

"No one questions your loyalties, Ny. We know you are not loyal to just one race, you are loyal to the people of Iryvalya, and that is what the Bringer of Peace should be."

When we got back to the building, I was surprised to see the main room of the building transformed. There were hanging vines with crystals glowing all over them to light the room, and replacing the seating area were bunch of small tables, five to six chairs at each table. The tables were simply decorated with seashells and coral candles alongside the plates and goblets. Jyngy saw us walk in, hurried over to me, and told me she liked my speech and she thinks The Drayks here thought it was honest and they have faith in me. I thanked her for her kind words and for the dinner, as I was quite hungry from only eating some bread before giving the speech.

Kaleyna waved me over to a table with five chairs and smiled at me. I walked over and happily sat down. Kaleyna sat down next to me on the left, and Prydos to her left. I sat quietly just enjoying the two of them talking to each other. It felt calm and normal for a moment. Prydos was picking on Kaleyna for her complaints about how much piercing her ears hurt when I heard someone come and stand behind me. I looked to Kaleyna and she gave me a wicked little smirk.

"Hello, Kylyan," I said confidently, knowing he had to be why Kaleyna smiled like that.

"Hello, my lady," Kylyan said, sounding surprised.

"Won't you join us?" I asked, not wanting to turn around. I was trying to appear sure of myself.

"It would be my pleasure," he said, stepping to my right and sitting down.

"How is your hand doing, Kylyan?" Prydos asked.

Kylyan stretched out his hand in front of himself and winced a little. "It is doing well. I figure if I can move it, it wasn't much of an injury."

Kylyan and Prydos continued into a conversation regarding injuries each of them had had in the past. While I was slightly interested in listening to them compare who was injured more, I was watching those moving around the room bringing food out to everyone and those sitting and talking at the tables. I could see Jyngy talking to Baysil. They seemed to be having a good conversation, as there were frequently smiles and laughter. Koyvean was sitting and talking to a male Elf whose name escaped me, though I remember meeting him at the feast, and also seeing him with Koyvean when Kylyan took me to get the viewing crystal made.

Then Rowzey walked towards our table and smiled at me as she got stopped by Ghily to talk. Rowzey nodded at me, letting me know she'd be over shortly and would hopefully sit with us. I looked over to Kaleyna and noticed that she was smiling at me. "What, Kal?"

"I was just thinking how much our lives have changed in such a short time."

"They definitely have, and I get the feeling there are more changes still to come."

"Have you decided yet what is going to happen with Jehryps?" she asked.

"Honestly I am not sure what should happen," I said to her, realizing I hadn't had a chance to tell her about Cliffside. "He was the one who informed the Elves to come to Cliffside, and Baysil told me tonight that Miaarya was badly injured and many of the Fairies were taken."

"Oh no," Kal said with a look of sadness on her face and the threat of tears in her eyes.

"Jehryps needs to be held responsible for his actions, Kal, but I do not know what should be done to him. His choices have caused so many people to be hurt, taken, and who knows what else."

"And do not forget what he did to you," Prydos added to our conversation.

"I haven't forgotten," I said quietly as an image of him grabbing me and pushing me against the wall flashed through my mind. A chill rand down my back and I realized again how close he had come.

"Yous okay?" Rowzey asked, sitting down next to Kylyan.

I snapped back to reality and smiled at Rowzey. "Yes, I am fine, Rowzey. How are you doing?"

"I's fine," she said with a smile. "I's am so proud of yous and Kaleyna for going through piercing yous ears."

"Thanks, but I am glad it is something I only had to do once," Kaleyna said to Rowzey with a light laugh.

"Perhaps. There are many Elves who have more than one in each ear," Prydos said with a smile.

"Why would anyone get more than one?" Kaleyna asked.

"Some get new ones when something big happens, like they learn a new power or like when they get tyed to someone," Prydos said.

"Okay, so we are good for a while then!" I laughed.

"You never know, you could always learn a new power," Prydos joked.

"It would have to be a pretty amazing power for me to want more holes in my ears," Kaleyna said.

Dinner was brought in for everyone, a decent assortment of chicken and meats from the Eastern Sea, vegetables and breads. After the dinner was finished, a dessert was brought out to everyone, something I had never tried before—fresh fruit covered in a hardened chocolate shell. It was so delicious and sweet, I drank a few goblets of water while enjoying them.

When everyone started to head to their rooms for the night, I realized I wasn't as tired as I thought I would be. I really wanted to soak in hot water, but did not want to soak in the hot spring room where Jehryps attacked me. I asked Kylyan if there was another hot spring room like that, and he said there was something even better. Prydos and Kaleyna asked if they could join us, so we all went to our rooms to change into some clothes we could wear in the water.

We met up outside the building like Kylyan said. He had us walk along the shore inside the cave. Once we got near the edge where the water reached, I noticed there was a ledge near the shore, and what looked like steps.

"Kylyan, where are we going?" I asked, a little nervous.

"You will see shortly."

As we walked along the ledge in the water farther away from the shore area, there was a slight shift in the cave wall. There was a hidden entrance that you could not see from the shore. We walked through it, and into a small dark pathway with seashells in the wall filled with oil that Kylyan lit as we walked.

Once we got to the end of the pathway, we were again walking on a sandy shore. When Kylyan moved aside, I could see a large hot spring. It had to be about three times bigger than the one in Xylonia, and it glowed a bright yellowish-green color. Kaleyna and Prydos rushed past me, tossing their robes to the ground, and jumped in splashing each other. It wasn't long until all four of us were in the amazingly warm water and having fun. It felt great to laugh and splash each other for a bit without having the eyes of everyone on me.

After a while, things calmed down and Kaleyna and Prydos ended up snuggling with each other and talking about their dreams of the future. Kylyan and I went to the other side away from them to give them some privacy.

After sitting quietly together, I turned to Kylyan. "Tell me about yourself, Kylyan."

"What would you like to know, my lady?"

"First, why do you keep calling me my lady?"

"Does it offend you?"

"No, I just was wondering."

"Because I was raised to give those I fight for the respect they deserve, and I could sense that you are not one to enjoy formal titles, such as Your Highness. I thought my lady would be a nice middle ground."

"You are correct, I am just not very comfortable with the special titles yet, but the 'my lady' doesn't make me feel uncomfortable."

"I am glad to hear that. What else did you want to know?"

"Where did you grow up?" I asked. "What do you like to do when you are not busy saving me from falling or being attacked? Whatever else you want to tell me."

"I grew up mostly in the southwest of Iryvalya on a small island with my parents. We moved around a lot because, like you, I am a mixed Elf."

"You are?" I asked, surprised.

"Yes. I do not tell many people, because I do not want my parents to be in any danger. They are actually with another Rebel group somewhere in the southern part of Iryvalya."

"It had to be hard growing up and having to hide."

"It wasn't easy, but my parents were always strong and told me that there is no reason that we need to be divided. They also told me many times that they were glad I was a boy, because they knew if I had been a girl, I could have been the Bringer of Peace, and they knew they would have had to give me up."

"Like my parents had to do."

"I can't imagine how hard that had to be for them, or you not knowing why your parents gave you up," he said softly.

"It was hard when I was young, and there are days where it still can hurt, but at least now I know why, and I know it was done to protect me and not hurt me."

"I can understand that. But to answer your other question, other than saving you, which I have enjoyed doing, I enjoy riding my horse and I like to cook also."

"Cook?"

"Yes, my mother taught me how to cook, and I helped a lot with the cooks we had with the different Rebel groups until I was old enough to actually fight or do other things to help."

We talked for at least an hour, mostly about how we grew up and what kinds of food we liked. We all decided it was time to head back, and I could feel my eyes getting heavier. The four of us walked back to our building, and after Kaleyna and Prydos went into their room, Kylyan stood next to me outside my door.

I opened my door and turned to Kylyan. "I just want to thank you again for everything today. I appreciate it more than I can say."

"If you need anything, just come get me or yell and I will hear you," Kylyan said as he took my hand in his and laid a gentle kiss on the top. "Goodnight, my lady."

"Goodnight, Kylyan," I said and went inside my room, softly closing the door. I changed into a sleeping gown and climbed into my bed. I lay there thinking about how I had made a major decision that would affect so many of us. As I drifted off to sleep, I could only hope I had made the right one.

᚜28᚛

THE MORNING AFTER MY SPEECH, we found that three people had packed their things and left in the night—two female Elves and a male Elf. Jyngy said she had been watching two of them, but the third one had surprised her. She told me the two Elves who she had been watching were named Kryvon and Sunorlyna, and the one she was surprised with was Eldreyva.

We were not worried about those who left, because right after my speech, Marselyus placed a spell over the entrance to the cave. Once they left the cave, they would have about an hour before the spell would start to work, and when it did, they would remember who they were and why they were leaving, but would have no idea where they had been. We knew they would have a general idea, as they would only be an hour out, but they would not remember the cave or the waterfall. One of the perks Marselyus added was that those who left would not remember the details of my speech, only that I gave one. It was definitely an impressive spell.

Over the course of almost four weeks, we had many meetings and several different training sessions. In the meetings, we had some of The Drayks from the south of Iryvalya come up, and they picked two representatives for the Nomydrac. They chose Balthyza, a male former Pyrothian Elf, and Xetyna, a female former Lumaryia Elf. Both seemed like very honest and likeable Elves. The Elves from Mylterias Cove had decided they only wanted to appoint one more to represent them, as they felt Jyngy was a perfect choice already. The second person they chose for the Nomydrac was Yorsot. He was a former Lumaryia Elf who came across very quiet and reserved.

The Nomydrac discussed at great lengths what should be done with Jehryps, and we had yet to reach an agreed upon decision. If one was not mutually agreed upon soon, what we would do with him would be up to me alone. He had been locked up in a building since his attack on me. He had received medical care and food, but nothing else. I was told he asked for me to come talk to him many times, however I did not think there was anything more I wished to hear from him.

I had been plagued with nightmares every night for a couple weeks about what happened between Jehryps and myself. While I knew Kylyan stopped him, my nightmares sometimes went further than what really happened. I talked to Kaleyna about it each time, and she helped me get a better handle on realizing that what he did was not my fault. The nightmares had not fully subsided, but now I had them only once a week at the most, so it was at least an improvement.

Baysil received word back from Louv that Miaarya and the other Fairies were healing well in Xylonia and they were welcome to stay with them as long as they wanted or needed. Louv also mentioned that Miaarya seemed to be in a big rush to heal and join up with us out here. The Satyr brothers lost the trail of the Elves who attacked Cliffside and took a bunch of the Fairies so, sadly, our efforts to free the taken Fairies were on hold.

Kylyan was training me in hand to hand combat. Prydos was helping me with improving my wind power, as he said it is very similar to his power with water. Baysil was actually teaching me and Kaleyna sword fighting. I never in my life thought I would ever know how to wield a sword with such ease. Even Koyvean was showing me how to shoot a bow and arrow. I was not great at that yet, but at least I had a general knowledge. Kaleyna, however, quickly picked up on the bow. She was able to hit her targets every time. I joked and told her that she would be our designated hunter.

Rowzey was busy helping Iclyn and Lydorea with something. They had not had much time to do more than share meals with everyone. I kept wondering if it was regarding Clyr, but I did not dare ask, in case someone overheard me.

Everyone had taken to calling me "Your Highness" now. Even Kaleyna and Rowzey said it to me when we were not alone. I understood the reasoning for doing it, but I still did not feel comfortable with it. It made me wonder if my mother was called by a title like that, and if so, did she enjoy it?

My thoughts were interrupted by a soft rapping on my door. "Come in."

Ghily opened the door and popped her head inside, smiling. "Jyngy asked me to come and get you. She said for you to meet her in her building."

"Thanks, Ghily, I will head right over there," I said, getting off of my bed.

I headed over to Jyngy's building, the one we first met her in. I went inside the first door, walked over to the next door and knocked.

"Please come in," Jyngy responded.

I opened the door and stepped inside. Jyngy was sitting on one of the chairs, and also in the room were Baysil, Kylyan, Kaleyna, Prydos and Koyvean.

"Hello, everyone," I said, surprised, seeing that everyone sat so that the only open seat was next to Kylyan.

"Ny, I am sorry to call a meeting on such short notice, but something has come up," Jyngy said.

"What happened?" I asked.

"One of Jehryps's guards had checked on him and said they noticed his wrist was bleeding. He had somehow managed to break off a piece of seashell and used it to try to kill himself," Jyngy said. "We have been able to stop the bleeding and he is now under a sleeping charm so he can't try anything right now. The thing is, we need to decide what is to be done with him and we need to figure it out now."

"The Nomydrac cannot decide on what to do, imprison him someplace or put him to death," I said flatly. "I knew it would come to me to decide what should happen, but to be honest, I am torn. I do not see any good coming of either option. I have been thinking about this, and I think that there might be an alternative idea."

"What would that be?" Baysil asked.

"I remember reading that Death Elves can sometimes possess the power to remove memory. Is that true, Koyvean?"

"Yes, I know of one who has the power to drain away memories," she said with a curious look on her face.

"Do you think it would be possible to remove all of Jehryps's personal memories? He would know basic things like how to walk and eat, but nothing personal?"

"It would be tricky, but I believe that can be done."

"Then, my idea is to have his memories drained away, and he can be sent back to Cliffside to help rebuild it and protect it."

"I think it is a good idea, but risky as well," Kaleyna said. "What if he remembers and tries to destroy Cliffside instead?"

"Do we want to vote on this?" Jyngy asked everyone.

"No, the Nomydrac could not decide," Baysil said simply. "It is now up to Nyrieve to make the final decision."

"If that is what Nyrieve thinks is best," Jyngy said, and I nodded to her. "Then that is what we will do. Koyvean, can you set it up to have Jehryps's memory drained?"

"It will be done before dawn," Koyvean answered.

"That was the only thing we needed to meet about," Jyngy said. "I'm sorry to have interrupted anything you were all doing."

With that, everyone got up and left the building. I walked with Kaleyna and Kylyan back to our building, when Kylyan asked if he could talk to me for a moment in private.

I wondered if he wanted to talk to me about our training. Things had been getting more intense with what he was teaching me. We had playful banter in talking, but I just kept thinking about how I would love to feel those soft lips he kept kissing my hand with against my lips. But every time I tried to talk to him about it, something would get in the way. I opened my door and stepped inside, allowing Kylyan to come in. I then closed the door for privacy and turned around to see Kylyan right in front of me.

Kylyan pulled me to him. I could feel the lengths of our bodies pressed together. His lips were so close to mine, I could feel the heat of his breath on my lips. I was trembling. All of my nerve endings felt like they were supercharged and I could feel each little movement, every breath I took raising my chest and lowering it. He traced his left hand through my hair and down my right cheek. Everywhere his fingers touched tingled, making me tremble even more. Everything in me wanted to cross that tiny gap between us and feel his warm lips on mine and run my fingers through his hair as he held me tightly against him. My heart was beating harder and faster with every moment that passed. I was looking into his eyes, trying to read them and know what it was he wanted, and to figure out if this is what I really wanted. Abruptly, Kylyan pulled back from me, looking at me as if trying to figure out what just happened. After he pulled away, I could feel the lack of his warmth against me, and all I felt was a deep longing to have that back next to me.

"Why did you pull away," I asked in breathless whisper, my heart still pounding in my chest.

"Because I do not want this to be something we would both regret. I truly care for you, Ny, but I do not want to be a distraction for you or end up hurting you." He looked as pained by this as I felt.

I opened my mouth to speak, and Kylyan gently put his warm fingers to my lips. "Wait... don't say anything. I am sorry, I have been holding back for a while, and seeing you tonight, just walking and smiling with Kaleyna, I don't know... I just wanted so much to kiss your full lips. We have been flirting back and forth for a while now, and I do not feel like it is only me who is interested, but my coming into your room like this and hoping to kiss you wasn't right. I am sorry for that."

He took my hands in his, and while looking me in the eyes, he lifted my hands to his lips and gently pressed a kiss into the palms of my hands. He softly let my hands drop away from his, and looked at me and smiled. Then he turned, opened my door and left my room, letting the door close behind him.

I couldn't believe what just almost happened. I wanted to kiss him, and yet I didn't know if it was the right thing to do. I quickly changed out of my leathers and into simple cloth pants and a shirt so I could go for a walk and think about the things I want and what I need to do moving forward.

I walked between the buildings for a while and then along the shore inside the cave. After about an hour, I stopped and sat by the water. I could faintly hear the waves outside the cave lapping against the rocks. It was a relaxing sound, and I found myself noticing little ripples dancing on the water. As I looked closer, I could see that someone was under the water.

I quickly jumped up and ran into the water to help whoever it was out there. I swam out to the area where I saw the person, but could not see them anymore. I dived down and looked to see if I could find anyone. I couldn't see anything. I dived down a few more times and still could not find anyone. I swam back to the shore to look for the person.

I could not see anyone out in the deeper water, but someone sat down the shore up to their waist in the water. I ran over to them. "I am sorry to bother you, but have you seen anyone else out in the water? I thought I saw someone under the water out that way." I pointed in the direction I saw the person.

"No, I am the only one who has been swimming in here tonight," the male voice said. I looked down and realized that he did not have legs, he had a tail. He was a merman.

"Oh, I am sorry, I thought you were in trouble out there."

"It is fine, Your Highness, I appreciate your concern," he said with a bright smile. "My name is Sudryl."

I reached down to shake his hand. "It is pleasure to meet you."

"The pleasure is mine," Sudryl said. "Would you care to sit with me for a bit? I can move closer to the shore if you would like to sit there to talk."

"Thank you, I would enjoy that." I walked back towards the shore and sat down as far out as I could with the water just above my waist.

Sudryl scooted back towards me and I saw he had very long, wavy hair. It went all the way down his back. It was a beautiful shades of blue and green, colors only seen in the seas. He had tan skin, showing he spent a lot of time out in the sun. His eyes were the same shades of blue and green as his hair, framed by pale yellow eyebrows. While he had a normal nose, along the sides of the bridge he had two small gills, which I guessed was what let him breath underwater. His tail was bright teal, quite long, and the scales were really shiny.

"I am sorry if I scared you, Your Highness, I just had finished dropping off a message for Jyngy and decided to swim about for a bit."

"Oh, please don't worry about it, I am just glad you were fine," I said. "To be honest, I have never met a merman before, and I did not know there were any here in Mylterias Cove."

"We are all over the place, even some up near Cliffside, but we do not like to come to land much if we don't have to. Things are much simpler under the water than above."

"I can imagine," I said. "Is there a reason I haven't met any of you yet?"

"We do not like to take sides among those on land. We are usually used as personal counsel, for when going through struggles or trying to decide what you truly feel."

"How do you help them know how they feel?"

"I am not sure how much you know about merpeople, but we can hear it when someone's heart is happy or sad or something else."

"I was not aware of that," I said, surprised. "That is an amazing power, though I imagine difficult as well."

"It is both. It is great to feel some things, but also sad and even disturbing at times," Sudryl said. "Can I ask you something, Your Highness?"

"Sure," I said, a little leery.

"Can you tell me why your heart sounds happy and also scared at the same time?"

"Oh," I said, completely taken by surprise. "I uhm… I am just trying to figure some things out and I have a lot I am responsible for right now."

"You do not know me, so I can understand if you do not wish to talk about it," he said, "but as a piece of advice from someone who has felt a lot of love and heartbreak from others, I want you to know that while I am not sure what kind of love I feel coming from your heart, I can tell you it is pure and true."

That took me by surprise. I did not know what to say. It was good to know the love was pure, but who was it for? Kylyan, Kaleyna, Rowzey, or even Iryvalya? I smiled at Sudryl and said, "Thank you, I appreciate that."

"I have to get going, before anyone starts to worry about me."

"It was very nice meeting you."

"It was nice meeting you too, Your Highness. And here," he said, handing me a small seashell, "if you ever need me, just place this in the sea and it will echo to me. I will come. It may take a while swimming, but I will come."

"Thank you, Sudryl, but why would you give me this if you do not take sides?"

"Because we believe in you, Nyrieve, and we believe you will bring peace back to Iryvalya," he said, and then quickly swam out to the middle of the water and dived down deep, disappearing beneath the waters.

I sat by the water for a while longer, wondering how people who do not even know me could believe in me so much and if I would be able to live up to their expectations. I know I am the Bringer of Peace, I am the one who is supposed to bring peace to Iryvalya, I just hope I have it in me to do just that.

☙29❧

WHEN I WOKE UP THE NEXT morning, I still had the small seashell in my hand. I set it in my bag next to the bed so I wouldn't lose it. I couldn't tell what time it was, being inside the cave, so to be safe I got dressed in my older worn brown leathers to go for another walk.

I walked along the shore again, and then back. I was trying to figure out Kylyan and myself. After spending a lot of time together since I arrived here, I couldn't deny that I had feelings for him. He is kind but also honest. When we trained, he was truthful to me if I wasn't doing well. He wanted me to learn how to protect myself, and wasn't afraid of upsetting me while doing it. He knew in the end I would be safer because of it.

At first, when he told me I was wrong or that I was being lazy, I would get mad and thought he must really not like me at all. It wasn't until we had a few practice fights with other Elves that I realized he had been training me to be the best I could. I remember getting knocked down pretty good a few times and having the sword knocked from my hands, which Baysil got after me for, but the thing I remembered when doing these practice fights was to always get back up. That is what Kylyan taught me, to always get back up and never give up. No matter how many bruises or cuts I had, I had to always get back up. Giving up is not an option anymore.

After walking and thinking about it, there was only one fear I had regarding a deeper relationship with Kylyan. I was worried that if anyone from either Elf Klayn knew about my relationship with him, he could be in more danger than he already was with being a Rebel. How could I live with myself if I brought him to greater harm just because I cared deeply for him?

"Ny?" Rowzey asked, startling me from my thoughts.

I spun around to face her. "Rowzey, are you okay?"

"I's was about to ask yous the same question."

"I'm fine," I said, lying to her.

"No yous not," she said. "Come with me, Ny. I's would like to sit and talk to yous a bit."

We walked down a path away from the shore, and there were some big rocks that we walked between. After a bunch of twists and turns we came into a small opening. There were some rocks in the middle, which looked old and worn, like people had been using this area to gather in for a long time.

"How did you find this place, Rowzey? I never noticed the entrance area whenever I walked by."

"I's didn't either. The Pixies found it and showed me it. They often see what we's can't."

"What did you want to talk to me about, Rowzey?" I sat down on one of the worn rocks across from her.

"I's promised yous and yous parents I's would always watch out for yous, but I's need to know that yous are okay."

"I am fine, Rowzey, just... nervous and a bit scared."

"Yous would be a fool not to be," she chucked. "So what all is yous worrying about?"

"How I am supposed to lead everyone, Rowzey? I know that the Elf Klayns must be aware of me by now, and that they will likely be searching and possibly harming others to get to me. I need to decide how to move forward, and I know the first move I make needs to be an act of peace. I just have no idea how to do it."

"As I's always say, Ny, yous cannot begin to decide to make the sauce until yous check and see if yous have all the right ingredients available. Once yous check if everything is there, only then can yous start to make the sauce, otherwise yous have to put it all back and figure out another sauce to make."

I thought about what Rowzey said. She always talks about the sauce, but it really means something much deeper.

"That's it!" I exclaimed.

"What's it?" Rowzey asked with a smile.

"I need to try to get the two Elf Klayns to meet with me first. I will somehow have to ask the leaders or representatives of the Pyrothian and Lumaryia Elves to meet with me and some of the Nomydrac. Even if it does not end with them agreeing to peace, we will at least have started showing what is important to us, peace and freedom."

"Yous have a wonderful idea, Ny." Rowzey said. "I's knew you could figure out what to do."

"Thanks, Rowzey, but it was actually your idea, and you already knew that," I said with a big smile on my face.

"I knew no such thing," Rowzey said lightly. Then her look became serious. "Yous need to decide what yous are going to do about Kyl."

I knew she meant Kylyan, she could not say his full name. My smile faded away as I asked, "What do you mean?"

"Ny, yous know that Elf cares about yous, and I's know yous be caring about that Elf."

"Yes, I do care for him," I said quietly, not sure where she was going with this.

"Then that is what yous need to tell him."

"I don't want him to get hurt, Rowzey," I said. "If he gets hurt because he was with me…"

"That is his choice, Ny," Rowzey said. "Yous do not get to make the choices for Kyl. Yous need to remember something. Yous cannot control what anyone else does, only what yous do. And if yous keep it from him that yous care about him, yous are trying to make the choice for him. Yous are better than that, yous know it is wrong to lie and yous can see what lies and trying to control others does to people. Iryvalya is in this mess because of people who wanting to make choices for others. Yous are not like them, and yous will never be like them."

"I know," I said softly. "The only reason I hesitate to tell him how I feel is because I do not want him to get hurt. I will talk to him, and I will be honest with him about how I feel and my concerns."

Rowzey leaned over and gave me a big hug, holding me tightly to her. "Yous and Kal make me so proud, yous know that?"

"We both want to make you proud, Rowzey."

"Yous do, and I's know you always will."

After our talk, I decided to go talk to Kylyan and tell him the truth of how I felt. Before I reached our building, I saw Jyngy outside, and she smiled and walked to meet me.

"Hello, Jyngy. How are you doing?"

"I am great, Your Highness," she responded. "I just wanted to come and tell you some good news."

"What is that?"

"It appears that Koyvean's friend was able to successfully remove Jehryps's memories," Jyngy said.

"That is fantastic news," I responded, happy to know he shouldn't have memories that would likely lead to him hurting me or others. "How is he handling not having real memories?"

"He keeps asking why he doesn't remember, so I gave him a small story to try to explain it. I told him that someone found him along the beach and he had a big cut on his head where it looked like he might have hit it against the rocks," she said. "I told him that he slept for a long time, and that in his sleep, he said a couple times, 'I am Jehryps.'"

"And he believed it?"

"He seems to, except he said he doesn't feel like that is his name, but he is comfortable with us calling him that."

"I guess that is good at least. Did Koyvean's friend say if there could be any side effects or anything we should be aware of?"

"He did say that he might recognize faces, but he will not know why or where he has seen them. He said it has something to do with how a person's image can be imprinted into our spirit, and that he cannot remove that."

"Has he recognized anyone yet?"

"Not as of yet, but he has not seen anyone he would have known in Cliffside."

"Okay, that is good to know," I said. "I appreciate you coming to tell me."

"My pleasure, Your Highness," Jyngy said with a smile. "Let me know if you need anything."

"Actually... I do need something."

"What can I do for you?"

"Can you please ask the members of the Nomydrac to meet tomorrow morning somewhere? I need to take care of some things today, and I would be very appreciative if you could set up a place and ask everyone."

"Of course, I will get it all taken care of, and I'll let you know where it will be."

"Thank you, Jyngy. I appreciate everything you have done for Iryvalya."

She smiled, gave a small bow, and simply said, "Volnyri," before she turned and left.

I continued to my building and went inside. Before I talk to Kylyan, I wanted to freshen up and try to look a little nicer. Ghily was leaving Kaleyna's room when she saw me. "Hello, Ny," she said.

"Hello, Ghily. Is Kaleyna in her room?"

"Yes, she asked me to bring her a different shade of makeup that I was telling her about. I guess she and Prydos were going to try to get a viewing crystal made as well."

"That is wonderful for them," I said, truly happy for my best friend, knowing that if all went well tonight, perhaps that would be me also. "I need to ask you a favor."

"Of course, Ny."

I had her come into my room so we could talk in private. I told her that I wanted to have a nice private dinner with Kylyan and I wanted to know if she could help me get ready and maybe have a nice meal sent to my room later for us. She said she'd be happy to help and had a huge smile on her face.

She left for a few moments to get something different for me to wear and also to request the food from the cooks. When she got back, she had a beautiful flowing gown. It was much simpler than the one I wore at the feast, but it was still just as beautiful and seemed more relaxed and simpler, like me. The dress went to the floor, but was just short enough so I wouldn't trip. It was a beautiful dark orange color, a slightly darker version of the color of Kylyan's shirt the night of the feast. It was layered in the softer thin silks and in a gauzy material in deep rich purples that faded towards the bottom of the skirts. It cinched just below my chest with a beautiful pearl belt that wrapped around me. This also had straps over my shoulders covering my one marking. Lightly draped over the shoulders was some of the gauzy material to wrap around me.

Once Ghily fixed my hair and makeup, she helped me into my beautiful dress. There were little silk slippers in the orange for me to wear. When we were done, I looked into the looking glass that was now permanently in my room, and I couldn't believe how soft and pretty I looked. Ghily had my hair twisted up with some of my hair in braids that wrapped around my head like a crown of sorts.

"Are you sure this isn't a little too much just for dinner in my room?"

"No, I think you look perfect," she said with a smile. "If you are ready, I can go get Kylyan for you?"

"Thank you. That would be lovely," I said, starting to get nervous as I dabbed a little of my perfume on.

Ghily left my room, and my heart fluttered. I was getting more nervous, knowing I needed to tell Kylyan the truth. My door opened, and I turned my face it, only to suddenly feel worried. Ghily was standing at the door with a frown on her face.

"I am sorry, Ny, but Kylyan is not in his room. When I asked around for him, I was told he was dining with some of his friends."

"Oh, it's okay Ghily. He did not know I was planning this, so it is my fault. I should have checked with him sooner," I said, feeling stupid for getting all dressed up without having asked him to join me.

"I have even more bad news," Ghily said.

"What is that?"

"Jyngy saw me and asked for me to have you meet her. She said it is very important. She wants me to take you up to the old lift that was used long ago when there was a castle on top of the waterfall. It still works, but no one ever uses it."

"Okay, let me change and I will go with you."

"There is no time to change. We have to go right now, Ny. What you're wearing will be fine. Just grab your cloak to make sure the water doesn't splash you too much and get it wet," Ghily said, pulling me out the door.

I followed Ghily down some paths I had never taken before near the entrance of the cave. We walked around a big rock wall, and hidden behind it was a lift. There was someone waiting at the top and the bottom to help pull the lift up to the top ledge. I looked at Ghily a bit nervously and she said it was safe and she had taken it before. The lift itself was a wooden platform that looked as if it had once been beautifully carved and decorated, but now it just looked old and worn.

I figured Jyngy wanted me to come and see the place for the meeting tomorrow, to make sure it'd be fine, as she always wanted to make sure I approved of things. When we reached the top, Ghily got off first and offered me her hand to step onto the ledge. We walked across the ledge towards an opening to the cave. I was surprised to see the flickering of a fire on the cave walls coming from outside.

When I rounded the corner to this exit, Kylyan, Kaleyna and Prydos all stood there dressed up similar to me. Kaleyna was in a dress like mine, but in a soft light pink color. The men were wearing dark-colored cloth pants and nice button-up shirts. They were all outside just smiling at me. Kylyan walked over towards me and turned to Ghily. "Thank you for getting Nyrieve up here."

"It was my pleasure. I will leave you all alone to enjoy your evening," Ghily said, sounding full of joy.

"I am confused," I said to Kylyan.

He took my hand in his. "I wanted us to have a nice dinner with our friends, and I wanted it to be a surprise. I know you haven't been outside at all since coming to Mylterias Cove."

I took a moment and looked in front of me, beyond my friends, and realized there were a couple fires burning to keep it warm and there was a table with chairs set up with a bunch of candles lighting it all. There was also a large blanket laid out on the ground with tons of soft-looking oversized pillows.

"How did you do all this?" I asked.

"I have my ways, Ny," he said with a smile as he took my cloak from me. With the fires lit, there was no need.

"Kylyan told us that he thought you could use a night with friends to relax a little and unwind," Kaleyna said happily. "It has been too long since we did anything fun, and I do not think we will have many more semi-warm evenings like this, as the harvest season is almost over now."

"And you know I could never turn down an evening with Kaleyna and you two," Prydos said.

"Thank you all for this. It is really a surprise and... I love it," I said, trying to not get emotional at how lucky I was to have such wonderful friends.

As Kylyan walked me further out, I could see we were inside the ruins of a beautiful castle. There were walls up on only two sides, the side facing the cave and the side to the west. Above us was a beautiful yet destroyed rotunda, which looked like it once had beautiful paintings on the walls. There were still ornate carvings in the pillars leading to the top of the broken rotunda, and I could see the stars above through all the broken walls and ceiling. There was a light blue cast to everything. The Rydison moon must be covering the Northern Sun, but from the way the walls were, I couldn't see it.

Before dinner, Kylyan arranged for another viewing crystal to be made of the four of us standing together. I stood with Kaleyna in the middle, Kylyan to my right and Prydos to Kaleyna's left. Once they were made, I was given one and the other was given to Kaleyna.

We sat down at the beautifully decorated table and Kylyan poured some water into the goblet in front of me. I took a drink and smiled. "Who told you I liked Peayalt?"

"While you have been busy leading The Drayks, I took some time to talk to Kaleyna and Rowzey to find out some of the things you like."

I just smiled at him and enjoyed the refreshing Peayalt. Some of the cook staff came out with trays of food. There was pasta covered in what had to be some of Rowzey's sauce, some pulled chicken in a red sticky-looking sauce, and now I wondered if Rowzey made all the food. We each took a bit of everything. I first tasted the pasta, and it was Rowzey's sauce. It had been in Cliffside that I last enjoyed her sauce, almost a whole season.

I decided I would try the chicken. I took one bite and I knew it was not Rowzey's. It was good like hers, but more spicy and much less sweet. "Wow, this chicken is amazing. I need to tell the cook it is the best I've ever had."

"You just did," Prydos said, laughing.

"What do you mean?"

"Kylyan is the one who made the chicken, Ny," Kaleyna informed me.

"I remember you saying you like to cook, but you never mentioned how great you were at it."

"My father had been one of the top cooks for the Elves, and he loved making food for me and my mother. He also enjoyed teaching me all his different recipes, and I always enjoyed getting to spend time with him in the kitchen," Kylyan said.

"It is delicious," I said. "Thank you for making it."

"It was my pleasure. I enjoy it when I can cook and not have to worry about anything else."

We spent the rest of the dinner talking and laughing about different silly stories about how we all grew up. I learned a lot more about Kylyan and Prydos, making me think even more highly of them both. Once we had filled ourselves on dessert, we made our way to the blanket and pillows to sit and look up at all the stars. I could not remember ever seeing so many before in my life. It was just beautiful, and the faint sound of the waterfall made it feel perfect.

Everyone chatted off and on about seeing a shooting star or what symbols we could make out of the star patterns. After an hour or so, Prydos said he was getting tired, so he and Kaleyna excused themselves, leaving Kylyan and me alone watching the stars. After a while of sitting in silence, Kylyan asked me if I wanted to walk around and see some of the ruins. He had been through them often and said there were some other great views.

"What happened to this castle?"

"It was destroyed during the Elf wars; however, it was destroyed by the owners."

"Why would they do that?"

"Because, the people who owned this place were of both Klayns, and they knew of the hidden cave below. So they figured to keep the cave hidden, and offer a place where people could hide, they destroyed their home to make it look like the Elves did it."

"I am guessing it worked."

"It did most of the time. There has always been a tracker here and there who gets curious and checks it out, but they usually never make it past the traps or charms set in place."

We quietly walked through broken hallways and rooms to see different exposed views of the mountains and the waterfall a bit. Kylyan led me to a spiral staircase that went up to what would have been a watchtower long ago. Kylyan kept in front of me and held my hand, making sure I was careful with each step.

I could not imagine how hard it must have been for the owners to destroy such a beautiful home. All the small details that you could still see showed me that someone really loved this place at one time.

When we reached the top of the tower, I noticed the roof was completely gone and over half of the walls were destroyed as well. I could see the Rydison Moon easily from here, but it seemed smaller being further away from Cliffside. Kylyan led me to one wall that had broken down to about the height of my waist and had me look off to the east.

The view was breathtaking. I could see the Eastern Sea and the reflection of the stars twinkling off of the water.

"Oh, Kylyan, this is so beautiful. I can imagine living right here in this spot."

"That was my thought as well the first time I stood here looking at the Eastern Sea," he said, standing behind me looking out over the sea.

I turned to face Kylyan. He was right in front of me, causing me to let out a small gasp of surprise. "Kylyan, I want to thank you for tonight. This really has been a magycal evening."

"I am happy you have enjoyed it."

"I have also thought a lot about last night and what you said. And I have decided that I need to be honest with you about how I feel."

"Oh, do I want to know how you feel?"

I smiled up at him, went up on my tiptoes to reach him, and wrapped my arms around his neck while looking into his eyes. His hands lightly touched the sides of my waist, helping me keep my balance. My heart fluttered and I knew in every bit of my being that I did care deeply about him.

I closed my eyes and leaned in enough to cross the small distance between us. His warm lips pressed against mine, so soft and tender. I felt the warmth of his body against me as he pulled me a bit closer and lifted me up enough to be able to kiss him with ease.

The wind swirled around us as we kissed, and I could feel both of our hearts beating against each other. It felt like a magycal current was running through me and into Kylyan and then back again to me.

The kiss felt like it lasted for hours, and when we finally pulled apart and looked into each other's eyes, Kylyan had a soft and sweet smile on his face.

"Ny, don't tell me that you are not the least bit interested in me now."

"Kylyan, to be honest, I thought it might have been best to have said that, to try to keep you safe, but that is not my choice to make. While I do not know where this will take us, I do care very much about you, and I would like to spend more time with you learning more."

"And I care very much for you, Ny. You are so different and similar to me at the same time. I know it is rather sudden, but I remember my mother telling me as a child that when soul mates find each other, they just know and nothing can or should keep them apart."

"You are such a good and sweet man, Kylyan," I said, running my fingers through his soft hair.

"Tell me something, Ny. Did you mean to have the wind swirl around us?"

"What are you talking about?"

"Do you feel any breeze at all right now?" he asked with a smile.

"No, I don't actually," I said, surprised.

"And there hasn't been one all night; it has been calm. You are the one who created that wind that swirled around us, Ny."

"I had no idea I could even do that. I have been working on my power, but never made that much air movement before."

"Sometimes our emotions tend to control our powers. This is a good example of what can happen when you are happy," he said, giving me a kiss on my forehead.

After about a half hour, we walked down the stairs and went down the lift and back to our building. Kylyan asked me if I wanted to come into his room for a bit to continue talking. We sat talking for quite a while about how he had been setting up the dinner for us without me knowing today. We cuddled on his bed talking for over an hour until sleep took us over.

"Nyrieve," Kylyan said to me, while lightly shaking my shoulder. "You've got to wake up."

My eyes fluttered open trying to focus on his face. "What is going on?" I asked, knowing we couldn't have been sleeping for long.

"Something's happened and we are needed right away," Kylyan said calmly, almost too calmly.

↔30↩

I SAT UP QUICKLY, REALIZING I was still wearing the dress from last night, even my shoes. I tried to get my head to clear up and leave the dreams of watching the stars with Kylyan. "What happened?" I asked.

"I am not positive. Baysil came here looking for you and said that he needed us to meet right away in Jyngy's building."

"Okay," I said getting to my feet, "let's go."

We walked quickly, hand in hand across the paths to the building Jyngy stayed in. I knocked quickly but quietly on the door, as I did not want to bring any attention to us from any of the other buildings.

Baysil opened the door and ushered us inside. Iclyn was sitting on a chair sobbing uncontrollably, which shocked me. I had never seen her out of control of her emotions before. Marselyus was sitting next to Iclyn holding her close, trying to get her to calm down. I looked to Baysil for an explanation, but he just gestured for me to go through the door to the room we had meetings in.

I walked over to the door with Kylyan behind me, opened it and walked through. It took a moment for my eyes to adjust, the light was brighter in this room than normal. Jyngy's back was to the door as she knelt down by the water talking to someone. When she turned to see who came in, I could see she was talking to Sudryl. When he saw me, he nodded in my direction.

"Jyngy, Sudryl," Kylyan said, nodding to each of them. "What is going on?"

Jyngy turned towards the wall to my left, where a blanket lay over the top of one of the couches. As I looked at it, I could see there was something underneath it. After a few moments, it dawned on me there was not something underneath the blanket, there was someone underneath it.

"Who is it?" I asked in a hoarse whisper.

Jyngy burst out crying, and Sudryl took her in his arms and held her. I knew she wasn't going to be able to answer me, so I forced myself forward to walk over to the couch. Each step felt like I had rocks dragging behind each leg, as if there were more added with each step.

I found myself standing over the blanket, and I slowly reached down and pulled the blanket back to reveal who was lying underneath. Her face was so pale, much paler then when she was alive. Tears fell down my face as the ground reached up to meet my knees when I lost the ability to stand.

"Lydorea?" I asked, knowing she would not respond to me. Her wet pink and purple hair spilled all over the side of the couch, and her cheek was as cold as snow. I moved the hair from where it was wrapped around her neck. When I had it all pulled away, I noticed strange markings on her neck.

"What are these marks from?" I asked, trying to keep the emotion out of my voice.

"What marks?" Kylyan leaned close behind me with his hand on my left shoulder.

"I didn't see any marks." Jyngy got up and walked quickly over to us. "Her hair was wrapped around her neck, I hadn't moved it."

"It looks to me like something was wrapped around her neck," Kylyan said, lightly touching the marks on Lydorea's throat.

"Who found her?" I asked Jyngy.

"I did," Sudryl said quietly. "I was swimming to meet Jyngy and I saw her floating near the shore. I tried to revive her, but she had been gone for a while already."

"Who pulled her out of the water?" Kylyan asked.

"Baysil and Iclyn," Jyngy said. "They were in here talking to me when Sudryl came in to see me."

I softly touched Lydorea's left cheek, wondering who could do this to such a wonderful person. She had never been cruel to anyone, and she always tried to help everyone. The same way she was trying to help me with finding Clyr. Then it hit me. Someone might have found out about Clyr and killed her to keep her from helping me find it. I slowly stood up, gently laid the blanket back over Lydorea's face, and walked back out to the other room. I walked over to Iclyn, kneeled down and hugged her to me. "I am so sorry, Iclyn. I loved Lydorea very much, and I can't imagine how hard this is for you."

Iclyn said between sobs, "She said she would meet us here... she was only ten minutes late when... when the merman came to say someone was... was in the water."

"Where was she going before meeting with you?" I asked gently.

"She said she was going to get some windoberry wine from the kitchen. We were going to relax, have a glass of wine and go to bed," Iclyn said between light sobs.

"Has anyone been back to your room to check if anything is out of sorts there?" Jyngy asked, coming through the doorway.

"No," Baysil said. "I can go check."

"No, Kylyan and I will go," I said, standing and walking over to him. "You need to be here for Iclyn right now."

Kylyan and I went back to our building quietly, but again hand in hand. When we got to Iclyn and Lydorea's room I paused for a moment, took a deep breath and entered their room.

A bottle of wine lay on the floor near the bed, and the sheets of the bed were thrown to the floor as if there had been a struggle. Lying in the middle of the bed was a piece of paper that had a seal on it. I leaned down and picked it up. The seal on it was of a flame. I broke the seal and opened the paper. The note was addressed to me.

Nyrieve,

Your attempt to erase my memory was futile. The memories that Death Elf took were mine, but only a copy. Do you really think I did not have precautions in place to keep something like this from happening? I was able to entice that Death Elf instead into helping me and is now leaving this wretched place with me.

As far as Lydorea dying, it was not intentional, but she did find me looking through your building trying to locate your room. When she confronted me, I accidently used her name, so she knew I remembered her. So I decided to take her to her room and have a little chat with her. I couldn't seem to charm her into being quiet, so I decided the only other option was to make her permanently quiet.

By now I should be long gone and on my way to fill in the Pyrothian Elves about you and your location. You should not have rejected me, Ny. We could have been powerful together, and now the only thing you can look forward to is the death of everyone you care about and yourself.

I will see you soon.

Jehryps

"No…" I said.

"Who is it from?" Kylyan asked.

I handed him the letter and let him read it. "This is my fault. I should have known that he would have figured a way around this. I shouldn't have been scared and should have just had him put to death," I said, getting angry.

"Ny, you did the right thing. You tried to handle the situation in a peaceful manner."

"Well you can be sure the next time I meet up with Jehryps, if I have my way, it will be anything but peaceful."

CR80

We showed the note to Baysil, and he gave it to Jyngy. Baysil explained that they gave Iclyn a sleep charm, and Marselyus took her back to her room to sleep.

"Neither will be able to lead anyone back here," Jyngy said.

"How do you figure that?" Baysil asked.

"The spell is still on all the exits, and they did not know it. So they both will be affected by the spell we have on the entrance. The only way to not have it effect you when you cross is to have the counterspell, and only I have it," she said.

"One less thing to worry about," I said quietly, thinking about Iclyn. I cannot imagine how heartbroken she must be.

"Would it be possible to get everyone in the Nomydrac together as soon as possible?" I asked Jyngy.

"I should be able to get everyone together within the hour."

"Okay, I want to have everyone meet up at the top of the cave in the castle ruins. I do not want anyone overhearing us," I said. "We need to go over our next steps and start moving forward."

"I will go get everyone and let them know," she said.

"Could you please also see if someone from the kitchen would be willing to make some food for us all?" I asked, thinking that waking people up would be better if they can get some warm food into them. "Just see if they can do some hot drinks and some muffins or something simple."

"Of course. We will all meet you in the ruins. I will also have someone go up and start a fire to get it warm up there," Jyngy said as she left the building.

"Baysil," I said, "I know Iclyn will want to prepare for Lydorea's funeral soon. If there is anything she needs or I can do, just let me know."

"I will let her know," he said.

"I am going to go and change into something warmer and I will meet everyone up at the top, and talk to Koyvean to see what this Death Elf might know that could cause us issues in the future," I said as I headed out the door. I felt Kylyan's hand on my arm, and I stopped and turned to face him.

"I know you need a few minutes to yourself to change and process everything, just know we will get through this, Ny. I promise." He hugged me to him and gently kissed my lips as he let me go.

"Thank you, Kylyan, I needed that." I gave him a weak but sincere smile.

I headed back to our building and to my room. I first changed into my black leather outfit with the green shirt. When I finished lacing up my boots, I looked into the mirror and noticed my hair was still pinned up and looked fancy. I took it all down and brushed it out. My hair was getting much longer, about halfway past my butt. I would need to get my hair cut pretty soon, as I could not see it being smart to have my hair this long if I needed to battle someone. When I finished brushing my hair, I put it into a long simple braid. It shortened my hair to the middle of my back.

I still had the makeup on, so I cleaned it off in the wash basin, and decided I should put some back on, but more simply. I only put on the charcoal stick smudged around my eyes, which seemed to make them bolder and stand out. I looked through all the makeup items Ghily had left for me, and I found a dark red stain to put on my lips. When I had everything set, I looked into the looking glass and stared at myself for a while. I couldn't believe that was me in the mirror. I looked like someone who was all grown and made important decisions, and I realized I did make important decisions. I guess I just hadn't fully realized that my life had changed so drastically and that it will never go back to the simple life I had in Cliffside. Though I was not sure if I really wanted it to go back to that, I enjoyed all the new people I had met and the places I had seen, and hoped that I could bring peace to our world.

I sat back down on my bed and thought about how much Lydorea had always been there for me. She had always been like a big sister. She was someone who Kaleyna and I could go to when Rowzey wasn't around or was busy. She had such beautiful powers and always seemed to be positive and full of a beautiful light that shined on everyone she was around. She also was willing to risk her life to help me find Clyr, and even though it was no longer possible to use it, I would one day find it and keep it in her memory.

I knew it was not my fault that Jehryps killed Lydorea, but part of me felt guilty. If I had just had Jehryps exiled or put to death like others wanted, she would still be here. There was nothing I could do to change what happened to Lydorea. The only thing I could do was make sure Jehryps paid for what he did. I did not want to become a person who would kill someone easily, but I was afraid that if I met up with him again, I would have no problems or reservations about helping him meet his death.

There was a light knocking on my door, and I got up and opened it. Kaleyna stood there with a worried look on her face. "Is it true? Is Lydorea gone?" Her voice trembled as she asked me.

I couldn't bring myself to say the words. I could only nod to her as she grabbed me into a hug. We both cried for a while and said nothing. After a while she stepped back and took a deep breath to steady herself. "Kylyan asked me to come get you. He said they were ready for the meeting."

I quickly fixed where the tears had worn off the black charcoal around my eyes, and then we headed off in silence arm in arm up to the lift and out to the castle ruins.

I couldn't believe that this was the same place we were at only a few hours ago enjoying the wonderful evening and getting to share my first kiss with Kylyan. Jyngy definitely moved fast at getting everything set up. There were chairs for everyone to sit in a circle, and off to the side were tables with hot drinks, muffins and other snack-like items.

Kaleyna let go and walked over to talk to Prydos. I was sure it was to fill him in on Lydorea. I walked over to the table and found that there was warmed milk with chocolate in it. I remembered Rowzey making this for me when I was young. It tasted so good and warm as I drank it, making me feel warm and reminding me of safety long forgotten.

"I's hope yous are not thinking that what happen was yous fault, Ny," Rowzey said behind me.

I turned to face her. She had been crying too. "I did at first, but Lydorea had decided to come here, and I could not control Jehryps's actions."

"Yous are right, the only person yous can control is yous, Ny," Rowzey said, taking my hand in hers. "And I's think yous are doing good, and making the right choices. I's know yous will do the right thing for Iryvalya and make choices when yous need to in the best interest for everyone." She patted my cheek with her other hand, and then grabbed a drink and a muffin and sat down near the fire.

Baysil walked over to me and asked if we could speak for a moment in private. We went to the edge of the ruin, and he said, "I am not sure right now if Iclyn will want to continue along with us, so I thought if she doesn't, we can make arrangements to get her up to Xylonia with Louv. I am sure he would make sure to keep her safe."

"I will support whatever decision she makes. I do not want her to feel pressure either way," I said honestly.

"Also, if we go by normal Fairy traditions, we would need to have the ritual for Lydorea in two days' time."

"I had honestly forgotten about the ritual," I said to him, realizing I had not seen one since I was young, as Fairies usually live to two hundred years old or more. "Do you know what Lydorea wanted her ritual to be?"

"I do not, but I am sure that Iclyn would have a good idea as to what she would have wanted."

"Do you want to check with Iclyn about it or would you like me to?"

"I will talk to her tomorrow when she wakes up. After the meeting, I plan to go and stay with her and Marselyus," he said. "I just do not want Iclyn to wake up and not be there for her."

"You are a good man, Baysil. I know you and Lydorea were really close friends."

"More than that, Ny. We never told anyone, because we only found out when we were older, but we shared the same father, just different mothers."

"She was your sister?"

"Yes, and I am going to avenge her death one way or another."

"And I will help you."

We walked back to everyone sitting and quietly talking. I sat at the chair that was left open, with Kylyan to my right and Kaleyna to my left. I guess it was time to get the meeting started.

❧31☙

I STOOD BEFORE ALL THE available members of the Nomydrac, took a deep breath and started. "Thank you, members of the Nomydrac. I appreciate you all coming at such short notice. The plan was to meet in the morning; however, there was need to gather everyone right away.

"Some of you may have already heard, but Lydorea was killed tonight." It seemed so strange to say those words out loud. I noticed a few surprised faces, and others who nodded quietly. "She died by the hands of Jehryps."

"What?" Relonya said.

"Why would he do that?" Koyvean asked, shocked.

"Apparently he never lost his memory," I answered. "He had a charm on him that gave your friend stored memories, but never making him lose his own."

"I have failed us," Koyvean said, hanging her head down.

"No, Koyvean, you did not know. I am the one who has failed us. I decided to take a more peaceful route with Jehryps and it was the wrong decision. Now he has killed someone that I and many others have cared deeply for and loved." I heard the shakiness in my voice. I pretended to clear my throat; I needed to be strong and not falter. These people were looking to me for leadership, not someone who would break down so easily.

"I's do not think it was yous fault, Ny", Rowzey said. "I's think yous tried the right way first, but now Jehryps proved that he cannot be given another chance."

"And he won't be," I said with force. "As of right now, if Jehryps is seen, I want him brought to me. Dead or alive."

Everyone nodded in agreement. I wondered how so much could change in such a short time. A few months ago I could never have imagined giving an order to bring me someone dead or alive, and now I couldn't imagine giving another order for him.

"While I am not ignoring what happened to Lydorea, there is another matter which we need to discuss. The original reason for our meeting," I said. "I know that the Elf Klayns must be aware of me by now. Those who left Mylterias Cove will have likely informed the Elf Klayns about me and what we are doing. While they will not remember our location, they will be sure to tell all they can remember about all of us.

"I have decided that we need to be the ones to make the first move. While I was wrong with my choice for Jehryps, I do believe that if I am the Bringer of Peace, I need to try to be peaceful in my initial actions," I said. "This is why I have decided that I want to arrange a meeting with the leaders or representatives of the Elf Klayns."

"Are you crazy?" Balthyza asked. "They will kill you at the first chance they get."

"I am well aware of this, and that is why we need to make the meeting on our terms and our way. We will send messages to both Klayns, and tell them that our wish is to meet to try to come to an agreeable solution. We will determine how many people they can bring, which will entail their representative and any guards. The locations we ask them to meet us at will not be the actual place. Once they arrive there, they will be given instructions on where to go from there. I want there to be at least three different locations they need to go through to get to the final location.

"We will have people hiding at each location, so we can monitor and make sure there is no one else following them. Once those who were invited for the meeting pass through to the next location, we will be setting up forgetful charms to keep anyone possibly following away and confused. In the final location, any of you who want to be there can come, because we will be trying to discuss a peaceful end to their fighting and allow Iryvalya to thrive in the peaceful freedom it used to have.

"Now, I know some of you might not wish to attend, as it could cause the Elves to strike out against your races as well. I will leave the decision up to you. I think you will make the right choice for your people either way. When we have the meeting, we will do everything very formally and show that we are extremely organized. We need to make sure they do not see any weakness in us, so if there is anything you disagree with me on, you need to bring it to my attention ahead of time or in privacy.

"We will have a few practice runs to see how we want the meeting to go, and have some of you portray the roles of the Elves to see if we can try to cover anything that might come up. I do not expect them to try to do an assassination right away, but I am sure they will at some point. That is why we will have guards around me at all times, and also all around the meeting area.

"Are there any questions so far?" I asked.

Everyone shook their heads no.

"Okay, so if the meeting does not end with them agreeing for peace, which I am not expecting them to do, we will make sure to let them know that while we want a peaceful resolve to this, we are willing to take un-peaceful measures to succeed."

Everyone nodded in agreement. We talked a little longer about minor details and also about the ritual that will be happening for Lydorea. After about an hour of discussing everything, the meeting officially ended and most everyone went back inside the cave and to their own buildings. We had set up several meetings to get things in place and would hopefully get the viewing crystals made to be sent to the Elf Klayns as soon as we decided where and when we wanted the first meeting.

Before I went back down, I asked Baysil, Kylyan, Jyngy and Koyvean to stay. Once we were alone, I asked, "Koyvean, what do you know about the Death Elf who helped Jehryps?"

"Truly I did not know much of him," Koyvean started, "only his name, Aloyc, at first. I have checked with the other Death Elves and Drayks here. He came here only a couple of seasons before we did, but he seemed to pull his own weight and made everyone think that he supported bringing peace to Iryvalya. He asked several times to be given more jobs around the Cove, but he was kept to doing only the basics of weapon sharpening and such. He was never entrusted with any information that could help Jehryps or either of the Elf Klayns that we know of. He must have had ties to the Pyrothian Elves, and he likely would have known who Jehryps was."

"If that is so," Baysil said, "then he must have set up the whole attack on Ny, knowing that if he failed and survived, Aloyc would help him by telling others of the powers he had."

"That is what I and the other Death Elves believe," Koyvean said.

"Well..." I took a deep breath, "as it is, there is really nothing we can do about it now, but it is good to know at least that Aloyc was not given sensitive information. I know it is possible that he spied and overheard things, but as it stands, he hadn't been made aware of much more than Jehryps already knows."

Kylyan added, "When they are caught, and one day they will be, we will make sure they pay for all the damage they have caused."

"I agree," I said, finishing our discussion.

When we got back to our building, Kylyan gave me a long hug and kissed me on the tip of my nose. "You are a great leader, Ny."

"Thank you, Kyl... I just hope my choices do not get anyone else hurt."

He smiled at me.

"What?" I asked him.

"You called me Kyl. People will call me Ky for short, but never Kyl."

"I figured Ky was too close to Ny," I said smiling at him. I loved his smile.

"I like it, something different, and sounds tough as well," he said. "I hate to leave you, but I need to go meet with Jyngy to help her get things prepared for the ritual for Lydorea."

"Is there anything I can do to help?"

"Not right now. It is just me helping get everything we need for it."

"Okay. I guess I will just go lie down for a little bit and then maybe figure out some ideas I have for the meeting with the Elves."

"Sounds good," Kylyan said as he leaned to me and lightly pressed his lips against mine. I wrapped my arms around him, keeping him close to me. My heart began to race again and I loved every moment of being in his arms like this.

When we finally parted he smiled at me and kissed me on my nose again. "You be careful, Ny, and if you need anything, come find me."

"You do the same," I said, smiling back up at him.

"I will," he said as he turned and walked back out of the building.

I went into my room and closed the door behind me. A letter rested on top of my pillow. I walked over to the bed and picked it up. On the outside was a note from Rowzey, telling me that she thought I should have this. The first thing I noticed after reading Rowzey's note was that the seal on the letter was a flame, just like the one on the letter from Jehryps. I quickly broke the seal and read the letter.

My Dearest Nyrieve,

Today is your tenth Leaf Day. I cannot imagine how much you have grown or what you look like, though I try to imagine it every day. I wish so much that your father and I could be there with you and spend this day with you and celebrate how much you have grown. I know you will not get this letter for several years, and I hope when you do you can forgive me for giving you up. There isn't a day that goes by that I don't wonder if I should have run away with you instead of sending you off to live with the Fairies.

I wanted to tell you a little about me, besides that I am your mother. As I am sure you have figured by now, I grew up with the Pyrothian Elves in Prax. My father, Legatey Rodyron, your grandfather, has been one of the three leaders of the Pyrothian Elves. Someone from his family has always been on the counsel since it was originally formed. He married my mother, Lyndrea, your grandmother, because not only was she a beautiful Pyrothian Elf, she also was a descendent of one of the five royal Elf bloodlines. Back before all the fighting began, the royal Elves were from the different elements of our world. They are Water, Stone, Air, Fire and Spirit. My family's royal lines came from the Air Elves.

This has allowed my family to hold high power within the counsel and always be considered leaders among our people. Over the last few years my father has become ill. It is suspected someone is poisoning him, but we have not found out yet who it is. Because he is no longer able to be on the counsel, they recently have appointed me to take his place. This scares me, since I am aware that the Bringer of Peace is alive and hiding out with the Fairies.

I am sure this news is not positive for you to hear, but I hope you under-stand that the only reason I took the position is in the hopes I can help steer the counsel to be more peaceful and to keep them from looking for you.

I hope someday our paths will cross in a positive way, my daughter. I know that you must do what is right for Iryvalya, and that you will. I just hope you will understand that if we ever meet in front of any of the Klayn Elves, I cannot acknowledge you as anything other than a stranger. It is safer for both of us that way. If we do meet someday, and I ask you about your name, please know that is my way of letting you know I am acknowledging you in my own way.

I wish you so much happiness and strength for everything that is to come. Trust in yourself and know that you have the royal blood of the Air Elves in your veins, which is a great and strong power, plus everything you get from your father as well.

I love you so much, my sweet daughter.

Love,

Your mother, Osidya

I sat down and reread the letter a few more times, soaking in every word and memorizing the names of my grandparents. So my royalty came from the Air Elves. This explained why my first power would be controlling wind, and made me wonder how much stronger this power could become. I looked at the lower righthand corner of the page and there was a small image drawn on it. It looked just like the swirl pattern on my shoulder. I pulled my shirt aside to see the image, and it was clearer now. It was faded shades of light blue now and it looked like swirls of lines. I needed to ask Rowzey if she knew what this symbol was for sure, but I was betting it had something to do with the powers of Air.

I took the letter, placed it inside a satchel, and walked over to Rowzey's room, hoping she would be there. I knocked and Rowzey said to come in. I slowly opened the door and walked inside her dimly lit room.

"Rowzey?" I asked.

"I's am over here," she said. I turned to look towards the corner and I saw her sitting on the floor with her reading cards spread out all over the floor in front of her. "Come and sit with me."

I walked over and sat down in front of Rowzey, making sure not to disturb her cards. "I got the letter."

"I's was guessing that was why yous came to see me," she said with a slight smile.

"Did you know what the letter said?"

"No, the letter was sealed and it was for yous, so I's didn't see a need to read it."

"It was from my mother. She told me she came from Air Elves."

"Yes, I's remember her telling me about that when we were on Troxeon."

"Do you know if the mark on my shoulder is a mark of the Air Elves? Because the same symbol was on the bottom of the letter from my mother."

"Yes, Ny, that is the symbol for the power of Air," Rowzey said. "The one on the back of yous neck is a vine."

I instantly touched the back of my neck. "A vine?"

"Yes, it is a vine wrapped in the shape of the triquetra encircled by dragon flames," Rowzey said with a sheepish smile.

"What... What kind of powers would be associated with these?" I asked, really confused.

"The vines in that pattern represent the past, present and future of Iryvalya, which is tied to yous," she said.

"Seeing as I am the Bringer of Peace, that would make sense, but why would they be encircled by dragon's fire?"

"It is a very rare thing. I's haven't seen it in... a very long time, not since I's was a young girl," Rowzey said softly.

"What does it mean?"

"Those who have the flames of the dragon can speak and give orders to dragons."

"But there are no longer dragons in Iryvalya."

"The last time I's saw that marking, there was..."

I smiled at Rowzey and asked a question I have asked a hundred times, knowing I'd get the same answer anyway. "How old are you, Rowzey?"

"Old? I's am younger than the Northern and Southern Suns, younger than the five moons... I's am still young!" Rowzey said with a laugh.

LeAnn Kelley

"I know you are, Rowzey," I said with a smile.

"Now, do yous see this card?" Rowzey pointed at one to my right. Her cards were old and fading, but the drawings on each of the cards were beautiful and always seemed lifelike.

"That is the power card, isn't it?" I asked, noticing a line that went through the center of the card, which had a hand on either side pulling the line each way.

"Yes, Ny, it is the struggles for the power. It used to only come up when I's would read the cards for anyone dealing with the Elves."

"Who are you reading now?"

"Yous, Ny," she said, looking at me.

"It makes sense, with me trying to meet with the Elves."

"Yes, for that it does, but this is a power struggle that has yet to be placed before yous," Rowzey said seriously.

"Can you tell what it is?"

"To me, it looks like yous will be given an offer to have power, but not the kind yous currently have."

"Do you know what kind of offer?"

"I's sadly do not, Ny. The cards only give a small glimpse of what may come. It's like looking down a river, yous see where it can end up, but yous do not always see the twists and turns it takes to get there."

"Are you worried that I will make the wrong choice, Rowzey?"

"I's am not worried about the choices yous make, my dear, I's am more worried about the consequences of the choices."

"Isn't that the same thing?"

"No, it's not."

"What is the difference?"

"Ny, think of it dis way, when I's offer yous a bowl of my sauce and Kal offers yous a bowl of her sauce, whose do you pick?"

"I don't know. I know you make the best sauce, but I also would know Kaleyna tried really hard to make sauce for me."

"Exactly, and yous know that if yous picked either of ours, one would be a little hurt but would get over it, right?"

"Yes, I would hope so."

"But not everyone is as understanding as we are, so when yous are offered something sometimes, and yous turn one down, that person

274

might not be as understanding and the consequences might be more than hurt feelings."

"I think I understand what you are saying," I said quietly, letting the idea fully process.

‑32‑

THE RITUAL FOR LYDOREA'S passing was a beautiful time at which we were able to recount the wonderful memories we all had of her. As with most Fairy rituals, Lydorea's body had been burned to ash to be spread out in the winds to continue to be a part Iryvalya. After almost everyone who knew her personally had spoken their memories of her, Iclyn spoke. She looked so pale, which, with how porcelain white her skin was normally, I did not think possible. She had her hair back in one long braid, and going down the whole length of it were pink and purple gems that Lydorea use to wear.

Iclyn stood next to the vase that contained Lydorea's ashes, placed her left hand on the top, and spoke to us all. "I remember the first time I met Lydorea. We were very young, I had just moved to Cliffside, and she was the first person who truly welcomed me. We became the closest of friends straight away, and stayed that way throughout our lives. Even when we realized we were in love with each other, our friendship always remained the foundation to our love. We had been tyed together for over ten Leaf years, and there isn't a moment with her that I would ever change."

Iclyn took a moment to compose herself, as she wiped away her tears. "There is one thing I need to read to you all, a passage Lydorea wrote in her journal.

"We have left Cliffside to try to meet up with the Rebel Elves, and I know many of the travelers are questioning if this is the right thing. I think even Nyrieve questions it. I, however, do not. I know that this is the right path to find the peace and freedom Iryvalya needs, and I have no doubt in my mind that Nyrieve will bring that peace to our world.

"I have, sadly, had more visions of the future that are not too promising for myself, but I feel that even if something should happen to me, I can find comfort *in the fact that I am living or dying for something that I believe in. This is what everyone of Iryvalya needs to believe in.*

"Our world was once joined in peace, and my only hope, even if I do not live to see it come to fruition, is that Nyrieve, the Bringer of Peace, along with anyone who desires the same, will fight for it as much and for as long as they need to. There is nothing in Iryvalya that is more important, and I am just proud that I am a part of this for as long as possible."

Tears ran hotly down my cheeks. Lydorea knew that she would not survive the trip in the end, but came anyway. When I finally looked up from wiping my tears away, I could see everyone else was moved the same as I was, even if they were not shedding tears.

Iclyn continued, "Lydorea never told me of her vision foreseeing her death. If she had, I am sure I would have tried to talk to her out of coming, but I know in my heart she would not have listened." She paused for a moment. "The truth be told, if the roles would have been reversed, I also would have still come along, as the reason we are here is bigger than ourselves, and the best way we can honor Lydorea's life is to ensure we do not give up on bringing peace to Iryvalya."

Iclyn looked at everyone, and quietly said, "Volnyri." And everyone repeated it back.

Once Iclyn finished, those of us close to Lydorea walked to the top of the cave and into the castle ruins. We went up to where Kylyan and I shared our first kiss.

There was no real wind to help Lydorea's ashes to blow away, so I pulled from deep inside of me and began feeling the wind stirring around me. I closed my eyes and focused on the wind pulling around us all, and when I opened my eyes I could see everyone's hair gently moving in the strong breeze I was making.

Iclyn took the vase and removed the lid and held it out in front of her. I could hear her whispering to Lydorea's ashes how much she loved her and would one day see her again and they would dance among the stars. I guided the breeze to the vase and could almost feel it reach in and pull the ashes with it into the sky, carrying Lydorea throughout Iryvalya.

Afterward, everyone met back inside where the cooks had made a lot of Lydorea's favorite meals. Rowzey even made a big cauldron full of her sauce, as it was one of Lydorea's most favorite things. Kylyan left my table to go talk to Jyngy about the arrangements that had been set forth for trying to arrange the meeting with the Elf Klayns. Iclyn walked over and asked if she could talk to me alone for a few moments.

We walked over near the waterfall and sat down on some of the large rocks there. "I am so sorry about Lydorea, Iclyn," I said to her, not knowing what I could possibly say to her that would give her any sort of comfort.

"Thank you, Ny. I know you and so many others loved her and will miss her too," Iclyn said softly. "I wanted to thank you for bringing the wind to carry her on throughout Iryvalya."

"Oh, well... I just wanted to help make sure the wind was strong enough to carry her," I said, surprised she knew it was me.

We sat in silence for a while. We both watched the waterfall and listened to the water fleeting down and then calmly flowing into the river. Lydorea told me once that it was important to stop and pay attention to nature, as it can teach us and will be there long after we are gone. Now Lydorea is gone forever.

"Ny," Iclyn said quietly, slightly startling me from my memories of Lydorea. "I have something for you, from Lydorea."

"What do you mean?"

"Like I said, she knew something was going to happen to her. I don't think she completely knew the exact moment, but she knew it was coming," Iclyn said. "She had been preparing a pack for you, and when I would ask her why she was rushing, she would brush it off as just wanting to be prepared. Now I know she was trying to make sure it was finished before she died."

"A pack?"

"Yes, I helped her with some items inside. She had other people help with other items as well. She also wrote you a letter that is inside the pack explaining everything inside it and what it does."

"Oh... that is... was... kind of her to do."

"She had written me a letter also. I found it this morning inside the pack as well. From things she said in it, she could have only written it a week ago at the most. She knew the time was coming and she wrote so beautifully about her life, memories that she cherished, and our love," Iclyn said as tears gently fell down her cheeks.

"That was very sweet of her," I said, not knowing what else to say.

"She said in my letter to make sure that, no matter what, I support you and help with anything the Nomydrac needed," Iclyn continued, "but I would have done that anyway, because we both wanted to see peace in our world."

"I cannot tell you how much you and Lydorea's constant support has meant to me lately and over the years as I was growing up," I said truthfully. While Iclyn was never one to be overly affectionate or someone I felt I could run to with silly problems, I always knew if I needed her help she would have been there without question.

"We have cared for you since you came to Cliffside. Lydorea was always better at showing emotions but we both always watched out for you. And I will continue to do so as well, Ny," Iclyn said, then surprised me by taking me into a hug that lasted a few minutes. Her tears dripped onto my shoulder and I knew mine must have been doing the same to her.

Iclyn continued to hold me, leaned close to my ear, and quietly whispered to me, "Ny, I will ensure the pack is in your room tonight. There are two letters for you inside. The one sealed with a dragonfly is the one that will explain all the items in the pack. The other is a blank seal. When you have read that letter, destroy it. You will understand after reading it, but do not let anyone else see it."

Iclyn let go of me and I just stared at her. Iclyn nodded to me, keeping me from asking any questions. Then she got up quickly and walked back to where everyone else was still eating and talking.

I went and sat down next to Kaleyna. She leaned over and asked if I was okay. I nodded to her, but said nothing about what Iclyn told me, as I didn't know if someone could be listening. After the food was gone, I decided to find Kylyan and see if any progress had been made in figuring out how to set up a meeting with the Elves.

I found Kylyan in Jyngy's building. They had come up with a few places to set up as the fake meeting areas and showed me two options for the actual meeting location. One was out in the middle of the water on an island with a few deserted manors. Boats would be used to bring the Elves to a small island called Lynawn. The second place was deep inside an old ruined castle. Jyngy was not sure who lived there originally, as it has been in ruins since she was born.

I sat down on one of her overstuffed chairs and thought about it. While the ruined castle would provide more rooms and places for us to hide, I couldn't help but think that the island seemed like the better choice. If we were out in the middle of the water, they could not ambush us without us knowing it with plenty of time to get out of there. Also, I kept thinking about how Sudryl said that the merpeople stay neutral, and it would be good to make sure that our meeting tries to convey to the Elves that we want peace and not that we are trying to force them into something.

"The island," I said confidently.

"You're sure?" Jyngy asked.

"Positive," I said. "It is in a neutral area, and when they make their choice, they cannot say that we tried to force their decision either way. How many manors are there on the island?"

"There are at least three that I recall," Kylyan answered.

"You've been there before?" I questioned.

"It has been many years, but yes. You can't see the island from the shore, the trees and rocks hide the buildings as you approach it. When I was there before it looked like it had been deserted for a very long time."

"Good. I think that will be best then," I said. "As far as the other false locations for them to meet, I will leave that for Kylyan to decide."

"Are you sure?" he asked.

I got up, walked over to him and looked him in his eyes. "Yes, I trust your decision and I know that you will pick the right places to allow them to get to the island without anyone following."

We sat and discussed the different locations, and eventually Kylyan picked which ones he felt would be the easiest for our people to monitor and to be able to ensure the safety of our people. When we had the majority of the details worked out, Jyngy suggested the way to invite the Elves for this meeting would be to make a viewing crystal for them both. This way we would show that we were serious and that I was not afraid of them knowing who I am.

I agreed to make the viewing crystals, but I still wanted to get some input on what would make the best impact. We decided to have a meeting of the Nomydrac tonight. Jyngy said she would go around and get everyone together for a dinner so we could discuss the details while we dined.

When I decided to head back to my room to relax for a while, Kylyan surprised me by saying that he was going to come with me. Jyngy gave me a hug before I left and said that she thought everything for Lydorea went very beautifully.

When I reached the door to my room, Kylyan told me that he was going to go get cleaned up and come back to my room if I was okay with it. I told him of course and gave him a kiss on his soft warm lips.

I went into my room, closed the door softly behind me, and decided to look into my mirror journal. There was only a small note from Rowzey saying that she enjoyed our conversation the other day and it reminded her of when I was young and in Cliffside. I put the book back into my bag, sat down on my bed and laid back to think, but before my head reached my pillow there was a soft tapping on my door.

I knew it was too soon to be Kylyan, so I got up and opened the door. Standing in front of me were two people I had never met before. "Hello," I said, almost as a question.

"Hello, Your Highness. I am Syviss and this is Crymson," the girl on the left said.

"It is a pleasure to meet you," I said, trying to keep formalities. "What can I do for you?"

"It is us who wish to do something for you, Your Highness," Crymson said in a light and fluttery voice.

"May we come in to talk to you for a few moments?" Syviss asked.

"Yes, of course," I said, backing up to allow them room to enter, remembering they would not have reached my room against the charms in place if they were dangerous to me. "Please come in."

Syviss walked in first, and I noticed she walked almost as if her legs did not want to move. She was shorter than me by a bit, had beautiful golden sun-kissed skin, and her hair was shades of bright and deep purples. Her eyes were swirled with two shades of purple, and framed by her purple eyebrows. Along the sides of her small nose were gills, just like Sudryl. She must be a mermaid as well, but she had legs. I wondered if that was why she was having a hard time walking.

The second girl, Crymson, walked in past me pretty quickly, as if to make up the time it took Syviss to walk in. Crymson was near the same height as me, her skin had a faint pinkish glow to it, and her hair was long and fell into loose curls down her back. Her hair was a few different shades of red, reminding me of garnets and rubies mixed together. When I looked at her face, I was surprised to see her eyes were swirled with the garnet red and also a very pale gold, and framed by darker red eyebrows.

Once I had shut my door, I faced both women, smiled and asked, "Would either of you like to sit down?" I wanted to give the mermaid a chance to rest her legs, which didn't seem to move underneath her with ease.

"No, thank you, Your Highness," Crymson said. "We do not plan to take up much of your time. We have only come here to bring you a message."

"A message from whom?"

"To be honest, Your Highness, we do not know," Syviss said.

"How do you know the message is for me?"

Syviss opened her satchel and pulled out a closed seashell the size of a plum. When she handed me the shell, I could see it had been sealed shut with wax and the only thing written in the wax was my name, Nyrieve.

"We used our powers to check it to see if there was a curse on it or anything inside it, but there is not," Syviss said.

"And my fellow Flower Nymphs and I did the same," Crymson said. "There is no malicious magyc tied to this shell or anything it contains. We even had some of the Elves and Fairies here check it before we brought it to you."

"How did the shell come to you?"

"I found it out in the middle of the Eastern Sea," Syviss said. "We have no idea how it got there or how long it had been there, but it called to me, and I had to bring it to you."

"Now we must go," Crymson said. "Syviss needs to get back into the water. She is new to having legs."

"One question before you leave. How did you find us here?"

"Merpeople are balanced, we do not pick sides, so we are able to locate anyone if there are no ill intentions in play," Syviss said.

"Thank you for bringing this to me," I said as the two women walked out of my room.

I sat down on the bed and took off Klaw to break the seal. When I finally got it off and was able to open the shell, I noticed a note with a small clear stone inside. I opened the note and read it.

Nyrieve,

This is a truth stone. Keep it with you. If it stays cool to the touch, people around you are being truthful. If the stone starts to get warm and becomes murky, people around you are not telling you the truth.
Volnyri

I checked the back of the note, but it didn't say who is was from. I decided to have the stone checked by Rowzey. She had seen a lot of things, and maybe she would know if it was real.

When I finally found Rowzey, she was with Baysil and the Pixie sisters. After exchanging greetings and asking how everyone was, I asked if any of them had heard of a truth stone. They had, but Rowzey had not seen one in many years. Baysil told me that he thought the Elves had had them all destroyed to keep people from knowing their true intentions.

I showed the small stone to them, and they looked at it in awe. I told them I had no idea who sent it to me, and wondered if having it would be a good thing. Rowzey decided we should test it to see if it worked.

"I's am going to say something untrue, and we will see if it reacts," Rowzey said. "I's do not make my own sauce. I's have always had someone else make it for me and I's say it's mine."

The stone warmed and the clarity of it became a murky gray color. "It works!"

We tried it a few more times, and it seemed to work each and every time. We decided I shouldn't let many people know about the stone. Rowzey said she would get me a ring I can put the stone in so I can wear it at all times. I decided I should go back to my room and wait for Kylyan, as he might already be wondering where I was. I thanked everyone for their time and took leave to go back to my room.

When I got back to my room, I found Kylyan lying on my bed and could tell he was sleeping. I decided not to wake him, but snuggled up next to him and joined him for a short nap.

The nap did not last very long. Someone knocked on the door, and I slinked out of bed to open the door. Koyvean was standing there smiling at me.

❧33❧

HELLO, KOYVEAN. WHAT is going on?" I asked, still trying to get my head clear and more alert.

"I was coming to get you. We have everything set up for the meeting to go over making the viewing crystals."

"I didn't realize it was so late already. I thought I had only fallen asleep for a few moments," I said, surprised. "Let me wake Kylyan up..."

"Too late," Kylyan said, groggy from sleep.

"Oh, okay. Well, where do we need to meet?" I asked.

"On top of the cave in the castle ruins," Koyvean said. "Jyngy figured there were already chairs and such up there, so it would make it easy."

"Okay, we will be up shortly. Thank you, Koyvean."

"Always," she responded as she turned and left.

I closed the door behind me, walked over to Kylyan and sat down on the bed next to him. "Sorry we woke you."

"No worries. I didn't mean to fall asleep, but I noticed you snuggling in with me, so I didn't want to get up. But when you got up to get the door, that is what really woke me, I missed having you in my arms," he said, pulling me back down next to him, wrapping his arms around me and nuzzling closer to my neck.

"That tickles," I said, giggling.

"Good," he said with a laugh.

After a short time of staying cuddled together, we got up and went to the top of the cave to the castle ruins. When we got there the members of the Nomydrac who were in Mylterias Cove were all there. Everyone was standing around talking and enjoying the warm fires burning.

Kylyan and I were the last to arrive, so once we were there the meeting started.

"Thank you all for coming, I appreciate it," I started. "What we are here for tonight is regarding the viewing crystals we will be sending out to the Klayns. We need to figure out what is the best message to send that shows our strength and resolve, and that might appeal to them too. Does anyone have some suggestions right off?"

Xetyna was the first to stand up. She was quite short, but with a lean muscular build. She seemed like someone most people would underestimate. She had chin-length hair, in beautiful multiple shades of light purple, and her eyebrows were the same purple as well. Her eyes were swirled with a deep shade of purple and an almost black shade of purple. She was fair-skinned, as if she were never out in the sun's light.

With a nod from me, Xetyna started to speak in a silky soft voice. "One of the first things that the Lumaryia Elves will notice is how you present yourself, if you stand tall and have eye contact. If you look unsure or stumble on your words, they will think that you are either not intelligent or you are afraid." She then sat back down.

Relonya stood up, and I nodded to her. "For the Pyrothian Elves, you will need to have very ornate attire. They are obsessed with looks and if you do not look perfect, they will not see you as anything more than a joke. They tend to underestimate those who are not afraid to get dirty." Relonya also sat back down.

I thought for a moment and said, "I would like those of you familiar with the Lumaryia Elves to help me go over how I need to hold myself and if there are specific things I should or should not say. Those of you familiar with the Pyrothian Elves, I would like for you to go over what I will wear, as well as the location and background image they will see."

Everyone nodded in agreement.

"The rest of you, I would like us to figure out everything we want to say. I want to make sure we do not leave anything out or happen to give up too much information."

We split off into three groups, and after about an hour or so, we regrouped and had figured out what I would be saying in the speech, and what I should wear. I will have tonight to practice a bit on the speech and by morning the clothing and location should be set up.

Kylyan and Prydos offered to help with getting the location set up, so Kaleyna offered to stay here and help me practice the speech. After about the fiftieth time of going through it, I decided it was as close to good as it could be.

"Kaleyna, I cannot go over it another time, I feel like I am just saying the words right now without meaning behind them." I repeated part of the speech in a flat voice, "We would like to welcome you to meet with us and to help us decide the fate of Iryvalya and the parts each of us are to play in it."

"Definitely sounds a little boring to me too," Kaleyna said with a chuckle. "And to be honest, I do not know why in the speech you keep saying 'we.' I know it is important to let them know you are not alone, but you should make it sound more like you are the one in charge."

"I was thinking that too... I don't know, Kal, I am too tired to even think about this. They want to make the viewing crystal first thing in the morning, so I should try to get some sleep, otherwise I will look tired and they will not take me seriously anyway."

We went back down inside the cave and walked through our building to my room. I turned and gave Kaleyna a hug. "Thank you so much for always being there for me."

Kaleyna hugged me close and said, "Of course. You are my best friend and spirit sister, there is no place else I would be."

"Are you going to bed as well?"

"No, I am not tired. I think I will go see if Prydos and Kylyan could use any help."

"Would you let Kylyan know I am going to sleep? He can come in if he likes, but I don't want him surprised if I am not awake."

"I will let him know," she said with a smile. "Now go get some rest."

She smiled, turned and walked back out of the building. I opened my door, stepped inside and closed it behind me. True to her word, Iclyn had a pack sitting on my bed with an unsealed note letting me know she left it in my room for me.

I took a quick look inside the pack. There were two sealed letters, both with Lydorea's handwriting on the outside. The first one read *Inventory*, and the second one read *Personal*. I decided the inventory could wait until tomorrow, but the personal one I wanted to read before going to sleep. I broke the seal on the letter and opened it, seeing Lydorea's elegant handwriting, and read what she wrote me.

Nyrieve,

I am so very sorry that this letter is my last way to say goodbye to you. You have been such a wonderful part of my life. I watched you grow, helped you with magyc and saw that inside you is the power and strength to be our Bringer of Peace.

I know you had your doubts along the way, I could see it on your face, but I also knew in the end you would choose this path. I know you can feel it in your heart that it is the right one.

I did know this was going to happen, that I would be killed at some point. While I entertained the idea, for a moment, of fleeing and hiding away with Iclyn, my heart could not let me do that. While I do love Iclyn more than anyone, I know that our love will never die, but I cannot say the same for the people of our world. To stay in this constant struggle would be the end to Iryvalya and all the good that could be accomplished.

In the pack are different items I feel can be helpful for you in the future. Do not waste your time going through it right now, you will have plenty of time in the future, and it will not be until then that they will prove useful.

I must ask two things of you, and seeing as I am no longer there for you to deny me, I will assume you will help me.

First, do not blame yourself for my death. I knew it was coming and I understood the risks set forth in following you. I chose to do it, and if I had the chance, I would do the same again.

Second, please help Iclyn whenever it's needed. She is sad now, and will need time to recover, but there is love for her again. I have seen it and I know it is a love she will fight at first, but help her see that it is okay to love again. A new love does not diminish an old love.

Take care of yourself, Nyrieve. Enjoy the love that you have found among friends. They are more like family sometimes than actual family can be. These people are the ones who will be there for you no matter what.

You have found something special in your friendship with Kaleyna. You both are connected in many ways, more than what you realize. Rowzey will always be there for you like a mother, she cares for you greatly. Cherish the magyc you have found with Kylyan. He is very special, as you will see.

While I was not able to help you locate Clyr, know that things that are meant to be will be.

And always remember that you must trust your instincts. Even if every-one tells you that you are wrong, trust yourself above all. Love and light, my dearest Ny.

Volnyri

Lydorea

I brushed the tears off of my cheeks and folded the note back up. I lay down on the bed and held her note to me. I knew I should destroy the letter, but I didn't want to ever forget what Lydorea told me. I decided I would destroy it later, but for now I tucked it away inside my mirror journal and then lay back on my bed thinking about Lydorea and all the things she said and did for me over the years. I would truly miss having her with me.

CBEO

I woke up curled up in Kylyan's arms. I lay there for a while just enjoy-ing the feel of his arms around me and hearing him breathe. After a slight change in his breathing, I figured he was starting to wake up. I turned my face towards his and placed a chaste kiss on his lips. He in turn pulled me closer and answered my chaste kiss with a much more passionate one and then a few more.

Soon we heard a knock on the door and I sighed. "I am starting to get tired of always having people knocking on my door."

"You are the Bringer of Peace, Ny, this is how it will likely always be," he said, placing a kiss on the tip of my nose causing me to wrinkle it up.

"I know… perhaps one day we will get to go someplace where we won't have constant obligations," I said hopefully.

"We will, I promise." He got up and answered the door for me.

Kaleyna and Prydos were standing there with big grins on their fac-es. Prydos asked, "We didn't interrupt anything important, did we?"

"No," I said, embarrassed by what he was insinuating.

"We came by to get you and let you know they have everything ready to make the viewing crystal," Kaleyna said. "So you need to come with us to get ready."

Prydos and Kaleyna gave me some privacy to get changed into fresh clothes while Kylyan went to his room to change. I picked one of the simpler gowns I was given—it was a soft green color—not caring, as I knew that my clothing would be changed soon for my speech.

When Kylyan and I arrived at the room Kaleyna and Prydos escorted us to, I was surprised to see only Ghily, Koyvean and the friend of hers who made the viewing crystals for me before. I had thought the whole Nomydrac group would be here standing next to me in the message we sent out.

"Hello, Koyvean," I said, walking towards her and her friend. "Is everyone else still coming?"

"Hello, Nyrieve. No one else is coming," Koyvean said, giving me a light hug, and turned to her friend. "I would like you to formally meet Zagnyon. She is able to make the viewing crystals, as she did for you before, and is also a Death Elf like me."

Zagnyon walked over to me as if she was almost floating just above the ground. She was wearing her black cloak again; however, she had the hood off. She was very short for an Elf, had light golden brown skin, and long wavy black hair that appeared to only be on the top part of her head, and underneath her hair was a pinkish purple that reminded me of the flower on a thistle. Her eyebrows were dark black and her eyes, like Koyvean, swirled with the two colors of her hair.

Zagnyon extended her hand to me and when I placed my hand in hers, she gently took it to her lips and placed a soft kiss on the top of my hand. "It is a pleasure for me to make these viewing crystals for you, Your Highness, and also to properly meet you, of course."

"It is a pleasure for me to officially meet you as well, Zagnyon," I said, taking my hand back after she let go. "And please, while we are working on this, feel free to call me Nyrieve or Ny."

"Of course, Nyrieve."

I turned to everyone else and asked, "Why isn't anyone else going to be here?"

"After some discussion," Kaleyna said, "Rowzey convinced everyone that you appearing alone would make the Elves wonder if you were truly as strong as you are trying to appear or if there are weaknesses."

"And how would that be a good thing?" I asked.

Prydos answered, "Think of it this way, Ny, they have to try to decide if you are a weak Elf or someone they need to worry about. It is the unknown."

Kylyan finished by saying, "The unknown is what will give you the edge. They will not know what to expect at the meeting, so all the control will be in your hands."

They were completely correct. We needed to have as much edge as we could over the Elf Klayns, and we needed it right away.

The first thing Ghily did was my hair. She lightly pulled it back in a long messy-looking braid that still looked very elegant. It made my hair look soft and almost ethereal. She put makeup on me that was quite minimal compared to what she had shown me before, only a little charcoal liner and some light pink color stain on my lips.

Ghily took me around a screened wall to get me dressed in an elegant but simple dress. It was a soft white silk, which was tight at the chest and flowed outwards. The sleeves were tight near the top of my arms and belled down to the floor, but were short on the top so my hands were not hidden. A thin silver ribbon wrapped around under my chest right before the skirt flowed out, and its tails flowed down my right side to the floor. She put me in flat white slippers that were very easy to walk in.

Once I was fully dressed, Ghily put on the same headpiece I had worn before with the moonstone gem. She smiled at me and whispered, "This is yours to keep, you know."

"It is?" I asked, surprised.

"Yes, it was made for you. Weren't you told?"

"No, no one told me that," I said. "Who had it made for me?"

"I do not know who, but it has been sitting and waiting for you to wear it for many years," Ghily said with a smile. "Just make sure to keep it safe and with you."

"I will, Ghily. Thank you."

Once I was fully ready, Koyvean had me stand in front of the plain cave wall. We had looked at different items we could put in the area for making the viewing crystal, but we decided to keep it plain and simple, while giving them no hints to our location.

Before we started, Kaleyna gave me a hug, told me I looked beautiful and that I could do this. Kylyan also hugged me and gave me a soft and sweet kiss. He didn't say anything, just smiled at me.

Zagnyon broke the silence. "I am ready, Nyrieve. I will be able to make both the crystals at once, so whenever you are ready, we will start."

"I am ready, Zagnyon."

"When I nod to you, you can begin," she said.

I stood there alone looking at everyone in the room, and realized that everything written for me to say in the speech was not me talking. In my gut I knew I had to speak from the heart. That is even what Lydorea told me. I just hope it is the right thing.

Zagnyon then nodded to me.

"Greetings, I am Nyrieve Vynlync. I am sure some of you have heard about me and have questions as to who I really am and what my intentions are. I am going to keep this short and simple for you. I am half Pyrothian Elf and half Lumaryia Elf. I am the Bringer of Peace." I moved my arm just enough to allow the mark of the Bring of Peace to show for a brief moment.

"I would like to request a meeting with both Klayns. You will find along with this message directions to a meeting location. I ask that you send those who can speak for all of you, but please do not send more than three representatives.

"While I am a simple person, please do not take me for a fool. I am not alone, and I am not afraid." Once I said those words, I knew it was a lie. I was very afraid, not so much for myself. I was afraid for all those that I loved and cared about, and for everyone who stood behind me.

"I look forward to our meeting and seeing how we can all decide to move forward with what is best for Iryvalya. Until we meet, Volnyri."

After a few moments of just standing there and seeing the surprised looks on everyone's faces, Zagnyon smiled and said, "They are ready."

"That was completely not what I was supposed to say," I said, starting to feel a bit nervous.

Kylyan walked up to me and smiled. "No, it wasn't what you were told to say."

Kaleyna joined us. "But it is definitely what you were supposed to say."

Now all I have to do is hope that the other members of the Nomydrac are not upset with what I chose, and also that both of the Elf Klayns decide to meet.

∝34∞

THE OTHER MEMBERS OF the Nomydrac agreed the speech I gave was from the heart and therefore appropriate. I was relieved and nervous when the messengers left to take the crystals to each location, which would take them approximately a fortnight to get to.

It did not take long to hear back from both of the Elf Klayns. We received bird messengers with notes letting us know. Both seemed eager to meet and agreed to the first meeting location we gave to them. The messengers who took the crystals to the Klayns would be escorting them to the first location and assisting them through to the next and then the final location.

A day after the messenger birds arrived, we were packed and leaving Mylterias Cove. I had mixed feelings about leaving. I had spent almost a whole season here, and it had started to feel familiar and began to have the traits of home. It was also the first place I had kissed Kylyan. I knew that I would try to come back here one day, but also knew even if that didn't happen, I would never forget it.

The cold season was already starting, and though it was far from freezing yet, I knew it wasn't far away. We rode the horses south for a day, stopping only to eat and sleep for a short period of time. We reached the boats that were waiting for us when the Nydian moon was at its highest, covering the Northern Sun.

The horses were loaded into the bottom of the boats, and we rode atop. The ride was a few hours long, and by the time we could see the island, the Northern Sun was peeking out from the Nydian moon.

I stood in the front of the boat with Kaleyna and watched the fog fade away from the small island. The closer we became to it, the more I realized it wasn't as tiny as I thought it was. I asked Kaleyna, "Is it just me, or do you think this is a lot bigger than we imagined?"

"I was thinking the same," she said. "Are you worried about it being bigger?"

"Not so much worried, as concerned."

"Why?"

"In case something does not go the way we plan, I want us to know the island enough to be able to get to some sort of safety," I said quietly.

"We could talk to Jyngy or someone to try to get a tour of the island and see what areas we could use for hiding or an escape if need be," Kaleyna said.

"I would rather not have anyone know of places we are looking to hide," I whispered to her.

Kaleyna looked at me for a moment, and just nodded in understanding. I knew she would press me more about it later, wanting more information, but she knew enough to just let it go while around others. That was one of the things I loved about my friendship with Kaleyna, we did not always need to use words to understand each other.

Once we reached the old worn dock, we were ushered off the boat first and then the horses were brought ashore. After allowing the horses a little time to get their land legs back, we mounted and rode again for about a half hour on an overgrown path through a thick forest.

There were in fact three large manors that were positioned a triangle shape. In the middle of the three homes was a large ornate fountain that had been taken over by plants. The fountain had a large smooth-looking rock in the middle, and on the face of the rock was carved a single spiral line, which looked just like the mark I had on my inner wrist. The spiral was in the middle towards the top of the rock and the end of it was pointing downwards. Coming up from the bottom were two small trees, one with ivy wrapped around it, one without. It almost looked like the spiral was trying to pick which tree to grow towards.

Seeing the same marking as the one I bore made me feel like this was a sign of sorts to reaffirm to me I am in the right place and hopefully moving on the right path.

Everyone was busy preparing the other two buildings for our guests, and I was told it would be good for me to try to relax. After getting settled in our rooms in our building, Kaleyna and I decided that even though it was raining steadily, we wanted to walk around to find different paths or locations in case we needed to make an escape. I found it amazing how old and untouched everything here seemed. I would have to ask Rowzey if she had ever seen a place like this or some of the markings we saw on the buildings and stone walls.

Once we were settled on a few different options, Kaleyna and I went back to our rooms to dry off and warm up. My room was the largest in the manor, which I argued that I didn't need, but everyone felt this was the best room for me and everything I'd need to be dressed for the meetings.

When I heard *meetings* I was a little surprised. I guess I failed to realize this could take more than one meeting to get things settled. While I was sitting in my room next to a large fire that Kylyan made for me to warm up by, there was a soft knock on the door.

"Come in," I said.

I was happy to see Baysil walking towards me with a couple of steamy cups of what smelled like peppermint tea.

"I thought you could use some hot tea to help warm you up," Baysil said as he walked in and sat down across from me in front of the fire.

"Thank you, it smells wonderful." I took the hot cup, enjoying the tingly feeling of it heating up my hands quickly. I took a small sip, the hot liquid warming me from the inside. "This is amazing. I don't think I've ever had it quite this flavorful before."

"It has to be over a hundred years old. I found it in the old kitchen and figured it couldn't be too bad," Baysil said with a smile.

"I love it. Thank you for bringing me some," I said, still wondering what the real reason was Baysil was visiting me. While I know he cares about me, I do not think he just wanted to sit and sip tea.

"So do you like your room?"

"Baysil, the room is fine. What I am wondering is what you really want to talk about."

"I know, I am not good at small talk," Baysil said with a half-smile. "I wanted to ask you how comfortable you are with the meetings. It has been a while since we had any time to just talk, and I wanted to make sure you were doing okay and ask if you had any concerns."

"Comfortable is not the word I would use for how I feel towards these meetings, more like... nerve wrecked," I said with a forced chuckle.

"I know this has to happen, I am just worried about anyone being hurt during this. Even if this doesn't end with everyone agreeing to peace, I want everything to start and end peacefully while we are on this island."

"You are very wise, Ny. I cannot imagine having everything that has been set before you when I was your age," Baysil said. "I wonder if it is just an Elf thing or a Nyrieve thing."

"I am not sure," I said, thinking. "Prior to finding out who I am, I never had anything that really challenged me or made me go outside my comfort zone. I know the first few hours after I found out, I was just a wreck, and to be honest, I did not know for sure if I was going to…"

"Be the Bringer of Peace?" Baysil asked thoughtfully.

"Yes, I didn't know if I could do this or if I wanted to."

"You have been doing everything wonderfully."

"I doubt everyone would agree with you on this," I said, taking another long sip of my tea.

"It doesn't matter who agrees with me. The only thing that matters is that you are comfortable with what you are doing," Baysil said with a warm smile.

"Can I ask you something, Baysil?"

"Of course, Ny. What is it?"

"Why did you have Klaw made for me, and why did you give up your life in Cliffside to help me?" I said quietly. "I mean, you aren't even an Elf, so what made you decide that you wanted to do this?"

He took a long sip of his tea and then a long deep breath before he started to explain. "To be honest, Ny, at first I did not do this for you. I knew you as you grew up, but as you know, we did not have lots of interactions with each other. To be honest, when I found out who you were, I was mad at you and hated you. Which is stupid, because you couldn't help who you were born as, but I did anyway."

"Why did you hate me?" I asked, confused.

"Because of the Elves, I lost my family," Baysil said somberly.

"Your family… I didn't know."

"Not many do, it's not something I like to talk about."

"You don't have to tell me anything, Baysil," I said, not wanting him to feel he had to.

"I'd like to share it with you, Ny. You have trusted me with so much, and I would like to trust you with something," Baysil said with a slight smile. "We lived in Everglyn Woods, and I had just been tyed to my long-time love, Maelyrra. We had even decided to start a family. She was due any day when the Lumaryia Elves invaded Everglyn Woods to hide out."

I sat there quietly listening as Baysil continued. "We hid in the cellar of our home and tried to not let them hear us. After about five days, we were running out of food and water, so I snuck out to get something for Maelyrra. Everything in our home was gone, so I went into a neighbor's house. I was only gone for a short time, but when I got back, there were Pyrothian Elves in my home and Maelyrra was gone."

"Gone?"

"They said they killed her quickly, so she wouldn't feel any pain," Baysil said with a tear falling down his cheek. "I struck out at them, but there were too many of them. They beat me, broke a few of my bones, and stabbed me at least three times. When they walked out of the house, they spit on me and said to say hello to Maelyrra for them."

"How did you survive?"

"Iclyn was a neighbor and a good friend of Maelyrra and myself. She came in after they left the village and helped me heal. Once I was able to walk again, we searched Everglyn Woods and helped everyone we could find leave and go to Cliffside. There were only seven of us who made it," he said. "My parents and siblings were all dead, as was Iclyn's family. When I came to Cliffside I hated all Elves, no matter what. And when you were brought here, Iclyn told me who you were, so I hated you as well. But... after the years of seeing you and knowing you, I started to realize that not all Elves were bad, and that some of them might be only following orders to keep those they loved safe."

"I'm so sorry. I don't blame you for hating all Elves."

"I've let it go. While I am angry at those who killed Maelyrra, I can't blame every Elf for it. Once I started to spend a little more time with you and Kaleyna, I knew that the hate those Elves had was taught to them, because you girls were always kind and good-hearted."

"Thank you for sharing this with me, Baysil," I said to him. "I appreciate it a lot, and I am so sorry for the loss of your family."

"Thank you, Ny. What you stand for and what we are fighting for is to keep something like that from happening to others."

"I hope that we can," I said, wondering if peace would actually be possible.

"We can, Ny. It might not come to us easily, but if we do not give up, it can," he said. "On that note, I am going to get going. I have a lot to do to get things ready for the first meeting. Just do me one favor please."

"What is that?" I stood up with him and walked with him to my door.

"If you ever at all feel that you are not being heard, make them hear you. What you have to say is important and worth listening to," he said with a smile, gave me a hug, and walked out the door.

I closed the door behind him and sat back down near the fireplace. I looked out the window. It wouldn't be much longer and the snow would take over the rain, and we would be fully into the cold season. We definitely needed these meetings in the next few days to go well. Otherwise we could end up stuck here until it got warm enough to leave.

CR8O

It was only a few days on the island before we heard that both representatives from each Klayn were on their way to the first meeting point. Once they reached that location, we received the follow-up message letting us know that they started going to the second location. It was no surprise to us to learn that they were both followed by a small group of warriors, but thanks to Jyngy's spell, they couldn't remember where they were going.

Once they had left the second meeting location, we were told there were no other followers and that they should be arriving in the next day. Everyone was busy making preparations for their arrival. They would be occupying the other two buildings along with some of our people as guards to ensure everyone's safety. We were planning to have a feast the night of their arrival in a large room off the back of the manor I was staying in.

For the feast I decided that we should have mostly Rowzey's amazing food, so she had been busy preparing for days in advance to get everything ready. I spent most of my free time in my room going over strategies for trying to get them to agree to peace, but I felt it was time being wasted, as we had no reason to believe these people would simply agree to peace.

We had received word that they would arrive in the middle of the day, so Rowzey went into a cooking frenzy, making sure everything would be ready for the meal. It was decided it would be best for the representatives to meet me for the first time at the feast. Once everyone was there and settled, I would come in and be introduced to them.

After the representatives arrived, Ghily came to my room to start getting me prepared for the feast. My clothing was as rigid as what I wore for the feast in Mylterias Cove. Though I had to admit, when she was done, I looked completely transformed again, this time in a soft silver color.

While I was again wearing a corset, my dress was not fully strapless. There were strategic straps and draping of thin gauzy material. The dress was tighter through my chest and waist, and then softly flowed outwards. It was made of only the gauzy material and gave an ethereal look. I almost couldn't believe it myself.

Ghily styled my green hair completely down with a slight hint of a wave to it. I hadn't realized how long my hair was now. I would need to make sure to pull it aside whenever I sat down. The only adornment to my hair was the silver headpiece, which helped keep my hair from falling into my face. She put minimal amounts of makeup on me, same as for the viewing crystals.

I did secure Klaw to my thigh before I put the slightly high-heeled shoes on. The shoes were also silver, but were not as hard to walk in as the ones before. Ghily said it was because these had a thicker heel to hold my balance better. After Ghily was done, she went out of the room and Kylyan entered. He just stood there smiling at me for a moment with his hands behind his back.

"What?" I asked him, checking the looking glass to see if something was out of place.

"You look stunning, my lady," he said as he walked towards me, "but there is something missing."

"What is missing?" I asked, concerned.

He brought his hands in front and I noticed a wooden box in his hands. He smiled at me and said, "This is what you are missing," as he handed me the box.

I slowly opened it, and inside was a beautiful necklace that had a silver rope chain and a single two-inch marquise-shaped rainbow moonstone dangling from a silver enclosure. "It is so beautiful, Kyl, thank you!" I gave him a big hug.

"It's nothing compared to your beauty, but I knew this would look perfect on you," he said as he stepped back and put the necklace on me.

I looked into the looking glass again, lightly touching the necklace and knowing he was right. I was missing something, and this necklace made me look completely finished and elegant.

"Where did you get this?"

"It was something I was given long ago, and now I know why. So are you ready to go and meet the Elves, Ny?"

I faced him with a half-smile and said, "I am as ready as I am going to be."

We walked outside the door, locked arms, and headed to the feast where the Elves were waiting.

☙35❧

KYLYAN AND I STOOD outside the double doors that led into the room where the feast was being held. I was getting more and more nervous by the moment, but Jyngy assured me that they would be back to open the doors soon and introduce me to everyone.

Kylyan squeezed my hand, which was sitting on top of his right arm. I turned and looked up to him. He was standing there strong and handsome as ever. He was dressed all in black and looked like there was nothing strange going on, that we weren't about to meet people that hated us just for being born. I asked him, "How are you so calm?"

"Because no matter what happens in the next few hours, at the end of the night, I will be walking you back to your room. I know that things might go crazy or they might be strangely similar to other feasts, but I just keep looking at you, how beautiful you are and how happy you make me just by being close to me, and that is enough to keep me calm."

I felt that butterfly sensation in my stomach. He always seemed to know the thing to say to help me look at the bigger picture. Yes, I was nervous about meeting all these people, and no, I did not know how everything would happen over the next few hours, but I did know that at the end of the night, Kylyan would be by my side.

"Thank you, Kyl." I leaned up to give him a quick kiss.

"My pleasure, my lady," he said, giving me a wink.

The doors creaked open, and the chatter from the other side faded into silence. The only noises now were Kylyan and me stepping through the doorway and Jyngy announcing us. "We are pleased to announce the arrival of Her Highness, Nyrieve Vynlync, and her escort, Kylyan."

As we descended a short staircase into the room, I noticed everyone was dressed in their fanciest attire. I found it so strange that these six people from the Elf Klayns would come with such formal clothing, but I guess I do not know enough about them to know what they would do.

Kylyan and I had discussed with Jyngy ahead of time how I wanted to proceed after the introduction, so he knew to lead me over to where the six Elves were standing, which was right where Jyngy arranged for them to be.

I stood before these six people—all exquisitely beautiful in their own ways, but complete strangers to me—who I needed to treat with care and caution.

"Good evening to you all," I said. "I want to thank you for coming to meet and discuss the future of Iryvalya, and for attending this feast to try to get to know each other at least a little before starting our talks."

They all took a moment to let what I said sink in, and then took turns nodding and agreeing with slight smiles. Jyngy stood to my right, as we discussed, and I nodded to her to make the introductions of the Elves in front of me.

"Your Highness, I would like to introduce you to all the Elves who traveled to meet with you," she said in a very formal voice. She started with the Elf on the far left of the three of us, right next to Kylyan.

Jyngy began going down the row of the Elves, moving towards her right. After each short introduction, I nodded to each in recognition.

"This is Oumryn Nordyl, one of the leaders on the Lumaryia Counsel." Oumryn was the same height as me, and had pale white skin. She had long pale blue and purple hair in a fancy braid. Her eyebrows were purple like her hair, and her eyes swirled the purple along with a shade of deep gray.

"This is Joynox, a member on the Lumaryia Counsel." Joynox was shorter than me, had pale brown skin, and he had shorter but shaggy light blue hair with streaks of light gold through it. His bushy eyebrows were the same blue and his eyes swirled of blue and gold.

"This is Zyrontax, also a member on the Lumaryia Counsel." Zyrontax was awkwardly taller and had a pale skin tone and a long braid of dark blue and light blue hair. His eyebrows were of the dark blue color and his eyes swirled the same colors as his hair.

"This is Fyra Aydrak, one of the leaders on the Pyrothian Counsel." Fyra was a striking woman. She was taller than me, very thin, and had a nice golden tan. Her hair was down to her waist. It was a bright red on top and bright orange underneath. Her eyebrows were thin and yellow, and her eyes swirled of red and orange.

"This is Roliyom, one of the members on the Pyrothian Counsel." Roliyom was also tall. He had dark skin and a lot of muscles. He had a single braid of various shades of orange. His eyebrows were also orange and his eyes swirled of two shades of orange.

"This is Osidya, also one of the members on the Pyrothian Counsel." When she said my mother's name I could feel my breath catch. I was standing right in front of my mother, and yet I knew I could not make any indication that I knew who she was. I remembered her letter saying she had been helping on the Counsel. Perhaps her father died and now she was a permanent member.

She was just as Rowzey had described her in her letter to me. She was taller than me and much thinner. She had a deep golden tan, and her long red hair faded to orange, hanging down straight. Her eyes swirled of the light and dark orange, but gave no indication she knew I was her daughter.

I took a deep breath to focus myself and to speak without any inflection to allow suspicion. "It is a pleasure to meet you all." Each of them took a moment to say typical pleasantries, talking about either my lovely dress or the beautiful room, but my mother only said, "That is a lovely name, Your Highness." She told me in her letter, if we ever met, she'd mention my name so I'd know she recognized who I was.

After a few more pleasant exchanges about their journey here and how they found their accommodations satisfactory, it was announced the meal was ready. We took to our seats. Kylyan led me to the head table and sat down to my left and Kaleyna sat to my right, helping me feel safe and grounded being near those I loved.

I couldn't say anything to anyone about my mother near the other Elves, but Kaleyna must have read my mind. She looked me in the eyes and asked, "Are you sure it is her?"

"I think so."

"Her?" Kylyan asked.

I shook my head at him. "Later."

We left it at that for the rest of the evening. The food was amazing. Rowzey had made her amazing sauce and so many other dishes. I also enjoyed having Peayalt to drink throughout the evening.

I was surprised by the pleasantness of everyone. One would have thought everyone were old friends and not enemies. Once the meal was finished, everyone said goodbyes and went to their own accommodations. I asked Jyngy if the Elves leaving so soon meant something, and she said she thought it was more to discuss their plans of action now that they have seen me and everyone else they think came with us.

When Kylyan walked me back to my room, I asked him to come in with me. Once inside, I had him help me unlace the back of my dress. After walking around a five-panel screen, I took the dress and shoes off, put on a more comfortable dress, and walked back around barefoot.

Kylyan was squatting near the fire. He had taken off his jacket and added a few more logs to keep the fire burning for quite a while. He looked up at me and smiled. "So do you want to tell me who 'her' is?"

"Osidya."

"And who is she?" he asked, walking over to me and wrapping his arms around me.

"She is my mother," I said softly.

"That is what I thought."

"Why did you think that?"

"It is very subtle, but you and she both have the same smile," he said, giving me a light kiss.

"I don't know what I should do."

"If you would like, I can make arrangements with all of the Elves for you to meet them all one on one. That way no one will question you meeting with just her."

"You don't think they will question it?"

"They might question you meeting each in general, but if you do not spend more time with her than the others, then it should not be overly suspicious."

"Thank you, Kylyan, you are the best," I said, giving him a kiss back, but not as soft as his. I kissed him deeply and wrapped my arms around him. He picked me up and carried me to the bed, laid me down on it, and lay down alongside me. For the longest time we just looked into each other's eyes and kissed off and on.

Kylyan looked at me and furrowed his brow. "What are you thinking, Ny?"

I looked up into his eyes and realized that I had never felt so safe or complete than when I am next to Kylyan. He didn't let me out of doing things I should do. He forced me to stand up for myself at times, and I knew, even if I got mad and yelled at him or stormed off angry, he was always there for me. And I was there for him when he did the same. He fit into my strange life perfectly, and he didn't ever seem scared away by everything that could happen. I needed to tell him all this, but when I tried to, I could only speak from my heart.

"I love you, Kylyan."

He smiled at me, placed his left hand on my cheek, and before kissing me passionately, said, "I love you too, Nyrieve."

I found myself kissing him back and holding his body close to mine. Our hands explored each other while we kissed and kept each other close. After a while we slowed down and looked into each other's eyes. He asked me, "Are you sure you are ready for... more?"

I smiled at him and nodded, and it was magycal.

03&0

When I woke up it was already morning and Kylyan was gone, but I could see he put more wood on the fire. I sat up and realized I was still completely undressed. I rushed behind the screen and put on something simple but warm to wear. I would have liked to wear my leathers, but I was told that if any of the Elf Klayns saw me, I should always be dressed softly and daintily, so they wouldn't think I was as strong as I am.

I was sitting on the bed finishing the tie on my braid when Kylyan knocked and came right in. When he saw me, he smiled brightly at me.

"Good morning, my lady," he said as he carried in a tray of food and hot tea.

"Good morning, my love," I said back with a smile as I got up and took the tray from him, set it down, and gave him a huge hug and kiss.

"I like the sound of that."

"Me too."

We sat and ate our food and Kylyan told me about how he had Jyngy arranging everything for me to meet with all the Elves. He suggested I have Kaleyna in with me, as it wouldn't seem so odd and she has the ability to read minds a bit, so more information couldn't hurt.

Kaleyna was happy to help me, and we were set up in a small room within our manor. Each Elf came in one at a time. There was small talk, questions about the weather, and compliments about our hospitality. The last Elf to come in was Osidya, my mother. When she walked in, I did not know what to expect, but once the door shut behind her she walked up to me, gave me a brief hug, and sat down as the other Elves did.

"I know who you are."

"I figured you would. Rowzey, I am sure, provided you my letter," she said in a very proper and stoic manner.

"I called the meetings individually to be able to have a short time alone with you, so we could talk and maybe get to know one another," I said. I was not getting the reaction from her I had been hoping for.

"And what exactly would you like to know about me that Rowzey, or myself in the letter for that matter, hasn't already told you?"

"Honestly I am not sure." I was starting to think this was a bad idea, but figured this might be my only chance to ever talk to her for long again. "I had hoped to learn more about you and what you like and what you do… if you ever still think about me…"

She took a deep breath sounding bored. "About me, I am on the Pyrothian Counsel, which does sum up about everything I do, but if you want to know the silly basics, I could indulge you. As far as foods, I like anything cooked on hot fire, for a color I like the color red. And do I think about you… yes I do, not as much as I did when you were younger, until recently of course."

"I see. Well thank you for your candor, Osidya. I am sorry that I misread the situation here."

"I do understand, Nyrieve, but the only thing I can say to you is that I hope you do what is right, and join with the Pyrothian Elves to lead Iryvalya into the world it was meant to be."

"So, you no longer feel like you did in your other letter to me, about hoping for peace."

"I was foolish and young, just as you are now if you truly think there can be peace."

"I am sorry to have wasted your time then. You may leave now," I told her sternly.

She got up, nodded, and walked back out.

Once the door closed I looked to Kaleyna, whose mouth was gaping open. I asked her, "Did that really just happen?"

"If I wasn't here, I wouldn't have believed it," she said. "Are you okay?"

"Yes and no," I said truthfully. "I was excited to see my mother, and had a silly hope of having a reunion of sorts, but I guess deep down I knew that wasn't possible. Besides, I already have someone who always cared for me as a real mother."

Kaleyna smiled and said what I was thinking. "Rowzey. She was always there for us as our mother, and we are lucky to have had her."

When I told Rowzey what happened with my mother, she looked heartbroken and hugged me to her. She said she had always worried if the power and corruption of the Elf Klayns would be strong enough to change her. I told Rowzey that it was okay, and that while it hurt on some level, overall I didn't feel as if I had lost anything. I already had a mother, her.

CK80

The next day, the first meeting of the Elves and a few members of the Nomydrac began. I felt it was not important for them to know who all the members were, so if some happened to be near them outside the meetings, information could always slip into our hands.

After four days of pointless meetings and each of the Klayns blaming each other for various crimes, I grew tired of listening to them. Neither wanted to take any actions that could create peace unless they were left in the seat of power to guide things in the direction that they felt was best.

I tried to reason with these people, but they kept treating me like I was a child, especially my mother. I tried to get them to move past their petty disagreements, but they always went back to the same thing over and over.

I decided at the end of the meeting today, tomorrow would be the last one. I talked to the members of the Nomydrac and explained to them that these people would never change unless forced. When I left the Nomydrac meeting, no one had unanimously agreed on what I should do.

I needed to take charge and make one last offer to bring our people together, but before I could do that, I needed to have the rest of my people ready. I told Kylyan my plan, and he agreed with me. He worked with Jyngy and Baysil to make sure the boats would be ready to take all of our people back to the mainland. We would be leaving boats for the Elves to return on their own, but we would not be waiting around for them to be ready.

Before I went to the meeting, I needed to do a couple things. First, I needed to talk to Rowzey for a bit, and second, check in with Kylyan to make sure everything was ready.

I found Rowzey in her room getting her stuff organized and ready. She told me the Pixie sisters were out listening for any information the Elves could possibly give up without seeing them. I had already told Rowzey a few days ago what had happened with Osidya, and she said she was so sorry and disappointed for me, but I told her not to be. I was at peace with the idea that Osidya gave birth to me, but that did not make her my mother. The person who was always there for me and cared for me was my mother, and that was her.

"So what is yous plan today, Ny?" Rowzey asked me after I sat down in one of the chairs in her room.

"Honestly, other than leaving at the end of the meeting to go hide out with everyone for a while, I don't know."

"Well yous got to know what yous are going to tell them, right?"

"I have no idea. I have listened to them for days, and nothing I say seems to get through to any of them."

"Yous might need to try to say it a different way," she said with a smirk.

"What do you mean?"

"Do yous feel yous have been yous true self in these meetings?"

"No, not really. I am dressed in fancy gowns, I talk quietly and wait my turn, and the whole time they ignore me."

"Yous need to make them see and hear yous," she said. "Now yous go get ready, and I's will see yous on the boat. Oh, and before I forget, Kyl gave me your truth stone last night, and I fixed it into a ring setting for you." She placed the simple ring in my hand, and I carefully slid it onto my left middle finger.

After I gave her a hug and walked out her door, I knew she was right. I ran to my room and was happy to see my bag still on my bed. I quickly changed into my black leathers with the green shirt, and after lacing up my black boots, I strapped Klaw to my thigh. I had been wearing Klaw under my dresses, but now there was no need to hide and pretend. I pulled my hair into a messy knot, but enough that it kept all the hair out of my way. I also took some of the charcoal stick and put some liner around my eyes to make them stand out, and the last thing I added was some of the dark red lip stain Ghily gave me. When I looked into the looking glass, I felt like myself and ready to go to that meeting.

Before I went, I asked Baysil to make sure everyone would head to the boats once the meeting started, and told him I counted on him to make sure everyone would be there. He seemed pleased to be in charge of that, and I knew he would get it done. For this last meeting, I asked only Kylyan and Kaleyna to come with me, and for everyone else to help get everything and everyone to the boats.

Once the Elves were all in the meeting room, I decided it was my turn to talk at this meeting, and everyone else would just listen. I stood outside the meeting room with Kylyan. Kaleyna was inside and would let me know when everyone had arrived.

Kylyan smiled at me as we waited. "You know you are wearing what you had on the day I first met you."

"I forgot that, but it's not like I have many black leathers," I said with a laugh.

"You know before I met you, I did not think I would like you."

"Why is that?"

"Because I never wanted to believe that one person could be the one to bring peace to our world."

"What made you change your mind?"

"When I realized you felt the same way," he said with a smile. "Do not worry, my lady, you will be great."

Then we heard the signal from Kaleyna that everyone was there, and it was now time for me to run this last meeting.

૦૩*૪૦

I shoved the doors open, grabbing everyone's attention. Their eyes followed me in shock from the noise and my appearance. There was no need to waste our time, so I got on with what I needed to say.

"I am not going to sit down and waste any of our time anymore, seeing as time has been wasted the last four days," I said as I walked in front of them all.

"Over the last four meetings, the only things I have heard out of any of you is what you want and what we should blame the others for. This is pointless, because in the long run, I do not care about you blaming each other or what you all think you deserve.

"The people of Iryvalya want freedom and peace, and none of you who represent your Klayns seem to want that for anyone other than yourselves. If we are to once again be one people, we have to care about those who stand next to us just as much as ourselves, if not more.

"As of right now, these talks are concluded. I have decided that we will no longer sit here and wait for you to understand that we will not change our minds and that we are willing to fight, bleed, and die for our freedom and the peace our people deserve. And if it does come to that, do not think for a moment your Klayns will be without bloodshed and loss, because those who fight for their freedom are much stronger and more determined than those who fight under orders of a hierarchy who will not fight for themselves."

Everyone sat silently with stunned looks upon their faces. I turned and nodded to Kylan and Kaleyna, who started to walk out of the room. Before I walked through the doors to head to the waiting boats, I turned and faced everyone one last time. I smiled and said, "Until we all meet again, Volnyri."

Glossary

Term	(Pronunciation)	Definition
Aloyc	(Al-oy-sea)	Name - Death Elf
Arnayx	(Are-n-axe)	Name - Male Elf
Ayllac	(Aa-lack)	Name - Female Pixie
Balthyza	(Ball-thee-za)	Name - Male Elf
Baysil	(Ba-sil)	Name - Male Fairy
Blackened Forest	(Black-ened Forest)	Island near Troxeon
Brydalwind	(Bri-dal-wind)	Meadow in the Stone
Callya	(Call-ya)	Name - Female Pixie
Cliffside	(Cliffside)	Village in the Stone Realm
Clyo	(Clee-o)	Name - Female Elf
Clyr	(Clear)	Amulet
Crymson	(Crimson)	Name - Female Nymph
Crystoval	(Cryst-o-val)	Mountains in the Stone Realm
Dalorvya	(Da-lor-vee-ah)	Destroyed Fairy village
Dazyen	(Daz-yen)	Name - Female Satyr
Demetryus	(De-me-tree-us)	Name - Male Gargoyle
Dymma Loycuvr	(Dim-ah Loy-curve-er)	Name - Female Elf
Eldreyva	(El-dre-va)	Name - Female Elf
Elyzia	(El-eez-ee-ah)	Name - Female Fairy
Eritsong Woods	(Ear-et-song Woods)	Village in the Stone Realm
Everglyn Woods	(Ever-glen Woods)	Village in the Air Realm
Fynnasla	(Fin-as-la)	Name - Female Fairy
Fyra Avdrak	(F-eye-rah Av-drake)	Name - Female Elf
Ghilyauna	(Gill-lee-au-na)	Name - Female Nymph
Grydios	(Gr-eye-de-os)	Village in the Stone Realm
Gwyndal	(G-win-dal)	Name - Female Fairy
Iclyn	(Ice-Lynn)	Name - Female Fairy
Iryvalya	(Eye-re-vale-ya)	World
Ivynilo	(Eye-vee-nill-low)	Moon
Jehryps	(J-air-rips)	Name - Male Elf
Joauxy	(Jo-aux-ee)	Moon
Joynox	(Joy-knox)	Name - Male Elf
Jyngy	(Gin-gee)	Name - Female Elf

Jynkins	(Jink-ins)	Name - Male Satyr
Jytt	(Jet)	Name - Male Gargoyle
Kaleyna Tarsys	(Ka-lee-na Tar-sis)	Name - Female Elf
Kelvyhan	(Kel-vee-han)	Name - Male Fairy
Kivesyon	(Key-ve-sy-on)	Mountains in the Stone Realm
Klaw	(K-law)	Knife
Klyan	(Clan)	Group of people
Knarfy	(Nar-fee)	Name - Male Satyr
Koyvean	(Coy-veen)	Name - Female Elf
Kryvon	(Cry-von)	Name - Male Elf
Kylyan	(Kill-ee-an)	Name - Male Elf
Legatey Rodyron	(Le-gat-ee Ro-die-ron)	Name - Male Elf
Leyhroi	(Lee-roy)	Name - Male Satyr
Louvyordal	(Lou-vee-or-dal)	Name - Male Gargoyle
Lowyll	(Lowell)	Moon
Lumaryia Elves	(Lou-ma-re-a Elves)	One of the Elf Klayns
Lydorea	(Lie-door-e-ah)	Name - Female Fairy
Lynawn	(Lynn-awe-n)	Island East of the Stone Realm
Lyndrea	(Lin-dre-a)	Name - Female Elf
Lyosx	(Lie-o-six)	Name - Male Elf
Maelyrra	(Mae-leer-a)	Name - Female Fairy
Magyc	(Magic)	Magic
Marselyus	(Mar-sell-ee-us)	Name - Female Fairy
Miaarya	(Mee-are-ee-a)	Name - Female Fairy
Montryos	(Mon-tree-os)	Name - Male Fairy
Mylterias Cove	(Mal-tear-e-es Cove)	Village in the Stone Realm
Nomydrac	(N-om-ee-dre-ake)	Group of people
North Sea	(North Sea)	The Sea in the North of Iryvalya
Northern Sun	(Northern Sun)	The Sun to the North of Iryvalya
Noygandia	(Noy-g-on-dia)	Town in the Water Realm
Nulya	(New-lee-a)	Name - Female Fairy
Nydian	(Nigh-dee-an)	Moon
Nyrieve Vynlync	(Nigh-r-eve Vine-link)	Name - Female Elf
Oryliout	(O-rye-lee-oat)	River in the Stone Realm
Osidya	(Oh-sid-ya)	Name - Female Elf
Ossyr	(Oss-er)	Bird
Oumryn Nordyl	(Ohm-ren Nor-dial)	Name - Female Elf
Pairyn	(Pair-ing)	Romantic Relationship

Peayalt	(Pea-y-alt)	Cucumber Lemon Water
Prax	(P-rax)	Town in the Fire Realm
Prydos	(Pry-de-os)	Name - Male Elf
Pyrothian Elves	(Pi-row-thee-an Elves)	One of the Elf Klayns
Reayondr	(Ray-on-der)	Name - Female Fairy
Relonya	(Re-lon-ya)	Name - Female Elf
Rhyon	(Rye-on)	Name - Male Gargoyle
Roliyom	(Ro-lee-ohm)	Name - Male Elf
Rowzey	(Row-zee)	Name - Female Unknown Origin
Rydison	(Rye-di-son)	Moon
Sangrynaw	(San-gra-naw)	Bird
South Sea	(South Sea)	The Sea in the South of Iryvalya
Southern Sun	(Southern Sun)	The Sun to the South of Iryvalya
Sudryl	(Sud-rile)	Name – Male Merman
Sunorlyna	(Sun-or-lena)	Name - Female Elf
Sweyton	(Sway-ton)	Name - Male Elf
Symiar	(Sigh-me-are)	Name - Male Fairy
Syngladen	(Sin-glay-den)	Village in the Fire Realm
Syviss	(S-ih-viss)	Name – Female Mermaid
Tyed	(Tied0	Married
Torgany	(Tore-gan-ee)	Name - Female Fairy
Troxeon	(Tr-ox-ee-on)	Island
Twyn	(T-win)	Intimate Relations
Volnyri	(Vol-nigh-re)	Old Iryvalya saying
Voynder	(Vo-ander)	Name - Male Gargoyle
Whyndal	(Wine-dal)	Name - Male Gargoyle
Windoberry	(Win-doh-berry)	Wine
Xetyna	(Ze-tee-na)	Name - Female Elf
Xylonia	(Zi-lone-ia)	Village in the Stone Realm
Xylota	(Zi-lo-ta)	Magical Berries
Yorsot	(Your-s-ott)	Name - Male Elf
Zagnyon	(Zag-nee-on)	Name - Female Elf
Zendiya	(Zen-die-ya)	Name - Male Gargoyle
Zyjoyvi	(Z-eye-joy-vee)	Name - Female Fairy
Zyrontax	(Zi-ron-tax)	Name - Male Elf

Acknowledgments

Special thanks to:

My remarkable husband Joe, without your love and support this book, and so much more, would have never been. You saw something in me, that even I could never see, thank you for never giving up on me. You have helped me become not only a better person, but the person I was meant to be.

My son Joey, your creative imagination and determination inspires me every day. You changed my world for the better the day you became my son.

My daughter Ivy, you have made me believe in miracles and see the magyc in the world. You completed our family, filled my heart, and you will always be my little girl. Always & Forever.

Richard & Teresa for providing me with different worlds to immerse myself in throughout my childhood with books.

Frank & Rose for your acceptance and support like I was always a part of the family.

Kelley, the flipside of my coin, for inspiring true undying love and friendship.

Aeriel for immersing yourself in my world and helping me fine-tune it.

Lem Montero, for bringing the cover of my book to life.

Lisa Gilliam, for your insightful edits and suggestions.

Rowzey… the sauce.

About the Author

LeAnn Kelley is the Fantasy Fiction Author of *The Tales of Iryvalya: Bloodlines*. She was born and raised outside Grand Rapids, MI in a small town named Lowell. She now resides in West Michigan near the lakeshore with her husband and two children. She has a degree in Psychology, and plans to continue her education in the future.

LeAnn always enjoyed reading and writing since an early age, spending all of her allowance on books and writing activities. When not writing, LeAnn enjoys spending time with her family, gardening, boating, kayaking or doing anything crafty (drawing, painting, jewelry making, pottery).

LeAnn is also an advocate for CHD Awareness (Congenital Heart Defects), as her daughter was born with a rare CHD.

Made in the USA
Columbia, SC
25 September 2019